HOME BEFORE DARK

SUSAN
HOME BEFORE DARK
WIGGS

MIRA®

MIRA®

ISBN 1-55166-673-1

HOME BEFORE DARK

Visit us at www.mirabooks.com

Printed in U.S.A.

First Printing: April 2003
10 9 8 7 6 5 4 3 2 1

Dedicated with all my love to Lori Ann Cross.
Even if you weren't my sister, you'd still be my best friend.

"There is in every woman's heart a spark of heavenly fire,
which lies dormant in the broad daylight of prosperity,
but which kindles up and beams and blazes in the dark hour of adversity."
—Washington Irving

$$\boxed{\text{P A R T} \quad \text{O N E}}$$

Before

"Our youth now love luxury, they have bad manners, contempt for authority; they show disrespect for elders, and love to chatter in place of exercise. Children are now tyrants, not the servants of their households. They no longer rise when elders enter the room. They contradict their parents, chatter before company, gobble up their food and tyrannize their teachers."

—Socrates (399 B.C.)

CHAPTER 1

That spike of panic a woman feels when the thought first hits her—*I'm pregnant*—is like no other. Sixteen years after that moment, its echo haunted Jessie Ryder as she drove through the Texas heat, having traveled halfway around the world to see the daughter she'd never met.

She could still remember the terror and wonder of knowing an invisible cluster of cells had changed her life forever, in ways she could not imagine. Sixteen years and uncounted miles separated her from that day, but the distance was closing fast.

Simon had tried to stop her—*It's madness, Jess, you can't just go dashing off to Texas*—but Simon was wrong. And this wasn't the craziest thing she'd ever done, not by a long shot.

For the hundredth time since flinging her belongings into a bag in an Auckland hotel room, Jessie wondered what else she could have done. There was no script for this, no instruction manual for putting the broken pieces of a life back together.

There was only the homing instinct, the tendency of the wounded animal to seek safe haven. And then there was the unbearable urge, long buried but never quite forgotten, to see the child she had given away at birth to the only person on the planet she trusted—Luz, her sister.

The front tire rippled over a line of yellow discs marking the center of the highway. Jessie's driving days were numbered, but a stubborn streak of independence, combined with a sense of desperation, made her defiant. She slowed, checked the rearview mirror—still getting used to driving American cars, on the right side of the road—and pulled off. She was lost again.

The glint of the sun over the jagged silhouette of the hills blinded her briefly, and she flipped down the visor. Grabbing the map, she studied the route highlighted by the counter clerk at Alamo Rent-a-Car. Southwest along the interstate to exit 135-A, State Highway 290 to Farm-to-Market Route 1486, following the little red thread of road to a place few folks had heard of and even fewer were inclined to visit.

Jessie had followed the directions. Or had she? It was hard to tell, and it had been so long since she'd traveled these forgotten country roads. As she traced a finger over the route, a movement on the road caught her eye. An armadillo.

She usually only encountered them as roadkill, as though they'd been born that way, with their little dinosaur feet pointed skyward. And yet here was one, waddling across her path like something out of a Steinbeck novel. An omen? A harbinger of doom? Or just another Texas speed bump? She watched the creature wander to the other side of the road and disappear into the low thicket of chaparral.

An oncoming car crested the steep hill ahead of her. She squinted at the approaching vehicle. A pickup truck, of course. What else did you find out here? As it slowed and then stopped on the opposite shoulder, she felt a slick thrill of danger. She was completely alone, lost in the middle of Texas, miles from civilization.

The window rolled down. Shading her eyes against the glare, she could make out only the outline of the driver—big shoulders, baseball cap—and, incongruously, a child's safety seat on the passenger side. A fishing rod lay across the gun rack.

"Everything all right, ma'am?" he asked. She couldn't get a good look at his face with the sun in her eyes, but that Texas drawl somehow put her at ease, evoking faint memories of lazy days and slow, neighborly smiles.

"I'm headed for Edenville," she said. "But I think I'm lost."

"You're almost there," he said, jerking his thumb in the direction he'd come from. "This is the right road. You just haven't gone far enough."

"Thanks."

"No problem, ma'am. You take care now." The pickup truck moved off, backfiring as it headed in the opposite direction.

You take care now. The friendly throwaway admonition lingered as she pulled back onto the road. She fiddled with the radio, finding mostly news and tears-in-my-beer country music. At last she discovered a decent rock station out of Austin and listened to ZZ Topp, turned up loud. She hoped the music might drown out her thoughts and maybe even her fears.

Austin's bedroom communities, with names like Saddlebrook Acres and Rockhurst Estates, were miles behind her, giving way to places with folksier appellations like Two-Dog Ranch. She passed a Texaco station with a hand-lettered sign: We Sell Gas To Anyone In A Glass Container.

Deep in the hill country, late afternoon settled in. The dark pockets of shadows hidden within the striated sandstone hills were not to be trusted. The waddling armadillo had reminded her that, at any moment, a jackrabbit or mule deer could leap out onto the road. She would hate to hit an animal. She didn't even want to hit a dead one, she realized, swerving to avoid a battered carcass that had not yet been desiccated into a grotesque kite of flattened skin.

The trip felt much longer than she remembered. Of course, years back, she couldn't wait to leave; now she couldn't wait to get home. Soon she saw it, the weatherbeaten Welcome To Edenville sign with its faded illustration of a peach orchard. Smaller signs sprouted in the field at its feet: The Halfway Baptist Church. Home of the Fighting Serpents. Lions Club meets on the third Saturday each month.

The tree-shaded town had the eerie familiarity of a half-remembered dream. Hunched-together storefronts lined the main square, which was organized around a blocky, century-old courthouse. Adam's Ribs B-B-Q and Eve's Garden Shoppe still stood side by side across from Roscoe's Hay and Feed and an exhausted Schott's discount outlet. Despite the addition of the Celestial Cyber Café, the place retained its midcentury, slow-moving character, a town content to lag behind while time sped past like traffic on the interstate bypass.

Right out of high school, Jessie had left for college. She'd loved Austin's urban bustle and suburban sprawl, its population of politicians, intellectuals, Goths, Mexicans, criminals and rednecks. Now she was back in the small town filled with everything she'd left behind, whether she liked it or not.

Despite the passage of time, she knew her way now. Five more miles along a narrow lane, past the preternaturally green Woodcreek golf course and driving range, and then a right turn onto the lake road.

She rolled down all four windows of the car and took a deep breath. She could smell the lake before she saw it—mesquite and cedar and the cleansing scent of air blown across fresh water. One of the few cold, spring-fed lakes in Texas, Eagle Lake was bluer than autumn twilight.

Areas of rounded rock, with hawthorn shrubs blooming in the cracks, plunged down to touch the water. The lake itself was a vast mirror with a forest fringe of the most extraordinary trees in the state. They called them the lost maples of Eagle Lake because everyone knew this particular type of tree didn't rightly belong in Texas. Maples grew in the long, frozen sleep of winter found only in the woods up north, not the unpredictable fits and starts of brutal cold and blistering heat of the Texas hill country. And yet here they thrived, nonnatives huddled together beside a picture-book lake.

Legends about the maples abounded. Indian lore held that they were the souls of long-dead ancestors from the North. Others claimed a settler had planted them for his Yankee bride to remind her of the New England autumns she missed so desperately. But all anybody really knew was that the trees were transplanted strangers that didn't belong, yet managed to flourish here anyway, bursting into hectic color after a scorching summer had sucked the pigment from everything else.

Each autumn, the maples blazed brighter than any forest fire, in colors so intense they made your eyes smart: magenta, gold, deep orange, ocher, burnt umber. For two weeks every fall, the Farm-to-Market Road was clogged with tourists who drove out to Lakeside County Park to take pictures of their kids skipping stones on the leaf-strewn water or climbing high in those God-painted branches.

As Jessie drew nearer to her destination, she tried to remember when the foliage reached its peak. Early November, she recalled. Homecoming season.

CHAPTER 2

The road surface changed to a jolting bed of caliche and crushed rock. Jessie clutched the steering wheel hard and concentrated. She had talked the Alamo guy into renting her the Ford Fiesta based on an International Driver's License. She'd convinced herself that, once she cleared the bustle and sprawl of Austin's tangled highways and headed out on the open country roads, she was a danger only to herself and the occasional hapless armadillo. A reckless impulse had compelled her to make this trip, and driving a car was one of many independent options she was about to give up. But not yet. Besides, she was almost there. A flurry of nerves stirred in her gut. She had come to fill a need as deep as Eagle Lake, yet she was terrified of reopening wounds she had inflicted long ago.

She counted the hills to the old place on the lake: one, two and three gentle rises on a slow-motion roller coaster. At the turnoff, she flexed her hands on the steering wheel, drew a nervous breath redolent of hill country dust and slowly moved forward, entering the property through the gate beside a huge, cloven monolith of sandstone. Affixed to it was an old wrought-iron sign: Broken Rock. As the story went, her grandad had built the place before there was a road leading to it, and he always told folks to turn at the broken rock. The name stuck and was now used to designate the old place on the lake.

The property had been handed down to Jessie's father, a remote and polite gentleman who had signed it over to her mother in the divorce settlement nearly three decades earlier. Glenny Ryder had kept only a few things from that first marriage. Her name—it was already engraved on a number of golf trophies—the lake property and her two daughters.

Jessie's childhood was like a colorful dream, filled with glaring sunlight, emerald fairways and long swift trips on the open highway, the world speeding by through the distorted rectangle of a car window. The soundtrack of that childhood consisted of the Beatles, the Beach Boys, Cat Stevens and James Taylor, crooning from the car radio between ads for Noxema and charcoal-filter Tarrytons.

After their daddy left, Jessie got the back seat of the 1964 Rambler all to herself, so she couldn't say she was all that sorry to see him go. Luz had cried and cried, but Jessie didn't remember crying. She just remembered the endless road.

Their lives were defined by their mother's tour schedule. When they stayed in a motel, there was always a king and a cot. Glenny took the cot and put Luz and Jessie in the bed. To this day, sleeping with Luz, knowing she was there in the bed next to her, was one of Jessie's most vivid memories.

After the divorce, Glenny had treated the lake house and outbuildings like a way station while she chased prizes that never lasted or brought her what she sought. Too many years and three husbands later, she had won only a handful of major titles. But she always did just well enough to stay on the tour, just well enough to pay her expenses, just well enough to keep her gone.

From a distance, the property appeared to be as Jessie remembered it. With a lurch of bittersweet emotion, she recognized the boxy, two-storey main house, the garage and boathouse, the dirt path winding through the woods to the three guest cabins they used to rent out to tourists. When they were girls, Luz and Jessie earned pocket money by changing beds and towels for the fishermen who came for the weekend.

Yet as she drew closer, she noticed differences. Unfamiliar vehicles—a dusty minivan and a Honda Civic parked under the car port. Gumball-colored toys littered the front path. She spotted a doghouse with the unlikely name Beaver painted over the opening. A flat of purple asters lay unplanted in the yard; a half-caned chair stood on the porch. Someone's partially eaten apple lay on the ground, swarming with fire ants. The place had an air of things left undone; Luz's family had dropped everything as though something had interrupted them.

They were about to be interrupted again. Jessie hadn't dared to call first. She'd been too afraid that she'd talk herself out of coming. Or worse, that she'd promise to visit and then chicken out at the last moment, disappearing as she had before, and disappointing everyone—again. The heartbreak that had sent her running long ago had never healed.

When she got out of the car and slammed the door, a throaty baying erupted. A gangly bluetick hound galloped across the yard, bristling neck hairs contradicted by the friendly swaying of a long tail. Jessie didn't know much about dogs. Because of the way she'd grown up, she'd never owned one. Their gypsylike existence in the back of their mother's pink Rambler had left room only for the occasional carnival goldfish in a clear plastic bag. One year a white mouse had lived for an entire summer in a Buster Brown shoebox before going AWOL at a motel in Pinehurst, North Carolina.

"You hush," yelled a voice from inside the house.

Jessie's palms were drenched in sweat. She wanted— needed—to pray but only the most childish of thoughts streamed out. Please God, get me through this.

The screen door of the porch opened with a creak and shut with a snap. Her sister Luz froze like a pillar of salt at the porch rail. Even in denim cutoffs and a bleach-faded pink T-shirt, Luz appeared formidable, in command.

"Jess..." Her whisper lingered over the sibilant sound, then she jumped down the stairs and raced across the yard. "Oh, my God, Jess."

They ran toward each other, arms reaching across time and distance and terrible words until the two sisters clashed in a tangle of limbs. As they embraced, a flood of emotion stole Jessie's breath. She batted back tears as she stepped away, shaken and battered and overwhelmed by bittersweet joy. Luz. Her sister Luz. The years had caused her beauty to soften like an oft-washed quilt. Her face bore the subtle lines of wear and tear. Her vivid red hair was paler in tone now, not so intense. She had borne three children, and it showed; she was rounder than the much younger picture of Luz that Jessie had carried in her mind.

"Surprise," she said with forced lightheartedness, then caught a flicker of concern in her sister's eyes. "I should have called first."

"Are you kidding? I don't mind," Luz said. "It's fabulous. And it's so *you.*"

Is it? Jessie wondered. Do we even know each other anymore? They'd kept in touch by phone and e-mail, but the sporadic contact was no substitute for being a part of each other's lives. She studied her sister's face, seeing an oddly distorted reflection of herself. Jessie and Luz had the same color hair, a faint saddle of freckles over their noses and eyes, their mother used to say, the color of a Scottish putting green.

A movement caught her eye as someone else came onto the porch—a tall, slender girl in shorts and a black tank top, with flame-red hair and eyes narrowed in curiosity.

Dropping her hands from her sister, Jessie gaped. Could this be her daughter, her tiny baby, this tentative young woman who matched her height exactly?

She cast a glance at Luz, whose smile was strained at the edges even as she gave Jessie a gentle shove forward. "Surprise," she whispered, echoing Jessie's lighthearted tone.

"Look at you," Jessie said to the girl. Then, with an irony only she understood, she added, "I swear, you're so beautiful, my eyes ache." She opened her arms wide.

For a moment, the girl stared. Frozen with fear, Jessie stared back, then slowly lowered her arms. She sensed but didn't see Luz make a signal to Lila, perhaps in some secret language of semaphores between mothers and daughters.

"Uh, hi," Lila said, her voice familiar and cherished from occasional overseas phone calls. She offered a tentative smile with all the wariness of a jogger confronting a large, unfamiliar dog.

You made this moment happen, Jessie told herself as the hurt settled in. This is your doing. She held herself still, her posture open. Nanoseconds before the awkwardness turned unbearable, Lila left the porch and walked toward Jessie. She hugged her uneasily, but Jessie couldn't stand it anymore and caught the girl in her arms.

"Oh, yeah, hug me, Lila," Jessie said through tears she didn't dare show. "Hug me hard."

The strong, slender arms tightened, and Jessie's heart soared. She was overcome by the lemony smell of Lila's hair, the youthful freshness of her skin, the warmth of her breathing. Holding her daughter for the first time was a huge moment in Jessie's life, and she wondered if her awe and enchantment showed. She realized her eyes were shut tight. Funny, that. When you held someone this close, you really couldn't see them, but all the other senses were filled to brimming.

She opened her eyes and saw Luz watching them. A cherry-red blush shadowed Lila's sweetly freckled cheeks. Jessie was drenched in wonder. It was like looking into a mirror, a particularly wonderful mirror that erased all the hard living and sleepless nights, all the mistakes and missteps of the past.

"Who is that lady, Mama?" A blunt, childish question broke the spell.

"Moi?" With her best Miss Piggy imitation, Jessie turned to face the little tousle-headed sprite. Though reluctant to relinquish Lila, she didn't want to make a scene here and now. "Who

is that lady?" Grabbing the little boy under the arms, she swooped him up. "I'm your long-lost auntie, that's who." She swung him around until he squealed with joy. "I know who you are," she said. "You're Rumpelstiltskin."

"Nuh-uh."

"You're Scottie and you're four and you have a dog named Beaver."

He nodded vigorously. Jessie set him down to address the other two boys watching avidly from the porch. "Your brother Wyatt is eleven and Owen is eight and he puts ketchup on everything he eats." Wyatt elbowed Owen, who gazed at her in amazement, clearly unaware of the telltale red-orange smear across his Animorphs T-shirt.

"What does Lila eat?" Scottie demanded, wanting more magic.

Jessie beamed at her. "Any damned thing she wants."

The boys' eyes widened, and they snickered.

"Mama!" Scottie spoke up first. "She said—"

"I said let's go inside before I die of thirst," Jessie interrupted.

The four children trooped into the house. Luz lingered to hug her one more time. Laughing, moist-eyed, she said, "I can't believe you're here. I can't believe I'm seeing you again." She paused to study Jessie from head to toe, taking in the swirling magenta skirt and marigold silk camisole from Bombay. "The kids already think you're Mary Poppins," she added. "Come on in. I'll see if I can't find my recipe for fatted calf."

Jessie felt the subtle sting of the barb. "I'm a vegetarian."

"And you weren't detained as a deviant at the Texas border?"

Jessie tripped on the bottom step and clutched at her sister for support. "Sorry," she said, laughing it off. "I think the jet lag is finally gaining on me."

She stepped into the unfamiliar chaos of a busy family. A TV, radio and stereo were all playing in various parts of the house. Kid clutter—lacrosse net, Rollerblades, schoolbooks and incomprehensible pocket-sized plastic toys—littered the main room. The smell of simmering spaghetti sauce spiced the air.

"We took a wall out and turned this whole space into a great room," Luz said, handing her a big tumbler of iced tea. "I can't believe you're here, Jess."

"Right in the middle of suppertime."

"I was putting the pasta on. Are you hungry?"

"Famished."

"I'll get busy, then, and you can keep me company." Luz led her to a stool by the kitchen island and offered her a seat. With negligent efficiency, she donned an apron, like a cowboy strapping on a gun belt. Jesus, an apron, thought Jessie. Her sister wore an apron.

As usual, Luz didn't mince words. "So what about Simon?"

Jessie hesitated. What *about* Simon? She'd known him for sixteen years, but had he ever really been a part of her life? He'd been teacher, mentor, lover, yet they had both cultivated the ability to set each other aside when something else came along. Even so, over the years their paths had kept crossing. They fell in and out of their relationship like time-share vacationers spending points. Then, in the past year, when the reality of her condition came crashing down, she'd dared to test the depths of their commitment. They'd both failed the test.

But it was all too complicated to explain, so she said, "Simon dumped me."

"Who's Simon?" Lila asked.

"Some pr—" Noting her sister's stiff posture, she said, "I mean, some jerk. He and I worked together, and he was my lov—boyfriend up until I— Until about a week ago." She suppressed a sigh of frustration. The thing about not being married is that you can't get divorced. So they didn't really know how to break up. Simon had bumbled around, muttering about a big new project in the Himalayas and how she shouldn't do anything hasty until she'd finally said, "Oh, come on, Simon, just be the prick you know you can be."

"Aw, Jessie." Luz patted her shoulder. "I'm sorry. What an idiot. What was he thinking?"

"He knew exactly what he was doing." Actually it hadn't broken Jessie's heart to leave him. She was good at leaving, and she'd left without regrets, simply bolted for refuge where she could hole up and heal. But it didn't feel like a refuge here, and she knew she would never heal.

"Lila, would you mind setting the table." Luz didn't ask it as a question. "You'll need to bring a folding chair from the deck."

Heartstruck, Jessie watched the girl respond to Luz's request with a belligerence she didn't bother to veil. Slamming open the sliding door to the deck, she brought in a chair and set it at the long table stretched to its limit by three leaves.

Lila. Jessie had sung the name to herself innumerable nights as she lay awake, thinking, wondering, wishing...Lila. A pair of liquid sighs, a sound as pretty as a spring breeze. Weeks after Jessie had walked out of the hospital, never to return, Luz had sent a picture of a tiny red-faced newborn that could have been any baby. On the back of the photo, Luz had written, "We named her Lila Jane in honor of the two NICU nurses who helped us so much."

Of course. They'd had more to do with Lila's survival than Jessie ever had. She had simply left, never looking back, with only the agony of her milk coming in, then drying up unused to haunt her with reminders of what she'd left behind. Jessie remembered looking at that photo for hours, trying to understand what she'd tossed into the wind, resisting the urge to gather it back. Oh, she used to ache with yearning and regrets, wishing she could hold her baby, witness her first smile, first tooth, first step. But that would only have deepened the agony. More than once in those early days, the physical distance and lack of funds had kept her from doing something foolish.

Luz assigned chores to each of the boys. Wyatt was in charge of slicing the bread, which he did with a stream of martial arts sound effects. Owen went outside to fetch his dad to dinner. Scottie was appointed chief napkin folder, and his airplane noises competed with Wyatt's Kiai until the place sounded like a war zone.

Lila must have felt Jessie's adoring, pain-filled gaze; she looked across the scrubbed pine table laden with chipped china and mismatched flatware and said, "This is not my life."

Jessie laughed, even though Lila didn't crack a smile. But Jessie thought, it is. It's the life I gave you. Tell me I wasn't wrong.

CHAPTER 3

A moment later, stomping feet sounded on the porch. "Intruder alert. Intruder alert," Owen and his father announced in a robotic monotone. Owen sat atop his father's shoulders, ducking down as they came through the door.

"Ian!" Jessie hurried forward as he flipped Owen head-over-heels to the floor. She hugged her brother-in-law briefly, a bit awkwardly.

He stepped back and grinned at her. He was one of those men who would look boyish at any age, be it twenty, forty... When he was sixty, he would probably still wear that Lone Star Long-neck T-shirt and the same size Levi's he'd worn in law school. Same blue eyes, same large gentle hands.

Jessie's skin prickled with apprehension. She'd known, of course, that by coming here she would have to face him, but she found herself unprepared for the sight of his lean frame, the abundant hair tumbling over his brow, the broad shoulders and generously smiling face.

"Hello, gorgeous," he said. "Long time no see."

"You look great, Ian," she said, feeling a rise of complicated emotion. For Luz's sake, they'd long ago put aside their old enmity and treated each other with good-natured familiarity.

"I smell like two hours of yard work." He paused to kiss Luz on the back of the neck as she worked at the kitchen counter. "You're a slave driver, Mrs. Benning." Grabbing Scottie like a football under his arm, he went to wash up.

Dinner was served boardinghouse style—pasta, red sauce with meatballs, meatless sauce hastily poured from a Ragú bottle, salad, bread. Luz seemed nervous, yet fiercely competent as she juggled glasses of milk and plates of spaghetti. Jessie felt like the main dish as the kids peppered her with questions. "Are you really our mom's sister?"

"Her baby sister, by three years."

"Are you famous? Mom told us you're a famous photographer."

"Your mom is being generous. My pictures are published in magazines but nobody knows who I am. Photographs are not for making the photographer famous. But it was heaps of fun."

"How come you talk funny?" asked Owen as he played with the croutons on his salad plate.

"I've been living in New Zealand for about fifteen years," Jessie said. "I probably picked up a bit of an accent. But you know what? They think *I* talk funny."

"Why New Zealand?" Lila asked. "How did you end up there?"

"That's a long story," Luz said quickly. "I don't think—"

"The fact is," said Jessie, feeling an unwelcome flicker of the old tension, "my very own sister made it possible." She settled her gaze on Lila. "I have a really generous sister. She and I were going to graduate from college at the same time, but there was only enough money to pay for one final semester. Luz insisted on being the one to quit and get a job."

"You had the higher grade point average, better prospects, a chance to work abroad with Carrington," Luz reminded her.

"I hope you're as good a sister as Luz is," Jessie said to Lila.

"She is," Scottie said stoutly. "She's the best sister I got."

Lila ruffled his hair. "I'm the only sister you've got."

The moment of tension passed. Jessie pushed back from the table and gave everyone a wicked grin. "I brought presents."

"Presents!" The boys punched the air. At a nod from Luz, they excused themselves and followed Jessie outside to paw through the boot of the rental car for the ANZAC bag containing the treasures. Even in her haste to leave, Jessie had taken the time to choose gifts for her family: a Maori waka figurine for Scottie, a fearsome carved swamp kauri mask for Owen and a small model of a Maori war canoe for Wyatt. For Ian, there was a kiwi bottlestopper, and for Lila, a set of paua barrettes, which gleamed with natural iridescence. She smiled a bit shyly, and it was all the thanks Jessie needed. Finally she gave Luz a carved greenstone pendant.

"It's the koru," she said. "A native fern. Regarded as a symbol of birth, death and rebirth. It represents everlasting life and reincarnation."

"So it pretty much covers all bases."

"Yep."

"I need all the help I can get." With a laugh, she leaned forward and hugged Jessie, a flash of good-natured envy in her eyes. "You've been to some fabulous places."

"This is pretty damned fabulous, if you ask me. I love what you've done to the house."

In the den, the phone rang, but no one sprang to answer it. Luz caught Jessie's look. "We don't take calls during dinner."

"But dinner's over," Lila protested.

"Not until the table's cleared." Luz ignored Lila's poisonous look.

The machine kicked on, followed by the sound of a distinctly male, adolescent voice.

The cherry blush returned to Lila's cheeks. She said nothing, but Wyatt piped up, leading his brothers in from the porch. "She's in *looove*. She's in love with Heath Walker," he said in a singsong taunt. Together, he and his brothers broke into the classic chant: "Lila and Heath, sittin' in a tree, *K. I. S. S. I. N. G...*"

Lila mouthed something that looked like *fucking morons,* threw her napkin on the table and stomped upstairs. Wyatt and Owen elbowed each other and giggled until Ian glared them into silence. Scottie chanted under his breath, "First comes love, then comes marriage, then comes Lila with a *ba*-by carriage!"

Jessie met Luz's eyes across the table. "Welcome home," Luz said.

Jessie sent her a pained smile.

The boys were denied dessert as punishment for the chanting.

"That means she didn't make dessert in the first place," Wyatt muttered, thus earning the extra chore of loading the dishwasher.

Owen and Wyatt were banished to the showers. Scottie grabbed a battered copy of *Go Dog Go!* and went in search of Lila to read it to him, certain his big sister had forgiven him already. Ian went to get one of the cabins ready for Jessie.

"Nothing like a nice relaxing meal with the family, is there?" Luz peeled off her apron and folded it over the back of a chair. She grabbed a bottle of red wine and two glasses and led the way out to the deck. "Now comes Merlot time," she said, imitating the old commercial.

She lit a citronella candle to keep the mosquitoes away. They sat down in a pair of Adirondack chairs and Luz poured. They weren't proper red wine glasses, they didn't match, but they were festive enough.

Luz held up her glass. "I'm glad you're back. And stunned."

Jessie raised her glass but instead of clinking against Luz's, she misfired and dumped half the wine on the deck between them.

"Damn it," she said through her teeth. "Sorry—"

"De nada." Luz gave her a refill. "With four kids, spilled beverages are my life, doncha know?"

They sipped their Merlot. Across the lake, the sun was a thread of fire on the horizon. The calm waters were glazed in beaten gold, with inky lines wavering across the surface. Lines she didn't trust. Didn't know which were real and which were not.

"Did you call Mom?" Luz asked.

"No. I suppose I should." Their mother lived in Scottsdale with husband number four. Stan? No, Stu. Stuart Burns. Jessie had never met him. She made a point not to get too cozy with her stepfathers, since none of them stayed around for long, yet Stu had defied the odds. These days, Glenny was the ladies' pro on a suburban golf course, and somehow she was just as busy as she had been when she was constantly on the tour.

Jessie and her sister sat without speaking for a while. There was so much to say that they said nothing, just listened to the sounds of the settling day: water lapping at the shore, bobwhites calling out for reasons no human could fathom, the swish of the wind through the bigtooth maples that grew along the south shore of the lake.

Luz drew her bare feet up to the edge of the chair and draped her arms around her knees. Her feet were tanned, the nails of one foot painted with pink polish. So much about her seemed half finished—projects, toenail polish, her garden. It was the story of her life. She'd left college before earning her degree to marry Ian and adopt Lila. Jessie wondered if this was a life half-lived, or had Luz left things undone because she had more important things to do?

Across the water, about a quarter-mile off, a vaguely familiar pickup truck pulled up to a wooden house set in the side of a broad hill. Jessie thought it might be the stranger who had given her directions earlier. "Are you acquainted with your neighbor across the way?" she asked, more concerned with filling the silence than with the answer.

"Not really. He's got a little girl about eighteen months old, I think. I heard he used to be a pilot in Alaska, but he moved down here when his wife died or left him or whatever. He's got a fancy Swiss-made airplane out at the county airpark. Ian's used his service for work before. His name's Rusty or Dusty, if I recall." Luz's face grew dreamy. "He's a grade-A hunka burnin' love, if you want to know the truth."

"Luz."

"I know, I know. But even we soccer moms have our fantasies."

"Is that a floatplane tied to his dock?"

"Yeah. He does lessons and tours, too, or so I hear. A regular jack-of-all-aviation. Maybe you could get him to fly you over the maples. That is, if you're going to be around for a while."

"Maybe." Jessie had hoped the wine would help relax the knots in her stomach, but it wasn't working.

The quiet lapping of the lake lent a sense of intimacy—though it was probably only imagined—to the moment. Luz didn't say a word, yet Jessie heard the question as clearly as though her sister had spoken it aloud: *Why did you come back?*

The wind licked across the surface of the water and sifted through the maple leaves.

Jessie took a deep breath. "I wanted"—*say it*—"to see her."

She knew what the next question would be before Luz asked it. *Why now?*

"I shouldn't have stayed away so long," Jessie said in a rush of nervousness and half-truth. "The years got away from me. But then I realized..." She took a deep swig of wine. Even now, long after she'd come to terms with reality, she was surprised by the terror that gripped her. She was at a crossroads in her life. Leaving Simon wasn't the only thing that was happening to her, but it had its own sort of importance. Struggling to hide her secret fear, she said, "Ah, hell. Simon and I broke up, and—"

"And?"

Not now.

"Everything went to shit. Nothing seemed right anymore. I wanted to see Lila and meet the boys, and...I missed you." The truth of it reverberated through her, the breeze shimmering audibly through the trees. "I'm sorry. What more can I say?"

"You don't need to apologize. God knows, I'm no saint."

"Yes, you are." Jessie had always known it, ever since Luz had played the Virgin Mary in the fourth grade Christmas play. Jessie, in first grade, had been in the hosanna chorus, with the sacred duty of ringing a bell on cue. She could still picture her sister, robed in blue, kneeling over a basket of straw containing a swaddled doll. Some artistry of lighting had suffused Luz's face with a glow of maternal piety that made the women in the audience reach for their husbands' hands, and even the gym teacher had to wipe away a tear.

Even then, thought Jessie. Even then.

Of course, their mother had missed the performance. Each December Glenny played in the Coronado Invitational in San Diego. Jessie couldn't recall which neighbor had looked after them that year.

"Luz? Is it that bad, that I came back?"

"No." She put a trembling hand on Jessie's. "It's that...I didn't really think you'd ever be back. The work you were doing over there sounded so fabulous... Perfect, like a dream."

Jessie took her hand away. "It was fabulous and perfect for a long time, but—" She hesitated. "It's over now." She gripped the armrests of her chair. "Luz, do you ever think about telling Lila?"

"Oh, *Jess*." The night shadows haunted Luz's face with mystery and pain. "Of course we've thought about it."

"But you never said anything."

"That was your idea," Luz reminded her, "and we agreed to honor that. We moved back here when she was three, so there was no chance of someone asking an awkward question in front of her. People still remark on how much she looks like me."

"She does look like you."

Luz nodded. "Like both of us. Once in a while, someone remarks that she looks like Ian. Can you imagine?"

Jessie took a swift gulp of wine. Yes. She could imagine.

"As a matter of fact, I have brought it up. The first time I tried to explain things to her was when I was pregnant with Wyatt. She was four. She asked me if I got so big when she was a baby in my tummy. It was simply beyond me to lie, even to a four-year-old. So I told her she was a baby in another woman's tummy, but the moment she was born, I became her mommy. She laughed and told me I was silly, so I didn't push the issue. It seemed cruel to burden her with information that would only confuse her. She never asked again and I'm sure she forgot the incident. And she was always a difficult child, given to taking dangerous risks."

"What do you mean, risks? Why didn't you ever tell me this stuff? It's not like I was incommunicado—we had letters, e-mail, phone calls."

Luz combed her fingers through her hair. "It was nothing *that* serious, but she's contributed her fair share of gray. The first thing she did when we moved out here was jump off the dock—and she didn't know how to swim. That same year, she went toddling out to the neighbors' cow pasture to pet a Charleroi bull. She broke her arm jumping off the Walkers' barn roof, flapping a pair of homemade wings, because she thought she could fly. I don't think I let her out of my sight until she started kindergarten. She loves extreme sports, white-water rafting, water-skiing—anything with a high degree of risk. Ever since she was tiny, she's had a wild streak running through her. I'm not sure why. Maybe because we worried and fussed over her so much when she was born, or—"

"Maybe she gets it from me," Jessie said, knowing the thought had crossed her sister's mind.

"I won't take that cop-out," Luz said. "I got the daughter I raised—that's how it works. Ian and I aren't perfect... Ah, Jess. Time slips by so quickly. I was always so busy when the boys were little. Even now, I barely have a moment to go to the bathroom, let alone psychoanalyze my daughter."

Jessie's gut lurched at the words *my daughter.* Leaning back in her chair, she absorbed the blow. With some barely acknowledged part of herself, she understood that Luz loved the idea of Jessie being fifteen thousand miles away. It was so much easier that way.

"She's been getting in trouble at school, acting out, that sort of thing. You saw how she acted toward me. My sweet little fairy child has turned into a demon, skipping school, sneaking out at night, climbing the water tower, rappelling off the train bridge, skinny-dipping in Eagle Lake. I keep telling myself it's a normal teenage rebellion, she'll get over it and we'll all survive, but it keeps getting worse. Her grades are going south, I don't know her friends anymore. She's going through all the things you read about in those scary books about adolescents. Ophelia is alive and kicking."

"So what are you doing about it?"

"We've been talking to the school counselor, but I don't know if it's doing any good."

"So does the counselor know—"

"Of course not. If we haven't told her, we're not about to tell some stranger. Only Mom knows, and she's never, ever mentioned it."

"Maybe Lila's having some sort of identity crisis."

"She's fifteen and a half. Everything is a crisis when you're that age."

Evening light fell over Luz. How different she was now. Yet how much the same. Over the years Luz had sent dozens of beautifully composed photos. Innumerable portraits and informal snapshots infused with the rich honesty that was Luz's trademark. Most pictures showcased the kids, but a few had featured Ian. He was always playing with them, flying kites, setting off homemade rockets, running along beside one of the boys on a new bike, paddling a boat. Luz's place had always been behind the camera. Like Jessie, she'd studied photography in college, and her photos were remarkable and crystal clear. Photography had been a passion for both sisters. Yet Luz had given up her ambitions to raise a family.

Jessie stood and stretched her arms toward the sky, arching her back. "I'm going to hit the hay. I don't even know what day it is."

Luz stood up and hugged her. "Ah, the jet lag. You must be bushed. I'll let you get to bed. Ian took your luggage over."

In the house behind them, lights glimmered in the windows, and the low hum of the air conditioner swished through the gathering twilight. The thump of rock music vibrated from one of the upstairs windows.

At the path to the cabin, Luz paused and squeezed Jessie's hand. "How long are you planning on staying?"

"I don't know. Look, if it's a problem—"

"Of course it's not a problem. You belong here for as long as it feels like home to you."

Jessie squeezed back, even as she bit her tongue. She'd never tell Luz, but this place had never felt like home to her. No place ever had. "I don't know what's next for me." It was probably the most honest thing she had said all night. "I called Blair LaBorde as soon as I landed in Austin." Blair was an old friend from the University of Texas, a fiercely ambitious failed debutante who didn't give a flip about the genteel past. After finishing her doctorate, she taught for a few years, then became the star writer of a glossy popular news magazine called *Texas Life,* working out of the Austin bureau.

Jessie was aware of the irony of looking for an assignment at this point, but she needed all the work she could get, and she needed it now. More than that, she needed the solace of work, which for so much of her life had been a refuge from issues she didn't care to face. When she took pictures, she could disappear into the camera lens and travel to sharp-edged, dramatic places where the real world turned into fantasy.

"You called Blair but not me?"

"I had to let her know I could use some work."

Luz relaxed a little; Jessie knew her sister understood practical matters all too well. "With her connections, she's bound to have tons of assignments."

"That's what she said. When I mentioned Edenville, she found a dead lead for a local story, and promised to see if she could revive it."

"Then it's as good as done. I wonder what it's about?" They stopped at the bumpy path that led to the three cabins on the property. "Not exactly the five-star hotels you're used to, is it, Jess?" Luz asked.

Jessie laughed, shaking her head. "You have an inflated view of my glamorous international lifestyle."

"At least you *have* a lifestyle."

"At least *you* have a life." Jessie laughed again as she said it, but she could feel the tension thrumming between them, as fresh as if she'd never left.

CHAPTER 4

Carrying the half-full bottle of wine and a borrowed glass, Jessie made her way along the path through the woods. She was eager for bed, hoping to push past the dizzy exhaustion of jet lag.

When she was little, the forest had held a thousand unseen terrors for her, and if she had to cross the woods at night, she would hold her breath the whole way for fear of inhaling the evil spirits that inhabited the darkness. She found herself holding her breath now, and the same old terror clawed at her, but unlike that frightened little girl with the messy braids, she knew what scared her. It was a lot more real than monsters hidden amid the sighing maples, shaggy mesquites and bony live oak trees.

Ian had brought in her bags and turned on a couple of lights and the window unit. Manufactured air that smelled faintly of mildew blew gently into the room. The cabin had a kitchenette, sitting area with a lake view and small bedroom and bathroom in back. A little, contained world, one that held neither threat...nor hope.

"Hello," she called out.

"In the bedroom," Ian said.

"Then I've got you right where I want you." Although everything had changed, Jessie forced herself to tease like the fun-loving girl he'd known so long ago. In the pine-paneled room, she found her sister's husband struggling with a hyper-elasticized mattress pad that didn't quite fit the queen-sized bed.

"Right," he said, flashing her a grin. "Give me a hand with this, will you?"

She eyed the messy wad of bedclothes. "But you were doing so well on your own." She grabbed a corner of the mattress pad and wrestled it in place. On the other side of the bed, he did the same. But each time they got one corner covered, the opposite one sprang loose. Finally Ian lay spread-eagled on top of the thing, holding down the corners while Jessie tucked them in place.

"The things I have to do to get a guy in bed," she muttered, finally succeeding with the mattress pad. She wrinkled her nose. "You were right earlier—you *do* smell like yard work." They worked together in companionable silence, and she was grateful for the ease she felt with her brother-in-law. There was a time when the two of them hadn't gotten along at all...and a time, before that, when they had gotten along too well. Now they simply got along, because to do anything else would upset Luz.

Everything about Ian Benning was larger-than-life—his looks, his voice, his laughter...his passion. That was what had drawn Jessie to him, so long ago, before he'd ever met Luz. Ian and Jessie had never loved each other, but youth and appetite had sustained them through a brief, incendiary affair that had flared up quickly, then burned to ash just as fast.

She and Ian never talked about that time and no one knew about it, not even Luz. It was all so long ago, she rarely thought about it. Especially since her heart guarded a larger secret, something even Ian didn't recognize.

He had been a third-year law student at UT, and Jessie a hard-partying photojournalism major who looked older than she was. Their affair had been simple biology at work, and Jessie had been known to base relationships on shakier foundations than that. She'd met him at a campus party and slept with him that night. For about three weeks, he was everything she'd ever hoped for—physically. But when not directly groping each other, they didn't have much in common. He thought experimental theater was something found at the Doyle Center on Sixth and Pine, and she thought a capital case was a character on her keyboard. They never officially broke it off, but in the middle of week three, as if by mutual agreement, they stopped seeing each other. She flung herself into a photography project taught by Simon Carrington, a visiting professor from New Zealand. She was fascinated by both the subject and the man.

Not long afterward, Luz fell in love. *He's perfect, Jess. I can't wait for you to meet him. And he's a law student....*

To their credit, Ian and Jessie covered their shock that first meeting. If Luz noticed the startled looks, the red-eared remembrances, the guarded glances, she never let on. When Jessie shook Ian's hand, she recalled that hand caressing her bare skin. When he gave her a fleeting smile, she remembered the taste of his mouth. It felt weird as hell. Not exactly like incest, but like some sort of secret that had no name.

Neither Jessie nor Ian ever said a word to Luz. Even then, they wanted to protect her because the idea of upsetting her was unthinkable. They both loved her, both wanted to safeguard her from the mistakes of the past.

"Where are you, Jess?" he asked, drawing her back to the present. "You look like you're a million miles away."

"Woolgathering," she admitted, fluffing the pillows against the headboard. Straightening up, she said, "Luz says Lila's been giving you a run for your money."

His face paled and his mouth tightened. Then he took a deep, uneven breath. "I never know what to do about Lila these days. Puberty hit like an eighteen-wheeler. According to Lila, I'm the bane of her existence. I love her, Jess. I love her with all my heart. But she's a teenager now and it's not so easy, figuring out the right thing to do."

She searched his face, seeking some hint that he knew the deeper secret. But he regarded her openly, and she saw no undercurrents buried in his eyes. He didn't know. Amazing. If Lila didn't know who her biological mother was, she couldn't begin to deal with who had fathered her.

When Jessie found out she was pregnant, Ian had cornered her in private and confronted her with the inevitable question: *Is it mine?* Simon had asked the very same question. And she gave each man the same answer, telling one man the truth and one a lie.

She had looked her ex-lover in the eye, that tall, good-looking man who loved her sister, and said, "No." What else could she say? If she admitted the baby was his, he would have been forced to choose between taking responsibility for the mother of his child, or keeping a secret from his wife. It would have been a nightmare for all of them, so Jessie had done the only thing that would keep the situation from exploding.

At the first doctor's appointment, Jessie discovered the date of conception coincided with a certain tequila-marinated night at a honky-tonk that ended on the screened-in back porch of the rambling old house Ian shared with other law students. But she never said a word. Luz loved this man, and Jessie would not be the cause of her heartbreak.

The rest of the pregnancy was taken up with discussing the adoption arrangements, getting a passport, making plans to live overseas as an expatriate. She and Simon were going to photograph the world's wonders. She was going to escape to the adventure of a lifetime. Ian was going to marry her sister, practice law, raise a family. It should have been so simple.

But at twenty-one, alone and scared, she hadn't understood that matters of the heart are never simple. She thought knowing the baby was with her natural father and Luz would dull the ache of loss. She thought sending all the money she could spare to help with the hospital bills would somehow exonerate her. But the hurt never quite faded.

As Ian turned on the hot water heater in the cabin, his pager went off. He checked the tiny display with a frown.

"Problems?" Jessie asked.

"Shoot. I was expecting this. I've got to get to Huntsville tonight."

He probably had to go file a last-minute appeal or something. Watching him, she could see he was already withdrawing, thinking about the case. Being a death row attorney in Texas was clearly a job with a number of built-in frustrations. "You'd better get a move on."

"Yep. Anyway, I need to go say good night to the family and get myself over to the airpark. Fellow there will take me to Huntsville tonight." He offered her a brief hug. "You need anything, let Luz know."

"I will. And thanks, Ian. Good luck." Standing at the door, she watched him head up to the house with a purposeful stride, a good man trying to keep a bad man from dying.

After he was gone, she poured the rest of the wine into a glass and went out to the broken little dock in front of the cabin to savor the last of the daylight. The water was dark and flat, the air refreshed by the cooling breath of night. Exhaustion crept through her, and her eyelids drooped.

But now she forced her eyes open; she had to look. Sixteen years ago, Jessie had left in a red haze of panic, before her premature infant's survival was assured, before the baby even had a name. Now Jessie was back, driven by desperation to face up to what she had done, to fill in the blanks of those lost years, to somehow find atonement and maybe even redemption. And it had to start with Lila.

She had to see her daughter, really see her. See the way the light fell on her hair in the morning, how her eyes looked when she smiled or wept, how her hands lay atop the covers when she slept at night, how her mouth puckered when she ate a slice of watermelon.

Jessie wished for the one thing she wanted above all else, the one thing she couldn't have—more time. She had consulted doctors and specialists from Taipei to Tokyo, but the prognosis was always the same. Her condition had no known cause...or cure. Once assured of the diagnosis, she'd done the only thing that seemed important. She had come back to see her child before the lights went out.

CHAPTER 5

The woman from *Texas Life* magazine was definitely getting on his nerves, thought Dusty Matlock as he stabbed the off button of the phone. Christ, how many different ways did he have to say no before she got it?

Blair LaBorde reminded him of his Jack Russell terrier, Pico de Gallo. Persistent as hell, immune to insult, didn't know when to quit. Over-the-top human-interest stories were her stock-in-trade. She needed them to make a living as much as he needed to fly to make a living. And the spectacular way Dusty's wife had died and given birth made him a prime target for the circling buzzards; he'd already turned down *People* and *Redbook*. Amber was almost two now, and he'd put his life back into some sort of order. The bleeding had stopped, the patient would live, but the scars would never fade. The pushy reporter wasn't helping.

The phone rang again, and he grabbed it. "Look, Miz LaBorde, what part of no do you not under—"

"It's Ian Benning from across the lake."

"Oh. Sorry, I thought it was someone else." Dusty didn't elaborate on his troubles with the nosy journalist, but maybe he should. Benning was a lawyer; he might know what to do about a persistent newshound. "What can I do for you?"

"I need to get to Huntsville tonight. Can you do it?"

Dusty didn't take long to consider. Immediate service was his stock-in-trade. "Can you meet me at the airstrip in an hour and a half?"

"You bet. Thanks."

Dusty was glad for the work. Benning had used his service a few times, and word of mouth on Matlock Aviation was starting to spread.

"Ay, mujer." In the next room, Arnufo gave a low whistle. "Come and see what I have found."

Dusty walked into the front room facing the water. The elderly Mexican stood in front of a tripod that supported a telescope, peering through the eyepiece. The scope was aimed at the dock in front of a cabin across the lake.

"Leave poor Mrs. Benning alone, you old *cabra*," said Dusty.

"It's not Mrs. Benning. Take a look. I think *La Roja* has a sister."

Shading his eyes, Dusty could see a woman seated on the dock, her long pale legs dangling over the side. The lowering sun highlighted a head of red hair. At first glance, she did look like Benning's wife. But at second glance...

His gaze clung briefly, then shifted away. "I think I passed her on the road earlier." He recalled a pretty, distracted-looking woman stopped at the side of the road, as though lost, in a late-model rental car.

"You should have introduced yourself."

He put the lens cap on the scope. "This is for looking at the stars, not spying on the neighbors."

Glowering, Arnufo straightened up. "We should bake a cake, go and introduce ourselves."

"Right."

A squawk from the playpen drew his attention. Amber was

standing up, her little fists grasping the webbing. Both men hurried across the room to her, and she greeted them with her best five-toothed grin.

"Hey, short-stuff." Dusty ruffled her white-blond hair. She reached up, opening and closing her hands in supplication. But her entreaty was aimed at Arnufo, not Dusty, which was just as well, judging by the smell of her. He stepped aside, saying, "She's all yours, *jefe*. I bet she's cooked up a little surprise in her diaper for you."

"You are a man of no honor."

"I am a man who needs to get a weather briefing and a flight plan. I'm taking Ian Benning over to Huntsville tonight."

"I'll fix you some *tortas* for supper." Arnufo Garza was a good cook, having learned to rustle grub during his bachelor years as a ranch hand in San Angelo. He picked up the baby. "Come to Papacito. I will not be intimidated by a diaper."

The three of them were an unusual family. Arnufo and his wife, Teresa, had been employed by the Matlocks since Dusty was a boy, as caretakers of the big house in the Stony Creek section of Austin. Teresa had practically raised him, because his mother stayed busy with his high-maintenance sisters.

When both Dusty and Arnufo were widowed in the same month almost two years before, Dusty had proposed the current arrangement. Now the old gentleman spent his days looking after Amber while Dusty got his business off the ground—literally and figuratively.

He patted his daughter's hair again, its softness slipping between his fingers, then headed out the back to the shed that doubled as a workshop and business office. To the dismay of his ambitious parents, he was in love with flying, not the petroleum industry. He earned his pilot's license even before his driver's license and had been flying ever since. By the age of twenty-one, he'd acquired a Pilatus PC-6 Turbo Porter, and for fifteen years he'd worked as a pilot in Alaska, flying mining, oil rig and pipeline workers to sites so remote that they seemed to be on another planet.

The wilds of Alaska would always call to the adventurer inside him, but with the birth of Amber, he'd had to make adjustments. Including leaving the frozen wilderness for his home state of Texas and the picture-postcard world of Edenville. The flying business was working out well here. Between Austin dot-com millionaires and good-old-boy oilmen, Dusty stayed plenty busy. But there was a jagged hole in his life, and he figured there wasn't any arrangement he could make to change that. His folks complained that Eagle Lake was too far from Austin; why didn't he find someplace closer?

They didn't understand. Karen had died in the autumn when the trees in Alaska took fire with color. She had always loved that time of year, when the first skin of ice on the lakes meant taking the floats off the plane and replacing them with skis. She would like the idea of her little girl growing up in a place where trees turned color as though touched by magic. The sight of those trees here in the middle of Texas was something special, like finding a pearl in an oyster, or a four-leafed clover. Rare, unexpected. Lucky, even. Discovering the maples here was like watching a bumblebee fly. Aerodynamically impossible, but they defied nature anyway.

From the window of the business office, he watched the woman on the dock. Though unable to see her in detail, he knew somehow that Arnufo was right. She was definitely related to Mrs. Benning. Where had she come from and why hadn't he seen her before?

You should have introduced yourself.

Arnufo was always handing out advice like that, but then again, life was a simple matter to Arnufo. So was death, come to think of it. In life, you made certain you did good work, took care of your family and kept your promises. If death happened to steal something from you—say, your wife of fifty-two years—well, then, you made a new sort of life for yourself.

Go and take what you want from life, Arnufo liked to counsel him. Don't wait for it to hand you something. Things given away freely are given away for a reason—because no one else wants them.

Dusty had tried dating a few times in the past few months, but he found the whole process depressing. His heart wore an armor of numbness. He had better luck when he stuck to running his business and raising his daughter. That's what he told himself, anyway.

"Introduce myself," he muttered under his breath, booting up the computer to log on for his briefing and clearance before gearing up for the night flight. "Hi, I'm Dusty Matlock, and I haven't been laid in two years."

"Some women would find that a great challenge," said Arnufo, joining him in the shop. On his hip, he carried a smiling, much more fragrant toddler. As she tugged at Arnufo's trademark bolero tie, she yakked away with the uncanny conviction that her babbling made sense.

"Yeah? Like who?"

"Bunny Sumner at the airpark, for one. She gave you a whole plate of brownies and you never called to thank her. And what about Serena Moore from the Country Boy grocery? The one with the *muy grande...*" With his free hand, he pantomimed a huge rack.

"Okay, I get your point. Should have introduced myself."

Arnufo swung the baby high in the air, crooning a little song in Spanish and earning a sweet chortle from her. The old guy was a natural when it came to Amber. The father of five grown daughters and a herd of grandchildren, he reveled in kids of any age.

Dusty smiled to himself as he worked at the computer terminal, yet he felt a vague stirring of unease. Arnufo was so comfortable with the baby. Dusty wasn't a natural when it came to kids. He loved his daughter, and perhaps the bond was even stronger because of what had happened to Karen, but that didn't mean he knew the first thing to do with Amber. The truth was, he handled her awkwardly, loved her awkwardly. He could read a German instrument panel, a Chinese flight manual or an aberrant weather pattern. He could compute climb and descent times and fuel burn in his head. But he could not read his daughter's face.

Arnufo watched him work in silence for a while. Dusty logged in to the weather and flight planning site and went through the drill. A seventy-one degree course, 192.2 nautical miles. Rhumb lines spidered across the screen, and the printer hissed out a chart.

"Take *la princesa.*" Arnufo held out the baby. "I will get you packed for the flight."

"I need to call the tower and get clearance over the Air Force base, then I'll be ready." Holding the baby, Dusty followed Arnufo outside. Sunset covered the lake in a blanket of gold. Amber made a sound of displeasure as Arnufo headed for the house, but she didn't cry as she sometimes did. Pico de Gallo came racing across the yard, distracting her and cheering her up. The dog was insane, but entertaining; Amber was nuts for him. She shifted in Dusty's arms, her sharp little elbows and knees poking into him. She smelled like flowers and sunshine and yeasty warm milk.

The baby made a gurgling sound and waved a star-shaped hand at the lake. The woman was a black silhouette now against the sinking light. When she tipped back her head to take a sip of wine, she looked like an antique French ad poster.

"Papacito Arnufo thinks I should've introduced myself to her," Dusty confessed to his daughter.

"Da," said Amber.

He perked up. "What's that?"

"Ba."

"No shit."

The purple sky, pricked by early stars, deepened to indigo. A clear night for flying. Across the way, the stranger on the dock stood and walked away.

Well, he was taking Ian Benning over to Huntsville tonight. Maybe he'd ask him a thing or two about the woman.

CHAPTER 6

God, thought Lila Benning, putting her hands over her tortured ears, what a stupid-ass lame family. Even with the stereo turned up as loud as she dared, she could still hear the Three Stooges in the next room, revving up for another night of being morons. Tonight's entertainment sounded like an armpit-farting contest. Lila dove for the bed, burying her head in a mound of pillows and stuffed animals.

Predictably, a shout from below created a momentary silence. "Pipe down up there."

Her father punctuated the command by thumping the wall with a fist, and the morons subsided. Then the inevitable whispers started up, like the munchkins in Oz peeping out from under their flower petals, the volume increasing until bunk beds rattled and giggles crescendoed with idiotic exuberance.

"Don't make me come up there."

Her dad's next command was followed by an even briefer silence and then an even louder song because, as everyone knew from the start, that was the whole point. To get Dad out from behind his paperwork and up the stairs.

His Timberland work boots thudded on the stairs with ominous slowness. "Fee fi fo fum..." With each step, he growled out a syllable. She heard him burst into the kids' room with a roar, followed by a chorus of porcine squeals and the rusty creak of bed springs as he wrestled the boys into submission. The ritual ended predictably. Dutch rubs all around, followed by Scottie's nightly reading of *Go Dog Go!* and then a "'Night, guys," and finally, blessed silence at last.

Lila crept out from beneath the pillows and waited. Dad tapped lightly at her door.

"Yeah?" she called out.

He stepped inside, hesitated. Her dad did that a lot lately. A pause, a measured beat of uncertainty that hovered between them like an unanswerable question. He never hesitated with the boys, but with her, he never plunged right in. The dim light from her computer screen saver outlined his tall, broad form. Her friends often remarked that her dad was a hottie, but she never saw him that way. She just saw her dad, who worked too hard during the week and went fishing on Eagle Lake every weekend and looked at her like she was a space alien.

"Hey, kiddo," he said.

"Hey. Where's Mom?"

He gestured vaguely. "She's helping me get a bag ready for Huntsville." He shuffled his feet. In Lila's room, plastered with deathrock posters, littered with schoolbooks and cheerleading gear and cosmetics, he never seemed to know quite what to do with himself, where to settle his gaze. The sight of a bra left out or—God forbid—underwear draped over a doorknob, always made him jittery. "So what do you think of your aunt Jessie?"

Lila gave a shrug of studied nonchalance. "Don't know. I just met her." The fact was, Lila was sort of fascinated. Her aunt, whom she knew only from the occasional scribbled note on the back of a postcard from Indonesia or Japan, an e-mail from an Internet café in Kathmandu and the Christmas phone call—which always came the day before Christmas because of the time difference—had never seemed quite real to her. She was a remote idea, more like a character in a book or a long-dead relative, like Great Grandma Joan. In person, Jessie was interesting and maybe a little weird. Her red hair was cut chin length, the tips bleached blond around her face. A younger, thinner, hipper version of her mom, without all of Mom's frustrated frowns, long-suffering sighs...and the veiled disapproval that always lurked at the back of her gaze.

"I guess you'll have a chance to get acquainted while she's here."

Lila shrugged again, pulled a stray thread from her cutoffs. "I guess." It was about damn time, she thought. About time something interesting happened in this family.

"'Night, kiddo. I'll see you day after tomorrow." Her dad planted a kiss on the top of her head and stepped out. She lay thinking about him and how strange it must be to go see a man's family while the state executed him. What did he say to them? What did he feel?

Most kids whose dads were lawyers were considered lucky. Their fathers made tons of money and drove BMWs and flew to Aspen or King Ranch in chartered planes. Lila's dad wasn't that sort of lawyer. She was old enough to know his work was important, but young enough to wish he got more out of it than write-ups in the paper and interviews on Court TV.

A few minutes later, her mom came in, carrying an armload of folded laundry. "Hey, sweetie."

"Hey." Lila wasn't sweet, and hadn't been in a long time. And both she and her mom knew it.

"Try getting these put away—"

"Before they go out of style," Lila said, taking the stack of folded shorts and crop tops and setting them on the end of the bed—on top of yesterday's stack. "I will."

Her mother sent a pointed glance at the stack, but said nothing. She didn't have to. Lila felt the familiar accusation.

Taking refuge in indifference, she said, "So what's the deal with Jessie?"

Her mom looked distracted, maybe nervous, although Lila had never really seen her mom acting nervous. She was always so sure of herself, so decisive. "I'm not certain what her plans are. She's going to do some pictures for a magazine, I think." Mom pushed a stray lock of hair behind her ear; she looked tired and harried. She always did, and that annoyed Lila. These days, everything about her annoyed Lila. The way she always wore faded shorts and giveaway T-shirts, the way she never put on any lipstick, the way she caught her thick red hair in a messy ponytail, the way she ate Scottie's leftover peanut butter toast for breakfast and never fixed anything for herself, the way she pretended to watch MTV with Lila but was really reading one of her bazillion travel books about Provence or Tibet, a dreamy look suffusing her face until something sexy happened on *The Real World.* Then her face would contract into a prune of disapproval. She was uncool and she knew it. Worst of all, she didn't care.

"So what do you think of her?" Mom asked.

"Dad wanted to know the same thing."

"And?"

"She's okay, I guess. Jeez, we had supper. Big deal. What, am I supposed to love her instantly because she's family?"

Mom blinked in surprise. For a second, she looked almost pretty. "I don't know what you're supposed to feel. Curious, I guess."

"Whatever."

Mom hesitated, then bent down and gave her a kiss. She smelled of the mom smell—cooking grease, shampoo, generic brand antiperspirant. "Make sure your homework is done."

"You bet," Lila said, knowing full well she wouldn't do the Spanish or the algebra tonight.

She had big plans instead. Luckily she didn't have long to wait. Dad would be off to Huntsville within the hour, and whenever he went out of town, her mom turned in early to fall asleep while reading *House Beautiful* or *Travel & Leisure.* Thank God tonight there would be no shuffle and squeak of bedsprings and soft giggles as her parents tried to be quiet. That sort of thing was excruciating to Lila.

Tonight she heard only the low murmur of their voices as Dad packed his bag. They were probably discussing Jessie and the guy on death row and maybe the meeting Dad would miss tomorrow with Lila's school counselor. She was glad of that. They kept trying to understand her "issues," and work on her motivation and self-concept—like those things were going to turn her into an A student with a perfectly clean room.

Sure thing, Mom.

After a while, she heard her dad drive away to the airpark and finally, finally the lights clicked off and the house settled.

A soft pinging sound alerted her. Heart thumping madly, she dashed to the window. The pebble at the window was an old trick, but it worked. She blinked her light three times to let him know she was coming.

By now, Lila had memorized the steps going downstairs. Numbers three, six and eleven creaked; she avoided them. She slipped out through the kitchen door and crossed the deck, and there he was.

Heath Walker. The only thing that made life worth living.

He was like a god, standing there, one hand on his hip, the other offering Beaver a piece of beef jerky so the stupid dog wouldn't sound the alarm.

Lila leaped at Heath, loving the feel of his arms going around her. His thick, wavy hair was made for her searching fingers. They kissed, hot slippery mouths and restless hungry tongues. Heath was ready to party. She could taste the flavor of purloined cigarettes and Shiner beer in his mouth.

"Let's go," she whispered, tugging him by the hand. "Hurry."

He tossed the rest of the beef jerky to the dog and they slipped away into the dark woods. He always parked on the other side of the property so no one would hear his Jeep or see the headlights.

"Oh, shit." Lila froze, clutching his hand.

"What's up?" he asked.

"We've got company. My aunt is staying in the cabin. Shit shit shit."

"Maybe she didn't hear."

They didn't speak as they crept along the path. Lila actually held her breath, not wanting to inhale bad luck from the atmosphere. There was one tricky thing about this. To get to the place where Heath parked his Jeep, they had to pass by the row of three cabins. If they were quiet, if they were lucky, she wouldn't see them. If they were unlucky, they'd have to make up some story about him borrowing a homework paper or textbook.

A single light burned in the bedroom window of the cabin. Please please please, Lila thought.

But no. The minute Lila and Heath stepped out of the shadows, there she was, standing in the doorway, shading her eyes.

"Lila?" she called softly, "is that you?"

Lila dropped Heath's hand. "Be cool," she said under her breath, then pasted on her best teacher-pleasing smile, even though Jessie wasn't anything like any teacher she'd ever known. Lila was a good faker, and she knew it. Her acting ability had kept her from flunking out of school, from getting caught shoplifting...but Jessie was a photographer, like Mom. A pang of nervousness rattled Lila, as she wondered, Can a photographer see things other people can't?

"It's me, Aunt Jessie."

"Come into the light, where I can see you."

Lila complied, motioning Heath to her side. Her aunt was wearing silky little shorts printed with moons and stars, and a spaghetti strap tank top. It was something Lila would have picked for herself.

"Um, this is my friend, Heath. He came over to borrow my chemistry book."

"Oh. Hi, Heath. Nice to meet you." She stuck out her hand, and for a second she aimed it in the wrong direction. She grinned, and her smile was beguiling. Her accent was unusual, as cool as the rest of her.

"Good to meet you, ma'am." Heath had perfect manners for meeting grown-ups, Lila thought with a surge of pride. The way he looked her in the eye, shook her hand, she'd never guess how toasted he was.

"So you must be a dedicated scholar, coming out so late to borrow a textbook," said Jessie.

"Hey, Aunt Jessie, give us a break, okay?" Lila sent her a wide-eyed look of appeal. "We're only going for a walk by the lake, I swear, that's all." She tried to sound desperate but not pathetic. But God, she had to get away with this. She had to. If Jessie ratted on them, Heath might drop her. He was a senior, captain of the football team and star quarterback. He could have any girl he wanted, and he might not want a girl who couldn't handle sneaking out on a school night.

Jessie hesitated, obviously trying to assess the situation.

"We're not doing anything bad, I swear it," Lila assured her.

Jessie pushed a finger at her lower lip. "Okay," she said at last. "I'll give you this one, girlfriend. I don't want to start our relationship on the wrong foot."

It was an odd turn of phrase. *Start our relationship.* Like this was the beginning of something. Lila would contemplate that later. For now, she wanted to savor her victory. She lit up with a smile and impulsively flung her arms around her aunt. It was weird to be hugging her, this person she'd never met until today. "Thank you," she said. "You're the best."

Jessie seemed surprised by the hug, then she clung hard for a second before stepping back. "Just don't screw up," she said. "And remember, if your mom asks, I can't lie for you."

"You won't have to, because I won't screw up, right Heath?"

"You bet. Nice to meet you, ma'am." He grinned that aw-shucks grin that made Lila's heart speed up, and it seemed to work on Aunt Jessie, too. She gazed at him with a sort of soft, melty look on her face, not with narrow-eyed suspicion like

Mom would have. Pride and gladness surged through her as she took Heath's hand and gave it a squeeze. This was one of those moments she wanted to keep forever, to remind herself how good life was.

They veered down to the lake, then took a circuitous route along the gravel driveway to Heath's Jeep. "Close call," she said on a burst of relief as she settled herself into the passenger seat.

"I'll say." He leaned across the console and kissed her again, and this time his hand stole downward to touch her breast.

She felt an electrical sting of fire, then reluctantly pulled back. He'd been pressuring her to have sex, and she'd been holding out, but pretty soon she knew she'd give in. One of these days they'd find the right time and the right place, and it would be perfect. "Everyone's probably wondering where we are. We'd better get a move on," she said.

"Yeah." He put the Jeep in gear and drove up past the broken rock, then pulled out onto the road. Lila pushed the power on the radio, and a gut-thumping beat filled the car. A short way down the road, they picked up four more passengers. Travis Bridger and his younger brother Dig, and Lila's best and second-best friends, Kathy Beemer and Sierra Jeffries. Travis, who was seventeen and looked old enough to buy beer in the next town, passed around chilled, sweaty cans of Shiner.

"Nectar of the gods, my friends," he announced, took a long gulp, then let loose with an impressive belch.

Turning around to the back seat, Lila clinked cans with everyone. "Cheers," she said, and downed a third of the beer in one pull. She honestly didn't care for the fizzy, bitter taste of it. But after the first beer, the second went down with ease, spreading its blurry chill through her limbs, softening the edges of the world and making her mouth tend toward smiling for no reason.

"Double your pleasure." Heath handed her a joint, and she used the cigarette lighter to spark it, inhaling and holding her breath and battling the urge to cough as she passed it to the back.

The sight of the four of them sitting there, with Kathy in Dig's lap because there weren't enough seat belts, cracked Lila up. She opened her third beer to celebrate the moment. There was nothing like the soaring joy of knowing she had friends like these four and Heath, who understood her even though she didn't have to say a word, who liked her even though her mother was lame, even though she didn't seem to know her father anymore, even though her brothers drove her crazy. They just *knew*. Sometimes she thought they existed in her life for the sole purpose of reminding her that every night could be a party.

The headlights of the Jeep threw a long cone of light along the empty road, the beam sweeping over scrub oak and mesquite and critters scuttling in the underbrush. The whole vehicle seemed to be buoyed along by beer and pot and laughter. When Heath reached out with his free hand to touch her cheek, she nearly burst with happiness.

"Where to, chief?" asked Dig, his voice croaking as he held in a toke.

"Seven Hills!" Lila shrieked, and Kathy took up the cry, too. "Seven Hills!"

Heath kept his eyes on the road as a priceless grin slid across his face. "You got it." He cracked open another beer, took a swig and set the can in the drink holder.

Lila felt a thrill of anticipation. Seven Hills was their favorite place to go ramping, and Heath's Jeep was the best vehicle for the job. His dad was loaded, and since the divorce he'd given Heath the best of everything, including a late-model Jeep, perfect for four-wheeling. And for launching.

The sport had grown so popular that they'd devoted an entire safety assembly at school to the topic. The principal and a DPS officer in mirrored sunglasses had stood at the podium, ignoring laughter and heckling as they expounded on the dangers of hill-hopping by crazed teenagers who drank and smoked weed. The tight-assed adults missed the point. It wasn't about danger and rebellion. It was about flying.

"Ready, gang?" asked Heath as they approached the roller coaster series of seven hills near an abandoned rock quarry in the middle of nowhere. The popularity of the place had increased lately as word got around, in the mysterious manner that things got around to teenagers. A few other SUVs and trucks were already out hill-hopping. She recognized Judd Mason's battered Bronco. There was an old pickup that might have belonged to anyone, but the flames painted on the sides and the *yee-haw* issuing from the open window were unmistakably Leif Ripley's.

Heath double-checked his seat belt. The back seat had only three belts, so he told Dig to let Kathy have the third one. "Brace your hands on the ceiling, man. *Hard.* You too, Lila honey."

With a sweet surge of admiration, she leaned over to kiss his cheek. He really was a safe driver. But safe didn't have to mean boring. Heath was proof of that. He revved the engine, blinked his lights to let the others know he was ready for takeoff and then punched the accelerator.

"Yeah!" Dig shouted from the back seat. "Go, Heath-man."

The Jeep shot up the hill like a bullet toward the sky, a perfect launch. Sierra and Kathy screamed, but Lila was mute with wonder at the breath-stealing speed. She pushed her hands flat against the roof, bracing herself.

And then it happened. The launch. At the crest of the hill, the Jeep took off, all four tires leaving the ground. The windshield formed a perfect frame for the endless night sky. It was like looking out of the Starship *Enterprise.* For a moment, everything slowed—time, breath, heartbeat—and even the shrieks from the back seat faded to the awed silence of shock and wonder.

Then came the inevitable bone-jarring landing. Heath managed it beautifully, with all the skill of a Hollywood stuntman in a Vin Diesel movie. Everyone celebrated with high-fives, and Dig, the idiot, decided to open a beer in celebration. The agitated beverage sprayed everywhere.

"Way to go, Dig." Travis cuffed his brother.

"My neck hurts," Kathy said. "My butt went three feet in the air."

Heath laughed and headed for hill number two. "Space," he said in a deep TV announcer voice. "The final frontier." Then he slammed his foot down on the accelerator. For a moment the back tires spun, filling the air with the harsh burn of rubber. Then the Jeep roared forward. They took the hill doing seventy, clearing the crest and bottoming out on the landing. Sparks shot from the undercarriage as the car careened along, bouncing crookedly. Lila felt a Fourth of July fireworks thrill as her shoulder slammed against the passenger-side door. Who cares if there's a bruise, she thought as she shouted with glee. This was the essence of life, and she was grasping it with both hands.

The next hill was her favorite, a long, straight shot up a sharp rise, followed by a landing on a steep slope. "One more," she begged. "Please, one more."

Heath gunned the engine. "That's what I like to hear," he said, and her heart burst with pride, because he was so special and he'd given her a compliment.

"This is the bomb," yelled Dig.

"I feel sick," Sierra whined from the back seat. "I bit my lip, and it's bleeding."

"Keep your mouth shut on the next jump," Travis said, tucking his arm protectively around her.

"Let's go, Heath. Hit it, man!" Dig said.

The Jeep raged forward. Lila had the sensation of leaving her stomach behind, like a feather on the wind. As they sped up the hill, the sky opened up before them, deep black and endless with possibility. She sensed everything with a heightened awareness— the sharp reek of rubber and road, the sound of her friends laughing, the rhythm of Second Wind pounding from the stereo, the crash of blood in her ears when the Jeep's four wheels left the pavement.

The vehicle flew higher than they had ever gone before. She knew it. She knew this launch was different when Dig pounded his knees and yelled, *"Awriiight!"* And when Kathy whispered, "I'm scared" and when Lila saw the sky begin to spin. And when Heath gripped the steering wheel and said, "Oh, shit."

Something was wrong, bad wrong. The knowledge flashed through everyone like an electric current, swift and shocking. Lila opened her mouth, but she didn't know if she was screaming or not. Her hands flailed, then she clutched at the armrest. Someone's—everyone's—screams filled the Jeep, the night, the world, the universe.

Time slowed and the car seem to float, suspended by terror and wishful thinking, and by prayers dredged up from Sunday school, over the road that wasn't there anymore.

It was over in the time it took to blink. Somehow, they'd taken off at a crazy angle, and there was no way they could land on the road. The Jeep crushed down to the ground, veering out of control, the windshield popping out like a contact lens. The car bounced and then rolled, and it was like the time Lila went kayaking on the Guadalupe River, and learned to roll the kayak, hanging upside-down underwater, so close to drowning that she saw stars until her mother had rescued her, hauling her to the surface by the scruff of the neck.

But there was no one to rescue her now. She was drowning in unspeakable pain, screaming pain, and the Jeep simply wouldn't stop rolling, kicking up a storm of caliche dust and tumbleweeds. Lila heard screaming and crying and *oh God oh shit* from the others—from Heath, from Kathy who was so scared and from Dig who thought all of life was such a joke. Someone flew out of the car—she couldn't tell who—and bounced like a rubber ball and disappeared. A lifetime flashed by before the Jeep finally shuddered to a stop like a dying dinosaur. Pain and fear and prayers pulsed with the music from the stereo, which played on as though nothing had happened.

The song ended and the DJ gave a rundown of the weather at the top of the hour. Lila wondered what hour. Thoughts drifted past and swam away from her like little colorful fish in an aquarium. She heard crying unlike anything she'd ever heard before. A thin, keening wail, not quite human. The sound of a creature in unspeakable agony, begging to be released from its misery. Her eyes were full of dust and grit, crushed glass and blood.

A beer commercial burbled from the radio: *Here's to good friends...make it a Michelob moment...* She smelled piss and shit and wondered if it was her and sort of hoped it was, because at least that would mean she was alive.

Lone Star Ford puts you in the driver's seat...

Move. She had to move somehow. She realized then that she was upside-down, hanging, held in place by the seat belt cutting into her. She swiveled her head, and pain burned like wildfire. The milk-white moon threw streams of light through the spiderweb cracks of the passenger-side window. The glove box hung open, having disgorged its contents, and a small lightbulb glowed within.

Heath. She couldn't see his face. It was turned from her, and his shoulder was jammed against the steering wheel. His silky blond hair looked like liquid gold. His hand hung limp and was flecked with dark spots. Blood.

Lila shut her eyes. Why was I mean to Scottie? Rude to Dad? Why didn't I keep my room clean? Please God, I'll do all those things, I'll be perfect if you just make this not be happening.

"I'm scared..." The tiny whisper came from somewhere else in the car.

The engine was still running and Lila could smell gasoline and exhaust. A clatter rattled through her head—the chattering of her own teeth. She tipped back her chin, feeling excruciating pain as she tried to make out the others in the back seat. Slitting open her eyes, she caught a glimpse of Kathy, who stared straight ahead without seeing and kept whispering, "I'm scared. I'm scared. I'm scared."

Someone else spoke. She wasn't sure who, but it came out as a distant, monotonous chant. "Please God please God please God..." A truncated plea from someone whose skill at praying was rusty.

She heard a distinct dripping sound and twisted to look, defying the screaming agony in her shoulder. Bodies lay strewn outside the car, but some were still strapped in. The back seat was a tangle of arms, legs, crushed beer cans, rumpled clothing, patches of dark, slick wetness she couldn't identify. She could see one face clearly. It was Dig, who'd given up his seat belt. His face shone like the moon, pale and round and distant and mysterious. His eyes were shut. A viscous black ribbon trickled from the corner of his mouth, another from his ear.

The clatter started up again inside Lila's head, only faster, harder. And through the steady rattle of her teeth, she managed to make a noise, sending through her pain and terror the only word that made sense to her, the only thought she had:

"Mommy."

C H A P T E R 7

Even before she answered the phone, Luz knew. It was the phone call every mother fears with the special dread reserved for people whose entire world is made of love for others. The call that signals her life has changed while she was sleeping.

She came instantly awake, grabbing the phone in the middle of the second ring. Adrenaline flushed all the grogginess from her by the time she had the receiver in hand. She mentally flipped through the gallery of possible horrors. Ian's plane had crashed. Mom had had a heart attack. Jessie... That had to be it. Simon was calling to grovel, and had no idea what time it was in the States. At least it was a school night, and the kids were safe in bed.

As she clicked on the phone, she glanced at the clock. The blood-red digits read 1:36 a.m.

"Hello?"

"Is this the parent of Lila Benning?"

Everything inside her turned to ice. "Yes," she said in a deceptively clear, calm voice. "This is Lucinda Benning." She almost never used her hated given name, but then again, she'd never had a phone call in the middle of the night.

"Ma'am, this is Peggy Moran. I'm a nurse at Hillcrest Hospital. Your daughter has been brought in..."

"Not my daughter. She's asleep in her room."

"...level two Trauma Center..."

Luz's mind seized on the information even as she burst into motion, tucking the cordless receiver between her shoulder and chin, bounding out of bed, throwing on clothes. "I don't understand. Lila's in bed."

"Ma'am, there was a motor vehicle accident involving a group of teenagers..."

"A group of...then there must be some mistake." Dizzying relief flowed through her like a drug. "It's a school night. She's here at home." Clutching the phone, she rushed into Lila's room, just in case. In case the nurse was wrong. In case Lila was actually safe and sound in her bed and this was all horrible nightmare. But no. The room was messy, but unoccupied.

"Ma'am, I'm afraid she's here. We ID'ed her from the learner's permit in her pocket."

The relief dried up, blew away like a child's lost balloon. Luz grabbed her purse from the doorknob as she passed. "Is she conscious? Can I talk to her?"

"She's in the radiology suite now."

"Is she—" Luz couldn't draw the words from the well of horror inside her. "I'm on my way. You understand, I'm forty miles from you. Do you need some sort of permission for treatment or surgery or—" She paused, reeling against the stair rail. She couldn't believe she was saying these things.

"It's too early to say for certain, ma'am." The nurse couldn't give her any more information, so Luz hung up.

What to do? What to do? She needed to get on the road. *Now.*

For the first time in her life, Luz wished for a cellular phone. Ian had one for work, but Luz had never cared for them, electronic umbilical cords that made it impossible to hide, even when you wanted to. Now she would give anything for one. She wanted to be able to drive down the road and tell Ian what was going on as she hurtled through the night toward her daughter. Instead, helplessly pacing the floor, she had to call the Huntsville TraveLodge, where he stayed when one of his clients was down to the wire.

Other attorneys' wives had warned her for years, *Never call your husband in the middle of the night when he's away on a case.* Death-row lawyers typically had any number of eager interns at their beck and call, and the ones with Ian's looks had plenty of becking and calling options. Interns tended to be young, earnest, idealistic, dedicated...and horny. All this flashed through her mind as a hotel operator took forever to pick up, then ring Ian's room.

"Ma'am, there's no answer. Would you like to leave a message?"

While she let the dog into the house, she spoke the unspeakable and left the name of the hospital. She rang off and alerted his pager. Then she tried his cell phone. He didn't answer, so she left the same message on his voice mail. *Damn you, Ian. Where the hell are you?*

She refused to think about that—about anything—except getting to Lila. Upstairs, she paused outside the boys' room, opening the door a crack to assure herself of what she already knew—they were fast asleep. The sound of their breathing, the smell of their sleeping bodies, filled her.

Jessie, she thought. Thank God she was here. She could look after the boys. Then Luz hesitated. Jessie didn't have the first idea how to get a gang of boys off to school. She would have to take it on faith that her sister could figure things out. The boys knew the routine.

Luz went outside, flung her giant purse into the car and started the engine. Leaving it idling, she made her way to Jessie's cabin, nearly tripping several times in the dark. "Jessie," she said, knocking at the door. "Jess, wake up." She pushed the door open to find her sister emerging from the bedroom, blinking in sleepy confusion.

"I'm sorry to wake you but something's happened," said Luz.

The sleepiness sharpened to concern. "What?"

"There was a car wreck. Lila's at the hospital. I need to get there right away."

Jessie's face turned pale. "Lila!"

"They just called. Hillcrest Hospital. I've already left word for Ian, and I'm on my way there now."

"Jesus. I can't believe this is happening." Jessie's voice shook, and she clutched at the door frame. "A car wreck? But that can't be. She—"

"Look, Jess, the boys are still sound asleep in the house. I let Beaver in. Can you go over and stay with them?" Luz realized her mind was jumping around, out of control. She was having trouble focusing. "And if I'm not home soon, can you get them up around seven and give them some breakfast? The school bus picks up Owen and Wyatt at the top of the hill at seven forty-five. Would you—"

"Go, for heaven's sake." With uncharacteristic bossiness, Jessie took charge. "Call me the second you know something." Jessie gave her a hug, then pushed her toward the door. "I'll take care of things."

Jessie's words rang in Luz's mind as she drove at a rampantly illegal speed, exerting a cold and perfect control over the car. She felt nothing during the endless drive. The mysterious yellow eyes of nocturnal creatures flashed now and then, and she knew she'd neither slow down nor swerve for the occasional deer or armadillo. It was as though she had given her mind a shot of novocaine, numbing herself to the soul-shredding terror that would seize her as soon as the body's natural anesthetic wore off.

She parked crooked at the hospital in a space marked Visitor. What else would there be at a hospital—a permanent resident? Then she rushed toward the main entrance under a grand porte cochere that made the hospital look incongruously like a five-star hotel.

Except for the ambulance bay on one side. Luz didn't permit herself to look, because if she did, she would be forced to imagine her daughter there, mummified in a cervical collar, backboard and fireproof blanket. Helpless, needing her mother.

The automatic doors swished open to a semicircular foyer swarming with people—highway patrolmen, EMS workers, hospital personnel in Easter-egg-colored scrubs. Women weeping in their husbands' arms, older people patting the hands of younger women, bewildered kids milling around in pajamas, everyone half-dressed and unkempt. Bad news left no time for good grooming, even in Texas.

As she jostled through the crowd toward a horseshoe-shaped reception counter, Luz recognized Kathy's parents and Heath Walker's mother and stepfather. She couldn't recall their names. When had she stopped knowing the parents of Lila's friends? They used to be the women she would sit with by the lake while their kids played in the shallows; the families they would invite over for barbecue and volleyball on Sunday afternoons. Parents used to stand on the sidelines during swim meets and soccer games, cheering each other's kids on. But as the kids got older, the parents drifted apart, needing each other less. Now they were simply people she nodded to politely at PTA meetings or church.

She leaned across the counter, which was littered with papers and charts, little containers of cheap plastic pens and paperclips. "Lila Jane Benning. I'm her mother."

"Yes, ma'am." A harried-looking receptionist clicked the keys of her computer. "Let's see. She's out of the Resuscitation Bay. They've moved her to exam room four. She's stable. You can go see her. I'll get an orderly to take you back, and—"

Luz didn't wait for the orderly but simply took off, passing a room labeled Trauma. With a swift glance, she saw doctors, nurses and technicians clustered around a draped gurney, their gowns spattered like butchers' aprons, the floor littered with bloody gauze and crumpled blue-and-white packaging. A branch off the main hall bore the ominous designation of Resuscitation Area. Hurrying past that, she found her way to a large oblong room surrounded by walls of wire mesh glass. Four beds were set up, all occupied and surrounded by a forest of rolling trays laden with instruments, IV poles hung with bags of some mysterious elixir, monitors punctuating all the activity with electrical blips. She spied her daughter immediately, an unmoving, supine figure shrouded in sheets, a limp curtain obscuring the upper half of her body. Only one slender hand showed, two of its fingers connected to some sort of monitor with clear clothespins and white Velcro. Luz knew that hand. Small and neat, like her own. Lila's eyes were closed, her face pale but unmarked, an alien-looking oxygen mask covering her nose and mouth.

"Lila," she said, rushing to the bedside. All of a sudden she was trembling, melting inside. The nurse said she's stable, Luz reminded herself, then said, "Baby, I'm here."

For a minute, it was just like when Lila was born, a tiny organism in an isolette, too fragile to touch. Luz remembered pressing her whole body over that clear cylinder, embracing it, praying, *Live, please live for me....*

She forced herself to stop shaking and held her daughter's hand, studying its wholeness and perfection as she thought about that newborn trapped in a nest of tubes in the NICU. Her tiny hands had been so transparent that every vein showed through, and sometimes Luz imagined she could see the blood flowing along the delicate vessels. So strange and beautiful, the nails clear ovals.

This was some sort of punishment, Luz thought with a sick lurch of her gut. Perhaps this was the retribution she had awaited with secret dread since the day Lila was born.

She had taken her sister's child. Never mind that it had been for all the right reasons and that Jessie had begged her to adopt the baby. Luz had always felt undeserving of such a gift and unequal to being the mother of someone so helpless and perfect and so close to death she was practically an angel already.

But Lila had survived. And thrived. Yet now Luz had almost lost her again.

She's stable. Luz wasn't sure what that meant. She caressed her daughter's head in a soothing, instinctive gesture. She felt dirt and grit, and something stiff and sticky in Lila's hair. She stank of vomit and blood and gasoline, offensive smells on this child, Luz's fussy little girl, who insisted on making special trips to the drugstore for vanilla-scented deodorant and antiseptic shower gel.

"Lila, can you hear me?"

"Mommy." The whisper was as thin and faint and sweet as birdsong.

Luz stiffened against a new wave of trembling, this one instigated by relief. "Baby, you're going to be all right. I'm here now."

Lila didn't open her eyes. Though she lay motionless, she seemed to drift a little, to withdraw.

"Sweetie—"

"You must be Mrs. Benning." A young man with a subtle accent and dusky skin greeted her. He wore a white lab coat over spotless scrubs, a tag hanging from his pocket identifying him as Roland Martinez. His manner was brisk and competent, his smile a flash of professionalism designed to reassure. "That red hair must be a family trait."

As he flipped open a chart, Luz felt a beat of panic. Dear God. What if they'd done some sort of test that showed Lila was not her biological daughter? Now was not the time to have to explain things to Lila. "What happened?" she asked.

"Your daughter was in a multiple-victim car accident along with five other young people. Lila was extremely lucky. Extremely," he repeated. "She was wearing her seat belt and suffered only minor injuries."

Reading from the legal-sized aluminum-backed chart, he said, "Dr. Raman, the trauma resident, admitted her. She was evaluated in one of the trauma bays and sent to radiology for X rays and a CT scan. There was no evidence of internal injuries. Nothing was broken." He gestured at a set of films. Lila's bones were fragile white ghosts backlit by the glowing box on the wall.

"She has a small laceration on one leg, a contusion on her shoulder from the seat belt, a few minor scratches from broken glass. You'll want to follow up with a visit to your family doctor, but the conclusion here is that she's your miracle girl, walking away from a wreck like that."

"Is that blood in her hair?"

"From one of the other victims." Dr. Martinez spoke very quietly, holding Luz's gaze with his. She didn't let herself ask about the other kids. Not yet.

"Why is she so out of it? Is she in shock?"

"Her blood alcohol level is 1.2, Mrs. Benning."

Luz breathed fast, staving off a new wave of panic. Drunk. Lila had been out drinking. Dear God, why hadn't she known? What sort of mother was she?

"Can you tell me how this happened?"

Dr. Martinez settled back on a wheeled stool and tucked the clipboard under his arm. "Mrs. Benning, do you know what hill-hopping is?"

"No."

"It's also called ramping and launching."

Numb, she shook her head.

"It's the latest craze in joyriding. The kids pile into a car or SUV and launch themselves at high speeds off the tops of hills. Like in the movies. Only what these kids don't understand is that professional stunts are completely different from launching. According to the preliminary DPS report, the Jeep went eighty feet through the air, then rolled another forty yards on impact. Lila was in the front passenger seat, still strapped in when the EMS arrived."

"I thought she was in bed, asleep." Luz shut her eyes, but quickly opened them again, forcing herself to look at her daughter. "Why would you do that, Lila?" she asked in an agonized whisper. "Why would you do such a crazy thing?"

Lila smiled a little. "I wanted to fly."

"Are you here by yourself, ma'am?" Dr. Martinez asked her in a sympathetic tone.

What he was really asking was, Are you all alone, did your husband dump you, is there no one here to pick up the pieces when you fall apart?

"My husband is out of town, but he'll be here as soon as he can," she said. "What happens next?"

"The highway patrol might want to interview her. She'll be discharged, barring any unforeseen changes in her condition." He handed her a clipboard and pen. "You'll need to fill this out."

Luz took the forms, and her teeth chattered as relief rolled through her. Then she forced herself to ask the dreaded question: "What about the other kids?"

"Four of them are being treated here." His dark eyes were thickly lashed, and soft with sympathy and secrets. "Another one of the victims was life-flighted from the scene to Brackenridge."

"Who?"

"I'm not at liberty to say, Mrs. Benning."

The constriction in her chest unfurled into ribbons of pain. She had read it a thousand times in the paper—The victim's name will be released pending notification of the family.... And then she dared to think the unthinkable. Thank God it was someone else's child and not mine.

Dr. Martinez's pager vibrated against a rolling metal table. "Would you excuse me a moment?"

Luz nodded, lost in her daughter again. Lila seemed to be dozing, or perhaps hiding behind closed eyes. It struck Luz to the core, how close Lila had come to dying or perhaps losing a limb, injuring herself permanently.

I wanted to fly. All her life, she'd sought things Luz couldn't give her. Flying was only one of them.

Forcing herself to concentrate, Luz worked her way through the lengthy, detailed forms. Medical history. Her hand shook as she began filling in the blanks.

Luz used to dream, too. Growing up, she imagined herself traveling the world, taking pictures of things most people would never see. The Taj Mahal, the caves of Lascaux, the Plains of Nasca. A husband and kids had never figured into that dream. But Luz had put her own dreams away years earlier to embrace a life she'd never anticipated for herself.

She had never believed in love at first sight until the day it had come knocking in the form of an earnest law student, smiling at her across a crowded library study table. In that moment, the color of her dreams had changed. They decided to get married right away. Luz would work while Ian finished his law degree, then she'd complete her own schooling. There was never any question but that she'd put his education first, as she had Jessie's. Luz had a talent for waiting. Maybe her mother had trained her to do that—to wait. All through her childhood she had waited—for a bus to pick her up, for her mother to notice her, for a check to come in...

Ian wanted to be a death-row attorney. She didn't really understand what that meant at the time. She thought marrying a lawyer meant stability, freedom from want. She envisioned a substantial house in a shady, old-Austin neighborhood, parties packed with interesting—no, fascinating—friends. Their future was set, golden with promise.

The one dark spot was the fact that Jessie and Ian disliked one another at first sight. They weren't rude about it, but...strained. When she asked them about it, separately, neither one really articulated the problem. Jessie said, "I want to make sure you'll be happy with a guy like him." And Ian said, "She's a flake."

Luz defended her sister, as she always did, but Jessie and Ian never did warm up to one another. Then, two weeks before Luz and Ian were to marry, Jessie had shocked everyone with the news of her pregnancy and the fact that she couldn't keep the baby.

When Luz asked who the father was, she simply said, "He's not an option." Luz assumed he was married. She offered to help Jessie. It wasn't as though Jessie would be the world's first single mom. Jessie admitted she truly wanted to have the baby, but it was impossible. She was so scared. She'd cried straight through an entire night; Luz knew because she sat up with her. "I couldn't even keep a goldfish alive," Jessie sobbed, referring to some long-ago childhood pet.

Simon had invited her to join a photography project underwritten by the BBC, which would begin in the fall overseas and end, perhaps years later, with a traveling global exhibit. The work would be hard for someone who was single and unattached. For someone trying to raise a baby, it would be impossible. Still, Jessie wanted to go. She had to go. It meant everything to her. It was a once-in-a-lifetime opportunity.

A *baby* was a once-in-a-lifetime opportunity, Luz remembered thinking.

Jessie had said, "I'm a terrible person. I'm so ashamed. But I'd be even more terrible as this baby's mother. That would be the real cruelty."

Luz told Ian she wanted them to adopt the baby when it was born. He turned white as flea powder and asked why. She told him she couldn't let Jessie give it away. Their unorthodox childhood had rendered Jessie incapable of being a mother. Yet it had the opposite effect on Luz. She wanted to mother the world. "That child is my own flesh and blood," Luz said.

Ian stammered out a question about the baby's father, and Luz explained her suspicions about Simon. Luz would always think of Ian's agreement as a surrender. She had won the battle. She was always secretly jealous of those adoptive couples who embraced the idea with a unified ecstasy. The truth was, she had dragged Ian kicking and screaming into fatherhood.

It had made her love him all the more. Instead of the planned honeymoon in Hawaii, they had a baby at Women's Hospital. They promised each other they'd take a trip later, when the baby was old enough to travel.

Seven months into Jessie's pregnancy, something went wrong. Weeks premature, the baby girl came almost without warning and was born too quickly for the doctors to stop the contractions. The newborn was put on life support. From the moment of the birth, Luz loved the tiny girl with a fiercely protective intensity that burned like fire.

Jessie went a little crazy when the doctors told her the prognosis. She insisted on signing the adoption papers mere hours after the birth. Since the chances of Lila's survival were so slim, Luz and Ian went ahead and signed, if only to give the baby two parents to grieve for her and a name other than Baby Girl Ryder. Luz asked Jessie if there was anyone she should call—meaning the baby's father. But Jessie only said, "He knows." Luz thought she was delirious.

Lila became her whole world, that helpless miracle encased in glass, defying the odds by surviving day after day. Luz sat vigil in the NICU, inseparable from the clear Lucite isolette that contained her baby. She celebrated every artificial breath pumped into the undersized body. She thanked God for every moment Lila survived without coding. Luz's devotion flowed into the baby like lifeblood from a gestating mother's umbilical cord. She nourished the struggling newborn with a love so powerful it was a pulsing, physical force.

The day they brought Lila home, Luz put away the travel books and set her dreams on the shelf. And, as exhausted by the ordeal as any woman who'd endured a difficult labor, Luz forgot that Lila had not been carried under her own heart. The unsleeping vigil gave Luz her own sort of fierce insanity, and she embraced a new dream—to see her child grow and thrive. And she did, turning into a magical little girl, an unasked-for gift for which Luz thanked God with tears of gratitude.

But Jessie was a part of Lila, too, Luz acknowledged as she made a row of checkmarks in the No column in response to the hospital questionnaire with its inevitable queries about family health history. What if she'd needed blood? Luz shuddered. The accident, coupled with Jessie's appearance out of the blue, was a slap of cold reality about Lila's biological parentage.

Then she filled out the inevitable "responsible party" information. Dear God, how simple it had been to honor Jessie's request to keep the adoption secret. In returning to Edenville, they reinvented themselves, reshaped their goals and dreams. They stopped planning trips—that seemed futile given all their debts and obligations. Then Wyatt came along, and Owen and finally Scottie. Not all of the pregnancies were planned, of course, but all were welcomed with a quiet, almost stoic joy. Ian worked hard and was a good dad, although he had always treated Lila differently than the boys. He was haunted by the nightmare of almost losing her at birth. In contrast, Luz loved her babies and loved being a mom so much she didn't realize she was losing herself.

Years and dreams faded away like the fall color in the lost maples of Eagle Lake, so gradually that she didn't notice until one day she looked up and all the brilliant pink and amber and orange had dissolved to a dull, uniform buckskin brown. She refused to allow herself to feel bitter. Every day was so full. She had so much, a husband who adored her, four active, healthy kids—

Luz bit her lip and completed the form. Then she watched Lila sleep for a while, growing restless as the minutes ticked by. Across the hall, she could see Heath's parents consulting with three doctors, and from the stricken look on their faces, she knew the news was not good. She turned away, hoping they wouldn't see her. Survivor guilt was its own kind of pain.

Setting aside the clipboard, she stood and paced, darting glances at Lila. She was like a Celtic princess, lying there, delicate and ethereally lovely. Yet she seemed to possess the same deeply embedded wildness of her birth mother, the same attention-stealing personality, the same beguiling mixture of cleverness and charm. Luz wondered how Jessie could be so...so present in a child she had left before seeing her first sunrise.

"Mrs. Benning?"

She looked up with a vaguely guilty start. The speaker tipped a felt cowboy hat in her direction, then removed it. He was a stocky man in the long sleeve blue shirt and tie and low-heeled cowboy boots of the DPS uniform. His badge identified him as P. McKnight. Strapped to his shoulder and hip were the classic tools of his trade—a holstered gun, handcuffs, a walkie-talkie, a nightstick. He exuded the confidence of a man sworn to protect and defend, but with an unreasoning anger, she had the thought that he'd failed to protect Lila from her own rebellious nature, or to defend her from the hazards of a carload of friends.

"I'm Officer McKnight, ma'am. I need to review some things in the accident report," he said. He told her more than he asked her, and they put together the likely scenario. Lila had sneaked out to join Heath Walker in his Jeep. They'd picked up the other kids and gone hill-hopping. Luz found herself squirming as Officer McKnight delved into her private struggles with Lila. The falling grades, the increasing truancy rate, the inscrutable silences, the bursts of shouting when frustration overwhelmed them. The beer and pot. How long had that been going on? For the life of her, Luz couldn't say.

She gazed helplessly into the highway patrolman's world-weary eyes. "I love my daughter. I never saw this coming. I never knew she was...that she would sneak out and drink beer and smoke weed."

His walkie-talkie burbled and growled, and he excused himself. Luz glanced at her watch—5:30 a.m. Lord, where had the night gone? And where the hell was Ian?

Luz stepped out into the waiting area, digging into her purse for change. She plugged a few coins in the pay phone and dialed.

Jessie picked up in the middle of the first ring. "How is she?"

"She's okay," Luz said hastily, trying to spare her sister the gut-tearing horror of the unknown. "A few cuts and bruises. They're releasing her as soon as— I actually don't know what we're waiting for. I couldn't get hold of Ian, but I left a message. I'm sure he's on his way from Huntsville." She hated how that

sounded, as though she couldn't find her husband and was making excuses for him.

"What happened?" Jessie asked.

Luz took a deep breath. She felt unexpectedly defensive as she twisted the silver phone cord around her index finger. "She sneaked out last night."

A long, tense hesitation hummed across the line. Luz couldn't read her sister's silence. Taking a deep breath, she went on, "She met up with some other kids, and they went hill-hopping." Luz shifted the phone from one ear to the other and wiped her sweaty palm on her pant leg, then proceeded to describe the latest fad activity to her sister. As she spoke, she pictured Heath's Jeep flying through the air, strewing children among the scrub oaks and tumbleweeds along the way. "Apparently it's a new extreme sport."

Another hesitation. Then Jessie said, "That's not exactly new."

"What do you mean?"

"Remember that El Dorado I had when I was sixteen?"

"Vaguely." She recalled an old green heap, one window stuck in the down position, rockabilly music blaring from a tinny radio. Then she recalled they'd had it towed to the salvage yard after Jessie drove it clunking home, its right front tire in shreds and the front end damaged beyond repair.

A chill prickled over her skin. "Are you saying—"

"Ridgetop Road, on the way to the quarry, right? Seven Hills? I guess stupidity must be a family trait. So you're sure Lila is okay."

"Yes. Shaken." Luz decided not to say anything about the drinking.

"What about the boy?"

"How did you know there was a boy? I didn't mention any boy."

"There's always a boy involved in something like this, isn't there? You said she met up with some other kids."

"She did. There were three boys and three girls in the car."

"Oh, God." Jessie sounded nauseous. "So is everyone okay?"

"I don't think so. One of them was taken to Brackenridge. I think—" She turned into the little nook of the pay phone and pressed herself against the wall, trying to disappear. "I'm afraid he's in bad shape, but nobody's talking. I'm scared for Lila. Afraid of how she'll cope when all this becomes real to her."

"She'll be all right," Jessie said. "We'll make it be all right."

"Thanks, Jess. We'll be home as soon as we can."

Luz hung up the phone, flashing on an image of her sister. What a shock it had been to see her walking up to the porch, a younger, more vivid version of Luz herself. Breaking into Jessie's own trademark thousand-watt smile, she had whirled into Edenville like a Technicolor tornado. Now she was in charge of Luz's boys.

Luz turned to scan the waiting area. She had brought Lila to the E.R. more than once, when she'd split her chin open falling from a rope swing, and when she'd broken her arm jumping off that barn roof. Wyatt had come in with a gash from a rusty nail one Sunday last year, and a few summers back, she'd driven herself here, not wanting to present that particular ailment to her hometown family practitioner.

Now the waiting area appeared chaotic, jammed with more and more people as time went on. When she recognized Mrs. Linden, the school counselor, she realized how big this was, growing bigger by the minute. There were six kids in the car. Six families, six mothers awakened from a sound sleep in the middle of the night. The effects of this would ripple outward like circles in water, radiating from a single dropped stone, getting larger and encompassing more and more each second.

People were crying, arguing, praying. The police were trying to question everyone. Nell Bridger collapsed into Mrs. Linden's arms, and something inside Luz curled up in horror. Nell had two sons, Travis and Dig. Which of them had been in the Jeep? Both?

She tried to navigate her way across the lobby to Nell, but her friend left quickly, leaning on the counselor. The noise rose in a crescendo of despair. Luz wanted to clap her hands over her ears to drown out the cacophony of fear and rage.

Into the streaming chaos walked her husband, worried eyes scanning the waiting area. Luz's heart rose when she saw him coming toward her. They met in the middle of everything and she clung to him, her safe harbor in a storm of confusion.

She said nothing, for she feared that bitter accusations might come out. Often his work consumed him. His job was no mere nine-to-five occupation. He'd missed birthdays and first steps, swim meets and teacher conferences because he'd been in court or in session, racing against time to rescue someone from being executed. She was proud of the work he did but sometimes— God, sometimes—she wished for more of him. For all of him.

"Is she okay?" he murmured. "Can I see her?"

Luz clenched her hands into his shirt. Her knees liquified, and she nearly collapsed against him. "She's going to be fine."

They embraced one more time and a flash went off. The media had arrived, hungry for anything that would sell papers or airtime. Grabbing Ian's hand, Luz wove through the crowd and into the hallway, then hurried on to the exam room.

Lila was sitting up in bed, sipping something from a plastic bottle. Her hair formed a ruby-toned nimbus around her head, and the cruel starkness of the overhead lights sucked all the color from her face. When she spied Ian, she cut her eyes away. "Daddy."

"Hey, sweet thing." Ian halted at the end of the bed and re-garded her with a sort of restrained reverence that was almost fear. He didn't touch Lila other than to put his hand on the starched sheet covering her leg. Ian rarely touched Lila anymore; since puberty hit, he regarded her as some exotic creature that could be handled only by trained specialists. "You're sure she's all right," he whispered to Luz.

"Yes. Stay with her." Luz ached to be away from the hospi-tal. She wanted to sweep her family out of the putty-colored halls, out of the exam room with all this frightening equipment for determining damage, life or death. "I'm going to find someone to help us get the hell out of here." She left him standing by the bed.

After the ordeal of coping with a premature infant, she knew how to handle the bureaucracy of a hospital. Her determination hardened to rudeness as she tracked down Dr. Martinez and informed him that if he failed to discharge Lila immediately, she intended to simply leave with her daughter. The doctor promised to see to it right away. Luz was always surprised when people found her intimidating. Yet her children made her fierce. They always did. They always had. From the first moment she laid eyes on Lila, Luz had been aggressively protective.

Armed with a sheaf of signed papers and forms, she marched into the exam room to give Ian the good news. While Dr. Martinez rattled off final instructions, he fitted Lila with a cervical collar, as a precaution. The high neck brace made her look like some sort of angry Egyptian goddess as she sat down, against her will, in the wheelchair for the ride to the parking lot.

The trouble started when they wheeled Lila out through the waiting room. Parents and relatives milled around, and clearly Lila was the first to leave. Some of the parents regarded her with yearning and veiled resentment. Her departure was a poignant reminder that their own children still remained.

As they approached the main door, a gray-faced, red-eyed woman approached. "I'm Cheryl Hayes. Heath Walker's mother."

Heath Walker. Lila's first love. Keeping their hormone-charged passion in check was like stopping the tide. Heartthrob handsome, with his Texas drawl and devastating dark eyes, he had beguiled their daughter away in the night, sought to impress her with his driving, put her at unspeakable risk, nearly caused her to die.

"Lucinda Benning," she said through a taut throat. "This is my husband, Ian."

The woman didn't acknowledge the introduction. Instead she focused on Lila, who looked up at her solemnly. "Mrs. Hayes, is Heath all right?"

"Of course he's not all right. His injuries are minor, thank God, but he's out for the football season. He'll miss homecoming! This is your fault, young lady." The accusation lashed like a whip. "Heath would never have gone out last night if you hadn't pressured him—"

"Just a damn minute," Luz burst out. From the corner of her eye, she saw Lila flinch, but couldn't stop herself. "It was your son at the wheel. You're not blaming this—"

"Excuse us." Ian cut her off with a smooth, quiet interjection and put his hand at the small of her back. "We've all got to get through this, Mrs. Hayes, but pointing the finger isn't going to help us or our kids. I wish you the best of luck with your son, ma'am." That lawyerly magic shut her up for a few moments, long enough for them to make it to the door. He escorted Luz and Lila outside with brisk efficiency, but not before Luz felt her face catch fire with delayed fury. "How dare that woman say those things?"

"She's upset," he explained. "People always try to find someone to blame when unthinkable things happen."

"She's right," Lila said, losing patience as a hospital orderly flipped the footrests of the wheelchair. She stepped over the metal footrests and got up to walk stiffly toward the parking lot. "I wanted Heath to launch the Jeep. It's one of my favorite things ever."

Luz's gut turned to stone as she handed Ian her car keys. "You drive."

He followed her to the car, holding the back door for Lila. Their daughter slid in, fastened her seat belt before either parent could remind her, wincing with hidden pain. She leaned back and closed her eyes.

"Heath was in the driver's seat," Luz said, sliding into the passenger side. "His conduct was his decision and his responsibility."

Lila yawned and sighed. Her lack of reaction to the situation was only a facade; Luz spotted the single tear that slid down her daughter's cheek and bled into the padded cuff of the cervical collar. She wore her attitude like body armor.

They drove away from the hospital in a terrible silence. Their daughter had just been involved in a trauma. She had not yet disclosed all that she had seen, heard, felt in those terrible moments. Her statement to the highway patrol consisted largely of *I don't remember* and whether or not that was the truth, Luz didn't know. What she did know was that she mothered by instinct and instinct told her that now, with the sunrise racing over the hills surrounding Edenville, was not the time for hard questions.

Ian lacked that maternal sensibility. He was a man, a lawyer and someone who was unflinchingly honest. "Things are going to change in a big way from now on," he said, his shadowed jaw ticking.

"We'll talk about it when we get home, okay?" Luz's hand shook as she pushed her hair back. Then she turned toward the back seat to find Lila with her eyes closed and mouth slack, fast asleep.

Reaching out, she rested her hand on her daughter's. The landscape sped by in a smear of asphalt roads and heaved-up sandstone hills, tortilla-yellow grass and blue morning sky. Roadrunners darted in and out of the hawthorn bushes and livestock gathered around salt licks put out by the ranchers. Trucks and bumblebee-colored school buses rumbled past. Cars turned into strip centers with video stores and Laundromats. For folks who hadn't spent the past night having their lives rearranged, it was just another day in the hill country.

"Where were you last night?" she asked Ian.

"We had a late meeting with the appeals team and the unit warden working graveyard shift. We'd ordered pizza and lost track of time. Then I got your message, and had to wake Matlock up to fly me back. The tower was unmanned that time of night so he had to get some sort of clearance. I came as fast as humanly possible, Luz. You know that. But I've never been quick enough for you, have I?"

"What?" She looked at him with a frown. Where had that come from?

"Never mind. We're both exhausted. Who's staying with the boys?" Ian asked, switching gears.

"Well, who do you think?" Luz figured it should be obvious. "Jessie, of course."

"I thought you might have called someone more—someone who knows the boys better."

"Jessie's right there. And she's their aunt."

"I guess."

"But you're not comfortable with her being in charge."

He glanced in the rearview mirror. "She's a flake. She's always been a flake. I'm not saying she'd harm the boys, but she might get...careless."

"Give her a break, Ian. She's not the same person she was sixteen years ago. None of us are. And in a pinch, Jessie comes through. She always has."

"Name one single time she came through for you."

"She saved my life. I never told you that, did I?"

"Jessie?" He lifted one eyebrow. "How much coffee have you had?"

"It's true. It was during a winter freeze when we were kids. The stock ponds had frozen over. Folks said it was the first time in fifty years the ice was thick enough to skate on. So of course we had to go check it out. It took a good hour to hike through the woods to Cutter's pond. We didn't have proper ice skates, but we managed to slide all day in our Keds. Jessie and I were the last to leave. All the other kids had to be home before dark but...well, you know my mother. She was more likely to tell us to be home by spring."

Luz hitched up one leg to sit sideways, so she could watch Lila sleep. Her goal had always been to be the sort of mother Glenny Ryder had never been. Other kids went home to warm houses with lights glowing in the windows and a kettle of soup simmering on the stove. Luz and Jessie went home to mind-numbing hours of bad TV and cold cut sandwiches.

"It was getting pretty dark," she continued, "but we wanted one more turn around the pond. Just one. I think it was the first time I ever beat Jessie in a race. But I fell wrong, skidded into a tree. My ankle wouldn't work, and my elbow bled like a fire hose. There was no way I could walk. The light faded, fast as a falling curtain. She built me a fire. I never knew until that day she could even build a fire, or that she always carried a pack of matches on her. She walked back to town to bring help. I'll never know how she found her way through the woods. She did the impossible and showed up in Edenville right when folks were turning on the six o'clock news. Everyone thought she was crying wolf, so she climbed into the sheriff's cruiser, started the engine and the emergency lights. I'll bet she would have driven straight into the woods if they hadn't agreed to go along. Jessie's strong when you test her. It's just that she's never been tested, not much, anyway."

"Because you've always made the tough choices," Ian muttered.

Luz's hackles lifted. "What?"

"You heard me." He took a deep breath, visibly groping for control. "I'm sorry, honey. But you've got to admit, you've been more than a sister to Jess."

Reaching out with her hand, she brushed a stray lock of hair from her daughter's brow. What an adventure it was, being Lila's mother. Sixteen years ago, Luz had made a left turn in the middle of her life, and she was still heading down that unexpected road into uncharted territory.

Ian drove with negligent precision, his wrist draped over the top of the steering wheel as he negotiated the rippling hills and unexpected curves. He swerved to detour around the carcass of a deer, scattering the crows scavenging a meal.

"You doing okay, Mrs. B?"

She nodded, though a wave of exhaustion rolled over her, heavy as cane syrup.

"So what're we going to do about our resident juvenile delinquent?" he asked, direct and lawyerly. "I say we ground her for life."

Luz nodded. House arrest. Still holding her daughter's hand, she vowed that everything would change from now on. She swore it. Things were going to be different. They were going to lay down the law.

From this moment on, nothing would be the same.

CHAPTER 8

"You're like my mom but you're different," Scottie declared.

Jessie's youngest nephew stood on a kitchen stool, wearing a Don't Mess With Texas T-shirt and nothing else. After a sleepless night, it had been all Jessie could do to get the other two fed and dressed and up the road to the school bus. Scottie had been parked in front of the TV, his head propped against the ribs of his sleeping dog, for the past forty minutes.

"I'm like your mom because I'm her sister," Jessie said, pawing through a plastic mesh basket of clean laundry she had found on top of the clothes dryer. "Aha." She produced a pair of Spiderman underpants. "I bet these are yours."

"Nope. Owen's."

"But you could wear them, for today."

"Nope." He regarded her with a solemnity that aged him beyond his years.

"What about these?" She plucked out another pair, these bearing a green cartoon character she didn't recognize.

"Wyatt's. Where's Mom?" The solemnity teetered on the brink of despair. Jessie knew without asking that Scottie had never before awakened to a house with no mother.

Sucks, doesn't it, little guy?

Jessie didn't know what she would do if he cried. With urgent movements, she sorted through the clean clothes, coming up with a wisp of lace—a thong.

"I bet this is yours."

"No way." A smile teased one corner of his mouth.

"No?" Jessie put on a baffled look. "You mean you don't wear pink lace undies?"

"Lila's," he said.

Yikes. Wasn't Lila a bit young for that? "Do you see any of your undies in here?"

"Nuh-uh."

"So you want to run around bare-assed all day?"

"You said ass."

"Is that bad?"

"We say bottom."

"Oh. I'll try to remember that." Scanning the cluttered room, she spied a tiny pair of swim trunks hanging from a doorknob. They were surfer shorts decked with navy hibiscus blossoms. "Scottie, I've had a brilliant idea." She pointed out the trunks.

"My swimsuit!" He scrambled down from the stool, his little butt hanging out as he crossed the room.

Jessie reached for the shorts. Her hand met empty air.

God, not now. She reached again, knuckles hitting the door. Concentrate. Focus. Grim with determination, she found her field of vision and reached again, this time seizing the shorts. "Voilà," she said holding them out.

"Wah-la," Scottie echoed, all smiles.

He was still smiling minutes later, long after Jessie had run out of patience. Her nephew insisted on putting the pants on all by himself, and did not seem to think that making it an all-day operation was much out of line.

God. Luz had gone through this with four kids. And she was still sane. How could that be? Yet as she watched Scottie inserting one foot, then another, into the leg holes, Jessie was seized by a sudden affection that brought a rush of sweetness through her as though she had gulped a mocha latte. The kid was beyond cute with his tumble of chocolate-colored curls, his little tongue poking out in concentration, his pudgy feet pushing against the fabric. She felt the loss of her years with Lila. *Dear Lord, what have I missed?*

"I'm so glad I got to see you, Scottie," she whispered, more to herself than to him.

"Huh?"

She smiled. "It's just good to see you. I feel like the luckiest auntie in the world."

He went back to dressing himself, taking forever to fasten the Velcro closure at the waistband.

While she was waiting, Jessie had found a bottle of pink nail polish and was doing her toenails, grimly proving to herself that the vision in her right eye still served. Through the diminishing field, her close-range acuity was nearly perfect. She glanced up to see Scottie watching her. Then, without a word, he stuck out his tiny bare foot.

With an air of somber ritual, Jessie painted his toenails. The look on his face filled her with an absurd gratification. Then his mercurial mood shifted. "Where's Mom?" he asked, looking worried again.

"She said we could eat Chee•tos for breakfast."

"Nuh-uh."

"And red Kool-Aid." Taking his hand, she brought him over to the fridge.

The guilt that had been gnawing at her since Luz had awakened her dug deep.

I could have stopped Lila last night. She reeled from the thought, wished she could race away from it, but she couldn't. She had colluded with Lila, covering up her deception as though it were a schoolyard prank.

We're only going for a walk by the lake, I swear, that's all.

Why hadn't she challenged the lie in those wide, green eyes?

Jesus, was she blind already? Why hadn't she heard duplicity in that pleading young voice? She should have, because it had been like looking at a mirror into the past. She used to lie all the time, used to run wild. The only one who had ever seen through Jessie was, of course, Luz. God. She would give up all of her vision right now if she could have that moment back.

"So where's the Chee•tos, huh?" Scottie asked.

She touched his silky curls. "I think I saw some in the pantry."

He trailed her across the kitchen. She lifted him onto a booster seat at the table, opened a small lunch-sized bag of Chee•tos and poured a cup of artificially red Kool-Aid. He dug in, eating fast before she realized her folly and fed him oatmeal instead.

Her heart pounded with a sick rhythm. Things were happening too fast and she didn't know how to slow them down. She never had. Neither, it seemed, had her daughter. Now she was feeding this child the most nutritionally bankrupt breakfast on the planet. She was going to burn in hell.

After opening the windows to let in the morning breeze, she sat next to Scottie. The sunny breakfast nook was smaller than her memory of it, though little had changed. It was the same tiger oak table she remembered, bearing a few more scratches and scars, perhaps. On a knickknack shelf on the wall was a small digital clock that read 2:26 a.m.

"That clock's wrong," she said. As if a four-year-old would care.

"That's the Jessie clock."

She frowned. "I don't understand."

But as he lifted his shoulders in an elaborate shrug, comprehension dawned. Luz had a clock set to the local time in New Zealand. Ah, Luz, she thought. Jessie used to phone at her own convenience, unwilling to calculate the time in Texas. But it seemed Luz always knew the time where Jessie was.

Some of their mother's old golf trophies sat on the shelf by the clock, though they now served as easels and props for framed photos of Luz's kids. An entire wall had been transformed into a mural.

"I bet your mama took all those pictures," she said to Scottie.
"Yup."

"I can tell," she said. "She takes the best pictures in the whole wide world, doesn't she?"

"Yup."

Jessie was particularly drawn to the shots of Lila. They showed her at various stages, from unsteady toddler into a breathtaking princess in an emerald-green dress with a Texas-sized corsage of mums and streamers, standing beside the outrageously good-looking kid from last night. Keith? No, Heath. The interesting half of Heathcliff. In anyone else's hands, the picture would have been a snapshot of a good-looking couple in the foyer, but as far as Jessie knew, Luz had never taken just a snapshot. Her work was seriously good. With her uncanny eye and sense of timing, Luz had managed to capture their very essence. Their youth and vulnerability, their beauty, their strength, their fearlessness. She wondered if they'd ever be fearless again, after last night.

"I remember when your mom got her first serious camera," she said. "It was Christmas, and she was twelve and I was nine. Our mama—"

"Your mama?" He looked skeptical.

"The lady with the tan," Jessie reminded him, wondering when Scottie had seen her last. "The one who makes you call her Miss Glenny."

"Yeah! And Grampa Stu takes me for a ride in his magic chair."

Jessie had no idea what he was talking about, so she went on with the story. "Anyway, Miss Glenny got an endorsement deal with Main Street Camera, and they let your mom have a real grown-up camera and all the film she wanted."

That year, the press had made much of Glenny Ryder's daughters, who shared her trademark red hair and lightning bolt smile. Luz and Jessie had followed their mother around like a miniature professional photographer and her assistant. That had been a good year. Jessie remembered an abundant Christmas at Broken Rock, a couple of shiny trophies to add to the collection.

She had a distinct memory of developing pictures with Luz. They'd turned the smallest guest cabin into a darkroom and they used to spend hours there. Magic happened when they dipped the paper into the developer, and the picture appeared. Photography was a miracle, an act of light and alchemy that fused into a lasting image. The ghostly blood-colored lamp in the watery cubicle painted the sisters' hands and faces and created a shadowy cocoon, making Jessie and Luz feel like the only people in the world.

Not long afterward, husband number two entered the picture, a blond, suntanned younger man who spent Glenny's money twice as fast as she won it, then left without a forwarding address for the creditors to find him. But Luz had always treasured that camera; it had started a lifelong love affair with pictures. Sometimes Jessie wondered, with a sting of guilt, if all of Luz's girlhood dreams had somehow taken hold of Jessie's heart.

Now Jessie understood what the trade-off had been.

Her gaze settled on a masterful portrait of all four kids together, playing in a field of bluebonnets. The children were as much a part of the landscape as the live oaks and rolling hills.

"You must be real proud of your mom's pictures," she said.

"Yup."

"Do you ever say anything besides yup?" She imitated him perfectly, coaxing a sweet grin from his Red Number Two lips.

"Yup."

She snatched him up and hugged him, savoring his compact warmth and puppyish smell.

A distant, plaintive cry captured her attention. A movement on the lake caught her eye. Through the broad bay window, she saw a flock of loons angling down from the sky to the lake.

"See the birds, Scottie?" She set him down and they watched in silence. The birds landed in V-formation, almost military in its precision. They glided toward the dock across the lake, where the green-and-white floatplane gently bobbed. "Have you ever seen that airplane fly?"

Nodding, he stood up on his chair. "Amber's daddy flies it."

The pilot. Rusty or Dusty, Luz had called him. "Is Amber your friend?"

She met Scottie's gaze and they said it together: "Yup," then burst into giggles. The uncomplicated mirth lingered as the birds took off with one mind, one motion. She could tell the moment the graceful spread wings caught air beneath them. She felt the sensation in her arms and chest, and her chin lifted involuntarily as the flock rose, leaving behind a sparkling diamond trail of water.

The birds crested the tops of the lost maples before banking and then flying out of sight. The image pierced her with a sharp ache, and she swallowed hard, fighting a sudden lurch of loss. What will I see when I can't see anymore?

"Aunt Jessie?"

She turned to Scottie, banishing the trouble from her face, a move so practiced and polished she did it without thinking. "Yeah, kiddo?"

"I need to pee."

"You know where the bathroom is."

He slid out of the booster seat and held out his hand, regarding her implacably. She took his hand, noting the fingers were now covered in Day-Glo orange powder. "I hope it doesn't come out red Kool-Aid," she said, leading him down the hall to the bathroom.

He climbed up like a cowboy to the saddle. There was a grid tacked on the wall and covered in stars: Scottie's Potty Chart. Oh, Luz, she thought. And you thought *my* life was exotic.

Digging around under the sink for a new roll of paper, she spotted a wrinkled drugstore bag and couldn't resist peeking inside.

A home pregnancy test, unopened. Never say her sister wasn't prepared.

Scottie leaped down as though an alligator had bit him in the butt. "Mom's home!"

He must have radar like a bat, Jessie thought, barring the door long enough to make him pull up his shorts and wash his hands. Wiping them on his swim trunks as he raced to the front door, he burst outside, followed by Beaver. He jumped down the steps, one at a time, his bare feet slapping on the planks.

The expression of pure joy on his face explained everything to Jessie in that moment. No glamorous career could ever compare to the look on a child's face, the sound of his voice, singing *Mom's home.*

Luz got out and caught Scottie up in her arms, hugging him tight. Over his tousled head, she regarded Jessie, and Jessie wasn't sure what lay beneath that look. Relief? Accusation?

Standing on the porch, Jessie was startled but not surprised to see a tall man unfold himself from the driver's side of the car. Apparently Ian had flown across the state last night to get to his wounded daughter. Did Lila know how lucky she was?

CHAPTER 9

As he regarded his sister-in-law on the porch, Ian Benning was reminded of something he'd never told a soul: his wife Luz was not the only beautiful woman he had ever slept with.

Seeing Jessie again, all these years later, confirmed it. That indisputable fact had not changed.

Not that he'd ever say so aloud, but it was true. Dressed in a short, flowing skirt and a tight top that made her look like a lingerie model, she had an exotic aura of drama and danger. The energy was different when Jessie was around. The air seemed to vibrate with the rare buzz of electricity before a lightning strike, drawing all the attention to a heated center. The mere fact of her presence made men want to perform feats of daring, capture prizes and lay them at her feet. During his brief, youthful affair with her, she'd never really let him know her—an aspect some men probably found intriguing, but it simply frustrated Ian. The moment the flame dimmed, she disappeared, off to the next adventure. He remembered feeling relieved. He'd dodged a silent, invisible bullet.

A few weeks after that, he'd nearly forgotten her, and then he saw her again. It was like being hit in the solar plexus. She was in the library, helping a deaf student with a biology paper—which should have clued him in immediately. When he moved in for a closer look, he realized it wasn't Jessie, but someone eerily like her. She caught him circling around, staring... So he introduced himself. She was Luz Ryder, and he immediately realized they were sisters. Luz shared Jessie's looks and voice, yet she lacked Jessie's hectic, unsettling beauty, her contagious energy. Everything about Luz was quiet and calm; she had a warmth that struck at the heart and brought comfort to the soul. Jessie might make a man want to slay dragons, but Luz inspired him to achievements that were more realistic and lasting—and therefore harder. She made him want to be a good man, to measure up to her vision of him. Ian loved her before the sun set that day, and he'd loved her ever since.

Meeting Jessie in a new context, as Luz's sister, was slightly awkward at first, then the awkwardness faded as both Ian and Jessie realized they had one thing in common—loyalty to Luz.

Then Luz dropped the bomb, informing him that Jessie was pregnant and Luz wanted to adopt the baby. Ian resisted. He wanted to start their lives together with a clean slate, not mopping up after Jessie's mistakes. But when it came to her sister, Luz had a core of solid steel. Refusal was not an option.

Ian cornered Jessie in private and confronted her with the inevitable question. He could still hear her answer, echoing across the years: "No."

He took the reply at face value. She was stormy and mysterious, and he knew she'd been seeing other guys. Sometimes the question nagged at him, but Jessie insisted he was out of the running, and on some level, he acknowledged it was easier to let it be. She'd been an indiscretion, a clash of hormones, nothing more.

From the moment of her birth, Lila had dominated the family. She presented every childhood challenge in the book. Ian tried to treat all the kids the same, but Lila demanded something different from him. He loved her with a fierceness that hurt, but his love was complicated. He didn't know what she needed from him. Or he from her.

"Daddeee!" Scottie brought Ian back to the present, launching himself like a human cannonball. Ian caught and held his youngest son. The kid reeked of junk food and juicy sweetness. Each of Ian's kids owned his heart in a unique way; Scottie's hold on it was forged of laughter and joy. Totally trusting of his father's grip on him, Scottie leaned back and flung out his arms so Ian could spin him around.

"Missed you, monster," he said.

"Aunt Jessie's been baby-sitting me." He gestured toward the house.

"So I see." He locked eyes with hers, and their gazes held briefly before breaking apart.

Jessie came down from the porch—bare feet, long tan legs, a couple of Maori tattoos in intriguing places—and hurried to the car. She patted his arm in a brief impersonal way, then brushed past him to the car. "Lila, are you okay?" she asked as the girl climbed out of the back seat.

"What's the matter with your neck?" Scottie asked.

"I'm fine." Lila waved away the hovering adults. "I'm okay. I'll be better when I can lose this." Before Luz could stop her, Lila ripped the Velcro straps of the cervical collar and discarded it. Beaver pounced, grabbing the thing and shaking it into submission.

"Hey, you." Jessie hugged Lila, holding her lightly as though she might break.

Ian tried to imagine what was going through Jessie's mind right now as she hugged her niece who was really her daughter.

"Is it your head?" Luz asked. "Are you dizzy?"

"No, Mom." Lila spoke with barely veiled exasperation. Her trembling chin hinted at the deeper reaction she was trying to hide. "I'm tired."

Scottie squirmed downward as though Ian's torso were the trunk of the tree. "Lila! Why're y'all dirty, Lila? What's the matter with your hair?"

The kid had always had a special affinity for his sister, though Ian was hard-pressed to know why. Lila always brushed him away as though he were a gnat. But when she thought no one was looking, she liked to cuddle with the little guy.

"Lila!" he persisted.

"Yeah, pest?"

"Lila, where did you get them fingernails, Lila?" Before she could escape, he grabbed her hand and inspected the flame-colored nails.

"I was born with these nails," she muttered.

"Nuh-uh."

"Was too."

"Was not."

The two of them entered the house, still arguing back and forth. The screen door smacked shut behind them. The gunshot slap of the door made Ian jump.

"You're white as a ghost," Luz said, rubbing his arm. "You'll be all right," she added, as though by saying it aloud she could make it so. "We're all going to be fine."

"Christ, how can you say that? Don't you get it, Luz? Everything fell apart last night. You know, I've lost cases. I've seen murderers die. I've even seen innocent men die for crimes they didn't commit. Held their grieving mothers in my arms. But this is worse. It's personal. My own goddamned family. I'm supposed to protect them, and instead, my own kid nearly gets killed. I failed to protect her."

"You didn't fail," Jessie said. "This is my fault."

Both Ian and Luz turned to regard her with anguished eyes. "What the hell is that supposed to mean?" he asked.

"Sit down. We should talk out here." In the shade of an umbrella-shaped live oak, they sat in metal chairs whose edges had started to rust.

Ian regarded his sister-in-law with both interest and suspense. The prodigal sister. The fact of her presence was still sinking in. Instead of welcoming her, he wanted to put up a wall. But no wall or any other barrier had ever been able to stand between Jessie and what Jessie wanted.

She looked like something out of a dream, sitting there, her bronze legs shiny as turned and polished wood. Her feet were bare, her toenails painted pink. A tribal symbol tattoo rode the crest of her right collarbone. Then he felt disloyal for staring at her and shifted his attention to his wife. "You okay?" he asked Luz. "Should I get you a cup of coffee or—"

"Let's talk to Jess," she said, sending her sister an encouraging smile. "I don't know why in the world you would say it's your fault."

"I saw her leave with her boyfriend." Jessie's voice trembled. "Last night. She even introduced me to the kid. And I sent them on their merry way."

Ian glanced at Luz, who in turn stared at her sister as though she had been kicked in the gut. He reached out and cupped the back of her neck with his hand, gently massaging the tense muscles there. Jessie crossed her arms around her middle. In that moment she didn't look so beautiful, merely lost, as though her steering mechanism had gone out. He had encountered people who looked that way in his work. They were not the death row inmates themselves, but the families of inmates—mothers and sisters and daughters who had traveled the twisted byways of the court and penal system, only to find a clinical cellblock and a chamber of death at the end of their journey.

"I was so jet-lagged, I didn't know what time it was," Jessie said. "But I heard them talking, so I stepped out, and there they were. I think I startled them more than they startled me. Lila introduced me to Heath and said they were just taking a little walk by the lake." She blinked fast, glancing from Ian to Luz. "I swear, there didn't seem to be any harm in it."

"A little walk." Luz's voice took on that harsh edge that had the power to cut so deep. Ian almost felt sorry for Jessie. Almost. "Since when does a boy just take a walk with his girlfriend at eleven o'clock at night?"

Ian kept rubbing her back but she didn't seem to notice.

"So I figured they'd do a little more than walk. But I never dreamed they would take off." Jessie shook her head. "I can't believe she lied to me."

Ian burst out laughing. "Where have you been living?"

"Why didn't you wake me?" Luz asked.

"She's not some toddler in danger of falling into the lake." Jessie looked her sister in the eye and Ian could see the effort it took. "I'm so sorry, Luz. I don't know how to tell you how sorry I am."

"So this all could have been prevented," Luz said in a low, incredulous voice. "If you had spoken up—"

"Hey." Ian surprised even himself as he interrupted her. "You know that's not how it works, Luz. Especially with Lila. If she was sneaking out, she would have succeeded whether or not Jessie informed us of it."

Jessie shot him a grateful look, but he dismissed it. He was more concerned for Luz. She was having a hell of a time with Lila lately, and when she got scared, she lashed out. Lila scared Ian, too, for that matter, but he was more realistic. People were going to do what they were going to do—stupid things, noble things, things that broke people's hearts—and there wasn't a hell of a lot even a mother could do to change that.

Luz pressed her lips and her eyes shut briefly and then he sensed her forcing herself to relax. He felt as though he had deactivated a bomb. And then he felt guilty for feeling relieved.

"He's right," Luz said at length. "You couldn't have known what they planned, and you couldn't have stopped them. But I wish—" She broke off and bit her lip, but Ian could tell Jessie heard the unspoken conclusion. *But I wish you had tried.*

"I never should have come back here," Jessie said. "Never should have tried to see her. It's like I brought a curse with me. I should leave immediately."

"That's what you're good at, Jess." Blunt honesty was Luz's specialty.

"Then why mess with success?"

"Because I need you here, damn it," Luz said, and her voice—her strong, unwavering voice—broke on a sob. "Can't you stick around for once in your life, just for a while?"

"Luz," Jessie whispered. "Ah, Luz, don't cry."

The sisters stood up and hugged in weary fashion. Standing off to one side, he could see their closeness and their desperation. They hadn't seen each other in years but that bond was still strong, a magnet whose charge had not diminished over time, but instead had grown stronger.

"You used to scare me, too," Luz whispered.

Jessie laughed unsteadily. "You were the scary one."

Luz pulled away, clearly not comprehending, although Ian did, perfectly. "We'd better get inside and deal with Lila," he reminded her.

Nodding, she took his hand in a gesture of sweet dependence that he had no chance to savor before it quick-hardened into resolve.

"Will you let me talk to her later?" Jessie asked.

"Yeah, you should," Ian said. "She owes you one hell of an apology for lying."

Jessie's temper struck like heat lightning. "What about the lie we told her? Maybe we're the ones who should apologize." Her fierce gaze locked with Luz's. "Yeah, *that* lie."

Luz stiffened. "Not now, Jess. That's not what she needs from us now."

Ian held his silence and his temper. It was easy for Jessie to come waltzing back after all this time, thinking they should suddenly reveal all to Lila, as though that would fix things. He couldn't understand why the issue was so important after all this time. Even before Lila drew her first breath, she had belonged to Luz and him in every way that mattered. Just because Jessie decided to show up now didn't change that—or so he hoped. "Leave it, Jess. Nobody's thinking straight now."

He could tell from the set of her chin that her surrender was only temporary.

Hand in hand, Ian and Luz walked into the house. Scottie was parked in front of the TV, turned up too loud. He was eating Chee•tos and drinking something red from his sippy cup. In one graceful movement, Luz managed to plant a kiss on his head, take away the Chee•tos and red stuff, turn down the TV. The kid never even knew what hit him. Scottie was by far their easiest child, and he settled back against the sofa cushions and turned his attention to SpongeBob Squarepants.

"We'll be upstairs with your sister," Luz said.

"Yup."

Lila was in bed when they walked into her room, but Ian could tell she was faking sleep.

"Your mother and I need to talk to you," he said loudly.

She blinked, opening her eyes to stare at them without expression.

"Sit up, please," he said. "This is serious, Lila."

"Like I don't know that." Scowling, she shifted in her bed to lean back against the pillows.

"We don't need your sarcasm," Luz said in her icy voice, rarely used, but it sent a chill down the spine.

"I don't need your lectures," Lila snapped, looking like an MTV groupie. "I don't need you to tell me I'm a screwup. I don't need you to tell me I'm grounded forever and how you used to be so proud of me and now you're ashamed and aren't I ashamed, too, and that the decisions I'm making now are going to affect the rest of my life and, thanks to my poor choices, I'm cutting off some of my best options—"

"At least we know she listened," Luz pointed out wryly.

"And if I don't straighten up and fly right, I'll end up in a polyester apron and paper hat—"

"That's enough." Ian rapped out the order, sounding eerily like the military father he had worked so hard to distance himself from. "Lila—" He stopped short of speaking his mind: *I've heard death row murderers who were more civil than you.* "I'm sure it hasn't escaped your notice that your whole world has changed overnight. But you're still our daughter. Your mother and I haven't discussed specifics, but there are going to be some serious consequences."

"There's a surprise," Lila murmured, unfazed.

Christ, where did she come from, the *Jerry Springer* show?

The phone rang, then stopped; Jessie had probably picked up.

Scrappy and defiant, Lila dove for her cordless extension. Luz beat her to it. "Hey," said Lila. "That might be for me. It could be news about my friends. I have to know if they're okay."

"I'll get that information for you. You're grounded from the phone. Also the stereo, TV and computer."

"I need to know what's going on," Lila protested. "You can't cut me off from—"

"You cut yourself off, Lila," Ian pointed out. "When you pulled that stunt, you put all your privileges at risk."

Her face turned paler than ever. "I'm sorry," she said. "I did a stupid thing and I'll never do it again, okay?"

"We agree on one thing—it was stupid." Luz's face softened as she put a hand on Lila's shoulder. "Honey, you're precious to us, you know that."

"Anything else?" Lila leaned back out of reach.

Luz dropped her hand, but otherwise made no response to the rejection. "This room needs to change." Luz started rattling off a list. "I haven't seen the floor in a year. The deathrock posters come down, and you're going to paint the walls—they haven't been done in years."

"So you're saying a Nine-Inch Nails poster caused the accident."

Luz ignored her. "I'm saying the posters go into the trash. You'll take the bus to and from school. No more riding with friends..." She enumerated the terms of house arrest, and she did so with a cold, controlled and focused fury that even Ian couldn't match.

Ian watched Lila's face, which reflected her emotions like the lake on a windless day. He was supposed to be good at evaluating the merits of the case, deciding whether or not justice had been done and persuading others that justice had or had not been served. In the case of his daughter, he felt helpless.

"What makes you think this will change a thing?" Lila demanded. "It will only make me hate you more."

Damn. She was definitely a Ryder woman, no doubt about that. Tough as rawhide from a longhorn. "Don't speak to your mother like that."

"Sorry," she mumbled.

"At least you'll be alive to hate me," Luz said, masking her hurt. "I don't expect any thanks for this but at least I'll still have my daughter." She turned and walked out of the room. Down the hall, the shower came on. That was where Luz cried, where no one could see her, where the water drowned out her sobs.

"Why would she even want me alive?" Lila said, not so adept at hiding her own tears. "She obviously hates me."

"You know better than that," Ian said. "We all do."

CHAPTER 10

"You're not meant to be alone, Dustin Charles Matlock. You know I'm right."

"I'm not alone, Mama," Dusty said into the phone.

"You're a young man in the prime of life," she said as though he hadn't spoken. "It's time to put the past behind you."

He eyed Amber, who was building a tower with her squishy blocks across the room. "Yes, ma'am."

"So anyway, Leafy Willis's daughter moved to Austin to do her residency, and she doesn't know a soul—"

"Give me her number, and I'll call her." He'd learned long ago not to argue. And a part of him agreed that his mother was right. For Amber's sake, he needed to get his head out of the past and start living. He was damned lonely sometimes—though not for the oozingly sweet huntresses his mother often sent his way. His widowed state was a babe magnet, but he kept attracting the wrong kind of babes.

She rattled off a phone number. "That's Tiffani with an *i*."

He paused as though writing it down. "Got it, Mama."

"She's going to be a neurosurgeon."

Dr. Tiffani, he thought. With an *i*.

"Anyway, call her. Take her out for a nice dinner. And you're still bringing Amber to see me this week, right?"

"Yes, ma'am."

"Good. Now, put Amber on."

"Mama, she doesn't speak English yet."

"If you don't let her talk to her grandma, she'll never learn," said his mother. "Let me speak to my granddaughter. I haven't seen her in two weeks. I declare, son, if you'd moved to Austin like we wanted you to—"

"I'll put her on." The last thing Dusty wanted was to argue with his mother about his decision to settle down in Edenville. Holding out the receiver to Amber, he said, "Here you go, short stuff. It's Grandma Weezy." His sister's firstborn had given Louisa Childress Matlock the name, and now all the grandkids called her that.

The baby grabbed the cordless receiver. As always, she had the uncanny ability to hold the earpiece in exactly the right place. Even more uncannily, she said, "Yah."

Then she cocked her head in a listening posture. Dusty stood back and watched. What did females talk about, anyway? He had been raised in a houseful of women—three high-maintenance sisters and an alpha-mother—so he knew they talked all the time, but for the life of him, he couldn't recall a single topic of conversation. In truth, he had never really been able to understand the rhythm of a woman's heart, or comprehend the workings of her mind, and that knowledge made him doubt his ability to raise a daughter. But that was exactly what he was doing. Once Amber learned to speak, what in the world would they talk about?

She babbled earnestly into the receiver, listened some more, babbled some more. Then, growing tired of the game, she set the phone aside and wandered off. Dusty picked up the phone and listened, but apparently his mother had rung off.

Arnufo came in with the mail, dropping everything on the table and heading straight for Amber. At his heels, Pico de Gallo trotted in, pausing to sniff at his food bowl.

"Nah," yelled Amber, tipping over the tower of blocks as she started toward Arnufo.

"And how is the *princesa?*" He swept the baby up, eliciting a sweet chortle from her.

"Talkative." Dusty sat down to flip through the mail. A tall headline on the front page of the *Edenville Register* caught his eye, and he picked up the paper. Seeing the story in print turned his blood to ice water. "Jesus," he muttered, scanning the article.

"Do not take the Lord's name in vain in front of your daughter," Arnufo said.

"Carload of kids flipped over last night out at Seven Hills," Dusty said. "That's why I got home so early this morning. The Bennings' daughter was involved, and Ian was in Huntsville. I had to fly him over to Austin." The way Ian Benning had looked, meeting him at the airstrip in the middle of the night, would haunt Dusty for a long time. He'd flown the man into a hell every parent dreads. As Dusty so painfully understood, this was the frailty of life. In a heartbeat, everything could change.

His gaze dropped down the page. "One of those kids was killed." *The victim's name has not been released pending notification of the family.* It can't be Ian's girl, he thought. No way. But that was the thing about accidents in the middle of the night. You never knew. He stared at the paper, the screaming headline illustrated by a stark photograph of the crushed Jeep. Only yesterday, those kids were doing homework, playing football, sitting down to dinner with their families, arguing with their parents.

Arnufo made the sign of the cross. Amber touched her head with her fist, trying to imitate him. He gave her a kiss, then set her down.

"Hell of a thing," Dusty muttered, putting the paper aside. "I feel so bad for their families. Goes to show you, kids'll break your heart every time. You can't avoid it."

Arnufo helped himself to coffee, offering a mug to Dusty and a juice box to Amber. "Why would you want to?"

"Because it effing hurts, *viejo*. That's why."

"So what? A true man bears the pain."

"A true idiot goes looking for it."

"A true coward avoids it." Arnufo picked up Amber again, holding her out by both arms as though she were a kitten. "What can you do, eh? Give her away to the gypsies?"

"I can...brace myself, I guess."

"Look, *jefe,* I have five daughters. Each one has broken my heart, many times. In this way, they show me I am alive, that I have a heart to break. This is not such a bad thing, eh?"

Dusty studied the full-moon face of his daughter, and Karen's spirit flashed mysteriously yet unmistakably through the baby's smile. "No," he said at last. "It's not such a bad thing."

"She will bring you comfort and joy," Arnufo promised.

"She will bring me sleepless nights and tuition bills."

"And you will thank God for that." He gave her a sip of her drink, then set her on the floor.

She was winding down, getting tired, Dusty could tell. Before nap time, she tended to do more crawling than walking, and she usually gave Pico a little peace. He turned his attention to the mail, opening first a large Express Mail envelope from Blair LaBorde. Hell's bells, he thought. The woman was persistent, he'd give her that.

It was a copy of the *Enquirer,* folded back to an article with the headline Dead Mother Gives Birth To Healthy Infant. The piece was illustrated by grainy photographs taken at the hospital in Fairbanks, pictures of him stripped of all humanity, pictures of a comatose patient and newborn infant that may or may not have been Karen and Amber. He stared, momentarily uncomprehending. Then he felt everything drain out of him. And finally, the lethal fire of a killing rage sparked inside him.

He crushed the paper into a ball and hurled it away. With the same motion, he picked up the phone and stabbed in a number he now knew by heart. "You're on my last nerve, Miz LaBorde," he said when she answered.

"Oh, good, you got my mail." She didn't sound surprised. The hound dog had known all along what his answer would be, eventually. "Putrid piece, wasn't it?"

"I didn't read it."

"Trust me, it's putrid. Scrapings from the bottom of a goat roper's boot."

"You would know."

Unfazed, she said, "You're a stubborn son of a bitch, Matlock. Do you want this to go unanswered? To be the final word on what happened? Look, I don't know you and I don't know your story. I only know you have one, and it's not the version some woman claiming to be your wife's best friend sold to that rag. Do you want your daughter to grow up and read the wrong version?"

"This'll be long gone by the time she grows up. It'll be long gone next week."

"Maybe, maybe not. People willingly tell lies for money. My publisher's offering you money to tell the truth. This could secure your daughter's future."

He wasn't even tempted. If he had been, he'd have sold his story to the highest bidder. Instead he had drawn a shell of armor around himself, barring everyone, holding them off. Early on, he'd threatened the hospital if word leaked out. For a time, his privacy stayed intact. But inevitably, the press, in the polished package of Blair LaBorde, had come to call.

"I will secure my daughter's future," he said.

"I don't doubt your intent, Mr. Matlock."

In his mind, he heard the words Blair LaBorde wouldn't say, didn't have to say. Karen would have made the same declaration with the same conviction. *I can take care of my daughter.* And why not? She was young, strong and healthy; she had every reason to believe she would do just that. The unspoken implication was that Dusty, for all his good intentions and noble declarations, could find himself as helpless as Karen. Anybody could.

His gaze wandered again to the offensive tabloid. That was Nadine Edison's story, disclosed for money and filtered through the long, grainy lens of intrusion. Amber would grow up and one day she would read about what happened. He hated that this rag was out in the world, that she might come across it.

"What's an exclusive?" he asked, sounding more weary than angry now.

"You don't tell your story to anyone but me."

"No risk of that."

"I'd only need a couple of days, no more. Maybe just one day."

He winced, envisioning several long conversations with this woman. "I'll let you know." Then he told her a gruff goodbye and hung up.

"You should do it," Arnufo said, clearly aware of the topic of conversation.

"You should mind your own business." But Dusty knew he wouldn't.

"I didn't know your wife well," Arnufo said. "But well enough to know she was a practical woman with a heart like a lion. She would think this story was wonderful. And Amber is proof that it is true."

Dusty couldn't dispute Karen's practicality. It had governed all the choices she had made in her life, right down to the last. Her love for him had been uncluttered and clean. She was the most honest person he'd ever met. He could hear her now, her voice a whisper on the wind: *They want to pay you for telling an amazing story that happens to be true. How bad can that be?*

"It's sleazy," Dusty said. "Exploitative."

Arnufo gestured at the tabloid. "*That* is sleazy. I like *Texas Life*. Good photography. Good recipes. Good politics." He finished his coffee with a sigh of satisfaction, then watched as Dusty paged through the contract that had been enclosed with the article.

"It is the right thing to do," Arnufo concluded. "You are telling the world of a terrible and miraculous thing that happened to you. The world can use a story like this."

"I don't give a shit what the world needs. This isn't about the world. This is about my daughter."

"Then tell it right, *jefe*." Arnufo headed outside for his cigar. He had a lawn chair and a coffee can filled with sand, and he sat very still, smoking and looking out at the lake.

In the end, it was Karen who made the decision. Amber crawled across the room like an off-road four-wheeler and clung to Dusty's leg, pulling herself up. The top of her head was even with his knee. She always seemed to have a special patience for him. And she tried, in her instinctive way, to help. Her fists clung hard, and she turned her head to pillow her cheek against his leg, making a little puppylike sound of contentment. Then she tilted back her face, and the wide, innocent eyes that stared up at him were Karen's eyes, the red Valentine mouth was Karen's mouth.

A wave of devastating love and protectiveness rolled over him with crushing strength. Amber was proof of how precious life was, and the strange way the world has of offering something unexpected when it takes everything away. He felt Karen's presence in that moment; he heard her heart beating as his own.

Without taking his eyes off the baby, Dusty reached for the phone.

CHAPTER 11

Jessie appointed herself official taker of phone calls. She wanted to shield Luz and Ian from anxious parents, school people and the local paper. Then a wire service and the Department of Public Safety. Then an insurance investigator. Growing ever more protective of her sister, Jessie set up a makeshift workspace on the deck at the umbrella table. She had a cordless phone, a notepad and pencil, a tall glass of iced tea and her youngest nephew whirling himself sick on a tire swing suspended from a nearby live oak.

Most people she spoke with thought she was Luz. Their voices were remarkably similar, although Jessie's Texas accent had been altered by little-known New Zealand phrases and cadences.

"I didn't know Luz had a sister," said an aggressive-sounding matron from the Halfway Baptist Church.

"I didn't know she had a church," Jessie said. There was so much she didn't know about Luz's life. Over the years, they'd kept in touch—Luz more conscientiously than Jessie, of course. But more of the phone calls and e-mail conversations consisted of Luz asking about Jessie, not vice versa. She winced, realizing how self-centered she'd been. She'd assumed her life was more interesting than Luz's and had expounded at length about her adventures. Some of her e-mail messages read like the work of a seasoned travel writer, bringing a place to life for people who would never get a chance to go there.

By the fifth call, she had perfected her spiel. Lila's injuries were minor, and the hospital had released her. She honestly didn't know the status of the others, and it really wasn't her place to give out names. She didn't know who was driving, or whose car it was.

That part was a lie, of course. It had been Heath, the teen heartthrob, in the guise of Heath the village idiot.

For the most part, the callers were caring, worried, supportive. But some were downright nosy, like the church lady. The straw that broke the camel's back was Grady "Bird-dog" Watkins, a personal injuries lawyer.

"Are you a friend of the Bennings?" Jessie asked.

"Look, I know this is a difficult time for the family, and I don't want to see it complicated by financial hardship."

"Of course you don't. So you propose to sue the driver, his family, the auto manufacturer, the tire company and the hospital. How's that for starters?"

"Ma'am, my job is to investigate and initiate action that will bring about resolution, justice and reparation for the victims of this terrible tragedy."

"And your fee for this would be...?"

"Negotiated with the victim and family," he said, very smoothly.

She hung up on him. Lawyers—the scum of the earth, her brother-in-law notwithstanding.

She jotted down the call on the list, drawing a scowling face next to it. The accident had rattled her in so many ways. Her first panicked reaction when Luz had awakened her had been a silent shrieking in her soul. What if something happened to Lila? What if the doctors needed important medical information about her, like who her biological parents were?

Ever since her outburst with Luz and Ian, the idea kept niggling at Jessie. She felt herself edging toward a growing conviction that the time had come to put the truth out there. Medical reasons aside, maybe Lila simply deserved to know the truth of who she was.

Lately, even Luz admitted things weren't so hot for Lila. Knowing the truth wouldn't turn her into a Rhodes scholar, but would it make things worse? And whom would it serve? Whom would it hurt?

Heaving a discontented sigh, she glanced at Scottie. Sitting in his tire swing, he kicked his feet into the fine dust of the yard, ineffectually trying to propel himself forward.

"Hey, chief," she called. "Want a push?"

"Yup." He squealed with delight as she pushed him high. Clutching the rope, he threw back his head and laughed.

"You hang on tight, now." Jessie felt a surge of apprehension. Only yesterday, she wouldn't have paused to consider the dangers inherent in pushing a little boy on a swing, but now her mind conjured up hideous disasters. This was something she hadn't anticipated—the understanding that life with kids was a constant, pressing, pounding worry about what disaster would come next.

"Are you hanging on?" she asked.

"I'm hanging on."

"Promise?"

"Promise."

As she pushed him higher and higher, a shadow haunted the edge of her vision.

Not now.

There was no pain, but a strobe followed by a pulse of black fog, obscuring her right field of vision.

Please.

She had never learned how to pray, but since the mysterious condition had stricken her two years earlier, she had taught herself. She prayed in the primitive, unschooled manner of a child, in broad and desperate supplications.

Please don't let this be happening to me.

She used to rage at the idea that her prayers were ignored. But maybe, just maybe she was praying for the wrong thing. The specialists she'd consulted reluctantly concluded that they couldn't fix this. No one could. And judging by her diminishing field of vision, she didn't have much longer in the light.

Soon, Dr. Tso had told her in his sleek, plush clinic in downtown Taipei. And Dr. Hadden in Auckland had gone even further—If there is anyone you should see, now would be the time.

If there is anyone you should see...

The words had driven her home. And so far, she had done nothing but screw up.

Scottie was oblivious as he soared, his face turned to the sky. "Look!" he yelled. "Look, Aunt Jessie. I can see the whole world."

"That's good," she told him. "You just look out at the amazing world."

"Amazing," Scottie said.

"Pump with your legs," she said. "I need to make a phone call." She dug her wallet from the zippered silk belt around her waist. Years of travel had trained her to keep everything she needed in a slender billfold.

An echo of the old restlessness reverberated through her as she extracted a forgotten boarding pass stuck like a bookmark between the pages of her well-thumbed passport. Ever since giving up her baby, she had traveled the globe, searching, always searching but never sure what she was seeking. For as long as she could remember, there had been something lacking, something missing from her life, her heart, her world. She was searching for a way to make herself whole, and she chose to do it by traveling, seeing untold wonders, majesty and squalor. She'd captured vivid images with her camera in a way that, while not making her rich, had allowed her to cover the hospital expenses, bit by bit.

If Jessie chose to fill the void by traveling the world, Luz found a more direct and obvious method. She married, had babies, moved back to the family home. Jessie wondered if Luz was truly fulfilled. She wondered if she had the nerve to ask her. Because what if the answer was no?

She sat down at the table and took a small white business card from her billfold. A graphic depicted a generic bird. Birdies were her mother's specialty.

The name was printed in shiny gold embossed letters: Glenny Ryder. Golf Champion. Those were the only words on the card, and that was probably appropriate. Those were the words that defined Glenny. No one, not even her daughters, could really think of her without including in the same thoughts "golf" and "champion."

Any other designation would be inaccurate. Glenny Ryder, mother of two, had never sounded quite right. She had given birth to her daughters; she even loved them in her own way. But as far as Jessie knew, she'd never mothered them.

She turned the card over and over in her fingers. How about Glenny Ryder: wife? That wouldn't fit, either. She had probably been married a total of thirty years, but to four different men. Glenny Ryder: serial wife.

Holding the card at an angle, she read the number she had never memorized because it kept changing and because she so seldom called. On the back, she had crossed out and rewritten three new phone numbers. She dialed the latest version.

"Hello?"

Jessie had to think for a second before her stepfather's name came to her. "Stu. Is this Stuart?"

"Luz?"

"No, it's Jessie."

"Well, now, Jessie. Isn't that nice. How are you?" He had a pleasant voice, one that reminded her of the host of a radio call-in show.

She bit her lip. "Fine. I'm back in the States, visiting my sister."

"Fantastic," Stuart said. "You must be having a great time, all together again."

"Uh-huh." Jessie shut her eyes, picturing him. Her mother had a talent for attracting and ill-advisedly marrying handsome, charming men who did irresponsible things with her money. Stuart was probably no exception. Luz had attended the wedding in Vegas a few years ago and had, of course, sent pictures to Jessie. She vaguely recalled a good-looking man seated at a bunting-draped table next to his radiant bride. He was not, thank God, visibly younger than Glenny. Their mother had worn an amber silk sheath, her athletic arms bare, her flame-colored hair too long for a woman her age. But the look worked for Ann-Margret, and it worked for Glenny Ryder.

"Is my mother around?"

"She's at the club."

"Of course she is," Jessie said wryly.

"She just gets better and better. You must be so proud."

"Oh, you bet."

"Anyway, she does carry a cell phone, strictly for emergencies."

She scribbled the number on the tablet. "Thank you, Stuart."

"No problem. Everything okay?"

She hesitated. "Just peachy. But I do need to speak with Glenny."

"I'm sure she'd love to hear from you."

Jessie rang off and drummed her fingers on the table. Strictly for emergencies. What did that mean, anyway? Her mother's emergencies meant a late check for commercial residuals, or her graphite driver needed reshafting.

The fact was, Glenny Ryder was not a bad person or even, for that matter, a bad mother. She'd simply given her girls an unconventional upbringing. From Augusta to Palm Springs, the three of them traveled the green highways of America, singing along with Jackson Browne or Carole King.

In places like the Springs, they lived like trailer trash, their car parked at some edge-of-town motel with a tired Vacancy sign and a name like the Starlite Inn. During the school year, they lived at the house at Eagle Lake, looked after by the haphazard kindness of neighbors and hired baby-sitters until they were deemed old enough to look after themselves. Glenny judged this to be when Luz turned nine and grew tall enough to reach the hide-a-key over the lintel.

Either through sheer luck or remarkably good insight, no overt disaster occurred. The girls raised themselves, Luz with an earnest diligence and Jessie with an angry wildness. Glenny collected both trophies and husbands, the former proving more productive and enduring than the latter. The girls learned to fix their own problems before Glenny found out about them. Jessie and her sister had always tried to take the tough decisions away from their mother. From the time they were very small, she had trained them to make allowances for her. The career put gas in the car and food in their bellies, so the career came first.

It quickly became a habit, an unwritten rule. Don't put too many demands on Glenny because she has a tournament coming up. If she doesn't make the cut...

Well, disaster was happening now, Jessie thought. On a scale she could never have prepared for. Somewhere in the world there must be a manual or list of things to do when your world falls apart. The first thing on the list would be "call your mother."

But Glenny Ryder wasn't like most mothers. She wasn't like any mother.

Hiya, Mom. I'm going blind, and Luz's daughter sneaked out last night and nearly got herself killed, joyriding with a carload of drunk kids. And how are things with you?

She stabbed in the number. While it rang, Jessie pictured the artificially lush golf course, its green-carpeted fairways rolling past stands of yucca and saguaro cactus, kidney-shaped ponds looking deceptively cool in the desert heat.

A hushed voice answered, "Glenny Ryder's service."

Only her mother would bring an answering service to the golf course.

"This is her daughter, Jessie. I need to speak with my mother."

"Jess? Hey, girl. You sound like your sister." Then Jessie recognized the voice of her mother's caddie. Glenny Ryder and Bucky McCabe had been together for over twenty years, making it the most successful long-term relationship thus far in her mother's life.

Jessie smiled. "Hey yourself. You still following my mother around?"

"Somebody's got to do it."

"What did I interrupt?"

"A real pretty tee shot. It's all right. Phone doesn't ring but it vibrates."

"Ingenious. Look, would you put Glenny on?"

"You bet." Bucky hesitated. "Sure would be nice to see you again, sweet pea."

"It would be nice to see you again, too," said Jessie.

A few moments later, another voice came on. "Jessica Didrickson Ryder, is that you?" Glenny was using what had always been known as her golf course whisper, designed to disturb no one.

"Hey, Glenny. I know you're in the middle of a round, but this is pretty important."

A beat of hesitation. "What's wrong?"

Christ, she didn't have a clue where to begin. "I'm back in the States," she said. "I'm staying at Luz's."

"Welcome home, champ. So what's the problem?" Glenny's voice was deep and sweet from nights of celebratory cocktails and Virginia Slims.

Jessie wondered why she had thought calling her mother was a good idea. "Luz's having a little trouble with Lila. And I'm—" She stopped, the words freezing in her throat. How did you explain this to anyone, even yourself? It had a name—AZOOR— and a pathology. The one thing it didn't have was a known cure.

She could find no reason to share that with her mother. "So anyway," she said, "Lila went out joyriding with a bunch of kids last night and there was a wreck."

"Oh, God—"

"She's not hurt," Jessie said quickly. "Some of the others were." She shut her eyes, wondering what Lila had seen, heard, felt. How long would the nightmare images haunt her? When would she begin asking the hard questions about the others? How would her fragile, mysterious, adolescent heart take bad news?

"Luz is pretty shaken up. I thought you would want to know."

"Well." Glenny exhaled loudly. "Poor thing."

Jessie couldn't tell whether she referred to Lila or Luz. "Everyone's been up all night," she said.

"Should I come?"

As far as Jessie knew, a mother wouldn't have to ask that question. A mother would know. *Should I come?*

She opened her eyes. "I don't know," she said with total honesty. "I suppose that's up to you, Glenny."

"Stu's got a conference in Phoenix next week.... If I showed up, I would probably only be in the way," she said, hedging already. She was practically begging for Jessie to agree, to tell her: *Of course that's true. Maybe you should wait until things settle down around here.* And naturally, that meant she would never come.

"You wouldn't be in the way," Jessie said. "With the three cabins, there's plenty of room."

"I don't know... You've never even met Stuart."

Jessie bit her tongue to keep from reminding her that in the past, her mother had brought home any number of men she'd never met. "All the more reason to come. I'd love to meet him."

"I'll see what I can work out."

Jessie knew what that meant. She'd used the phrase many times herself. It meant you had a terrible time saying the word no, but no was the only answer you gave to people who wanted something from you. It meant you didn't want to get involved.

It meant there was nothing the other party could say to change your mind.

The call-waiting signal beeped. "I have another call coming in," she said.

"I'll let you go, then."

You did that a long time ago, Glenny.

Keeping one ear tuned to Scottie at all times, she pushed a button to receive the next call, and ended up taking half a dozen— more friends and neighbors, more school officials, people at Ian's law firm. Still no word from the families of the other kids. She dutifully jotted down numbers and offered a truncated explanation of the accident, then thanked each caller for expressing concern.

Meanwhile, she performed a half-panicked check of her vision. By now she was used to the field drill, holding out a finger at arm's length and slowly moving it to the periphery, marking the degree where it moved out of range.

"Whatcha doing?" Scottie caught her in the middle of the experiment.

She managed to smile. "Watching my finger until it disappears."

He imitated her, but swiveled his head in the direction of his finger.

"That's cheating. You have to keep your eyes straight ahead."

"Why? If I keep my eye on it, I can see it longer."

She laughed. "Maybe you've got a point, cowboy. If you can't see something from the corner of your eye, then turn and look at it."

"Yup."

Who would have thought that hanging out with a four-year-old could be so enlightening?

Unlike Scottie, Lila was neither straightforward nor simple. She had proven herself to be complex and crafty, manipulative and untruthful. At the same time, she was charming, funny, caustic and beautiful. She had a streak in her that Jessie recognized. It was the same reckless abandon that had driven Jessie to do the stupidest things of her life—to sleep with men she didn't love, give up too easily, leave too quickly. To let panic and heartbreak drive her decision about her child.

At the time, she believed adoption was the best possible choice for the baby, but the plan seemed to be backfiring now. Why? Why? She'd stayed away, kept her distance. Wasn't that part of the bargain she'd made with God? She had given her child the calm, steady influence of her sister. Jessie wanted to ensure that Lila didn't turn out like her.

Yet that was just where Lila seemed to be heading.

Scottie wandered over to the rope swing, and the phone rang again.

"Benning residence."

A hesitation. "I'm calling for Jessie Ryder, please."

She lifted her eyebrows in surprise. "This is Jessie Ryder."

"It's Blair LaBorde, from *Texas Life*."

Jessie recognized the round and mellow drawl of her former journalism professor. "I didn't expect to hear from you so soon."

"I didn't expect to find something for you so soon. It's in your own backyard, as a matter of fact."

Jessie's blood heated. "No way. You don't expect me to cover the wreck—"

"Wreck?" Blair's voice sharpened. "Who said anything about a wreck?"

Jessie stood and paced, wishing she had kept her mouth shut. "This isn't about the accident?"

"No. But it could be. Maybe it should be, hon."

"Not on your life." Jessie owed Blair more of an explanation than that. She'd find out soon enough, anyway. She gave a quick, unsensational summary of what had happened.

Blair gave a low whistle. "Six kids. Hell of a story, there."

"This is a tight-knit community. People are taking it hard." She decided not to reveal just how close she was to the situation. "So what is this about?"

"That cold lead I told you about. Something I've been hound-dogging for a while. Could be a big story."

That was code for, Maybe we'll actually make a little more than the usual pittance. Jessie perked up at the prospect of an assignment. One of the psychologists who had screened her for the Orientation and Mobility program in Austin had suggested that Jessie clung to work because her psyche had rationalized that if the camera took her into darkness, perhaps some grand design would save her from having to go there herself. Of course, a career that relied on being able to see was not going to make sense anymore. But maybe she had one more assignment in her.

"I'm listening."

"The magazine wanted a feature on a resident of Edenville, Texas a while back, but we dropped the lead. When you mentioned you were going back there, I looked into reviving it."

Jessie's heart sank. Christ, what if it was Ian? Ian Benning, the noble, penniless death-row attorney, fighting injustice despite the opposition of his conservative politician father. He was the stuff of David-and-Goliath stories; he always had been. "You're kidding. So who is it?"

"Nobody famous. A human interest piece. And it's a crack-erjack story. I'm waiting on an answer from the guy. I know what it'll be. He's a stubborn SOB, but he's no fool."

"Human interest? Then why me? I photograph mountains and suspension bridges, not—"

"So it's not a suspension bridge. It's a local guy named Mat-lock."

A shadow loomed in front of Jessie, and she shrank back before realizing the darkness was cast by the big live oak across the yard. "Fine. Give me the scoop and let's do it."

CHAPTER 12

Lila slept all day, the way she used to when she was little and had an ear infection and a fever. Except that now, when she awakened to a blaze of late-afternoon sun streaming through the window, she didn't feel any better.

She could hear the activity going on below—the phone ringing, her dad pacing the floor and talking to her mom in a low rumble, her aunt's lightly accented voice chiming in now and then. Mom sounded totally stressed out, because she couldn't get hold of her best friend, Nell Bridger. Trying not to think about the last time she'd seen Dig and Travis, Lila squeezed her eyes shut.

Some time later, after more drifting, she heard Owen and Wyatt getting home for the day, slamming the door and being shushed. Scottie asked to go see Lila, whining a little when denied. Lila wished the little guy would come in anyway—or was she on restriction from him, too?

She lay unmoving, hot and groggy, wishing she could be little again, cocooned by the hazy comfort of her mother sitting on the edge of the bed and smoothing her hand over Lila's brow. She yearned for the salt-sweet tang of brackish Gatorade from a sippee cup, the earnest hilarity of *Sesame Street*, the sense that the smiling world would wait for her to get better. But she wasn't a kid anymore; her mother and father had made that perfectly clear when they'd laid down the law. Yet in the same breath, they'd grounded her as though she was Wyatt, in trouble for hitting golfballs into the lake.

They didn't get it. She was the oldest, the only girl. She was always having to baby-sit and clean up and put up with the Three Stooges. No wonder she sneaked out, drank beer, partied with her friends.

Frustrated, she lay appraising her memories the way she had assessed her injuries in the moments following the accident. Some of her recollections were ice-sharp, others were vague, as though someone had breathed on a mirror, melting the details into a diffuse blur. The agonizing moments of lying there, listening to the blare of the radio and smelling the reek of dripping gasoline, had been endless. Someone—Kathy, she thought—had turned hysterical, screaming and crying with the sort of roaring savagery you might hear in a zoo.

Lila remembered putting her hands over her ears as she let the tears run unchecked down her face. She offered up not only prayers, but detailed, intricate bargains to God—a 3.5 GPA if nothing was broken, volunteer hours at the Hill Country Care Alzheimer's facility if she didn't need stitches, a lifetime of uncomplaining household chores if no one in the Jeep was hurt at all....

Finally a fire truck and ambulance—maybe more than one—arrived, bathing the area in artificial white light. Paramedics and big-shouldered firemen swarmed over the hill like an army of fire ants. Grim faces appeared in every window. Gruff voices barked orders and talked about a "plan of extraction" and called for backup.

Judd Mason, who'd witnessed the accident because he was out doing the same thing in his Bronco, had appeared at the Jeep window, tipped his head sideways to peer inside. Before the rescue workers could peel him away, he said aloud what they were probably all thinking: "Ho-lee doggone shee-it. Look who's been whirled around in the Bass-o-Matic."

One fireman, so young he hardly needed to shave, grabbed Judd by the back of the collar and shoved him away. All cockiness gone, Judd fell to his knees and vomited. The young rescuer looked inside, too, and Lila remembered how close his face was, his features distorted by the cracks in the glass, his angel eyes filled with heartbreak. "This one's conscious," he called, his gaze never leaving her, never wavering. "Hurry up with that stretcher."

More rescue workers closed in, asking Lila all sorts of questions: Did she know what had happened to her? What day was it? What year? Where did she hurt?

The strange thing was, at the time she had believed with every shred of herself that she was dying. She was a floating corpse, breathing underwater.

That's what shock does to the body, Dr. Martinez had explained to her much later. She felt like she couldn't catch her breath. She felt like she would never breathe again.

She didn't really recall the "extraction," as they called it, or the ambulance ride to the hospital. She had lain on a gurney for uncounted minutes before being questioned by the highway patrol, X-rayed, cleaned up, given some sort of IV and parked in an exam room to wait for her mother.

Hurry, Mommy, hurry.... Maybe she'd said it aloud, maybe not. She wasn't sure.

The moment her mother had burst into the room, Lila had known she would survive. But she didn't break down, didn't sob with relief even though she wanted to. If she did that, her mother would know how scared and confused she was. She'd been fighting forever to prove she was her own person, and now this. So she put up her usual defense—anger, defiance, sarcasm—and prayed she could get the hell out of there.

According to the doctor, she was the lucky one of the bunch.

"Shaken, not stirred," the technician who did the CT scan had cheerfully proclaimed.

The lucky one. What was so lucky about surviving an accident when the boy you love and all your best friends were...

She scrambled from the bed and snatched up the phone receiver. Dead. The cord to the phone jack was gone.

She slammed down the phone, then grabbed the edge of the dresser as a wave of dizziness caught her. She felt like Dorothy in the swirling house, spinning out of control with no landing in sight. Feeling her way back to the bowl-shaped Papasan chair in the corner, she drew her knees to her chest and wrapped her arms around them. She smelled her own sweat and puke and someone else's blood and realized she hadn't even bothered to shower before collapsing on her bed and sinking into sleep.

What about Heath? Had he taken a shower? She let out a wavering little moan.

"Hey, are you all right?"

Lila dragged her head up. "Aunt Jess. Where's Mom?"

"Busy with your brothers, I imagine. I thought I heard you moving around up here and figured you were awake. Do you need anything?"

Lila leaned her head back against the cushion of the big round chair and stared at her aunt. She looked like a tattooed, red-headed pixie. The image spun gently. She was like Mom but she wasn't. Mom on Ecstasy, maybe.

Do you need anything?

Yeah, Aunt Jess, how about we figure out a way to rewind the past twenty-four hours?

Then the dizziness stopped and she focused on the cordless handset clipped to Jessie's waistband. "I have to make a phone call," she said. "I need to find out what happened to my friends. Kathy's my best friend. We've known each other since kindergarten. She was so scared in the car last night. I just want to hear her voice."

Jessie indicated the turquoise plastic phone by the computer. "So make the call."

"My phone is out of order," Lila said. "I think the battery's dead. Can I borrow that one? Please?"

Jessie moved closer. She didn't seem to see the stack of willfully neglected schoolbooks on the floor in her path. She kicked them over, nearly falling on her face. "Damn," Aunt Jessie muttered. "Your folks were right about one thing. This room needs a big cleaning."

Great. She'd already gone over to the Dark Side.

"So can I borrow the phone?"

Jessie sat on the vanity stool and swiveled to face her. "Lila, you lied to me last night. Just remember that. Last night started with a lie. I was stupid enough to believe you. I have to live with that. I have to live with what happened because I believed you. My mother's caddie used to say, 'Fool me once, shame on you. Fool me twice—'"

"'Shame on me,'" Lila said, repeating the old phrase with her. "I've heard it."

Jessie sat silent, watching her. She had the weirdest way of looking at a person. She didn't just look with her eyes but with her whole body, like she was a dry sponge and you were water and she wanted to absorb you so you'd no longer exist apart from her.

Fool me once, shame on you...

Was she ashamed?

She was supposed to be, so she did what you were supposed to do when you're ashamed of yourself. "Aunt Jess, I'm real sorry about what I did."

Last night started with a lie.

She swallowed, and felt the first truly excruciating physical pain since the wreck. "I'm sorry," she repeated.

Jessie sat there, motionless. "It's not just me you should be apologizing to."

Tears pressed at the back of Lila's eyelids, and she fought for control, crushing them shut. She'd vowed recently to quit crying, because crying let people know you cared. Caring gave them power over you, and then you ended up doing things to make them happy instead of pleasing yourself. It was a harsh assignment to give herself, but life was harsh and she just wanted to have a good time.

She opened her eyes. "So you came in here all offended because I lied, but you don't want me to apologize."

"It's not that you don't owe me an apology," Aunt Jessie said. "I need for you to mean it. I know you're damned sorry you sneaked out with your boyfriend and got in a car crash, but are you sorry you lied to me? I don't think so. You don't even know me. What do you care whether you lied to me or not?"

"I don't want to care." The desperate whisper came out of its own accord. Then the tears followed, hot and humiliating, more defiant than her vow. They burned her cheeks with their heat, their quiet power. "Please, Aunt Jessie. I don't want to care."

She pulled herself into a miserable ball of shame, wishing the chair would swallow her up. Aunt Jessie came across the room to her, stumbling again over a stack of folded clothes Lila hadn't put away. Jessie sat down and put her arms around her, holding on tight even though Lila reeked, and for some reason that made Lila cry harder.

Once she started, it was impossible to stop. She just sat there and cried and cried while her aunt held her, and somehow she ran out of steam and started to feel a little better. She never hugged her mom or dad anymore. She was always mad at them or getting ready to be mad at them or getting over being mad at them. But she had no history with her aunt, no connection, nothing at stake. Somehow that made it possible to cry and not want to die at the same time.

"I was so scared," she said, sniffling. "I was so scared." She said it over and over again while Aunt Jessie stroked her hair and then handed her a towel from her cheerleading gear bag. Pulling back, Lila was amazed to see that her aunt's cheeks were streaked with tears. "Why are you crying?" she asked.

Aunt Jessie's mouth trembled. "Oh, baby. This is the first time I ever got to hold you in my arms and rock you."

Lila didn't know what to say to that, so she took the towel and dabbed at her face. Sharing a corner of the towel, Aunt Jessie wrinkled her nose. "This thing is a biohazard."

"My whole room is a biohazard."

"Is that how you like it?"

"Of course not. But I don't like cleaning it, either."

"I think you should clean it."

Lila thought of the way her aunt had stumbled over things. "I have to. My parents are making me. I'm just waiting for the workers to come and install the bars on my window. I'll never see the light of day again."

Something like panic flashed across her aunt's face. "Don't ever say that."

"It's true. They're going to keep me in jail until I'm old enough to vote. They don't care if I rot from boredom."

"If your parents didn't care, they would cut you loose and let you drift away, maybe sinking out of sight."

Lila rose from the chair. She felt achy and fragile, even though she wasn't supposed to be injured. She started picking through clothes mounded on the floor, tossing them in a laundry basket. Aunt Jessie watched for a while, then took out a slip of paper with phone numbers scribbled on it. She turned on the phone and stepped out into the hallway. Lila instantly glued her ear to the door.

Aunt Jessie identified herself as a family member of one of the victims and asked about the other kids. She listened carefully, saying "uh-huh" a bunch of times. Then she said, "Is she awake? Would it be all right to ring her room? I see. Yes. I'll hold."

Lila couldn't stand it any longer. Whipping open the door, she said, "Kathy?"

Aunt Jessie nodded and came back into the room, crossing to the chair and sitting down. She looked like an angel, surrounded by colorful pillows, her short-enough-to-be-cool skirt draped over the edge of the chair. She froze, holding up a hand. "Is this Kathy? Just a moment, love, there's someone here who wants to speak to you."

Pure elation bubbled up in Lila and she seized the receiver. *Thank you,* she mouthed at her aunt, then said, "Kathy? It's me, Lila. Are you okay?"

"No." Kathy's voice sounded tired and weak. "My leg's broken in two places. Broken ribs, too, and stitches under my chin where I banged it. Hurts like a bitch, or it did until they gave me something. I'm dying of thirst, but they said I'm not supposed to drink anything."

"Have you seen Heath?"

"No." A long pause.

"Kathy, what?"

"My mom said Sierra had to have surgery to stop some kind of internal bleeding, and her foot was crushed."

Lila clamped her eyes shut. This wasn't happening. It wasn't. "She's on the track team."

"Not anymore." Kathy's voice sounded slurry and strange. "Where're you?"

"They let me come home," she said. "I'm grounded for life."

"Me, too, probably. As soon as the parental units quit feeling sorry for me."

"If they're like mine, the pity won't last long."

"That sucks."

"Yeah. Have you heard about the others? What about Travis and Dig?"

The phone was snatched from Lila's hand. Her mother stood there, her face as hard and white as marble.

"Hey," Lila said, taking refuge in defiance. "I was talking."

She pressed the off button.

"I had to find out how my friends are doing," Lila snapped.

"In the future, I'll get that information for you." Her mom wheeled on Aunt Jessie. "She's not allowed to use the phone until further notice."

"I thought hearing from her friend would be reassuring," said Aunt Jessie.

"You thought—" Mom stopped and took a deep breath.

"Look, the phone's off-limits for a reason. And Lila, you won't...God, how do I say this?" Her voice wavered and she stopped talking, which worried Lila. Her mother always knew what to say. She wasn't harsh and angry anymore, but troubled and sad. "Honey, I didn't want you getting the facts from your friends, over the phone."

"Kathy was telling me—" Lila stopped. Lately she didn't hesitate to contradict her mother, but there was something weird about the way Mom held her lips pressed together as though holding something back that had to come out no matter how much she might want to keep it inside. "What?" Lila whispered, wishing she hadn't used up all her tears on Aunt Jessie.

Mom reached for Lila, but Lila stepped back. Mom lowered her hands to her sides, still holding the phone. "It was a really bad accident. Everyone's saying it's a miracle you weren't hurt at all. But the other kids weren't so lucky."

"I know about Sierra's foot."

"Some of the injuries were...more extensive."

Lila couldn't breathe. Somehow she managed to gasp out, "Heath?"

Mom shook her head as she clipped the phone to the waist-band of her shorts. "He'll survive." Her hands kept moving nervously, picking things up, setting them down. "But...honey, it's Albert Bridger—Dig." She paused, and her face turned even whiter. "His injuries were extensive, and he was life-flighted to a level one Trauma Center. They did everything they could to save him." Mom swallowed hard. She looked totally wrung. "Ah, Lila-girl. Dig's dead."

Jessie took a whispery little breath, but Lila didn't breathe at all.

No. No. No. She didn't say a word, yet her mind screamed. Her heart screamed. And then she completely rejected the idea. Not Dig. Dig was only in ninth grade; he was the youngest in the family. He had just made junior varsity on the football team. He was saving up to buy a dirt bike. She'd known him since the day his mother had plunked him down in the sandbox at Spring Valley Park and, only three, he had uttered one word over and over again: Dig. Dig. Dig.

He couldn't be dead. He couldn't be.

Lila nearly doubled over in pain, but she refused to react. Refused to show any sign at all that she'd heard her mother. If she didn't howl, cry, throw things, tear at her hair, then it wasn't real. Dig could not be dead.

"Sweetie," her mother began.

Lila held out a hand as if to fend off a blow. She knew what was coming next. Her mom would shift into that familiar oh-so-practical mode. She would explain to Aunt Jessie who Dig was and how long they'd known the family and why this was all so sad. And then she'd start compiling a verbal list of things to do, like make a casserole and order some flowers and think up something trite and sentimental to do, like planting a tree in his honor in front of the school.

Mom stared at Lila's hand. "I'll sit with you for a little while."

Lila nodded, then changed her mind. "I think I need to be by myself."

"You're sure."

She nodded again. *Please.*

Mom and Aunt Jessie looked at each other. Then Mom walked out of the room, motioning for Jessie to follow. Aunt Jessie looked back over her shoulder at Lila. Her eyes were funny in a way Lila couldn't explain to herself—seeing and not seeing, looking and not looking. Maybe that funny way she had of looking and seeing had to do with the fact that she was a famous photographer.

Then she stepped out, leaving the door ajar.

Lila hugged herself as a sudden chill took hold, even though it was probably seventy-five degrees in the room. She shut her eyes and a picture of Dig appeared, his head thrown back, Adam's apple bulging from his skinny neck as he hooted with laughter and gave up his seat belt to Kathy. Heath had just handed him a joint; Lila had just loaned him her graphing calculator, and it was still over at his house. Had he finished those algebra problems? Had he petted his dog, made a wish on a star, heard the new Actual Tigers song? She could hardly stand to think of all the things he would miss. He'd never make the varsity football squad, never get up the nerve to ask a girl to prom, never see the autumn leaves reflected in the lake or sit around a bonfire, laughing with his friends.

A horrible whisper started in a back corner of Lila's mind. *This is your fault, young lady.* The whisper grew louder and stronger until it became a shout that filled her head, drowning out everything else. Mrs. Hayes was right. If it hadn't been for her, Heath never would have gone out last night, and Dig would still be alive, and Sierra would still have her foot.

"...the main reason I grounded her from the phone." Her mom's voice drifted from downstairs.

"Okay, so I get it now." Aunt Jessie sounded edgy, confused.

"I'd appreciate it if you would respect my rules when it comes to Lila."

My rules. The way she said it, you'd think they were chiseled into a stone tablet up on a hill somewhere.

Jessie said something indistinct, but Mom's reply rang clear: "Don't you dare leave now, damn it, Jess. I need you."

Wow. So Mom nearly ran her off already. This had to be a record. Still, those last three words were something Lila had never heard from her mother before. *I need you.*

"...kid who died?" Aunt Jessie was asking.

"I've known his mother forever. She's not married, lives in a double-wide at Two-Dog Ranch..." Her mom went on like this and then said the inevitable: "I'm going to take a casserole over..."

Lila pushed the door shut, leaned against it and covered her ears. She didn't want to hear any of this. The more she heard, the deader Dig got.

CHAPTER 13

Jessie had been legally blind in one eye for over a year. She was losing the vision in the other eye, too, but fierce denial and dogged determination had delayed the inevitable. Yet now, even her stubborn will wouldn't hold back the future. She had to surrender to her condition, which was progressing with increasing velocity. Yet even while making arrangements as coldly and rationally as possible, she felt as though she'd stepped off a cliff. It was a long fall to nowhere.

She made a phone call to the Beacon for the Blind in Austin where she'd already preregistered from overseas. In a toneless voice, she set an appointment, then took a shower, thinking she would cry herself sick. Instead she could only stand there in shock, the water beating down on her as she struggled with a terrible sense of unreality.

Perversely her vision had stabilized for now, at least. She'd experienced the same thing in her left eye, nearly a year ago. She'd suffered months of vitreous floaters, mysterious flashes, blurred smears of light like rain on a window. And then one day, the symptoms receded. Inflammation subsided, retinal dysfunction went into remission and she managed to see with remarkable clarity out of part of her eye. This miracle filled her with the cruelty of hope, making it all the more devastating when all vision disappeared only a few days later, never to return.

Her remaining vision in the right eye was excellent, but now she knew better than to hope. As she stepped from the shower and dried her hair in front of a mirror, she blinked several times, looked from side to side, up and down, checking all the benchmarks the doctors did as they studied her condition.

As if there was anything they could do that hadn't already been tried.

AZOOR stood for acute zonal occult outer retinopathy. But what it meant was the end of her life as she knew it. She lost count of the days and weeks she'd spent in specialty clinics, her head immobilized by a padded vise, her electroretinograms showing nothing but bad news, her hopes grinding down to grim determination and, finally, despair. Like misinserted film lying at the bottom of a camera, her retinas were fast becoming useless.

At the Dalton Eye Clinic in Christchurch, they'd done all the tests technology and experimentation would allow. But peripapillary scarring had accelerated the foggy gray obscurity in its relentless descent over her vision. The most eminent specialists in the Far East had declared that there was nothing further they could do. The doctors she had seen so far, the specialists and experts, had reluctantly categorized her as one of the unlucky victims of disease. While many recovered their vision within three years, a select few failed to improve. Jessie was in the latter category. It was time, she was told, to face the truth and make plans accordingly. They advised her to enroll at the Beacon for the Blind, an international organization which had a major facility in Austin.

While the specialists tried to explain this as a phenomenon of nature, chance and science, Jessie had her own theory. This was a force greater than her will, her desire or any doctor's desperate treatment. Perhaps it was retribution. She used people, turned her back on people, left people. This was the price she would have to pay.

Now she worried that her curse was infectious; it might taint the very person she'd come halfway around the world to visit.

She'd wanted to see Lila before she couldn't see anymore. And then when she showed up, Lila nearly died. Jessie ought to simply disappear. Except for what Luz had said: "Don't you dare leave now, damn it, Jess. I need you."

When Lila had lain sobbing against her chest, Jessie had finally learned what it was like to love a child, to hold her so close their hearts melded, to accept her even when she'd done a terrible thing, even when she smelled of blood and vomit and motor oil.

Perched at the end of the bed, she touched up her toenails with Capri coral polish. She put on a beige tank dress and then her work vest, a marvel of engineering in khaki canvas, riddled with pockets, grommets, loops, ties and zippered compartments. Very Margaret Bourke-White.

She wasn't quite sure how to gear up for a shoot like this. What lenses would she need? Fast film or slow? Print or digital?

The thing that surprised her was how nervous she was. You would never know her published credits numbered in the thousands, that she'd been short-listed for all the major prizes including a MacGregor from Australia, that her work appeared on billboards and the sides of buses all over the Far East, that she'd had several single-artist shows. Today she simply had to shoot a guy across the lake. Big deal. Yet deep down, she knew something she would never tell a soul—she was ending her career as a photographer. This was the last subject she would ever shoot.

A few minutes later, dressed, geared up and edgy, she appeared at her sister's door.

"Aunt Jessie!" Scottie launched himself at her, clinging to her thigh like a barnacle as she walked inside.

"Hey, big guy." She ruffled his curly hair.

"He's a gi-irl," Owen teased. "He's got pink toenails."

"I bet you want pink toenails, too. You and Wyatt both."

"Eew!" Her elder two nephews howled over the sound of the too-loud TV set.

From the kitchen, Luz yelled, "Turn that thing—"

Wyatt hit the mute button.

"—down."

"Hi, guys." Jessie was relieved to find a more normal routine after the weekend. There had been a special sort of pain in the dazed and mournful worship at the Halfway Baptist Church, everyone walking around shell-shocked and empty, little kids squirming and misbehaving and apprehensive at seeing grown men and women weeping and hugging each other. Jessie had sat far in the back with Lila, squeezing her hand. She could tell the girl wished she had opted out of the service, but Luz wouldn't hear of it, of course. As quickly as she could, Lila had slipped out and hurried to the car, preferring to stay alone and silent, dealing with unimaginable grief and guilt and God knew what else.

Things seemed calmer now. In deference to the tragedy, the tiny school district had declared attendance optional. Extra counselors would be on hand at all levels. Luz had apparently decided to keep Owen and Wyatt home. Lila refused categorically to go to school. She claimed they'd mob her, accuse her of being the cause of everything.

"What are you guys up to today?" she asked her blissfully young, uncomplicated nephews.

They stood silent and bashful, their attention riveted on her, the uninvited stranger. She wondered if they would always associate her arrival with disaster. "I bet you're going on a pirate ship," she suggested. "No? Maybe you're going to trap an armadillo in the woods."

Owen, the middle boy, definitely looked intrigued by that one.

"Or how about digging a hole through the earth to China?"

"Yeah!" said Scottie.

"How about you clean your room," Luz said from the kitchen. "Inspection's in fifteen minutes, and we're leaving to do errands. If your room's clean, I'll take you to McDonald's for breakfast."

The boys' faces blossomed, and they headed for the stairs, nearly tripping over each other in their haste.

Jessie walked into the kitchen. "Now, where did you learn that trick? Dr. Spock?"

Luz bent to take a bubbling, cheesy casserole out of the oven. "Hey, that guy could learn a thing or two from me. Bribery is a power tool."

Jessie bent over and sniffed, shutting her eyes as she inhaled.

"King Ranch Chicken," Luz said. "For Dig's family. There's a funeral planned, Nell's got relatives coming to town and they're going to have to eat. Anyway, I thought I would drop this off when we're out today." She jotted reheating instructions on a Post-it note and stuck it to the lid of the Pyrex dish.

Jessie had to get used to the idea that Luz had a separate life here, with friends Jessie didn't know, friends who now knew Luz better than Jessie did. "Are you and Nell Bridger close?"

"We are. I've known her since the kids were little." She set the casserole in a double paper bag, lines of grief pulling at her eyes and mouth. "Those boys are her whole world. I've taken their picture for the Christmas card every year since they were tiny."

Dig and Travis. The elder boy's extensive injuries would keep him in hospital for a long time.

"I don't know how she'll get through this." Luz sniffled, brushed at her cheek. "And all I can think to do is bring her a casserole."

"She'll want to see you," Jessie assured her, "casserole or not. Where's Ian?"

"He drove to the capital early today." Luz spoke casually; this was obviously routine. "He took the rental car to Austin to return it, and he'll get a ride back with an associate who lives in Marble Falls."

"And Lila?"

"I'm letting her sleep in. Then...we'll see."

"She's got to rejoin the living one of these days."

"Not today." Luz looked at Jessie while untying a wrinkled Kiss The Cook apron. "So you're off to work."

"Yep."

"That was quick."

"You know Blair. She's always got something up her sleeve. And I have to make a living."

Luz smiled. "What, you're not doing this to express your artistic soul?"

"I'm doing this to pay off my Visa bill." She hesitated. "I'm not so keen on photography these days."

"Are you kidding? It's your life."

It was. Jessie forced a smile. "People change careers all the time. I've been thinking of trying my hand at writing. Or maybe basket-weaving."

Luz laughed, clearly thinking it was a joke. Jessie glanced up at the family photos displayed on a rack over the breakfast nook. "Now *that* is for the soul," she said.

The richness of her sister's life was apparent everywhere, expressed in little details most people would take for granted: Owen's I ♥ U Mom card, stuck to the fridge with magnets. A cross-stitched potholder with the slogan, Luz's Kitchen Is Warmed By Love. And, of course, the picture mural of faces bright with laughter or solemn with concentration and oblivious to the camera, action shots, still shots, kids frozen in motion or sound asleep or brandishing an award or sports trophy.

"Right." Luz wiped down the butcher's block kitchen island. "I never got around to framing stuff, so I started slapping prints up on the wall. Ian put the sheet of Plexiglas over it, and now it looks intentional." Her gaze touched Jessie. "You seem nervous."

"I don't have much experience photographing people."

"Oh, come on. That's like me saying I don't have much experience shooting monuments or land formations." Setting her hands on her hips, she studied the mural. "Come to think of it, I don't." Then she laughed. "I guess that's the thing—in order to take pictures of exotic places, you have to actually go somewhere."

Jessie pointed out a photo of Wyatt dressed up like a killer bee and brandishing a Star Wars light saber. "You don't call this exotic?"

"I call it bizarre." As they finished their coffee, they reminisced about their long-ago days at college. If Jessie was Ansel Adams, Luz was Annie Leibovitz. Jessie would insist on driving clear out to Enchanted Rock and waiting for the perfect sunset, while Luz preferred sitting at Barton Creek Park, capturing family picnics, kids playing, old couples sitting on benches. They discussed Jessie's equipment, from the latest digital upgrades to the old classic Nikon FM she'd had forever. It was the most companionable time they'd spent since Jessie had arrived, but it was over too quickly. It ended with a thud and a "Mo-om. He took my—"

A honking horn sent the herd thundering to the door. The dog bayed a greeting.

"Someone's here," Scottie yelled.

"We know, moron." Owen shoved him aside to open the door.

"I'm not a moron."

"Are so."

"Am not."

"Are—*whoa.*"

Owen stepped out onto the porch, motioning for Jessie and Luz to follow. A cloud of caliche dust swirled around a late-model Cadillac with gold and white trim and vanity plates reading Chi-O 4-Ever. A tall woman in an Escada suit emerged and went around back to the trunk.

Blair LaBorde had not changed much over the years. She still had blond hair of a volume and tint only a certain class of true Texas women ever achieved. It was the shade of champagne left out overnight, and had been fluffed into the sort of coiffure made famous by socialite Lynn Wyatt.

A good quality lipstick outlined a mouth with a hardworking smile and a set of well-tooled teeth. She wore a look of determined optimism that functioned as a mask for some sort of deep and bitter discontent and the ruthless ambition that ran rampant in Texas women of a certain age. She had nervous hands and a nose that twitched as though she was about to sneeze. Jessie noticed all this in the few seconds it took to walk outside to the driveway. She had cultivated an uncanny ability to suck up visual images quickly and file them away.

"Jessie Ryder," said Blair, talking in a suburban Dallas drawl as she opened the trunk of the Cadillac. "And Luz. Lord, but the two of you have hardly changed at all. I swear, you need a theme song to start playing when the two of you show up together."

"The Good, the Bad and the Surgically Enhanced," Jessie suggested.

"Surely not." Blair lifted a perfect brow.

"Not yet, anyway," Jessie said.

"And not on my budget," Luz said.

Blair hugged Jessie and then Luz. She had been their mentor years earlier, for under the homecoming queen exterior lay a keen intelligence—and a Ph.D. in mass communications. "God, it's been a grandaddy coon's age." She waved at the wide-eyed boys clustered on the porch. "Yours?" she asked Luz.

"My bundles of joy."

"And your daughter?"

"She's going to be all right," Luz said. "She's the lucky one."

"I heard. Hon, I'm so relieved for you."

Luz stepped back. "I'll let the two of you get to work."

"Ready?" Blair asked Jessie.

"I think so."

"I love your work, by the way. I've seen it here and there over the years."

Jessie put her camera bag in the trunk, noting that it was cluttered with clippings, e-mail printouts, a banker's box stuffed with files. "You've seen my work?"

"Nope, just saying that," Blair admitted without the least twinge of guilt. She took out a card of gum squares, popped one out of the back and put it in her mouth. "Nicorette?"

"No, thanks."

With a shrug, Blair popped a second piece into her mouth. "One of my major food groups these days. So are you ready?"

Jessie nodded, trying to ignore the flurry of nerves in her gut. This was another assignment, nothing more. She'd photographed the wonders of the world. Shooting a man and his daughter would be a cakewalk.

"So anyway," Blair said, cracking her gum, "I've heard you're the best there is."

Jessie laughed as she got in the passenger side. "I've heard the same about you."

"Good to know. This ought to be fun, anyway." As she eased her car up the drive and turned onto the main road, she said, "Pretty around here." She drummed her fingers on the steering wheel. The nails of her right hand were perfectly manicured and painted an aggressive, shiny red. On her left hand, the nails had been bitten to the quick.

She flexed her hands on the steering wheel. "Quitting smoking is hell."

"Yeah. I've done it a few times myself," Jessie admitted. "How long have you been working on this story? You didn't tell me much except to say it's local and human interest."

"I've been after him for over a year. He was a big holdout. They all are, claiming to want to protect their dignity and privacy. But those are commodities that can be bought for the right amount of money. This guy held out longer than most. I was almost going to have to go with an account given by a third party who talked to the press in the first place, but he finally decided to cooperate."

"Sounds complicated. Most of my subjects aren't in a position to negotiate."

"What are your subjects?"

"Asian rain forests. Coral reefs in the South Pacific."

"How long were you out of the country?"

"I was overseas fifteen years."

Blair gave a low whistle. "So you probably haven't heard about the Matlock case." She eased the car onto Springside Way, heading toward the south end of Eagle Lake.

"Not really."

Blair cracked her gum and flashed a grin. "Boy howdy. Are you in for a treat."

She turned down a driveway leading to the Matlock place. The rambling house sat low into the brow of the bank sloping down to the lake. A sizable boathouse sagged into the water. A newly built dock projected out into the lake like a straight blade. Moored to one side was the green-and-white floatplane.

"I usually like to schedule the interview and photo shoot separately," Blair said, "but this one was hard to pin down. Pain in the ass, actually. So we'll get it all done today and then get out of his hair."

She parked in the shade of an overgrown crape myrtle and got out. A little terrier sprang from the bushes like a stone from a slingshot, yapping for all he was worth. The dog was followed by an older man, small of stature, with leathery skin and calm brown eyes. He shushed the dog in Spanish and nodded to Blair.

"You must be Mr. Garza," Blair said. "Mr. Garza, my photographer, Jessie Ryder."

The man greeted her with an unhurried but perfunctory nod of his graying head. "He is down in the shop, fixing a motor."

"Thanks. We'll find him there."

As they headed down the steep bank, Blair muttered, "Great. He's probably a mess, and he knew we were coming today."

"It might be fine," Jessie said, trying to sound reassuring. "Sometimes you can get a lot more out of a person when he's doing something routine. My sister says he's a hunk."

"Then what are we waiting for?" Outside the workshop, Blair paused to refresh her lipstick. She offered the tube of scarlet to Jessie, who shook her head. Then Blair knocked, although the door was ajar.

"Mr. Matlock? Dusty," she called in her best debutante voice.

"Come in." He spoke over his shoulder, remaining bent over something on the workbench, which gave them an unparalleled view of a flawless male butt.

The workshop smelled of motor oil and sunlight streaming through the windows, and held the heat of the day already in its grip. A small oscillating fan blew its quiet breath across the benches and tools. The man straightened with unhurried grace, and stood still, backlit by the glare from the windows.

Inside Jessie, awareness sprang to life. The fall of light created a lyrical precision of line and form, etching that image indelibly in her mind. He had dark hair laid in the sort of thick waves a woman's fingers itched to plunge into. In scuffed work boots, he stood over six feet tall. He wore a pair of jeans and a plain T-shirt, plastered to his torso by sweat.

His arms were brawny with hard-worked muscles, his stomach flat as the top of a six-pack. His eyes, Jessie saw when he stepped into the light, were bluer than Eagle Lake at its deepest point.

Damn. She wished she had borrowed that lipstick after all.

CHAPTER 14

Dusty had tried his best to forget that the woman from the magazine was coming. He was already regretting his decision to let her do the story. Now her Cadillac was parked in the drive, and here she was, in all her overpriced glory. Blair LaBorde, a big-haired, hungry-eyed woman, had been the bane of his existence ever since hearing about Amber's unusual birth. She had the harsh brilliance of a cut and polished gem, and ten years earlier she could have passed for one of the models in the ads of her glossy magazine.

But it was the assistant rather than Miss LaBorde who caught his attention. Even wearing an elaborate fly-fishing vest and standing amid the small motors, blades of all sizes, power tools and spiderwebs, she wasn't merely pretty. She had the sort of face you saw on movie posters thirty feet across. Yet at the same time, she looked familiar. And up close, he could see an unexpected grace that softened the perfection of her face, giving her a humanity that made him stare at her longer than politeness allowed.

"Thank you for agreeing to meet with us," Blair said, giving him no time to examine his reaction to her companion. "This is

Jessie Ryder," she added. "She's the best we have—you won't be disappointed."

"The best what?" He kept studying the woman named Jessie, and recognition nudged at him again. "Have we met?"

"I'm visiting my sister, Luz Benning. She lives across the lake. You know her husband, Ian."

Now it came back to him. The lost traveler on the road, the woman on the dock. His gaze slipped over her, and she shifted away as though avoiding an uninvited advance. Yet, perversely, her edginess drew him.

"Lots of folks mistake Jessie for Luz," LaBorde explained.

"I don't make that kind of mistake." Then he felt guilty about his brusqueness, given what the Bennings were going through. "Dustin Matlock," he said, wiping his hand on a greasy rust-colored rag and then holding it out.

"Good to meet you," she said, apparently pretending not to see the hand.

"I'm sorry as can be about what happened to your sister's kid. Is she going to be okay?"

"Yes. We're all relieved about that. I'm sure Ian will call you when he gets a chance. Thank you for getting him to the hospital in the middle of the night."

Nice voice, he thought. Texas and something else, something a little exotic.

"I'm glad the girl's not hurt," he said. Ian Benning was a client, possibly a friend. Ian's kid had to be all right, Dusty told himself, feeling a little light-headed with relief. Otherwise his sister-in-law wouldn't be here, working. "Tell Ian I asked."

He went to the door and stepped outside. Pico ran across the yard, harassing a mockingbird. Amber toddled along behind him, giggling as Arnufo pretended to chase her. The baby wore a sagging diaper, a soiled Dallas Cowboys T-shirt and nothing else. Arnufo had planned to get her all dolled up for the reporters, but apparently he was running behind schedule. Amber babbled and hurried over to Dusty, clinging to his leg as she peered at the strangers. He ruffled her hair, brushed the grass with his foot to make sure there weren't any fire ant nests nearby, and then she toddled off.

Jessie Ryder rummaged in the trunk of the Cadillac. A few moments later, she emerged with an elaborate camera, immediately aiming it and snapping a series of shots, accelerated by a whirring motor drive. For several seconds, Dusty felt completely disoriented. Then hunted. Yet even as she worked, she had the strangest effect on him. He had an almost irresistible urge to touch her skin, smell her hair, stay up all night talking to her. It was a strange way to feel about someone who was in the enemy camp. What was it about this one? She shook him, not because she was trying to take his picture but because she made something inside him pay attention to things he hadn't let himself feel in two years.

Interesting, he thought, but he arranged his face in a scowl as he turned to Blair LaBorde. "You didn't tell me this was going to be an ambush."

"I told you I was bringing a photographer."

"No, ma'am, you didn't."

"Well, surprise, then." She oozed Southern belle charm. "Pictures make up seventy-five percent of our features."

"I don't read your features."

"You're giving the world a wonderful story because you're a loving husband and a proud father," LaBorde persisted. "I'm sure you'll want pictures to—"

"You know goddamn good and well why I'm giving you this interview," he snapped. "It's because Karen's so-called friend blabbed to your competitor, and I'm setting the record straight. But you'll excuse me if I don't want pictures of me and Amber plastered all over your rag."

Blair was unfazed, regarding him with cool self-possession. "Our photo editors are the best in the business, and Jessie Ryder has an international reputation. And, I assure you, I am an excellent journalist." She failed to flinch at his ferocious expression, and he felt a reluctant admiration for her. "Mr. Matlock, I've faced gang leaders, accused murderers, adulterous evangelists, armed survivalists, you name it. I'm not easily intimidated." Blair LaBorde was polite, firm. "I'll publish the truth. I can make you that promise, so long as you don't hold out on me."

Jessie Ryder didn't bother with the politeness. "So what'll it be?"

Damn, thought Dusty, looking at her. There was no denying it. He liked the challenge she offered. And, perversely, he liked her straightforward manner with the camera. She didn't hide in the shadows, invading his privacy with a telephoto lens as the tabloid photographers had back when the story got out.

He hefted the baby onto his hip, and her little fist curled into the sleeve of his sweaty shirt. "I'm going to get cleaned up."

CHAPTER 15

Blair turned to beam at Jessie. "He likes you."

"Ah, Blair, you still have such deep insights into the human heart." Jessie couldn't help staring as Dusty Matlock walked toward the house, faded jeans molding to his hips, the tiny child latched on to him like a limpet.

"It's a gift."

"You didn't tell me he was camera shy."

"Honey, there is nothing shy about that man."

True, thought Jessie. He exuded confidence and something more. Some indefinable sense of her that went beyond mere interest. Her on-again, off-again thing with Simon had given her plenty of opportunity to meet all kinds of men, but already she knew she'd never met one quite like Dusty Matlock. She had blown it completely, taking pictures right out of the gate. But she was unused to subjects that actually had temperaments.

The older man, Arnufo Garza, brought out an Igloo cooler filled with ice and Cokes in small hourglass-shaped bottles. He set the cooler on a weathered redwood picnic table on the deck. "I hope you don't mind being al fresco while I straighten up the house. We didn't realize you would be taking pictures today."

"I could come back," Jessie suggested.

"We would all like that very much. But you should stay. I am sure Dusty will want to get right to it."

She felt a ripple of warmth that culminated in a blush. She'd never understood why she still had a tendency to blush, after the sort of life she'd lived.

He opened two Cokes, gave one to Blair and held out the other to her. With a slightly unsteady hand, she helped herself to the bottle, its familiar shape reassuring.

Blair rummaged in her bag. "Mr. Garza, could I ask you something?"

He smiled, clearly more at ease about the interview than Matlock. "Of course, senorita."

Blair took out the digital recorder, no bigger than a pack of cigarettes, and set it on the table. "How long have you worked for Mr. Matlock?"

He calmly regarded the recording device. "On or off the record?"

Blair took a seat in a faded lawn chair. "Your choice."

"Doesn't matter. I have always wanted to say that. Why do you assume I work for him?"

"Don't you?"

"Why wouldn't you ask how long Dusty has worked for me?"

Blair had the grace to flush, though only for a moment. Then she was all business. "I apologize. So does he work for you?"

"No." With a twinkle in his eye, he smoothed his neat, salt-and-pepper mustache. He focused on the recorder. "My name is Arnufo Carlos Chavez y Garza. I am sixty-nine years old. I was born in Jalisco, Mexico, and emigrated legally to el Norte in 1974. My wife died two years ago and I am here because Dusty and Amber need me, because I need to stay busy and because it is pleasant for me."

"So what was Dusty's state of mind when he lost his wife and gained a daughter?"

"That is a question for him, not me." He faced the lake, the breeze lifting his steel-colored hair. He turned abruptly, and Jessie realized he'd heard the sound of the opening door before she had.

"Incoming, Arnufo." Dusty's voice called from inside the house.

"La tengo," said Mr. Garza.

The baby waddled purposefully to him, reaching out with chubby hands, a dandelion puff of pale hair framing her cherub's face.

Blair made a sound of dismay. "What the hell is she wearing?"

Jessie suppressed a grin. "I'll bet that's her best dress." The tiny child looked like a birthday cupcake frosted in pink, the satin overlaid by cheap lace. It was the kind of dress you saw for sale at Fiesta Mart or weekend mercados, the kind a little girl might wear for her first communion, the kind a fond but clueless man might choose.

Arnufo lifted the baby in the air to make her laugh. Instinct alone took hold of Jessie as she raised her camera and snapped away. The motor drive buzzed as she took several tight shots of the pair of them—the kindly older man so focused on the child, and Amber with her head back, enjoying the ride. "Thanks," Jessie said. "I think we got some good ones there."

"There is no such thing as a bad picture of a baby, eh? Or a good one of an old man."

She winked at him. "Tell that to Sean Connery."

Matlock came out of the house. Jessie noticed that he'd showered in record time. Dark and gleaming curls spilled over his brow. A fresh denim shirt, open at the throat with sleeves rolled back, brought out the vivid blue of his eyes. On the pocket in machine stitching was a logo with a pair of wings and the moniker Matlock Aviation Services.

Amber squirmed and cooed when she saw him coming. Matlock took the baby, his hands splayed in the froth of lace and satin. With a curiously adult patience, Amber clutched his sleeve and waited for him to have a seat across from Blair. "So let's get going."

Jessie felt absurdly nervous. "All right."

He nodded curtly. "Anytime now."

"Just ignore me. Pretend I'm not here." She heard herself babbling but couldn't seem to stop. Something about him...the more brusque he was, the more fascinated she became.

He checked her out with unabashed interest. "Yeah," he said, "I'll ignore you."

"You won't even know I'm here."

He set his ankle on the opposite knee and placed Amber in the crook of his knee. She babbled and grabbed for the logo on his pocket.

Blair clicked on the recorder again. "Okay, Dusty. This is your shot. We want your story, start to finish."

He took a long, deep breath, held it a moment, then let it go. Jessie viewed him through the camera lens and was grateful for the artificial distance between them, because the expression that shadowed his face was so intense she wanted to look away.

He stopped and shut his eyes briefly, and when they opened, he seemed to have gone away somewhere, far away. Then he started to speak. "There was nothing unique or special about Karen and me. We met, we fell in love, we got married. Ran a flight service up in Alaska, and made plans for our first child. Like I said, nothing special at all. Until she died, two months before giving birth to our daughter."

C H A P T E R   1 6

The cold black eye of the camera faltered a little, and that surprised Dusty. In her handling of the equipment, Jessie Ryder appeared to have the confidence of long experience. He pictured her snapping away with cool professional ease at politicians, small-town heroes and victims of industrial accidents. Yet her wavering aim with the fat, expensive-looking lens betrayed a set of nerves too close to the surface.

"Sorry," she murmured. "Your last statement startled me."

Even now, nearly two years after it happened, Dusty felt Karen's presence as though it were yesterday. She was wry and funny and unfailingly honest, and he had a feeling she'd be intrigued by all of this. "That's why it's going in your magazine," he said.

Color misted her cheeks, and he realized he was intrigued as well, by a woman who seemed so worldly yet blushed so easily. For the first time in two years, he felt something he hadn't expected to feel ever again—that rare and powerful beat of attraction for a pretty woman. For that alone, he felt like thanking her. It was his first indication since Karen's death that not only was he alive, but he damned well wanted to stay that way.

The awakening he'd felt when he'd first met her was no aberration. As the minutes passed, his certainty intensified. Why else would he sit here and bare his soul and his life without falling apart?

Maybe the heat was getting to him. But maybe it was her. Then he sensed LaBorde watching him watch Jessie. Down boy, he told himself. They were here for a grim business, and he'd agreed to go along with it.

"Whenever you're ready." LaBorde sounded unexpectedly compassionate.

He shifted his thoughts to the painful past and turned his focus to the small box on the table. Would the recorder capture the terror of Karen's ordeal, the sense of loss that lay over his soul, every minute of every day, since then?

"Karen and I had everything to live for, and every reason to expect a long and happy life," he said. "She was young and strong, a pilot in her own right, but she grounded herself when we found out she was pregnant. In her sixth month of pregnancy, she still walked three miles a day." He could picture his vibrant young wife, soft blond hair gleaming in a sun that beamed with the unique intensity of summer in northern Alaska, walking amid the boreal forests of birch and spruce, or the Jurassic-sized flowers of their garden. The foxglove and hollyhock grew fast and huge, blossoming with fierce abandon, before the early winter killed them.

On the day everything had changed, the late-summer sun was as intense as her smile, the breeze as sharp-edged as a scalpel. She came in from her walk looking fresh and happy, the tip of her nose pink from the chill air. He remembered the way she pressed her hand to his chest, right over his heart, and leaned forward to kiss him, as she had a thousand times before. Did she seem a little breathless? Unsteady? Had he been too distracted to notice?

He had been going over some long-range business plans. They would be moving to the city before winter took hold. The summer station had its rustic charms and brutal challenges, but caution overruled adventure when it came to the birth of their first child. In busy, urban Fairbanks, they had taken a sublet on a temporary apartment close to North Star Hospital, where the baby would be born, and they intended to stay until the spring before flying home. A simple, workable plan. In a million years, he never dreamed so much could go wrong, so quickly.

That day, a subtle note in her tone pierced through his absorption in whatever business documents or flying data drifted across the computer screen.

After she kissed him, her mood shifted. "I don't feel so good. I have a headache."

"You want to lie down? I'll bring you some of that herbal tea—"

"I don't want to be a scaredy-cat about this, but it's not a regular headache. Something's wrong. I have to go to the doctor. Now."

The urgency in her soft tone had seized him. Something was wrong.

He swiveled in his chair, stood to hold her. "Is it the baby?"

"No." She hesitated, looking uncharacteristically helpless and confused as she whispered, "It's me."

Going to the doctor was not a matter of driving down the road to a strip center clinic. He flipped on the radio and the laptop, alerted the two-man ground crew at the airstrip. To get her to the doctor, he would have to fly for forty-five minutes. They left the house unlocked, chopped tomatoes lying on the counter next to Karen's grocery list written in purple ink. While he sped to the runway, she called her doctor on the mobile phone. He could hear her struggling to be calm and clear as she described her symptoms: *sharp headache...the pain is strange, hard to describe...no contractions, but this headache....* In her taut, pale face, he could see terror mingling with confusion. Why was this happening?

Dusty was an experienced pipeline pilot. For five years, he'd ferried oilmen, boomers, company executives and millionaires along the jagged cold spine of Alaska, over a white wasteland as beautiful as it was treacherous. He had delivered lifesaving serum to native Inupiats, evacuated men who'd fallen down holes or roughnecks who'd had their noses smashed in barroom brawls. Two years earlier, he'd even flown a woman in labor and her scared young husband to the hospital. They'd counted together through the contractions and laughed nervously between them, debating whether to name the baby Del Rey for the city of his conception or Macon for the parents' hometown. The woman had been even younger than her husband, but she'd never once said, "Something's wrong."

Those two words had changed Dusty's world, his entire future, and on some level he'd known that, even as he zipped on his flight jacket and helped Karen into hers. He wasn't sure whether or not he imagined it, but she felt very fragile to him at that moment, her arm almost birdlike as he guided her hand into the sleeve of the jacket.

His ground crew was the best in the state and they were at their best the day Karen left the Alaskan wilderness for the last time. Even then, some bitter unacknowledged part of him understood that she would not be back. It was written across her pain-pulled face; it lurked deep in her eyes.

He flew as fast as the state-of-the-art Pilatus turboprop would allow, not caring about drag or fuel conservation of all things. Karen sat virtually unmoving, strapped into her seat, eyes shut, sweat beading on her upper lip.

In the other passenger seat rode Nadine Edison, a bush schoolteacher whose unimpeachable qualification was that she was Karen's best friend. She'd been keeping Karen company and adding to the excitement of planning for the baby. She talked constantly, reassuring Karen all through the flight. She told Karen how much she was loved, how perfect the baby was going to be, what a proud, honorary aunt she would be.

Dusty paused in dictating his narrative to the tape recorder, a gurgle and cry from Amber bringing him back to the present. "The only thing Karen's best friend hadn't told her was how much money she was going to get for selling the story to the tabloids."

He glanced at his daughter, who resembled a giant pink carnation in her lacy dress. Arnufo had bought it at the Mercado del Sol down in San Antonio. It was hard to imagine Amber being old enough to read this stuff one day, but he knew that time would come.

"So you trusted Nadine Edison."

"Karen did. I didn't have much of an opinion of her either way."

"All right. So take us back to that day. Your wife was quiet during the flight."

He nodded. The brackish, polluted sky over the city had never looked more welcome, the homely block of the Northward Building more beautiful. But, even before Karen passed out, he felt a premonition of how wrong things were going. "I told her I loved her. I told her that a bunch of times." He stared down at his hands, flexed and unflexed his fingers. "I reckon that's what you say when you're losing hope, when there's nothing more to do, nothing more to say.

"She told me three things before we landed." He remembered seeing the brightly lit cluster of emergency vehicles waiting on the tarmac. These people knew him and Karen; they were friends. Everyone at the airpark wanted to do his part.

"There's a recording of our last conversation." If the situation had been different he might have laughed at Blair LaBorde's expression. "The flight data recorder got it all. And yes, I'll let you listen to it, and yes, I'll give you a transcript. I'm not ashamed of anything I said."

"What were the three things?" asked Blair.

"She told me she loved me and the baby. She told me to save the baby, no matter what." He paused, took a deep swig of his Coke. "And she told me she thought she was going to die."

* * *

Dusty stared off into the distance, memories melding with the present moment in a way that was almost surreal. Across the water, the Benning place looked busy as usual—kids running all over, folks coming and going. In his mind, the last moments with Karen crystallized for him and then shattered.

He shot a glance at Jessie Ryder. She had walked into his life uninvited, and yet she seemed to belong here. She was turning his grief into a public spectacle, but at the same time, she was making a record of it for Amber. One day, his daughter would be old enough to see the images Jessie was making today, to read the words he was speaking.

"That was the last thing she said—ever," he continued.

The flight data recorder had picked up his strained and frantic, "Karen. Karen. God, she passed out. Goddamn it, do something," he said to Nadine. She'd stayed on the radio with the ground, where an ambulance would be waiting.

Karen had lost all color and life, yet somehow he kept flying while his whole world disintegrated at eighteen thousand feet. During the frantic transport from touchdown to hospital, panic and denial screamed through him. Yet his heart began to ache with things he knew were true, even before the doctors rendered their verdict. A massive cerebral aneurysm had burst, the trauma team declared her brain dead. All that remained was to decide when to pull the plug. He heard what they were saying, saw the flat brain waves on the monitor, but he couldn't accept it. That was his heart, his wife, his future, lying on the gurney.

He glanced at Jessie Ryder again. She sat perfectly still, riveted. She hadn't taken a single picture. The only movement was the river of tears coursing down her face. When their eyes met, she made a visible attempt to steel herself: straightening up in her chair, gripping the arms, swallowing with visible effort.

"What's with you?" he asked, surprised.

"I don't know your story," she explained. "I've never heard it." When Amber laughed, she looked in the direction of the baby, then turned back to Dusty. "She's the reason you agreed to do this, isn't she?"

Her swift comprehension gratified him. What a strange time, he thought, to feel this way. The currents between them were almost tangible, a thick tension in the air. "I owe it to her to get the truth out there. I guess I'll never figure out why the public's fascinated by the crude and brutal facts of the case."

"People read about a stranger's tragedy in hopes of avoiding their own," Blair said. "Maybe it's a talisman against their own suffering. Believe me, it's a lot easier to deal with someone else's tragedy than it is to deal with your own."

Dusty figured he only imagined the shadowy grief that flickered over Jessie as Blair spoke. Suddenly he wondered if the wreck was even worse than she'd let on. Yet she seemed totally focused on him. Not in the newshound way of Blair LaBorde, but in the way of a listener around a campfire, equal parts sympathy, horror and partisan interest. He ought to be used to that by now, but in Jessie Ryder, the concern had a different quality. She made him want to stop, explain, take out his heart and sift through the ashes of it, to see if any life spark could be revived.

He finished his Coke and addressed the digital recorder again—a neutral device that cushioned his emotions. "There comes a time during pregnancy when the baby becomes real," he said. "Do you believe that?"

Blair shrugged. "I've never been pregnant."

He glanced at Jessie. She opened her mouth, closed it. Her cheeks turned red, but she said nothing.

"One of the duty nurses at North Star told me this. She claimed there's a moment during gestation when everything becomes real. That day hadn't happened for me yet," he told her. "We planned to do all the shopping and preparation for the baby in the autumn while living in the city, waiting for the big day to arrive. So we hadn't really done anything about...well, anything." Still he didn't want to say it. They had barely discussed names, announcements, and it had never occurred to them to discuss arrangements in case the unthinkable happened.

"Then when Karen—" He stopped, regrouped. "I was sitting at the side of her bed. I'd just had about the hundredth meeting with the hundredth set of doctors and counselors and what have you. They told me she was gone." Although the hours of anguish seemed fused together, he vividly remembered his sleeping-beauty wife, the way her hand felt and the smell of her hair. He tried to convince himself that she had gone away somewhere, never to return. But she was still so...present.

"The organ donation counselor said that when the brain dies, everything else wants to shut down, so they had to get a decision quickly. They made a big deal about how healthy she was, the fact that she was known to be a generous person, that she'd signed an organ donor card—hell, didn't we all? And they were right. She had. I had no problem agreeing to it. She would have made the same decision for me."

He took a deep, rib-stabbing breath. "The trouble was, she wasn't really dead...yet. That's when it came to me. Here they are telling me she's a life-support system for a heart, lungs, kidneys, corneas, skin, you name it—and nobody mentioned the other life she was supporting."

He saw the moment comprehension dawned. Jessie's face expressed shock and sadness and finally, when she glanced at Amber, a deep and genuine appreciation. She made him remember the hard choices he'd been forced to make. They could deliver the baby immediately and remove Karen's life support, leaving him a widower with a premature infant. They could let Karen die, taking the baby with her. Or they could keep Karen alive as long as possible in the ICU, monitoring the baby's progress until it was healthy enough to be delivered, probably six to eight weeks down the road. But despite options for the baby, there was no hope for Karen. Dusty's world had blown apart. He'd hated his promise to her, and maybe he'd even hated the baby a little for prolonging his grief.

"I wasn't real civil to the duty nurse who kept talking to me about the baby. I yelled at her, a lot. And the whole time, I'm sitting there holding my wife's hand." He paused, swallowing and looking off into the distance again. The forest fringe along the lakeshore trembled and blurred, but not with tears. His tears were private. This story was going out into the world.

He looked back at Jessie. He could read her heart by the tender set of her mouth, the tremble of her eyelashes. He suspected nothing in her experience approximated what he'd endured with Karen, yet he saw something in Jessie's face. He regarded her with a peculiar and heightened awareness, feeling a tremendous affinity for her. She was a stranger, yet her heart seemed to him like familiar territory. It was the oddest sensation. He knew it with the same powerful intuition that guided his pilot's hand when he flew. Since the incident, women had tried to console him, to share his pain, to seduce him into numbness, but it never worked. Now, without seeming to be conscious of the fact, Jessie offered something different. An acceptance of his hurt, and somehow, the unspoken promise that healing was possible.

Arnufo came out of the house and picked up Amber, taking her out to the middle of the yard to play with a bright red ball. Neither woman moved.

"My wife was pronounced legally dead," Dusty said. "For two months, I visited her every day, talked to her as though she were actually there, played the music we used to dance to. They kept telling me she was dead, gone. But she was warm, and beautiful, and I sometimes let myself believe she was only sleeping. When I held her hand, I could feel her pulse. And the whole time, in the back of my mind, I knew they would come for her. They would take the baby, and Karen's organs, and then they would take her away from me." He'd gone a little crazy, watching Karen's stomach grow as her lifeless body gave life to a tiny, unseen stranger. The long goodbye had passed in a blur of agony.

"When the time came, her O.B. supervised the whole business, start to finish. It was a marathon, keeping everything monitored. The doc let me listen to the baby's heart sounds and told me how it would all play out. But nobody told me how you survive something like that."

The moment he held his newborn, he realized the wonder of his sacrifice. He named the baby Amber, the color of Karen's eyes. He would have called her Karen, but he didn't know if he'd ever be able to say the name without sadness. He pinched the bridge of his nose, taking a deep breath. This was a tell-all, so he might as well tell it. "At one point I considered giving the baby up for adoption."

Jessie gasped as though she'd burned herself. Cheeks flaming, she fumbled with something on her camera.

"Why didn't you?" Blair asked.

"Actually, I came pretty close. But...my heart wouldn't let go. It was something I had to do, was meant to do, hard as it was going to be. Giving her to someone else to raise wouldn't work."

Amber's early months were a sleepless haze in Dusty's mind. He didn't drink, because drinking only made him sadder, but he felt like he had a constant hangover. Grief and fury and even resentment tangled his heart until sometimes he couldn't breathe, until he had his hand on the phone, ready to call the lawyer he'd spoken to about a private adoption. But he never made that call. The baby's utter dependence on him kept him going, sometimes only minute to minute. It was a way to get through the night, and then the months, and now almost two years had passed.

In the silent wake of his story, he felt raw and exposed, but also...lighter. It was absurd. He knew almost nothing about this woman, yet he'd found himself glad he'd met her. She had come to invade his privacy, but she looked as raw and exposed as he felt. Phony compassion emanated from LaBorde, but not Jessie. Jessie's reaction was far more interesting to him. She wasn't staring at him with pity in her eyes. She was looking at Amber. And she was smiling.

Though she couldn't know it yet, she was a new element in his story, not just a hired gun who'd come to document the bar-ing of his soul. She was a stranger who had stepped into his world, and for some reason he could look at her and life looked good to him once again.

CHAPTER 17

There were simply no words. Jessie felt as though a vise had grabbed her heart and squeezed. She pictured Dusty seated at his wife's bedside, playing music, holding Karen's hand and talking endlessly, as though she were still there. The image haunted Jessie. How would it feel to love someone like that? To lose her? To know the precise date and time her breathing would stop and her still-warm heart would be lifted from her chest and given to a stranger?

She couldn't bear the terrible, compelling way he was watching her, so she turned to Blair LaBorde, with anger burning in her eyes. *You didn't tell me...* She'd been told only that he was a widower returned from Alaska to raise his child, not some tragic figure forced to endure the unendurable.

"Excuse me," she said, getting up from the table. Checking her film load, she walked across the lawn to Arnufo and the baby. This was why she photographed tree specimens, rock formations, ancient mosaics, monuments of lost civilizations. She never should have taken this assignment. She'd never be able to do justice to this man and his suffering. The shots she'd taken earlier of Arnufo and Amber were inadequate. She knew that now. Her work lacked that indefinable real quality it would have had if she'd taken the time to see with her heart as well as the camera's eye. She had to try again.

As she approached, the baby hid behind Arnufo's knee. Jessie didn't know much about babies, but she did know they could sense a person's mood. Maybe, like horses, they could sense fear. Slowing her steps, she composed her face into a warm smile.

"Does Amber like having her picture taken?" she asked Arnufo. As she spoke, she switched lenses and added an extension tube.

"Of course," he said with a fond grin at the little towhead. "She is used to it. She has a lot of admirers."

Jessie sank down on one knee. "Is she used to strangers?"

"Not so much, now. But she likes people."

"Hello, little one," Jessie said in a soft voice, holding out her hands. The doll-like face was, for a moment, as mild and bland as a full moon. Jessie considered what she now knew—that this child had been delivered from a dead woman's body. She was a product of both love and sacrifice; her very existence was a mystical gift. She put her hand into Jessie's, and her tiny fingers fluttered like the wings of a bird. Jessie imagined Lila at this age, and she inadvertently closed her hand.

Amber's face contorted with apprehension, and she howled. Arnufo waved at Dusty to let him know things were fine. Then he picked up the baby and motioned for Jessie to follow. Speaking over the child's cries, he said, "In this way, she is not a bit like her father. She won't let you get close until she trusts you."

She glanced at Dusty. "How is that different from her father?"

"He lets everybody close. He trusts everybody until they prove otherwise."

It took a certain kind of bravery to be that way, Jessie thought. Or a willful innocence. Both of which she surely lacked. She remembered Dusty's face when he said Karen's friend sold the story of his wife's death to a tabloid. The sense of betrayal had been milder, actually, than the sheer surprise of it.

Turning her attention to the more cautious Amber, she thought of the portrait wall in Luz's house and wished she'd studied her sister's technique more closely. But like much about Luz, her technique was invisible. The resulting deeply layered studies of the children's faces, open and revealing, were fresh and uncontrived. Arnufo was right—trust was the key. She couldn't treat this kid like a statue of Napoleon or a Tuscan vineyard, for Lord's sake.

"I wouldn't mind taking a few more shots of you," she said. "Or don't you trust me, either?"

"I am too old to trust such beauty," he said, "and too foolish not to."

"God," she said with a laugh. "Where have you been all my life?"

"Raising five daughters as beautiful as you."

She turned away to hide her expression. Rarely in her life did she feel the lack of a father, but sometimes it hit her like a hammer.

"We are ready," said Arnufo. Shifting the baby to the side, he stared directly at the camera and struck a curiously old-fashioned, almost military stance. She knew a posed portrait would be an unorthodox choice, but there was something deeply appealing in the composition of this steel-haired, mustachioed older man holding the baby like a delicate flower. The contrast of his leathery skin with her petal softness embodied the difference between youthful innocence and hard experience.

She fired the shutter several times, savoring the decadence of burning film. Years in remote places with a fully manual camera had trained her to be careful with her compositions and stingy with her shots; she no longer had to do that.

Yet in this case, as soon as the shutter clicked the first time, she knew she'd gotten lucky. The portrait would be a stunner. She took a number of shots, gaining confidence as she went. She captured Arnufo surveying the property from a lawn chair. With the big sky behind him, he resembled a Spanish hidalgo from another age. The baby gradually got used to her, and even seemed to like her a little, bringing her found offerings—a twig, a feather, a fallen leaf. Jessie followed along, motor drive purring. There was an unpredictability to the child's movements that she found intriguing, even charming. She got a shot of Amber laughing at the little brown-and-white terrier, and several others of her standing at the water's edge, pointing out the sky. The child's wonder lent a sense of freshness to ordinary things, and once again, a sense of loss stabbed at Jessie, the missed chances of choices not taken. Raising a child was one adventure she had never experienced, and perhaps it was the grandest adventure of all.

"I get worried when she wanders near the lake."

Jessie straightened up, turning to see Dusty Matlock coming toward her. "Sorry."

Arnufo said something in Spanish she didn't catch.

The baby let out a squawk of greeting and headed toward him.

"I've got her, *jefe*," Dusty said. "Go and fix some iced tea for the lady with the big hair." He grasped the baby under the arms and picked her up. "You like kids, Jessie?"

The question caught her off guard.

He grinned at her hesitation. "It's not a hard question, ma'am."

She lifted the camera to her face. "I've never spent much time with kids." She squeezed the shutter even though it was a nothing shot. She needed to put something between her and Matlock. Everything about him challenged her, including the fact that he'd actually considered putting his baby up for adoption, then dismissed the idea. Though he didn't know it, they were the flip side of each other's experience.

She watched his hands. Squarish, strong, sure of themselves in all things...except when it came to holding his baby. The lacy dress rubbed up against his chest, the scalloped hem brushing his chin. Dusty Matlock looked as lost as a man who had inadvertently stepped into the ladies' room at Neiman Marcus. He was ill at ease, yet at the same time, his face bore a look of helpless adoration. She tried to capture that, rucked-up dress and all.

"She's beautiful," Jessie said. "I bet people tell you that all the time."

"They do."

This wasn't working. The chemistry was all wrong. And Jessie knew exactly why. "Mr. Matlock—Dusty—before we get started, I want you to know how sorry I am about your wife."

"People tell me that all the time, too."

"Does it help?"

"No."

"Does anything help?"

"Yeah."

She held in a breath of relief. If he'd said no, she'd know for certain the guy was a walking, talking ride to nowhere. Not that it should matter to her, but it did. "Amber, right?"

"Yeah. And other things. Lately."

"Could you...maybe elaborate on that?"

There was magic in his slow, deliberate smile. He got under her skin with his unpredictable ways, his shifting moods. He was like the weather on the lake, stormy and bright, choppy and smooth. And right then, she found the picture she was looking for. He had that knee-melting smile on his face, Amber was gazing up at him as if he had invented the sunrise and, at that moment, the sunlight glanced off the baby's head. Jessie got off one shot, and it was all she needed. But even after she lowered the camera, he was still grinning at her.

CHAPTER 18

On a rainy afternoon, Luz and Jessie went into town together, but they were on separate missions. Jessie wanted to use the dye sub printer at the local computer shop to create some digital images from the photo shoot. Luz was going to visit Nell Bridger.

Luz put the car in gear, then rolled down the window. "You boys mind your sister," she yelled. Owen, who was playing on the porch swing, waved at them.

Jessie fastened her seat belt. "Does she baby-sit a lot?"

"She's the oldest. It's her job."

Jessie bit back her opinion that Lila needed time to be a kid. It wasn't her call. She listened to the hiss of the rain outside, the occasional rumble of thunder rolling and cracking across the countryside. Shifting uncomfortably in her seat, she indicated the parcel beside her. "Another casserole for your friend?"

"Yep. Lasagne."

Luz's compassion for Nell was both genuine and powerful, and Jessie felt proud to have a sister who cared so much. Luz didn't just care, but she acted on that compassion, heading straight into the center of the crisis, knowing she'd probably suffer bumps and bruises along the way but willing to take on other people's burdens. Had she always been that way? For as long as Jessie could remember, she had. "She's lucky to have you as a friend," Jessie said.

"Well," said Luz, "I appreciate the vote of confidence, but I don't know what good it will do Nell. There is nothing I can do or say to fix this for her."

"It isn't yours to fix, Luz. Have you thought about that?" She bit her lip, then added, "Not all problems can be fixed."

"I know that. I'm not naive. I'm doing what I can to make things better."

And that was what Luz was all about, Jessie reflected. That was why Jessie couldn't bring herself to tell Luz what was happening to her. She'd try to fix it, she'd knock herself out doing everything she could. She'd never let Jessie learn to live on her own.

Shifting again, Jessie forced herself to gather the courage to tell Luz what she really wanted. Wind combed through the weedy roadside chaparral, scaring a jackrabbit from its hiding place. A red hawk circled, perhaps hoping for an easy meal of roadkill, but the rabbit veered deeper into the field. "I need to talk to you about Lila."

Luz stared straight ahead, watching the wet pavement, pocked by large raindrops. Damp, moldy-smelling coolness blew in through the air conditioning vents. Her arms stiffened as though she were bracing herself for impact. "What about Lila?"

Her defensive tone rang with an unspoken warning. Luz was not going to make this easy. Well, fine, thought Jessie. It sure as hell wasn't easy. But for once in her life, she wasn't going to back down from her sister. "When you told me about the accident, one of the first thoughts I had—when I could think at all—was that she might need blood, or tissue or something that would show—"

"I thought about that, too," Luz confessed.

"And?"

"And I'm relieved the issue didn't come up."

"But it might have."

"It didn't."

"What about tomorrow? The next day? The day after that?"

"What about the past fifteen years?" Luz clipped off the words in the bossy, big-sister way Jessie had always hated.

Then she caught Luz's anguished expression and amended, "I mean, things can change at the drop of a hat. Chances slip away and you can't get them back. I've been thinking long and hard about who Lila is. And whether you like it or not, I'm part of her."

The approach to town was heralded by tall, bony pecan trees, their drying leaves astir in the wind. A few ripe nuts pelted the car as they passed under the arch of branches. Luz pulled in a shaking breath. "Of course you are, Jess. There's so much of you in her. She's our sunshine, she always has been. You know that. Even when she's out going crazy and doing dangerous things in cars, she's still our Lila. We couldn't love her more if—" She stopped, searching.

"If you had given birth to her," Jessie supplied.

Squared shoulders again. Stiff arms. Defensive posture. But what, Jessie wondered, was Luz defending herself against? Hurt? Betrayal?

"Would you argue with that?" Luz asked.

Tension thrummed between them. "Of course not." She could tell her sister wanted to end the discussion, but she forced herself to push them both past the comfort zone. "I know that when I—when she was born and you adopted her, I surrendered everything to you and Ian." She shut her eyes, inhaled the rain-scented air from the blowing vent. "Even the truth."

"That was your idea, Jess."

"I thought knowing the truth would only confuse her and make her feel...different."

Her sister nodded, some of the tension easing out of her. "Ian and I agreed to honor that."

"Well, after the accident, I started thinking... Shit. This isn't coming out right at all."

Luz hesitated, and Jessie felt her struggle. It was funny how, when you knew someone like she knew Luz, you could feel what she was feeling. And what Jessie sensed right now was complete dread.

"Just spit it out, Jess," Luz said finally, apparently discarding her chance to change the subject. "Tell me what you want."

All right. Here goes, thought Jessie. She planted her hands on her knees, shut her eyes and took the plunge. "I think we should tell Lila I gave birth to her."

The windshield wipers batted rhythmically into the long silence humming between them. Fallen leaves drifted down. Luz's hands tightened on the steering wheel. Her fear was so palpable, Jessie believed she could smell it, tangy and slightly acrid, like fresh sweat.

"This was the last thing I expected," Luz said. "I never dreamed you'd change your mind about this."

Jessie felt a new wave of anxiety emanating from Luz, and she wondered at its source. Did she have some outmoded concept of adoption? "Luz, it's not like I slunk off, had a baby, then got rid of it. Secrecy and shame have nothing to do with adoption anymore. This idea of kids feeling dirty or abandoned just doesn't hold water. We chose adoption out of love for a child, not because a child was unloved."

"God, Jess. Do you think I don't realize all that?"

"Then you should realize people don't make a secret of adoption anymore. They haven't for a long time."

"What people?" An edge sharpened Luz's voice. "We're not talking about people. We're talking about Lila. After all this time, how is Lila to believe she wasn't abandoned? How could she forgive me for not telling her the truth before? Is there a blueprint for this sort of thing? A how-to book? Can I look in the index under 'What to do if your daughter doesn't know she's your niece?'"

"I don't know. It seems wrong." As soon as the words were out of her mouth, she wanted to snatch them back. "God, Luz,

I didn't mean it like that. You adopted my baby when I couldn't keep her. When she was born so sick we didn't know whether she would live or die. I gave up any right to have a say in raising her. That's why I never came back. But...I'm back now."

Luz took a shuddery breath. "So you want to tell this rebellious, out-of-control girl she's adopted."

"Maybe she's out of control because she doesn't understand herself, and maybe knowing her identity will clarify things."

"Maybe she'll blame me for lying to her. Maybe she'll resent you for abandoning her."

"So we should keep this from Lila because we're afraid of her reaction?" Jessie asked, then rushed on before Luz could answer. "She's practically grown. She deserves to know. I'm not bringing this up lightly, Luz. I've thought and thought about it, long before the accident."

Luz drummed her fingers on the steering wheel. She breathed in quick, shallow gasps. "Do you think I haven't?"

"And?"

"All I know is that there is nothing simple about this situation. Adoption is only part of the issue."

Jessie heard the rest in the silence that followed, punctuated by the hiss and thump of the windshield wipers, the occasional thud of a falling pecan. Trust and betrayal, secrets and deception complicated the matter.

Jessie clenched her hands in her lap. She wished there was a way to be certain of what she was doing. Did the truth need to be brought to light, or was it better left in the shadows? Was she fulfilling some selfish fantasy of reclaiming a little part of her child, or giving Lila the gift of her true identity?

Lila's first question was bound to be who fathered her. The information could blow Luz's world apart. But then again, it was the truth.

"Luz?" Jessie said, desperate to know what her sister was thinking.

Luz whipped her head around so fast, the car wobbled in the

roadway. She brought it back into the center of the lane. "I need to talk things over with Ian."

A chill crept over Jessie's skin. Now she knew how Pandora felt. She reached forward and aimed the air-conditioning vent away from her. "What'll his opinion be?"

"The same as it is with everything about Lila these days. He'll want me to figure out what to do about it."

"Do he and Lila have problems?"

"What father doesn't, with his fifteen-year-old daughter? Ian's solution is to hand everything over to me. I wonder if all men do that after their kids hit puberty. We don't know what it's like to have a dad, do we, Jess?"

Jessie let out a long exhalation. "No, we don't. Ah, Luz."

Luz turned her eyes from the road to face Jessie. "I'm going to need some time to think about this. We should talk more—"

From the corner of her eye, Jessie spied a movement. Not trusting her vision, she blinked, and the image resolved into a small gray squirrel, idiotically darting into the road. "Luz, watch out!" she yelled.

Luz swerved, the tires humming on the slick pavement. The back end fishtailed, momentarily out of control. The lasagne on the seat between them flew forward. Without thinking, Jessie snatched it back.

Luz quickly straightened out the car, but not before an ominous thump sounded. She pulled off to the shoulder. "Damn," she said through gritted teeth, looking at the rearview mirror. She pounded the steering wheel with the heel of her hand. "Damn, damn, damn. I'm going to burn in hell."

Still clutching the lasagne, Jessie turned around to see a small furry heap in the middle of the road. "Uh-oh," she said.

"God, you always do this," Luz said. "You always pick the worst possible time to say something upsetting, and now look what happened."

"That's right, Saint Luz. Blame me. Even though you're the one behind the wheel." But Jessie's temper dissolved when she saw the look on her sister's face. She fell silent, hurting for Luz, who wouldn't intentionally harm a soul. "I saved the lasagne," she said softly.

"That's good." Luz let out a long, weary sigh.

"Poor little Squirrel Nutkin," Jessie whispered. Then she couldn't help herself. She burst out laughing. Luz did, too, and for a few minutes they laughed like a pair of evil witches.

"We're awful," Jessie said.

Luz pulled onto the road and slowly headed onward. "Well, I guess nothing worse will happen to me the rest of the day."

"Yeah," said Jessie, "but you can't go around running over small animals just so your day will get better from there."

In the café next to the computer shop, she spotted Dusty Matlock. He was seated in a booth, nursing a cup of coffee while Amber sat across from him in a booster seat, using a French fry to draw swirls in her ketchup. Jessie's reaction to him was instantaneous—a jumble of apprehension and anticipation unlike anything she'd ever experienced. It was more than a response to a sexy guy who displayed a healthy interest in her. It was an untimely attraction that mocked her with its undeniable strength. Complicating that was a flood of tenderness as she listened to the baby chortling mindlessly.

She was tempted to flee before he noticed her. Her protective instincts warned her to get out now before she did anything stupid like fall in love. She and Dusty Matlock were the last thing each other needed. He was dealing with single parenthood, while she was facing the fight of her life, and neither was in a position to do the other any good.

Yet she couldn't resist. Particularly when Amber looked up and yelled out an incomprehensible greeting.

"That's toddler for 'Have a seat, ma'am,'" said Dusty, getting to his feet.

"How could I resist?" She slid into the booth next to Amber, who offered her a limp French fry. "Thank you," she said, and made a show of savoring it. The baby watched her with total absorption, then chuckled with good-natured humor. When Jessie studied her face, she felt intensely curious. Who would this little person be years from now? What would be important to her? Who would she love? What did the world hold for her?

An unbidden fantasy crept through Jessie. She pictured herself watching Lila's first smile, her first tooth, her first step. She wondered what Lila's first day of school had been like, how her first date had gone. She felt a flash of unholy envy for Luz, who had not missed a moment of Lila's life. But then she focused on Amber. All those experiences were still waiting for this little soul. Jessie wondered who would be there to live through them with her.

Amber offered her another French fry, and Jessie accepted with a smile. "So I was working with some of the digital pictures I made for the *Texas Life* piece," she said, indicating her bag. "Would you like to see them?"

"I'll pass." His voice was low, suppressing emotion.

"Your story was incredible. Blair will do a good job. You'll see." Ah, she wished she could take his pain away, but she sensed that wasn't what he wanted from her. "I hope you don't have any regrets about doing it."

"Of course I have regrets. But you made it worthwhile," he added.

"I did?"

"If not for LaBorde's article, we never would have met. I want to get to know you, Jessie. I really want that."

"No, you don't." She tried to shore up every defense she had. "I'm too footloose for a responsible dad and man of business."

"That's one of the things I like about you."

"Dusty—"

"No, let me finish. There's something going on here. We both know that." He gestured at Amber, whose head lolled onto Jessie's shoulder. "Between all of us."

"That can't be," Jessie said swiftly. "I'm as sorry as can be about your wife, and I wish you all the best, but—"

"Let me tell you about my wife. I loved her. I loved her with everything that I am. Everything I could make myself be. When she lay there in that hospital bed, I used to beg God to take me instead, to use my corneas and my kidneys and leave her and the baby be. So yeah, I loved her. Then I lost her, and I'll never get over that. The grief won't go away. It's a part of me, like loving her was a part of me."

Jessie braced herself. Surely he was leading up to the heartbreaking disclosure that, in his short time with Karen, he'd loved enough for a lifetime, and now he'd never love again, but that didn't preclude screwing around.

The expected recitation didn't come. Instead he said, "I want to love someone again, Jessie."

Shock stole her breath. "Why are you telling me this?"

"I thought that, before we go any further, we should discuss it," said Dusty.

She blinked. Everything this man said surprised her. How could a guy possibly be as wonderful as this one seemed? "That's supposed to be my line."

"You wouldn't have initiated the discussion."

Unsettled, she folded her hands tightly on the tabletop. "Yeah? How would you know that?"

He gently and deliberately disengaged her fingers, covering them with his. His touch was familiar, intimate. "Because I can tell you're protecting yourself. You don't want to get involved."

"What makes you the expert, Matlock?"

"Because up until we met, I was just like you."

"What are you like now?"

"Ready. And surprised as hell that I am."

CHAPTER 19

Since meeting Jessie Ryder, Dusty hardly slept at all at night. He couldn't stop thinking about her. She'd struck him like a bolt of lightning, and his nerves buzzed at the prospect of getting to know her—quickly, deeply. She inspired a curious urgency in him, a sense of time running out. For the past six months, he'd tried to feel this way about a woman. A few times, he'd given in to his mother's attempts at matchmaking and had arranged several dates on his own. But nothing had felt quite right. He'd met nice women, pretty women whose heartbreak over his situation was sincere, who cooed over Amber and sent out signal flares of availability. Yet he hadn't felt that lightning bolt, cracking open his heart again—until now. It wasn't a comfortable feeling, but he welcomed it, wanted it. Old sadnesses, fears and frustrations were untangling in his heart in a way he'd never expected.

In the morning, he drank his coffee in silence while watching Amber with the sunlight in her hair and then he thought of Jessie again and his chest actually hurt with wanting to see her. Horniness was one thing; this was much different. This was going to change his life. Hers, too. He wondered if she knew that yet.

Scooping up Amber, he did something he hadn't done in a long time. He went to the closet and took out a well-worn Matlock Aviation jacket, size extra small. He could still picture Karen wearing it, grinning and giving him the thumbs-up sign from the pilot's seat. His Karen, who loved flying, and adventure, and her husband.

Gathering the jacket to him, he caught a light, ineffable fragrance so evocative that he nearly sank to his knees. "This belonged to your mama," he told Amber, putting her down and sitting on the floor to show her the jacket.

"Mmm." She clutched at the slick fabric of the lining and peered up at him with Karen's eyes.

"That's right. Your mama. And this—" digging in the inner pocket, he took out a gold wedding band "—will always belong to me." He put the wedding band on and showed it to Amber. "Too big," he declared. "Arnufo doesn't cook like your mama did." Slipping off the ring, he held it at an angle and studied the engraving inside: Love Never Dies. When they had chosen their rings, the phrase had been nearly meaningless. Now he felt the weight of it, every day of his life. Karen was gone, and the love he'd borne her now belonged to Amber, just as the love his wife had borne him shone from the baby's eyes each time she looked up at him.

He slid the ring back into the pocket of the flight jacket and zipped it closed. As he did so, a curious lightness slipped over him. Maybe it was wishful thinking, but he felt Karen's approval like a blessing.

He used to think Amber was enough, but he was fooling himself. Karen had been on life support until Amber was born. Now he realized he'd been on life support ever since Karen had died. Meeting Jessie Ryder forced him to face that. "I need to do this, short stuff," he said to the baby. "Can you understand that?"

"You afraid of heights, Miss Ryder?"

Jessie blinked sleepily at the visitor on the doorstep of her house. "At seven in the morning, I'm afraid of everything."

"It's after nine."

"Oh. Then no. But what the hell are you doing here?"

Dusty Matlock's gaze caressed her, and suddenly her silk tap pants and camisole seemed insubstantial.

"I'm kidnapping you," he said.

"I've had training," she warned him.

He grinned. "So have I. That's a great outfit, but you should get dressed."

This was absurd, she thought, yet at the same time, she felt totally drawn to him and deeply intrigued that he'd shown up out of the blue like this.

"I've got coffee," he said.

"Then how can I resist?" She ducked inside and took her time getting ready, even though she wanted to hurry. Her eagerness to be with him bothered her. "Down girl," she muttered.

He was deeply appealing to her. Taking his picture was the most challenging assignment she'd ever attempted. Photographing real people with real emotions demanded something from her that she wasn't used to giving. The encounter with him and Amber had given her a glimpse of a sweetness that could never belong to her. For that she ought to resent Dusty Matlock. But when she stepped outside into the autumn sunshine, she was glad she'd met him.

"Well, come on, then." He started walking toward his blue pickup truck.

She followed him, feeling things she had no business feeling. "Where are we going?"

"Trust me, I'll have you home in time for dinner. You have your camera, right?"

She patted the much-used leather bag. "Trust you?"

"With your life. You won't be sorry."

Swept up by his irresistible energy, she went with him. He turned the radio up and rolled the windows down as they made the short drive to his house. Parking the truck, he led the way down to the dock where the floatplane was moored. He flipped open the tiny, flimsy-looking hatch and offered his hand, palm up.

"Ma'am?"

Her whole body responded to the deep invitation in his voice, in his hand extended in welcome. She took his hand. "I thought you would never ask."

"So now the truth comes out. You're only interested in my machine."

"Right."

He held the plane steady as she stepped on a pontoon and climbed in. The thing dipped and shifted, catching her with one foot in the cockpit, one still on the dock. But he was there behind her. Strong hands gripping her around the waist, his body a wall between her and disaster. Clumsily she hoisted herself into the plane and landed squarely in the passenger seat. The plane was like a child's toy; small planes always seemed that way to her. Everything was crammed together in miniature. The wings and hull were flimsy, insubstantial as a whirligig made from an aluminum beer can.

"Thanks," she said, eyeing him with a combination of interest and suspicion. It wasn't like her to feel flustered by a man.

"No problem." He didn't seem at all perturbed, but openly attracted and very focused on her. Then his attention shifted as he went through a routine, checking gauges, valves, buttons, levers and a GPS screen with an air of long familiarity. "So did your pictures come out okay?"

"There's genius in those shots, I swear," Jessie said. "Blair's happy, anyway."

"She's a real charmer," Dusty said.

"Being charming is not a priority with Blair."

"You work with her a lot?"

"No." She caught his eye as he unmoored the plane from its cleats. "You're my first."

"Does that make you want to come back for more?"

She looked him in the eye. Her vision wavered—or maybe it was the motion of the plane. "I think I got everything I need the first time."

He grinned. "Nope," he said. "Not by a long shot." He let the comment linger in the air between them, then flipped on a radio monitor. He finished his inspections and preparations and shoved the plane away from the dock, riding a pontoon and grasping a wing-shroud as he pointed the nose away from shore. With a practiced, unhurried grace, he climbed into the pilot's seat. She reached around and found a seat belt, drawing it across her lap and clicking it in place.

"You don't seem to be too nervous about flying," he commented.

"Should I be?"

"With me? No way."

"Then I'm not. To be honest, I have more experience flying in small planes than I do taking pictures for *Texas Life.*" She'd been transported in rattletrap tuna cans and patched-up puddle jumpers from Kashmir to Kathmandu. She had flown screaming between jagged Himalayan peaks with the pilot laughing and stoned out of his gourd on hashish. After what she had seen and done in Asia, this felt pretty tame.

Except that it didn't, somehow.

With a stroke of a lever, a turn of the key, he brought the engine roaring to life, propellers bursting into motion. He turned to study her for a moment while the plane drifted.

"Just so you know," he said, raising his voice over the chugging engine.

"Know what?" The flurry of awareness inside her stirred again.

"We're starting something here."

Jessie frowned. "I don't know what you mean. Starting what?"

His grin was wicked. "Us."

A shiver rippled over her skin. "Oh, come on."

"I mean it, Jess. Everyone swears it's Amber who keeps me going. But it's more than that. I'm still here, and there are things in life I won't get from my daughter. So I need to do more than stand around taking up space."

A dizzying hope spiraled through her, but she forced herself to face facts. He needed to face them, too. "Don't tell me you're over losing your wife, Matlock."

"I'll never be over her. But there's room for more. Listen, I thought Karen was the love of my life."

"What do you mean, you *thought?* Wasn't she?"

He adjusted a small, shiny lever on the dashboard. "I loved her like crazy. But she wasn't the love of my life. If I called her that, then it would mean my love life was over when she died." Unexpectedly, he cupped her cheek in his hand. "As you can see, I'm not quite ready to give up."

Jessie let out an involuntary sigh and sat back in stunned amazement as he turned the Cessna Caravan and accelerated. He plucked a pair of Serengeti aviator shades from his shirt pocket and put them on. The motor engaged with a loud nasal whine. His hand lightly controlled the rudder to navigate forward. The plane taxied out and weathervaned into the wind. The motorized buzz intensified. As nimble and delicate as a water strider, the craft turned to the open water, the engine noise deepening to a growling sound. She could tell he was an experienced bush pilot from the practiced way he lined up, applied full up-elevator and full throttle. He relaxed the elevator to neutral, then applied it up again until the floats left the water. The noise crescendoed, and she could feel the moment the wind caught beneath the delicate wings. The plane went aloft as though a large hand scooped them up and transported them, angling toward the sky. Leveling out to gain airspeed before completing the climb out, he aimed toward the headwaters of Eagle Lake.

A shudder passed through the Cessna as they cleared the bank, and then the ride smoothed out. A few moments later, they were floating along like a boat on calm water.

Jessie knew she ought to be looking out at the scenery, but her gaze kept being drawn to Dusty Matlock's face. He put on his headset but the earpieces were set back, the mouthpiece angled away from his lips. That mouth.

"Do you do this often?"

"A few times a week, at least. Only I usually head north first, circle up over Marble Falls. But today I wanted a longer ride. I reckon you don't mind."

"That's not what I meant."

"So what did you mean?"

Damn. He was going to make her say it. "I meant grabbing a woman you just met, shanghaiing her to God knows where—"

"I thought we would take a look at Lake Travis and Enchanted Rock. It's pretty this time of year."

"So do you?" she asked.

"Do I what?"

"Do this often?"

He grinned. "Would it matter one way or the other to you if I did?"

"No." The truth popped out of its own accord.

"Good."

They banked and then soared with the sun glinting on their wings, the landscape racing along in a blur of umber and green and the light blue smear of the river cleaving through the hills. The very tops of the lost maples had barely begun to turn, and they resembled a forest of red-tipped matches, not yet struck to fire.

Dusty flipped a switch, and the old Texas swing sound of Asleep at the Wheel filled the cockpit.

Jessie shut her eyes. Her mouth eased into a grin she couldn't control.

"What?" he asked, an answering smile evident in his voice.

"We're musically compatible."

"There was never any doubt."

She knew whatever it was he intended to start with her was going to be short-lived. She'd be gone before anything serious happened. He gave her the sensation of looking down into a flickering well with the sunlight glinting on it, offering tantalizing glimpses of mysterious depths, gleanings so elusive and quickly gone, flashes and floaters of deceptive allure.

Even without looking at him, she knew he was grinning with

an air of irresistible charm and self-confidence. She scarcely knew the man, yet there was such a sense of recognition between them that she could already picture him perfectly in her mind's eye. White teeth, tanned skin, eyes a shade too blue, hair a shade too long, curling over the collar of his shirt. More than that, she could picture something she'd glimpsed in his eyes the very first time she'd seen him. She had no name for it yet.

She blinked her left eye open to foggy nothingness. Before panic set in, she opened her other eye and let out a breath of relief. She refused to let this day be soiled by dread, and turned to the window, looking at the overwhelming beauty of the view. Taking out her Nikon F5 with an image-stabilized lens, she slid open the window and fell into her element, photographing the scenery. She'd always had the uncanny ability to keep a straight horizon. Her bestselling image, a sunrise over the Seychelles, had been taken without a grid screen.

The landscape rolled out in all the staggeringly lovely variety of the Texas hill country. High clouds formed whipped cream castles with feathery turrets. Sheer canyons and domelike rock formations, sculpted by time-worn geologic faults, were scored by the flashing ribbons of rivers and creeks. The toy county courthouse presided over a pristine town square. Closer to the distant city, she could make out a pattern of hypercultivated emerald golf courses, fringed by abnormally large houses. They flew along Lake Travis and over Enchanted Rock, an amber granite batholith a half mile in diameter. Its domed surface was creased by mysterious fissures, dividing it into lobes like a great brain.

In her travels, Jessie had seen wonders beyond imagining, had gone to places so exotic no one had ever heard of them, yet only here, in the heart of Texas, did she actually feel the landscape. It was woven into her heart and soul, as much a part of her as her mother's wanderlust and her father's poor judgment. There was really only one word to describe what she felt as she looked down at all the complicated magnificence fifteen hundred feet below—home.

"So what about you? Do you do this often?" Dusty's voice broke in on her thoughts.

"I've been known to. I once toured Luxor in a biplane. Nice ruins, but I couldn't get a comb through my hair for a week."

"I don't mean the flying."

She knew exactly what he meant, but she asked anyway, "Then what do you mean?"

"Having sex on the first date. Do you do that often?"

"Who says I'm going to—"

He ran the flat of his hand over her thigh in an indecent, intimate caress that should have offended her, but didn't. "I say."

"The plane! The plane!"

Jessie couldn't hear her three nephews, of course, but as they ran hell-for-leather down to the dock, she imagined their ecstatic Tatu-like cries as they watched the green-and-white floatplane drifting toward shore. The bluetick galloped along with them, no doubt baying loudly, though Jessie couldn't hear that, either. As the plane taxied to the dock, she shut her eyes briefly and tried to imagine not being able to see them. How would she know they were there if she couldn't see them?

Then Dusty cut the engine, and instantly, the hound's baying and the boys' shouts of excitement rang across the water. She could picture them jumping up and down as they waited for the plane to approach.

"Am I that boring?" he asked with a chuckle in his voice. "I've put you to sleep?"

She opened her eyes, angling her head to see him past a shadow she didn't want to think about. "I demand a high level of entertainment."

Cocky as a high school quarterback, he said, "Then you came to the right place." Climbing out onto the pontoon, he expertly moored the plane, closely watched by a rapt audience. Jessie was grateful for his steadying hand as she disembarked and made it high and dry onto the dock.

"Jessieee!" Scottie leaped at her, grabbing her leg. His little torso was encased in a high-tech life vest, which Luz made him wear if he was going anywhere near the lake.

"So this is Dusty," she said, and told him each boy's name and age. "He took me on a sightseeing tour today. We stopped for lunch at a barbecue place on Lake Travis."

She might as well have spoken in Maori for all the attention they paid her. The boys swarmed the plane, fascinated, while Dusty showed them around and Beaver growled and sniffed at the alien craft. The afternoon warmth had given way to the cool breath of early evening, and she tilted her face to the sky. The boys' voices seemed to fade into the background as she focused on the soughing chime of the wind through the trees, the plaintive call of a loon going to roost.

After a while, Luz came down to send the boys in to wash for supper. "You're staying, of course," she said the moment Jessie introduced her to Dusty.

He gave her the once-over. "Yeah?"

"My sister, Luz," Jessie said. "She's always been bossy."

"I like that in a woman."

"When Mr. Garza called to say you'd gone flying, I invited him and your daughter, too," Luz said, and Jessie wondered if she only imagined the heightening mist of color in her sister's face. "I've been wanting to meet you—Ian loves flying with you. We're having vegetarian King Ranch Chicken." She seemed to see no contradiction there.

Dusty looked from Jessie to Luz and back again. "Damn, life is good."

Supper was a noisy, messy affair that underscored Dusty's conviction that not only was life good, but it was worth living. Luz and Ian Benning presided over three exuberant boys who went nuts for Amber, falling all over each other to make her giggle at their antics. The family resemblance was strong in this handsome bunch. The teenaged daughter in particular bore a startling likeness to both her aunt and her mother, though she had Ian Benning's thoughtful mouth. Lila was quiet and maybe even sullen, but Dusty figured that was to be expected, given the ordeal she'd survived. But even she cracked a smile when Amber, overwhelmed by all the attention, simply reached out with both hands and tried to hug the very air itself.

Arnufo caught Ian's eye across the table and raised his long-neck bottle of beer. "You are surrounded by blessings, amigo," he said, his words all but drowned out by the chattering of the children.

"Don't I know it." Ian took a sip of his Shiner. Then he frowned down at his plate. "Except maybe this casserole," he added, adding a forkful of jalapeno slices from a jar. "It definitely needs something."

"Maybe it needs a more grateful husband to eat it," Luz said.

Dusty had liked Luz instantly. She was the sort of woman you wanted to view from different angles. In many ways, she seemed like a typical busy, even harried, wife and mother, but he sensed something more there, beneath the surface. If Ian Benning knew what was good for him, he'd never overlook that.

"It's delicious," Jessie said. "Isn't it, Lila?"

The girl had been gazing idly out the window, silent worries hovering in her green eyes. "Hmm? Oh, yeah." She pushed the food around on her plate.

"I stopped by your school today," Luz said. "Your teachers said not to worry about homework. Your math teacher gave me a list of assignments, but said to take your time."

"Okay. Thanks. I've decided to go to school tomorrow, anyway." She and her mother regarded each other with a quiet tension that seemed to hum audibly between them.

Then Amber, who was perched in a booster seat, reached over and clamped a dimpled hand on Luz's arm. "Mah," she said.

A bittersweet ache rose in Dusty's chest, even though he knew it was a random syllable. Beside him, Jessie tensed, and he slipped a hand under the table to rest it easily on her thigh. She tensed even tighter, but didn't bat his hand away. It was damned good to feel the shape of a woman's thigh beneath his hand, to feel her shoulder brushing against his at the crowded table, to inhale and catch the scent of her hair. There was nothing in the world like the smell of a woman's hair.

It was hard to believe he hadn't known her forever. He felt completely at ease with her, yet at the same time, she excited the hell out of him. There was a remarkable simplicity and clarity about what he felt for Jessie Ryder, what he wanted from her.

Everything.

CHAPTER 20

Jessie felt unaccountably wistful as Dusty thanked Luz for dinner and said goodbye to Ian and the children. This day had been filled with unexpected gifts and unanticipated emotions. Each child around the dinner table represented an age she had missed with her daughter. She had missed the flower-faced Amber stage, the unquestioning acceptance of Scottie, the shy inquisitiveness of Owen, the coltish awkwardness of Wyatt.

And then there was Dusty. The last thing she needed right now was this jolt of yearning she felt for a strong, sad man who had endured so much. Perhaps it was a good thing that he was leaving. He had to take off before nightfall in order to get the Cessna docked at his place. Even Lila showed some color in her cheeks when he told her how sorry he was about the accident and how glad he was that she was okay. She smiled a little as she offered a subdued word of appreciation.

"See you later," he said in a low, intimate aside to Jessie.

She walked outside with him, Arnufo and Amber, taking the baby around to the passenger side of the pickup truck to put her into her car seat. Amber felt sturdy, a firm lump of humanity. Although Jessie carried the child on her hip, the toddler held herself at a decorous distance, pushing back with her hands. Her solemn expression and the way her gaze clung to Arnufo hinted at a low-grade but as yet unvoiced distress. She was waiting, giving Jessie the benefit of the doubt.

"Don't worry," Arnufo said, sitting patiently in the driver's seat. "She is starting to like you. I can tell."

"I like her, too. She's a good baby."

The older man smiled. "All babies are good."

I wouldn't know. Jessie felt it again, the impact of what she'd done all those years ago. Dear God, what had she given up? The right to gaze into a face like this, to dream of a future for someone whose future was in her hands.

She studied Amber a moment longer as she grappled with the mystifying web of buckles and bumpers that made up the car seat. The complicated potential in that little face both intimidated and excited her. When she considered the miraculous way this child had been born, waves of wonder overcame her. "I'm glad I got to do the pictures."

"She is the gift he received. A miracle," Arnufo said. "I will always believe that."

"Hell of a sacrifice," she said.

"Hell of a gift," he said with a wink. "Listen. God takes things from us. Precious things. We do not know why. It is not for us to question. Sometimes the reward seems too small for a sacrifice so great. Still we go on. What choice do we have but to go on?"

Jessie brushed her fingers over Amber's white-blond fluff. "You're really something, Miss Amber."

"Yah."

Stepping back, Jessie made certain all fingers and toes were safely inside before shutting the door.

Down at the dock, her nephews and the dog were screeching and howling in wonder as the plane taxied out and took off. Shot through by sunlight, the droplets of water off the pontoons made a trail as hard and bright as yellow diamonds, showering in its wake.

"Yes!" the boys shouted, giving each other high-fives and

leaping around in some sort of tribal ritual. Even Ian joined in, six feet of pure goofiness.

Jessie returned to the house and encountered Lila on the porch. "So what do you think of your neighbor?"

"Mom says he's already falling for you. I think she's right."

"You and my sister are hopeless romantics, then."

"My mom?" A humorless laugh burst from her. "No way. When she says some hot guy is hitting on you, she means business."

"He's hot?"

Lila nodded.

Jessie fanned her face. "So it's not just me."

"Mom says all the hot guys were always after you. Were they?"

Jessie looked away, remembering. "Maybe that's how it looked to Luz. I never really thought about it." The sun had sunk below the line of hills and Dusty was taxiing to his dock. "I suffered through some really bad dates, but I had this irrational horror of being without a guy. Dumb, huh?"

Ian came walking up to the house, draped in boys. Scottie rode his shoulders, his knees around Ian's head in a wrestling hold. Owen was on his back while Wyatt clung to his leg, riding Ian's foot like a surfboard.

"What's dumb?" Wyatt asked.

"Boys," Lila said.

"Are not."

"Are so."

"Are—"

"Beam us up, Scottie," Ian said, his signal for him to open the door. Ducking beneath the lintel, he dragged himself and the boys inside before the argument escalated.

Jessie saw the way Lila watched them, and her heart lurched. "Your dad and brothers are really something, aren't they?"

Lila sat down on the porch swing, hugging one leg up to her chest while the other leg dangled, bare foot brushing the floor. "Something. I'm not sure what."

Jessie wasn't certain how she knew, but Lila's yearning to belong was a palpable thing. "Is it hard, being the only girl?" she asked.

"It's not like I have a choice." She brushed at her cheek, a swift, furtive movement. "They all—they're always having such a good time together. He's never like that with me. After what happened, I know he never will be."

"Some things are simply not reversible. You're old enough to know that. But other things, well, they can be fixed."

"Whatever. It's dark already. I'd better get going." She stood up, staggered a little and grasped the chain of the porch swing.

"Are you all right, love?"

"I should get to bed early. School tomorrow."

Jessie kissed her temple, savoring the brief contact. After Lila went upstairs, Jessie straightened the downstairs, accompanied by the busy *swish* of the dishwasher. She could hear a car, but saw no one, so she turned her attention to wiping down the counters. Thumps and outbursts came from upstairs as Luz and Ian got their children ready for bed.

"'Night, everybody," she called from the foot of the stairs. "I'm heading over to my place."

"See you in the morning," called Luz.

"I'm taking the rest of the Merlot," Jessie said, pushing the cork into the bottle she and Luz had opened at dinner.

"It's all yours," Luz yelled. Then her tone changed. "Owen Earl Benning, you take that toad outside this minute."

Jessie walked out with her nephew, lingering as he whispered something into his cupped hands, then squatted down while something hopped away in a rustle of leaves.

"What did you whisper?" Jessie asked.

"I told him it wasn't personal. Mom hates critters. You should have heard her when I brought in the rat snake."

Jessie leaned down and kissed the top of his head. "Do me a favor. No more snakes indoors."

"'Kay." Wiping his hands on his pajama bottoms, he went inside.

The strong smell of roses reached her, making Jessie's skin prickle. She wondered...could it be? She went to the far corner of the porch to see if Luz's old rosebush still grew there. She'd tended it since before memory began, declaring it the bush that wouldn't die. Even in the dead of winter when the bitter winds of blue northers ripped across the state, the old rose always clung by the porch. It might surrender a leaf or two, but never its whole self.

And sure enough, it had endured. Peering through the night shadows, she saw the clusters of cream-colored blooms nodding in the chill breeze. This late in the year, the flowers were nothing special, but their perfume was a cloud of pure heaven. Reaching out, Jessie picked one to take over to her cabin.

As she headed off down the wooded path, she realized she was still afraid of the dark. Her heart pounding, she focused on the glimmer of light from the cabin's porch. It was only one tiny point of light, yet it was enough to see her safely through the woods.

She shut her eyes to make the light disappear. Almost instantly, she stumbled and fell to her knees. Somehow, she managed to keep the wine bottle from breaking, but the impact jarred her teeth together and scraped the tender flesh of her knees.

"Bloody hell," she muttered. "Bloody goddamn hell." Picking herself up, she made her way to the cabin, focused on the light and forced herself to think of other things. She felt frustrated, empty, dissatisfied with the conversation she'd had with Lila. Jessie wasn't sure what she'd been expecting—that they'd magically be best friends—but the fact was, they were strangers bound by blood and maybe a couple of mysterious flashes of recognition. Lila was almost eerily similar to Jessie at that age. Jessie used to sneak out at night and go driving around, or simply walk down to the dock and smoke pot, sometimes by herself, until Luz invariably awakened and made her come inside. What did they used to talk about? What made her feel better?

Concentrating on putting one foot in front of the other, Jessie pushed through the dark tunnel of the woods, heading toward the light. She knew she'd stay up too late, too wired from her day to relax. Who wouldn't be, after the way she'd spent the day? Yet still she felt frustrated, empty. Anxious about her plans for the future.

An ominous shape detached itself from the shadows and moved swiftly toward her. Jessie sucked in her breath to scream, but before she made a sound, he laughed at her.

"You weren't planning on drinking alone, were you?"

"Matlock. You scared me. What are you doing here?"

"I figured you'd be expecting me."

"Why would you figure that?"

"I said I'd see you later. It's later." He gently pried the wine bottle from her grip and held the door open for her.

"What the devil are you doing?"

"I'm going to have a glass of wine with my new woman."

She couldn't help it; she laughed. "No, you're not. You're going home. I am not your 'woman,' new or otherwise. I didn't invite you here."

"Sure you did."

An incredulous laugh burst from her. "You really are something, Mr. Matlock."

"So are you." Taking the single rose from her hand, he did a quick scan of the cabin. "Nice," he said, "but it's stuffy in here." He stuck the rose in a glass of water, adjusted the screened windows to let in the night air, then found a pair of wineglasses and poured. "I want you to know, this is not some ritual seduction to prove I'm ready to start dating again."

Actually, ritual seduction didn't sound half bad. "Then what is it?"

He handed her a glass of wine and touched the rim of his to the rim of hers. "A beginning. And this is going to be so good." His stare never strayed from her face as he sipped his wine.

A beat of panic struck Jessie. "What do you mean, this?"

"I mean us." He grinned, that slow and sexy spread of his lips that made her forget the whole world. Without warning, he put his hand behind her neck, pulled her toward him, settled his lips firmly over hers. And despite her vast, sometimes regrettable experience, Jessie had never been kissed like this before. This kiss was direct, aggressive, openmouthed. A wicked flutter of his tongue imparted a dizzying suggestion of sex, but only a hint.

How could all that happen in a kiss lasting no longer than three heartbeats? Yet even before her thoughts caught up with the rush of sensation, she knew exactly what he intended. She could taste it on his lips, feel it in the firm insistence of his embrace. Just when she relaxed, all too willing to succumb, he pulled back.

"So anyway. That's pretty much what I have in mind."

She felt obliged to assert herself. She could safely say that, even though she was no shrinking violet in the sexual fling department, he had taught her something new with his kiss. She had a serious case of dry-mouth but she spoke anyway. "What about what I have in mind? Or doesn't that matter?"

He laughed and touched her under the chin, reminding her that her mouth was hanging open. "Honey, I know exactly what you have in mind. And believe me, it matters."

And then he kissed her. It was like the previous one, which up until now had been a kiss she thought she'd dream about forever. This was better—a personal best. His lips were tender and sweet with wine, and insistent with unspoken promises. His intensity held her spellbound. She was gripped by the insatiable hunger that had possessed her years before and had set her off to wander the world. But everything was different now. This need for him was so much deeper and therefore so much sadder. And she wanted him badly enough not to care what morning brought.

Still, honor demanded that she warn him. "I can't be...what you want me to be."

"What do you reckon I want, Jessie?"

"Someone who knows how to stay in one place, who can seriously be part of your life."

"We *are* serious."

"We are?"

"We agreed to have sex. I intend to take that seriously."

He grinned again and she melted some more. She felt as though they were speeding through the rites of courtship, and the greedy, needful part of her was glad, because she didn't have time to take this slowly. She sensed the wanting in him and it matched the wanting in her.

She felt a stirring inside, a softening. The air felt thick and alive, pulsing with his next words even before he spoke them.

"It hasn't been easy and it sure as hell hasn't been pleasant. But in the past couple of years, I've discovered that I'm just a guy who fell in love and had a great marriage and then lost it. But I'm going to live again." He crossed the room in two strides and held out his hand to her. "And I'm going to love again, maybe even better than I did the first time around."

"Whoa, slow down. This is rebound stuff."

"Nope. Something happened when I met you. I think you felt it, too."

She bit her lip, unable to contradict him. This was insane, but he was incredible. Simply being with him gave her a glimpse of a different world, a world of precious, quiet safety.

"Look," he said, "if I seem in a hurry, maybe it's because I've been waiting so long."

Her fingers trembled as she took his hand and rose to her feet. "You're very sure of yourself."

"It's the pilot in me. I make quick decisions and I can't afford to be wrong." He pulled her through the doorway into the bedroom, pressing her against the wall as he undid the row of buttons down the front of her tank dress.

"And what are your instincts telling you?"

He skimmed the dress down over her shoulders, letting it pool on the floor. "That you're the one."

She felt trapped, vulnerable, pressed between the paneled wall and his body, between his expectations and her impossibilities. What was it that he saw in her, two years after the most wrenching tragedy a man could suffer, that made him capable of looking her in the eye and saying those words? She realized that she wanted to know him, yet even so, she felt compelled to warn him off. "I'm not good for you."

"I'll be the judge of that."

"I'm a disaster waiting to happen. Trust me, it would be a mistake to get involved with me."

"What do you mean, you're a disaster?"

"I'm— I have plans, and there's no room for anything else. I can't stick around. You need to know that about me. You see...I tend to keep my distance from people. I never set out to do it, but I...leave things behind."

"I've never been put off by a challenge." He unhooked her bra and discarded it, then bent down to kiss her exposed flesh. "Nice tattoo."

"I don't want to challenge you." What she wanted was to fall for him with every ounce of her body, but she couldn't be that cruel. She'd be gone soon. She had no choice. "I'm not kidding," she said, her voice growing fainter. "I can't stay around—even for you."

"I'll make you a deal. You quit worrying about that and I'll shut up and get down to business." He took out a packet of condoms and dropped it on the bedside table.

"I can't quit worrying." But even as she spoke, she shut her eyes and took in the exquisite sensation imparted by his mouth, his hands. It was more than mere wanting; it was discovery. And not only of him—his taste and smell and intense physical presence. She was also learning things she'd never known about herself, or things that were perhaps lost in her youth. She cataloged every texture and taste and smell of him, his unique essence, and it had a devastating effect on her. She felt him turn her, lower her gently to the bed.

"Fine, then just lie there and let me make love to you. Trust me, you'll like this."

CHAPTER 21

Jessie shone. Luz could see a certain aura about her sister as Jessie walked into the kitchen. "Good morning," said Luz, setting out four lunch bags assembly-line style on the counter. "You're in a good mood."

Jessie's dazzling smile percolated into a laugh. "It's a good day." She wandered over to the coffeepot and helped herself to a cup, adding sugar and enough cream to spill on the counter. Without seeming to notice the spill, she went and stood at the bay window overlooking the lake. Sunrise painted the flat water pink and gold, and mist haunted the low spots and clung to the water's edge. Across the lake, a truck sped away.

With automatic movements born of long practice, Luz assembled lunches as she watched Jessie. "That grin of yours wouldn't have something to do with a certain pilot who spent the night with you, would it?"

"It would. But he wouldn't be the first guy to leave me at first light."

"He'll be back. I was watching him last night. I know."

Jessie turned, and the sunrise outlined her slender form. She wore exotic silk pajamas—low slung bottoms and cropped top—

and when lit from behind, she looked as fresh and carefree as she had years before, a college girl in search of a life.

Luz struggled with an old, familiar demon. Envy. Jessie wasn't beautiful; she was luminous. Her gifts were so many, and they came with such ease. But as always, Luz battled the demon with her most powerful weapon. She loved her sister. How could you let envy interfere with love?

The sound of the shower drumming upstairs, the radio blaring Nelly Furtado, told her Lila was up, and evidently serious about going to school today. Another issue—Jessie was waiting for an answer. The discussion about Lila's adoption hadn't gone away. It hovered, waiting to land. As life returned to relative normalcy, the lingering questions would recur. When would they tell Lila? What would they tell her? How?

Yet this morning, Jessie's mind seemed to be elsewhere, turned inward, perhaps. With the ease of a blackjack dealer, Luz laid out slices of bread. "He was that good, huh?"

Jessie hugged herself. "Boy howdy. You have no idea."

Twiddling a butter knife around in a jar, Luz extracted the last of the peanut butter. She made no comment as she thought about the last time she'd awakened with that peculiar, unmistakable glow that followed a night of incredible sex. Last June, maybe?

"On a scale of one to ten," said Jessie, "it was about a ninety-eight."

Luz dropped tiny bags of chips into each standing lunch bag, along with fruit—apples today—and a cup of pudding and a plastic spoon. Four bags, four lunches, four kids, four reasons to tell Ian, "Not tonight, dear."

Jessie leaned against the counter where Luz was working. "Looks like everyone is headed to school today."

"Even Scottie. He's got playgroup until noon. I make him a lunch like the others so he'll feel grown up." She bent over, scrawling on paper napkins with a ballpoint pen.

"What are you doing?"

"Love notes to go in the lunch bags." She spoke as she wrote, illustrating each one-liner with a happy face and heart. She stuffed a napkin note into each bag, labeled the bags with the kids' names, and felt Jessie's attention on her. "What?"

"You do this every day."

"Every day there's school."

"Four lunches."

"One for each kid. Sometimes Ian gets one, too."

"You amaze me, Luz. You always have."

Luz couldn't help herself; she laughed. "For this I had three-and-three-quarter years of college." Walking to the bottom of the stairs, she yelled, "Is everybody up?"

"Yes, ma'am." Scottie's shrill voice. Ancient pipes quivered and shrieked as Lila shut down the shower.

Lunches complete, Luz prepared breakfast, putting out pitchers of milk and juice, boxes of cereal.

"You know, Amber's in Scottie's playgroup at the church," she said. "Dusty signed her up for the toddler room. Maybe you'd like to drop Scottie off this morning."

Jessie turned quickly away to refill her coffee mug. "Amber's going to her grandma's in Austin today." She sloshed coffee onto the countertop as she poured, creating her second spill of the day. "I'm not totally at ease, driving. I got so used to driving on the other side of the road overseas."

"Okay. It was just a thought." Luz wiped the counter.

Jessie sipped her coffee and stared unfocused across the room. "So what do you think of Amber?"

Luz considered her sister. Jessie had never made a lasting commitment, not even to Simon. Maybe, just maybe Dusty would be the one. Lord knew, if he and Amber couldn't win her heart, nothing could. "An angel. And those two guys treat her like one. Can you grab the canister from that cupboard on your right? The sugar bowl needs refilling."

"Sure." Reaching up, she grabbed the aluminum canister and slid it across the counter. As Luz measured out the sugar, Jessie took something else from the cupboard.

"Is this what I think it is?"

Luz felt an odd prickle of foreboding, as though Jessie had unearthed something private. Forcing her hands to keep steady, she filled the sugar bowl and carried her coffee to the table to enjoy it during the lull before the breakfast stampede. Jessie followed her, bringing the treasure she'd found.

"I'd forgotten all about this," Jessie said.

"Me, too," Luz admitted. "Sort of."

"Our wishing jar." Jessie lifted the lid of the old engraved metal container and stuck in her hand.

Just that image brought memories rushing back through Luz's mind. Their mom had brought the trophy cup home after a tournament. It was inscribed with Longest Drive and the date and place: Fandango Woods, September 9, 1974. It was arguably the ugliest trophy their mother had ever won and no doubt would have wound up in the attic except that it had a lid. Mom hadn't been fond of it because she hadn't won the tournament.

That year had been particularly hard. Their mother's winnings were slim and she'd missed qualifying for the tour. Luz could still remember standing in the school cafeteria line with the light blue perforated tickets for free lunches.

Of the three of them, only Luz knew how to face facts. Their mother managed to find a dozen reasons not to go to Social Services and stand in line for food stamps. Although only a child, Luz was the one who had to swallow her pride and take the forms to the welfare office. She made excuses for her mother, saying she was out of town, ill, unavailable. At school, she gritted her teeth and used the blue tickets. Jessie was more likely to skip lunch and shoplift Twinkies and cans of Dr Pepper from the 7-Eleven.

One morning, all those years ago, Luz was mending her favorite shirt right here in this kitchen, seated at this old battle-scarred table, when their mother had taken down the not-quite-a-trophy and said, "This is a wishing jar."

Jessie, always the more whimsical of the sisters, instantly said, "Can I make a wish?"

"That's what it's for." Mom handed them each a slip of paper, a pencil and a coin. "But it'll cost you. You write your wish on the paper, wrap it around a penny and drop it in. Next time I get a check, we'll pull one out and make it come true."

And so the tradition was born. The girls put their coins, wrapped in wishes, into the jar. Jessie took the exercise to heart, even adding a whispered prayer and kissing the wish before secreting it away. Sometimes when their luck came around, Mom remembered her promise. They got to close their eyes and pick a wish.

The things they wrote on those little slips of paper were sometimes specific—a Nikkor adjustable tripod. Sometimes whimsical—a unicorn. Sometimes irrelevant—a Captain and Tenille album. Sometimes poignant—a daddy. And often impossible—world peace. Even into their adolescent years and early adulthood, they'd kept up the tradition.

It had been Luz who had come home from her after-school job cutting fabric at Edenville's Heavenly Haven of Cloth one day and written, "a college education."

"So do you still do it?" Jessie asked, yanking her back to the present. "Do you still make wishes?"

Luz took a sip of black coffee. "Sometimes. But with four of them, the wishes always outnumber the chances to come true. Ian doesn't win prizes. He brings home a paycheck, and that's generally spent by the time he gets to the bank." It was staggering, how much simple day-to-day living consumed.

"Well, that's the idea," Jessie said. "You always need to have more wishes than you can possibly grant. That's what gives wishes their power." She took the lid from the trophy. "So let's have a look." She reached in, withdrew a tightly folded scrap of paper, carefully unfolded it and pushed it across the table.

Luz glanced at it. "Wyatt's hundredth request for a Sony PlayStation. I keep thinking if we put it off long enough, he'll outgrow his need for it, or they'll invent something cheaper. But judging by the handwriting, this is a fairly recent addition."

"Let's try another."

It was a mystifying tribal symbol, probably scrawled by Scottie. "Not sure," Luz said. "It's either a pet rat or a Krazy straw."

The next wish they unwrapped made Luz blush. "That's just Ian being...Ian." Before she could crumple it up Jessie snatched it away, holding it to the side, reading it at an odd angle. "It says B J. Does this mean what I think—" She burst out laughing. "Typical guy. He never stops trying."

Was Ian typical? Luz couldn't be sure. He was the first and only man she'd ever loved. In high school, boys had found her studious, diligent ways off-putting. She used to see sixteen-year-old mothers toting squalling babies through the Country Boy Grocery and vowed she'd never get knocked up and trapped. Keeping that vow meant staying away from boys and partying.

Instead Jessie got knocked up, but it was Luz who got trapped. The thought made her feel guilty and she quickly wiped it away. "Next."

Jessie stopped giggling and opened another. "Something from Lila." Luz recognized the flourishes of her daughter's calligraphy.

"What does it say?"

"A real tattoo."

"That's simple enough."

Luz glanced at the amber-colored scroll peeking over the edge of her sister's pajama top. "Uh-huh."

Unaware of her scrutiny, Jessie extracted another wish.

Luz recognized her own scrawling handwriting. "My B.A."

"As in the degree?" asked Jessie.

"Yup. As in Bachelor of Arts, preferably summa cum laude. Eleven more credits and I'd have it. I bet that thing has been sitting for ten years. Lately this jar's a place to park my spare change, that's all."

"You parked your dreams there. You should go back and finish," Jessie said.

"College? Just like that?" Luz laughed. "Sure. I'll get Ian to cancel all his court dates so he can watch the kids, board the dog at a kennel, forbid Scottie to get an ear infection, grab a few grand out of thin air and head for the city to be the world's oldest living coed."

"If it's important to you, you'll do it."

"I've got four kids—"

"And how did that happen, Luz? By accident?"

"As a matter-of-fact, not all of them were planned."

Jessie nearly choked on her coffee. "Hey, I can believe one accident. God knows, one was mine. But you've got three boys, Luz, and you're not stupid. You wanted babies more than you wanted some piece of paper."

Luz had no answer for that. Her response to each pregnancy had been shock, followed by a rush of joy so intense it almost knocked her over. She'd even loved being pregnant and giving birth, regarding swollen ankles and varicose veins as badges of honor. She loved nursing, loved being immersed in the warm, milky scent of herself, and the sense that her body had the power to produce exactly what the baby needed, making no mistakes.

"I guess I thought I could have both," Luz said. Her coffee had turned cold and bitter and she pushed the mug away, reaching across the table to stick her hand in the jar. The sheer volume of folded-up wishes startled her. She dug to the bottom and pulled one out.

"A trip to Mexico. Hmm. It's in your handwriting, Jess."

"Yeah?"

"You must have written it before you took off."

"I never took that trip."

"That's why it's still in the jar. But there's still time."

Jessie crumpled the wish and tossed it aside. Luz started to do the same with the B.A., but at the last minute, folded it around a penny, pressed it to her lips in the age-old ritual and put it back in the jar. She grabbed a pen and the grocery list pad. "Let's make a wish right now, Jess."

"All right." Jessie scribbled something, her pen running off the edge of the page and scoring the old pine table.

"Jeez, you ought to think about getting your eyes checked, Jess."

"As a matter of fact, I—"

"I'm going to be late," Lila said, clomping down the stairs. "No time for breakfast."

Luz shot up, folding the lunch sack and dropping it into Lila's bookbag.

Lila looked pretty. Beautiful, actually, with her hair damp and slick from the shower. Despite the perpetual disarray of her room, she always managed to look as though she'd stepped from the prom pages of a Delia's catalog.

"You've got seven minutes before your bus." Luz knew instantly it was the wrong thing to say. She knew even before her daughter hunched up her shoulders and narrowed her eyes. Lila did not take the bus. Since the start of the school year, Heath Walker had picked her up. She always went to school in his red Jeep, riding a wave of prestige and acceptance that meant far too much to her.

"Maybe you'll make new friends on the bus." A lame attempt, but Luz couldn't stifle herself.

"Great, Mom."

"Good morning to you, too, doll-face," Jessie said.

Lila scowled. "Whatever."

"I have a better idea for getting this kid off to school," Jessie said. "I'll kick her ass all the way to town."

"Good plan," said Luz.

Lila studied her reflection in the sliding glass doors. Though she put on a brave face, her nerves were taut and close to the surface. Luz could sense it like a force field around her daughter.

The pipes groaned as Ian started up his shower, and she felt a flash of irritation. Couldn't he have waited to see their daughter off today, of all days? She'd survived a fatal accident that had disrupted the whole school. She needed every bit of love and support they could muster. Didn't Ian realize that?

"Sweetie, we know it's going to be hard. I can't tell you how much I respect you for getting back to your routine so quickly." She winced at her own platitudes. She sounded like a radio talk show host.

"Whatev," Lila said again.

"I'm proud of you, too," Jessie said loyally. "No matter what happens in life, school goes on."

Lila nodded, then slid a glance at Luz. "Homecoming's this weekend."

Homecoming was a big deal in a small Texas town. Even the fact that the Edenville Serpents' star quarterback had crashed his car wouldn't stop the time-honored tradition. By Friday, Luz knew, the excitement would reach a fever pitch. Girls would parade around, sporting corsages of dinner-plate-sized mums in school colors—purple and black—trailing ribbons as long as the girl was tall. Boys would climb the water tower to spray paint the year on its already grafitti-covered tank. Every cookie baked by Paradise Bakery would have a megaphone shape, and cheerleaders would deck the houses of the players in colored streamers.

Lila had made varsity cheerleader this year.

Luz bit her lip to keep from pointing out that Lila was grounded and would not be allowed to go to either the homecoming game or the dance afterward. No sense in dumping the painful reminder on her now, when she was about to head off to school.

"Bye," Lila said hastily, and rushed out the door.

With a sigh, Luz sat down at the table. Jessie pushed the paper and pen toward her. "Make a wish, sister."

CHAPTER 22

Lila had lived in Edenville all her life, but today she felt like an illegal alien as she bounced along in a school bus that reeked of diesel fuel and gym bags. Gazing out a smudged window at the postcard-pretty town square, she realized the world had changed overnight. The last time she'd seen Edenville, it had been through the eyes of a girl who knew only sunshine and laughter, friendship and fun. She was returning as someone who had looked death in the face. In the bright autumn morning, people rolled out awnings, swept sidewalks, greeted each other with waves and smiles.

Who were these strangers with their easy laughs and carefree lives, these people who slept well at night instead of dreaming about being tumbled in a rolling Jeep like frogs in a blender?

No one spoke to her on the bus, though she garnered plenty of nosy stares, some nasty whispers. The other passengers were mostly underclassmen who hadn't gotten their licenses yet, kids who were too poor to afford a car, or loser girls whose boyfriends had dumped them. The bottom-feeders of Edenville High.

And now there was Lila. Since walking away from the wreck, she had been cut off from the world. She didn't really know where she fit in anymore, and that was the worst feeling in the world. The things Heath's mother had said—*It's all your fault*—haunted her day and night. What if Mrs. Hayes was right? What if Lila was to blame? Maybe if she hadn't gone out that night, hadn't encouraged Heath, no one would have been hurt. She yearned to flip the calendar forward, turn sixteen and drive away forever. She had her learner's permit, and once she passed the road test, her dad was going to let her have the old Plymouth Arrow that had been parked in a shed on the property ever since she was little.

Dodging the stares and whispers as though they were spitballs in civics class, she wished for today to be like every other day, with Heath picking her up for school, solidifying her position on the invisible but oh-so-important popularity chart. Now, grounded deeper than the Treaty Oak, she had no idea where he was, at home or still in the hospital, or if he'd be at school today. Her mother had turned into a phone Nazi, even disabling the modem so Lila couldn't sneak a look at e-mail or receive instant messages.

When the bus lurched along the street in front of the school, Lila felt disoriented. It seemed as if she'd been overseas in a foreign country without phones.

Edenville High—Home of the Fighting Serpents—was a typical old-fashioned American high school, the sort you saw in nostalgic movies or read about in the AAA Driving Guide, which characterized Edenville as "The Town that Time Forgot." The school's front lawn was planted with magnolias and live oaks. The brick and concrete building was both imposing and reassuring in an ageless, traditional way. It had been here forever, and would still be standing decades from now.

It was weird to think that her mom and her aunt had gone to school here, but impossible to escape that fact. There were even several teachers who'd had them in class. Her English teacher, Mr. McAllister, constantly reminded the whole world about the Ryder girls and how Lila looked exactly like them both, right down to the last eyelash. Last spring, Lila had browsed through the yearbook archive only to find that for four years, credit for the best photos in the book went to "L. Ryder." L for Lucinda. Odd. You'd think Jessie would be the one taking all the pictures, seeing as how she grew up and became a world famous photographer. Yet all the yearbook photos had been taken by Lila's mother. It was totally bizarre to think about her mom being anything other than her mom, but you'd have to be blind to miss her talent at taking pictures. Maybe, a long time ago, her mom had thought about doing it professionally, as a job.

Of course, Lila had never asked her.

She wondered if the saying was true, that by the time you were in high school, your life's work had found you. Mr. Grimm, the college and career counselor, said that the talents and tastes that emerged during high school were likely to be the key to what you were going to do with the rest of your life.

Lila's own talents and tastes were still emerging—at least, that's what she told herself. She liked cheerleading, alternative rock, vintage clothing and Nacho Cheese Flavored Doritos, which girls with boyfriends could never, ever eat because they gave you bad breath. She was good at doing backflips and walkovers, making out with Heath Walker and sitting in the back of class, being invisible.

She had no idea how these skills would serve her well later in life.

In the side parking lot, the bus chugged and shuddered to a stop. Lila jostled her way up the aisle and jumped out, free at last. Someone behind her whispered, but when she whipped her head around, she only saw two girls she barely knew, innocently organizing their school bags. Then it came to her—the heavy one was Cindy Martinez. Lila had once borrowed her Spanish homework, and after that, Cindy had tried to be her best friend, but Lila had given her the big chill and she'd backed off.

Slinging her backpack over one shoulder, she trudged across the cracked and buckled parking lot. Nearby, seniors in the Fast-

Track Program—those who were taking career training as well as high school classes—were arriving for the day, some of them organizing carpools to Llano Junior College in the next town. For a moment, Lila yearned to go with them and never come back. But she forced herself to approach the school.

Like a well-founded rumor, the furtive aroma of a stolen cigarette crossed her path. A knot of Goths and Eurotrash huddled at the west entry, where no self-respecting regular kid would dare to be seen. Never before had she been so sensitive to the way people at this school segregated themselves, with invisible ribbons around their groups that shouted, "Police Line—Do Not Cross."

In front of the stadium quadrangle, she spotted a small group of 4-H Clubbers meeting on the green. They were with three little yellow Labrador retriever puppies wearing green pinneys that said Guide Dog In Training, so people would let them into shops and restaurants and history class. Those kids were okay, she supposed, but they were weird in their own way, and just as segregated. In addition to breeding goats and rabbits, they raised puppies from some famous breeding program in Round Rock. The way it worked was that a kid would adopt an adorable baby Lab, raise it by hand, housebreaking it and bonding with it, sleeping and eating with it and everything. Then when the pup was grown, they'd hand it over to some institution in Austin for training with the blind. Lila didn't get it. Why would you give all your love and affection to a puppy and then let someone else have it? How could those kids stand it? Of course, she reminded herself, some 4-H-ers routinely sent animals they'd raised to the slaughter, so maybe their hearts were different.

As she neared the front of the building, she felt a keen sense of anticipation. This was her school, her world, the place she belonged. She even dared to hope that Heath had returned, that she'd see him today.

Black and purple streamers hung from the spreading oaks near the front entrance, and a huge banner proclaimed, Go Serpents.

Homecoming was going to go on as planned because this was Texas and in Texas no one would dream of canceling homecoming just because the co-captain had wrecked his car and some kid had died in the crash.

It occurred to Lila that she was grounded, and she knew her parents. They wouldn't relent. Still, they were sound sleepers. She would sneak out and go to homecoming. Heath would be all better. He'd give her one of those dorky corsages the Serpent Boosters made each year and she'd wear her new dress, and for years afterward she'd keep that corsage like a museum relic in its molded plastic container.

She might complain about school but the fact was, she loved it. Loved the noise and laughter, the reek of the cafeteria and the aroma of coffee streaming from the teachers' lounge, the crackle of announcements over the loudspeaker and the chalky smell of old classrooms, the walls lined with ancient books, the hallways with banging metal lockers.

Finally she smiled. She was glad to be back.

She even heard a choir of angels singing in the distance. Then, with a start, she realized they weren't angels at all, but the Edenville High Chorus for Christ, a club of born-again students whose scrubbed faces were always smiling and whose attitude was always good.

They were gathered at the flag pole in front of the school. The giant American flag and the even bigger Texas flag both flew at half-mast.

Dig, she thought, her smile disappearing as she hurried forward. What she saw stunned her. She had never seen so many flowers in her life. Store-bought bouquets still in their cellophane, cut flowers stuck in jelly jars, Indian paintbrush and sorrel blossom gathered from fields—all were strewn and stacked and propped in a giant pyramid around the base of the flag pole. There was a single sunflower in the middle, and at the moment, a scruffy crow was pecking rudely at its seedy center. There were notes and cards and snapshots, even hand-lettered signs attached to bouquets and dime-store teddy bears and footballs and trophies. Lila spotted a pumpkin on which someone had written, "I miss you, Dig" in black magic marker. Overlooking the whole heap, displayed like a grotesque black-and-purple scarecrow, was a football jersey hanging from a rough-hewn wooden cross. The jersey bore the number 34 and the name Bridger in blocky letters across the back.

"We are high on Jeee-zuz," sang the chorus. They held hands and swayed as they sang, looking ecstatic with eyes closed and faces raised to the morning sky.

Watching them, Lila felt a beat of resentment. When Dig was alive, these holier-than-Swiss-cheese kids wouldn't save his soul if it were a Kmart blue-light special. The kids in this club were exclusive, all-white, pretending the black and Hispanic kids, and kids like the Bridgers who lived in trailer parks, didn't exist except when they needed to trot one out to prove their diversity.

But now that Dig was dead, they were ready to accept him as one of their own.

Lila's skeptical thoughts must have disturbed the holy firmament, because when the song ended, "I'm so high on Jesus, I can see the face of heaven," a few of them turned and saw her.

The news of her presence spread like a computer virus, but she was focused on one person and one person only.

"Heath!" His beloved name burst from her on a wave of relief. She hurried over to him. "Oh, thank God you're here."

Propped between two crutches, he stood flanked by kids she barely recognized. Ignoring them, Lila rushed forward to hug him, but the crutches got in the way, and she held back. Still, he was here, and he looked wonderful.

She eyed him with increasing caution. Ordinarily he'd hug her and maybe steal a kiss, and she'd sort of hope people saw because, even on crutches, he was the hottest guy in the school.

But today, there was ice in his eyes, pure ice, and it stopped her like an invisible wall.

"Heath?" She spoke more softly, tentatively now.

He offered her a tiny motion of his head. "Hey."

His lower right leg was encased in a high-tech, Velcro-strapped cast. Her confidence dimmed. "So you broke your leg."

"Duh," someone behind her said.

She ignored the voice. "Heath, I'm so sorry I didn't call. I'm grounded from everything, absolutely everything. My parents might not even let me go to homecoming this weekend. But I promise I'll find a way." She was babbling but couldn't stop herself. "I won't let you down."

"My leg is broken. I'm out for the season."

"But we can still go to the game, and then the party and dance afterward." She stepped forward, thinking that if she could touch him, the ice would melt and they would be fine.

"You don't get it, do you?" he asked.

She froze. Her stomach knotted tight. "Get what?"

He pointed a crutch at the strewn flowers. The air was thick with the scent of rotting sweetness. "This changes everything. You can't pretend nothing happened."

"I'm not pretending anything, but we have to go on, figure out a way to make sense of what happened."

"I have," he stated. "I've found forgiveness."

She frowned. "I forgive you, Heath."

"That's not what I mean." A strangely benign expression softened his face as he regarded his new companions. "I've accepted Christ into my heart as my personal savior."

"Oh, for Pete's sake. Overnight, you're a changed person?"

He glared at her. "I've been forgiven for the things you made me do that night."

"I made you sneak out? I made you go hill-hopping? I made you wreck your car?" Lila was incredulous. "That's a cop-out. You were driving, and if finding religion helps you stop feeling so guilty, fine. But I'm not getting born again. I was born right the first time."

"Then you're going to hell. But you'll go alone."

Humiliated and on fire with hurt, Lila moved away, staggering a little as though someone had hit her. She spotted Tina Bor-
den, co-captain of the cheerleading squad, and relief washed
over her. Tina was with two other cheerleaders. You almost
never saw cheerleaders by themselves; they felt naked without
at least one on each flank.

"Hi," she said, gathering tattered shreds of pride around her.
If her parents didn't let her cheer at homecoming, she would die.
Completely die. "So what about the big game?"

Tina's eyes narrowed. "You need to see Miss Crofter."

Miss Crofter was the faculty adviser of the cheerleading
squad. "Why?"

"You missed a game and two practices in a row, so that means
you don't cheer at the next game, even if it's homecoming." She
and her companions headed toward Dig's memorial.

"Hel*lo*." Lila stalked after them. "I was in a major car wreck.
It's not like I was skipping out."

Tina flipped her hair over her shoulder. "Rules are rules."

The three of them walked away.

"That's ridiculous." But they weren't listening. They whispered to each other as they headed off to where the singing was.

And Lila knew she wasn't going to hell. She was already
there. Blinded by tears of rage and humiliation, she walked
away from the school, her backpack feeling heavier with each
step she took. She had no idea where she was headed, and she
couldn't see where she was going, anyway. Without warning, she
slammed into a tall guy in a uniform.

"Whoa," he said, stepping out of the way and steadying her
with a hand to the shoulder. "I only want to talk to you, not slam-
dance before nine in the morning."

She blinked, trying to orient herself. Buff-colored shirt,
crisply ironed. Some sort of insignia on the pocket. "What?"

"Didn't you hear me calling?"

"Calling what?" The letters under the round badge spelled
A. CRUZ.

Taking her by the elbow, he steered her to a nearby concrete bench facing the quadrangle. "Maybe we should start over."

She regained her balance then. Okay, so he was some sort of volunteer fireman or rescue worker, maybe. But what really brought the world back into focus was his face. He looked like a movie star's favorite son—perfect black hair, white teeth, caring dark eyes. "Good idea," she said.

He handed her a handkerchief—a real cloth one, folded into a square. Nobody on the planet carried a cloth handkerchief, did he? It was no use pretending she wasn't crying, so she wiped her face with the clean white cloth. "Thanks. Um, am I supposed to give this back to you now? It's kind of gross."

"You can wash it and bring it back to me. Just make sure you iron it."

She could tell from his grin that he was teasing. A. Cruz had a great voice, a great grin that made her feel both shy and intrigued.

"Right. I'll iron it."

He put out his hand. "Andy Cruz."

"Lila Benning." She touched his hand briefly and studied the uniform. "Do you go to school here?"

"I'm a senior. This semester, I'm training with the county rescue workers. The reason I yelled at you to wait up is that I think I might have something of yours or your friends—from the accident. I was at the scene."

She stared at him then, and remembered the moments after the wreck. Someone with a flashlight. Angel eyes filled with heartbreak, never leaving her, never wavering. Voice firm and commanding beyond his years: *This one's conscious. Hurry up with that stretcher.*

"Anyway," he said, "there were a few things left at the scene, and they're at the fire station now. Did you lose something that night?"

"You have no idea," she said.

"I might. If you want to talk about it..."

She hesitated, passed her gaze over the face, the crisply ironed uniform. He was a senior. A rescue worker. "Okay," she said. "Maybe I do."

CHAPTER 23

Jessie needed to go to Austin to keep the appointment she'd made in secret, from overseas, many weeks earlier. The trouble was, her vision had deteriorated so quickly that she couldn't even think of driving. Just making the proof sheets and prints from the photo shoot had been an ordeal.

The solution had come to her from an unlikely source—Nell Bridger, the mother of the boy who had died. Apparently she had contacted Blair LaBorde to say she was interested in making a statement for a *Texas Life* article about the accident. Not only that, Nell and Blair were coming to discuss the accompanying photos.

Jessie found Luz in her big, sunny kitchen, wiping the counter with one hand while changing a lightbulb overhead with the other.

Jessie felt a rush of love so sharp and sweet that it pierced. "How many of my sisters does it take to change a lightbulb?"

"Not even a whole one." Luz tossed the sponge into the sink. "I learned multitasking back when Windows belonged on houses."

They discussed Blair's idea over coffee in the quiet morning lull after the kids had gone to school and Scottie to playgroup. "At first, I couldn't believe Nell would want to put her story out there," Luz said. "I mean, to go public with her grief seemed so incomprehensible. But I talked to her for a long time last night, and I think I understand. She wants to get the word out about hill-hopping, maybe reckless teen behavior in general. That's her way of coping with her loss."

"What do the parents of the other kids think?"

"I think she has every right to go public, and I promised to support her. Kathy Beemer's family feels the same way—getting the word out could save a life. I haven't spoken to Sierra's or Heath's folks. What do you think, Jess?"

She remembered how she'd felt that night, when Luz had awakened her to say Lila was in the hospital. It was, bar none, the most terrible sensation she'd ever experienced, as if all the air had been squeezed out of her, and she would never breathe again. "I wouldn't wish this on anyone, anywhere. So I suppose I agree with Nell. If making people aware of this keeps even one kid safe, then it's worth doing."

"Good, because I'm sure she'll want you to do the pictures."

Jessie tried to find the words to demur. As she was fumbling for an explanation, Blair LaBorde arrived. "I brought Krispy Kremes," she said, offering a red, green and white box.

Jessie trailed her hand along the railing of the deck as she stepped down to greet Blair. "Our thighs will never forgive you."

"I made a fresh pot of coffee," Luz said, leading the way inside. She set steaming mugs with the cream pitcher and bowl of sugar on the table, and the three of them sat down to wait for Nell.

"Good Lord, that's fantastic," Blair said.

Jessie could tell from Blair's voice alone that she had spotted Luz's photo collage and the framed pictures lining the breakfast nook. She beamed with pride. "Luz is pretty good, huh?"

Blair sipped her coffee. "Incredible. So what have you done professionally?"

Jessie could feel her sister diminish, somehow, as she sank down opposite Blair. Only Jessie recognized the strain in Luz's voice as she said, "You're looking at it, Dr. LaBorde. Kids and dogs. School plays and peewee football."

"You should be published," said Blair, and suddenly Jessie realized what this was leading up to. The possibility had been percolating beneath Blair's polished surface the whole time.

Luz shifted on her chair. "I don't have any credentials. I never even finished my degree."

Blair drummed her fingers against her mug. "I wasn't aware of that."

"I got married, and Ian and I— Lila came along right away."

Jessie pressed her hands together beneath the table. She wondered about Blair's memory of that time. When Jessie finished school, she'd been five and a half months pregnant. She hadn't advertised the fact, but she hadn't hidden it, either. What did Blair remember?

"You should have come to me back when I was on the faculty," Blair said to Luz. "I would have worked with you to finish your coursework."

Jessie touched her shoulder. "Luz never goes to anyone for help."

"And you do?" Luz's voice was defensive, edgy. But somehow resigned. "It's our mother," she explained, addressing Blair. "A psychoanalyst would have a field day with us."

"What, did she lock you in the basement for months while you were growing up?"

"No, that would mean she'd have to remember that she even had kids," Jessie said.

"Ah, Jess, she did the best she could," Luz said, ever the mediator. Sometimes Jessie wanted to grab her by the throat and shake her. To Blair, Luz said, "She was on the pro golf circuit, and had to travel a lot. During the school year, Jessie and I lived here, and in the summer we went on the road with her."

"Well, I'll keep you as busy as you want for the magazine,

and we'll see what we can do about those pesky graduation requirements."

There was a moment of stunned silence, then a sigh exploded from Luz. "What are you, my fairy godmother?"

"I wave my wand, honey, and make it all better. Right, Jessie?"

Jessie nodded vigorously, hoping neither would notice her preoccupation. She had to deal with what was happening to her. Her doctors overseas had arranged everything in advance, sending her records to the Beacon with a detailed case history and vigorous recommendations for including her in the special program. Today's interview would move her toward the next step in learning to live as a blind person. The very idea made her dizzy, but time was short. She knew that. Soon, she'd be gone for good.

To distract herself, she laid out the proofs from the photo shoot of Dusty Matlock and his baby. Though Jessie could only see them through the narrowing field of her right eye, she knew they were technically sound and would make a handsome addition to the article. But compared to Luz's work, they lacked soul. It was a flaw so subtle that few would notice. Two of those few who would sense the difference were sitting right here at the table with her.

"You should have hired Luz." Jessie voiced the opinion neither woman would admit to. She spoke without malice or envy, just stated simple fact. "Families, kids. That's her thing."

"I couldn't have taken that shot," Luz said with laughter in her voice, pushing an outtake across the table toward her.

Jessie tilted her head, needing only a glimpse to remind her of the shot. It was Dusty standing alone with one elbow propped on the wing of the Cessna, his eyes, his stance, everything about him exuding sex. Just before she'd taken that picture, he'd brought up the topic of their sleeping together on the first date. His blatant suggestion had affected her timing, and she'd hit the shutter almost by accident. It was, far and away, the best picture in the lot.

Just the thought of him caused a series of warm, smooth ripples to spread through Jessie. He had the most hypnotic effect on her, even when he wasn't around. In his absence, Jessie absolutely ached for him. She craved more of him, more than one night. At the same time, she felt relieved to have some time on her own, because her feelings for him were so intense. She needed to numb herself. She was headed for a destination where she could bring nothing along. She couldn't drag him to the place she was inexorably going.

"I can't use it, alas." Blair pushed the glossy closer to Luz. "Too sexy for the theme of the story. But Lord have mercy, look at him."

Jessie rested her chin in her hand. She couldn't stop the dreamy smile that softened her mouth. "I know."

Blair popped a square of nicotine gum out of its foil packet. "You didn't."

"I did."

"Really?"

"Really," said Luz. "So you should actually take credit for being their matchmaker."

Blair described the article and layout to Luz, showing her what she'd prepared for the editorial meeting. "It's going to be the cover story," she declared. "It's absolutely heart wrenching."

"'Matlock's Miracle'?" Luz read from the shout line.

"So it needs a little work," Blair admitted. "But it will be fine. Jessie, you'd better stake your claim to this guy, because when word gets out, he's going to be beating the women off with a pipe. Even Arnufo is going to be bombarded with propositions. 'The distinguished Mexican male nanny.' He's outstanding." Blair popped her gum. Then she put her hand over Luz's. "Hon, I hate to say it, but the article on the wreck is going to materialize with or without us."

"Blair has very few boundaries," Jessie explained.

"I work for a magazine with a circulation of two million," Blair stated, unrepentant.

"See?" Jessie said, gesturing at the pictures scattered across the table. "My God, this is about a man taking a baby from his wife's womb and then cutting off her life support. You think she'd hesitate to write about the accident?"

Blair said nothing further. She never made excuses for herself.

"So dead teenagers sell magazines?" Luz asked.

"Unfortunately, yes," Blair admitted.

"But we can control this," Jessie said, using her sister's favorite word.

As Blair gathered up the proofs and slides, Nell drove up in a pockmarked old Dodge Charger. Jessie followed her sister outside and waited while Luz and Nell embraced, then stepped forward. "My heart goes out to you, Nell," she said, wincing at the inadequacy of the words.

"I appreciate that." Nell gave her hand a squeeze.

Jessie studied her. How was she even able to stand, to breathe, given the magnitude of her loss? And yet here she was, forced to face a future without her boy. She was a heavyset woman with strong features that Jessie supposed looked ten years older than they had just weeks ago. Her no-nonsense hands had short fingernails and no rings. She wore a dark, straight jersey dress adorned only with a sterling James Avery cross hanging from a thread of leather. The scent of lavender and sleeplessness clung to her. "I've been wanting to meet you, Jessie. Luz has told me so much about you." She stepped back, her haunted eyes studying her. "Wow, you do look alike."

They went inside, and Nell moved through the house in familiar fashion. Jessie knew without asking that she was a frequent visitor. Nell took out a folded newspaper and slapped it on the table. Inch-tall letters proclaimed, Teen Dies In Twisted Tragedy. The piece was illustrated by stark, tasteless pictures of the mangled Jeep, candid shots of the victims' friends and families and one of Nell herself, making her look like a homeless woman. "Here's what's been published so far."

Then she opened another folder. "This is Luz's work," she explained to Jessie and Blair. "I was never good with a camera, so Luz took lots of pictures of my boys over the years."

Jessie wasn't surprised to discover the same sensitive humanity that characterized Luz's shots of her own family. That was her trademark. These were the type of photos that would make perfect strangers call Luz and tell her about their lives, about their kids and the trouble they got into and the hurt they had caused, and the way they managed to survive after terrible things happened.

Nell gazed steadily at Luz. "I want you to do the pictures for the article."

"Nell, no." Luz's voice was low and taut with urgency, and she cast a look at Jessie.

"That wasn't my idea," Jessie said. She could feel the distress coming off Luz in waves. "I swear it."

"I need for you to take the pictures," Nell said. "I want people to know what happened, but not like that." She gestured at the newspaper. "It's the only way I can give any sort of dignity to what happened to Dig."

"I can't do the pictures," Luz objected. "People in this town are not going to stand for me poking a camera in their faces, invading their privacy. The other victims already resent Lila for surviving unscathed, and they're not going to be any happier with her mother."

Nell shook her head. "That's Cheryl Hayes talking, because her son's missing the rest of the football season. Everybody else feels the way I do. You're one of us, Luz. You've suffered with us, cried with us. You won't make us look like a bunch of backwoods hicks."

"Nell is right," Blair said with assurance. "People want their grief portrayed. Remember Oklahoma City? Columbine? They want their story told, and they want it done beautifully. Trust me on this."

"And you're writing the piece?"

"Actually, I was going to give that over to Jessie."

Jessie held her breath, waiting. Luz put a hand on Nell's shoulder. "Nell?"

"I think that would be fine," Nell said softly.

The tension buzzed between them, thick and uncomfortable.

Blair took out her gum and wrapped it in a napkin. "I need a real cigarette."

Nell stood wearily. "I'll join you."

As soon as they were gone, Luz turned on Jessie. "Why are you being so pushy about this?"

"Because I'm entitled to be pushy for a change, damn it."

"What do you mean, 'for a change'? Are you saying I'm the pushy one?"

"Hey, if the shoe fits."

"I can't believe you think I'm pushy. You're the one trying to manipulate the situation."

Jessie almost laughed. "Look, Luz, we both know how it is between us, how it's always been. I screw up—you pick up the pieces. It's always been that way. I skip school. You forged the note from home. I need money for tuition—you put your own education on hold to work. I have a baby out of wedlock—you adopt her. Just a few examples of you bailing me out. So how about I do the bailing, just this once?"

Luz leaned against the counter, stunned into silence. "Where'd all this come from, Jess?"

"Try a lifetime of being the screwup younger sister. Luz, you put your dreams on hold for me. Hell, when was the last time you put a wish in the jar? You're going to do this, like your friend asked you to. You're going to take the pictures for the article I'm going to write."

"That makes no sense."

"It does, and you will." It felt good to be the bossy one for a change. "If you don't step up to the plate, we'll lose the opportunity, and even Nell Bridger knows that. Without your pictures, we're going to wind up with sensationalist, tabloid dreck."

She gestured at the photographs on the wall. "Luz, you can use your talent to do some good and maybe make a little money to boot."

"Spoken as a true mercenary." But the waver in Luz's voice indicated capitulation.

Jessie hurried over to the cabin to grab her things before Luz changed her mind. Jessie was learning to feel the way through space, almost against her will. The people at the Beacon had advised her to enroll in their program as quickly as possible, before she formed habits of gait and posture that were undesirable. As she crossed the yard, she gave a thumbs-up sign to Blair and Nell. She grabbed the soft leather portfolio filled with her records, then hefted her camera bag. She brought it back to the house and set it before Luz.

"You're going to be needing this."

"I can't take your equipment." She spoke with a hushed reverence as she handled the cameras, lenses, filters and gadgets Jessie had amassed over the years.

"You can, and you will. Listen to me. You know this stuff, Luz. You always have. You're the only one Nell trusts to do this right."

Luz took out a camera, lifting it as though it were the holy grail. Only Jessie understood fully what was happening. She was handing Luz her dream and would never snatch it back. Jessie would never again take a photo, never heft the solid body of the camera in her hand, feel the smooth snap of a lens seating itself in place or hear the satisfying click of the shutter capturing a perfect shot. The passing of the camera equipment signified the end of a chapter. She watched Luz's face, memorizing her sister's expression down to the last detail. She was desperate to observe everything and imprint it on her memory. It was as much a form of self-preservation as it was defiance.

She concentrated on simply breathing, and hoped her emotions didn't show. She was at a turning point, but for now, she wanted it to be a private transition. She was ending the only life she knew, and leaping blindly, in every sense of the word, into the unknown. There was something both gratifying and appropriate in passing the tools of her trade on to her sister.

Luz looked ready to burst into tears. But she didn't. Luz never burst into tears.

The phone rang, disrupting the moment. Jessie grabbed for it. Since the accident, she'd adopted the habit of running interference for Luz.

"Benning residence."

"Mommy?"

The word froze Jessie, and for a moment she fell into the fantasy. "Lila? What do you need, love?"

"Oh. Aunt Jessie." The change in the girl's tone flattened Jessie. "Can I talk to my mom?"

"Is there something I can do for you?"

There was a tragic sniffle that cut straight through the phone line and grabbed Jessie's heart. "I'm in the nurse's office at school," Lila said miserably.

"Are you sick?"

"This is the *nurse's* office. The refuge of outcasts."

The raw hurt in her voice clasped even tighter around Jessie's heart. "You're an outcast?"

Lila hesitated. "I don't feel so good."

Jessie tried to put together the scenario. Lila had come home from school yesterday and gone straight to her room, claiming she had homework. She'd scarcely spoken at dinner and resisted all efforts to draw her out. This was the first crack in her shield.

"What's the trouble, sweetie?" Jessie asked.

"Oh, Aunt Jessie." She caught her voice in a sob. "I can't be here today. It's too hard to be at school right now. I've got to get out of here."

Despite everything else that was pressing at her today—the day she was going to take a major step toward a dark and frightening future—Jessie didn't hesitate. She was quickly learning a fundamental law of nature. When a child needed you, there was no time for a personal crisis. "You sit tight, love. I'll get you out."

* * *

"Thanks for offering to give Lila a little TLC," Luz said, hugging Jessie as Blair started the car. Nell had already left to meet with her pastor and some of the other families about the article. "I don't mind letting her have a day off for some girl time in the city. You're a lifesaver."

"Lifesaver." Jessie snorted. "I've never rescued anyone in my life."

"Bullshit. Remember the time I broke my ankle in the woods and you went for help?"

"Just like Lassie," Blair said.

"Okay, that's once," Jessie conceded. "Name another."

"You don't get it. Once is all it takes. If you hadn't saved me that day, I'd've died."

"Well, in this case, I don't think Lila's life hangs in the balance. She needs a day away. A day in the city might be the thing. I'll take her to lunch, then see if they can work her in at Galindo's—maybe a haircut and manicure? If there's time, I'll let her buy a new CD, and then we'll catch a ride home tonight with Ian."

"That sounds good, Jess. But..." Luz bit her lip, and her brow creased in a way that made Jessie want to scream.

But what? Don't tell her I gave birth to her?

"She might ask to go see Travis Bridger—he's still in the hospital. I'd rather she didn't visit with him yet."

Jessie let out a breath she didn't know she was holding. "Fine. We'll steer clear of all hospitals. Got it."

"I didn't mean to sound so bossy," Luz said.

Yes, you did.

"She's going to be okay, Luz. A day off, and she'll come back a changed person."

"I pressured her to go back to school too soon after the wreck. I thought getting her back into a routine would be good for her. Instead I made things worse."

"God, Luz, why don't you take responsibility for the anthrax scare and the Middle Eastern situation while you're at it?" Jessie said. "Look, you did nothing wrong. A bunch of kids screwed up royally, something terrible happened and we have to help them deal with it as best we can. Lila is going to be okay because you raised her to cope. I'm doing my small part. Working on this article is going to be therapeutic—for both of us." It felt strange, offering solutions to Luz, who always knew all the answers. Jessie added, "We'll both be new women at the end of it all."

"Implying there's something wrong with the old women."

"They're old," Blair shouted from the driver's seat. "Let your sister get in the car, hon."

Jessie hugged her again. "We'll be home with Ian tonight. Take some time for yourself. Make friends with the camera again."

She got in and gave Blair directions, guiding her through the shaded hills of Edenville and past the Gothic courthouse, which presided over the central square, its bell tower sandy yellow against the sky.

"So this is your hometown," Blair commented, navigating the Cadillac along Aurora Street.

"My old stomping grounds."

They passed the Halfway Baptist Church, an old-fashioned wooden building with white siding and a perfectly groomed lawn. Nell's Charger was parked at the side. The notice board in the front proclaimed, Our Angel, Albert Bridger, 1989 to 2003.

The Sky★Vue Drive-in Theatre still stood at the far edge of town, the back of its towering screen painted in a Lone Star flag motif, red-brown streaks streaming under the bolts like rusty tears. The marquee read "Cl sed 4 the Seas n."

"I bet you made your share of trouble there," Blair remarked.

Jessie offered a rueful smile. She remembered cars that smelled of motor oil spilt over engines that ran badly, and the cheap, thin taste of beer stolen warm from a pallet behind the

Country Boy Grocery. She could still recall the sensation of a boy's curiously timid hand settling on her thigh. Or another boy, whose decidedly untimid hand captured her breast as though it were a fly ball out in right field.

Blair surveyed the outlying, empty fields of layered rock and chaparral only a few blocks from the main square. "No wonder you left this place."

"Some people can't imagine being anywhere else. It's a town where all the neighbors know each other and none of the kids can get away with anything because everyone's watching. But the trouble with some kids is that knowing they're likely to get caught is no deterrent. It's part of the game."

They parked in a visitor space at the school and stopped at the bizarre shrine to Dig—a mound of flowers and memorabilia that was already looking tired and forlorn. "We'll want pictures of that," Blair said, gesturing at the football jersey fluttering in the breeze.

"Luz will do this right, Blair. I swear it."

They went into the high school. It was not exactly as Jessie remembered, but close enough. Locker room smells, disinfectant, coffee, hollow noises. A hallway gleaming from its nightly buffing. Hand-lettered signs bearing announcements: Homecoming '03. Go Serpents!

Leaving Blair to inspect the hallowed halls of Edenville High, Jessie went in search of Lila. The main office still rang with the busy chaos of a postal substation. And the attendance clerk, Mrs. Myrtle Tarnower, had not moved from her spot at an obsessively neat oak desk with its green blotter. Jessie thought her unreliable eyes were playing tricks on her, because it was impossible to conceive of Mrs. Tarnower sitting there year in and year out, keeping track of who was sick and who was late and who was truant, phoning parents to verify claims of the missing. Mrs. Tarnower must have called the Ryder place many times in search of Jessie.

"I'm here to pick up my...Lila Jane Benning," said Jessie to a woman wearing a black-and-purple booster ribbon. "My sister Luz—"

"—just called about her." The receptionist handed her a clipboard, then waved her toward the nurse's office. It was still in the same location it had been two decades before, when Jessie used to stop in for a Band-Aid or a Midol, or to hide out when she didn't have her algebra homework done. She went down a side hallway, stopping at a heavy door with a thick pane of frosted glass.

Jessie knocked lightly, stepped inside and encountered a husky boy with acne, sitting on a stool in the corner, holding a blue gel pack around his hand. Moving past him, Jessie peeked into a side room. There sat Lila on a low bench, her face pale and intense as she studied a bilingual choking chart on the wall.

"Hey, kiddo."

"Aunt Jessie." Lila exploded with the word as though she'd been holding her breath. "Thanks for coming."

"I'm glad to do it. Let's go." They emerged from the nurse's office to find Blair in the foyer of the building, interviewing a pair of wide-eyed underclassmen. When they spied Lila, they excused themselves and hurried away, as though her misfortune was contagious. Pretending not to notice, Jessie introduced Lila to Blair and said, "So are you really sick, or sick of this place?"

"I pick answer B."

"That's what I figured. Listen, Blair and I are going to write an article about the accident. It's going to be published in *Texas Life*."

"No way."

"Way. Mrs. Bridger and Mrs. Beemer both want to be in it. So we have some things to do in the city. She's going to take the idea to her editorial board, and I've got a few errands. How about you come along? There's something I think you'll like, guaranteed to heal the sick. Ever heard of Galindo's on Sixth Street?"

"It's only about the most famous salon in the city. Are we going there? Really?" Excitement animated her voice.

"I'll treat you to lunch and then a half-day spa routine. But I have to warn you, it includes a massage."

Lila settled against the pink leather upholstery of the back seat. "I've never had a massage before." She fell silent until they passed the green-and-white sign: Now Leaving Edenville. Then she let out a long sigh.

"Talk to me, love," said Jessie, swiveling sideways on the front seat and reaching for her hand. She gestured at Blair. "Dr. LaBorde is a professional. You can say anything in her presence, as long as you understand she has no respect for privacy."

"I respect telling the truth," Blair said. "Not everyone can handle the truth."

"The whole school knows anyway," Lila burst out. "Heath dumped me."

Good. Jessie bit her lip to keep from saying it, but getting rid of the kid who had nearly killed her didn't seem like a terrible idea.

"I'm sorry, love," she said. "I know you'll miss him. Listen, about that article—your mom's doing the photographs."

"No way."

"Way."

"I thought you were the photographer."

"Not anymore." The finality of saying it aloud appalled Jessie, but she held her feelings in check. This must be how Luz did it, she realized. This was how Luz controlled her world. She erupted inside and kept the same shell on the outside. "So is that okay with you?"

A shrug. "I guess."

"People want to know about the town, your friends, your life. But if you don't want me to say Heath broke up with you, I won't."

"However, the fact that he dumped his girlfriend on homecoming week says something about his character," Blair added.

"What's that?" Lila asked.

"That he's a spineless weasel who won't take responsibility for his actions," said Jessie.

A tiny, gratifying giggle escaped Lila. Jessie absorbed her lovely smile and filed the image away in her heart.

"I had a boyfriend in college who dumped me two days before the Aggie-Longhorn game," Blair said. "What a prick."

Lila looked startled and pleased by her salty language. "What did you do?"

"My sorority sisters and I gave him the hairball treatment."

"What's that?"

"We all cleaned out our brushes and stuffed the hair through a crack in his car window. It made quite a pile, right on the driver's seat, as I recall."

Lila laughed and brushed at her tears, but the levity was soon crushed beneath the dead weight of worries. "It's not only Heath. I'm suspended from cheering because I missed practice—like, well, *excuse* me for getting into a car wreck. It's not like I planned it. But it's worse than that. Since this happened, Heath started hanging around with the religious kids."

"What?" Jessie frowned.

"A group at school. They're all like, if you don't walk with Jesus, you can't sit at my lunch table."

"I hate when that happens," Blair murmured, cracking her gum.

"Heath barely went to church in his life, and now he's going around saying he's forgiven and saved. In the meantime, they all blame me, and I wasn't even driving."

"So why do you think they blame you?" Jessie asked.

"Because they need to blame someone who's not the star quarterback of the football team. He told everybody it was my idea to go out to Seven Hills that night, and my idea to go launching. He even said I told Dig to give up his seat belt to Kathy. They're all treating Heath like some kind of war hero."

"Never mind that, love. Today is your day."

* * *

On the way into the salon, Jessie spotted a familiar book in a shop window, and insisted on buying it.

"Pat the Bunny?" asked Lila.

"For Amber. It's the perfect toddler book—you read it by touch. I bet you don't remember that I sent you one for your first Christmas."

"Nope. You're dating him, right?" Lila asked with a sly smile. "Amber's dad."

"Is one date considered dating?"

"It is if he looks like that."

Jessie laughed. She wanted to tell Dusty he'd passed the Lila test. She wanted to tell Dusty everything. If she was smart, she'd avoid him completely.

Ah, but she wasn't smart. She'd never been smart.

The spa restaurant served everything in tiny, artistic portions. The food came painstakingly stacked, with lines of raspberry vinaigrette drawn on the plates. They dug into their lunches, Lila savoring every fussed-over bite, Jessie barely eating at all. No wonder people spoiled their kids, she thought. Taking delight in the pleasure of the child created a quiet satisfaction she'd never before experienced. Lila's obvious enjoyment of the meal and her anticipation over the salon were only the beginning. With her photographer's eye, Jessie took memory pictures, studying Lila's hands, face, expressions. It was strange and sad and fitting, Jessie reflected. She was spending her last official day as a sighted person with her daughter.

She left Lila for a half-day treatment, giving her a hug as a woman dressed as some sort of New Age acolyte brought a glass of herbal tea and turned on a set of magnetic chimes.

"This is *so* awesome," said Lila.

"It's supposed to be three hours of awesome. I'll meet you back here around four. We might have time for a little shopping, and then we'll take a taxi to your dad's office."

"Aunt Jessie?"

The tentative note in Lila's voice put Jessie on alert. "Yes?"

"As we were driving in, I noticed—well, we passed the hospital. So I was wondering—"

"Don't ask, Lila. Please, don't ask."

"I just—"

"No." Jessie knew she had to put her foot down. Why was that so hard? Then she wondered if Lila might sneak out of the spa and go to the hospital on her own. With everything else Jessie had to do today, she couldn't afford a crisis with Lila. "Don't betray me," Jessie said. "I need you to not betray me."

"Jeez, you're turning into a drama queen."

Jessie took a panicked breath of air and summoned up a cocky grin. "I've been wanting a change of careers."

CHAPTER 24

The salon was a stroke of genius. What a perfect cover, Jessie thought as she walked the four blocks past the UT main campus to the Beacon Eye Institute. She wouldn't need to explain her errands in the city at all.

The concrete edifice of the building dominated an entire city block. She entered through swishing automatic doors and stepped into an extra-wide, accessible hallway with polished floors and sound-cushioned ceilings. Feeling like a rat in a labyrinth, she followed the color-coded stripes and arrows on the hallway floors, eventually finding her way to the ophthalmology wing. A long bulletin board outside displayed information about Eye Health. The *E*s were stenciled backward to imitate the symbols on an eye chart.

"Cute," she muttered under her breath, and entered through the glass door. She shut her eyes as she waited, not wanting to acknowledge the pamphlets and brochures about the importance of wearing safety glasses and getting regular eye checks. Ten Facts You Need To Know About Retinitis Pigmentosa. Living With Ushers Syndrome. Controlling Diabetes. Managing Anger. Oh, there was a good one.

There was a word she didn't see printed on any pamphlet or brochure, but it was like an elephant in the room. *Blind.* Such a simple word, used so frequently. Blind ambition, luck, rage. Venetian blind, duck blind, double blind. Blind fucking date. Taste tests, random samplings, justice. So many things were blind. She'd be in good company.

At the outset, her appointment was entirely predictable, almost comfortable simply because it was so familiar. She knew exactly when and how to jut her chin on the brace of the slit lamp. The devices and tests, the questionnaire on a clipboard. Dr. Margutti had prepared herself by reviewing the mountain of data and history forwarded from the facilities in Taipei and Christchurch. She carefully documented the progress of the blindness, working with a perfect balance of competence and compassion. The doctor in Christchurch had provided nearly everything they needed in advance—physical and psychological tests, a complete case history, enthusiastic recommendations regarding her potential. "He probably couldn't wait to get rid of me," Jessie said. "What did he write? Jessie Ryder will make a great blind person?"

Margutti ignored her sarcasm. She had the gentle, sensitive hands of a concert violinist and the firm voice of an experienced lecturer. The tests were a case of déjà vu, as was the sinking feeling in the pit of Jessie's stomach. Nose to nose with the doctor as Margutti evaluated Jessie's almost nonexistent visual field, she braced herself for the electroretinogram—the numbing drops, the hour-long exam in the dark. The probes resting on her eyes felt like eyelashes.

"The response to the flash in your right eye is significantly diminished."

"Yes." Jessie wanted to despise the doctor for being unable to offer hope. Instead she maintained a neutral attitude as Margutti explained the things she already knew. But the moment of truth, though expected, came without warning.

"You'll have to use an occluder to obscure the last of your vision during training. The sooner you start, the better. If you'd like, we can enroll you early at the Beacon."

"No." Jessie's answer was swift, angry. Months ago, she had known this day was coming, yet the terror was as fresh as ever. She hated that this scared her so. She had scaled impossible mountains, sailed treacherous seas. She had dined with international criminals and traveled in the company of dangerous men. She had survived malaria, tsunamis, dysentery and body cavity searches. This was simply another thing that was happening to her, another thing to survive.

"Ordinarily a member of our staff makes a home visit," said the doctor.

Jessie thought about bringing a stranger to Luz's place to poke around, ask nosy questions, point out hazards and shortcomings. "At the moment, I don't have a permanent residence. I'd like some help finding a place after I finish the program," she said.

"Of course."

"Thank you." Jessie had coldly and dispassionately determined that the most important thing in her life was her independence, and had sought out the best way to reclaim it despite what was happening to her. One of the most successful programs in the world happened to be right here, at the Beacon. It was an eight-week program—the first four in residence, training with a guide dog, followed by four weeks of intensive independent living classes. Everything was all set to go.

Everything except Jessie.

"All right," said Dr. Margutti. "You'll want to take full advantage of your visit today. My receptionist will show you how to get to the working campus. You'll have a tour of the facility and meet some very special people."

Down the elevator, across a footbridge and into a shuttle bus for a short ride to a low-key residential campus. A sign designating it as the Beacon For The Blind, Est. 1982 flanked the main gates. She'd seen pictures of it, but she could never envision herself here. Who would ever imagine a stint at a place like this?

The compound was dominated by a large building which housed common areas, classrooms, laboratories and a student and instructor wing. Footpaths of brick and gravel and packed earth crisscrossed the area, some of them marked with orange cones and obstacles, and through it all wound a busy paved road. She felt the hard bite of angry resentment as she walked down the halls to meet her doom. Each splash of color, each movement on the grounds, with their stately pecan trees, manicured lawns and contoured hills, fed her rage.

Even though she had begun planning this months ago, Jessie balked at the door. *I don't belong here. This is a place for blind people.* She bit back a scream of protest, passed through the foyer and entered a conference area that resembled a cozy living room furnished with an overstuffed sofa and chairs and an adjacent lounge and dining room. French doors framed a cedar deck.

A woman crossed the foyer. "Jessie? I'm Irene Haven."

Jessie recognized her voice instantly from their many phone conversations. "So here I am...at last."

They shook hands. Irene's grip was as calm and strong as her voice. She had clear green eyes, abundant dark hair, olive-toned skin and a face that was both attractive and kind in a no-nonsense way. "Let's go out on the deck. I told Sully we'd join him there. We're having such beautiful sunshine today."

Jessie had also met Malachai Sullivan, the assistant director, via phone and e-mail as well. When she and Irene stepped outside, they found him seated at a large round table draped with a bright red cloth and littered with paperwork.

He was good-looking in an older-guy-in-shades-and-Levi's way. "So you made it, little lady," he said, greeting Jessie with a genial smile. He seemed to be a classic Texas gent, with a lazy drawl and engaging manner, and an intent way of focusing on Jessie as she took a seat across the table from him and Irene.

"I made it," Jessie said. "I can't believe I'm here." She was awash in uncertainty and fear. This wasn't happening. This couldn't be happening. She didn't belong here, with blind people stumbling around, stripped of dignity and purpose. Except that she didn't see anyone stumbling around. In the distance, two people walked along together, crossing the street, but they didn't appear to be blind. Somewhere, the sound of barking dogs erupted, but she didn't see the herds of noble, hardworking, harnessed beasts she'd expected.

"I know you're familiar with our program," said Irene, "but this is your first visit, so Sully will give you the VIP tour, as we do all our prospective clients." She poured three glasses of iced tea. "Jessie, Sully, here you go. Welcome to the Beacon."

Jessie took a sip of her tea, and Sully drank his practically in one gulp. "All right," Jessie said. "Now what?" She laughed at the nervousness she heard in her own voice. "My God. I haven't felt like this since rush week at UT."

Consulting a thick file of notes about Jessie's case, Irene said, "You've been through a lot, but you have strong advocates in Dr. Hadden and Dr. Tso. Both of them supported your application vigorously, Margutti signed off on you, so you're good to go."

"You mean you actually reject people?" Jessie was incredulous.

"Absolutely. The success of the program depends on effective use of our time and resources, and it simply doesn't work for some people. So. Here are the essentials. The goal is to provide you with strategies for independent living."

"Independent. How can I be independent if I can't even fucking drive?" Jessie snapped, her anger spilling out.

"For one thing, you'll redefine independence for yourself," Irene said calmly. "What's driving, anyway? It gets you from point A to point B. Sitting behind the wheel of a car isn't the only way to do that. You'll learn to look for other options. With your instructor and our staff, you'll cover every aspect of living, from the moment you get up in the morning to the moment you go to bed. After four weeks on campus, you're launched."

"You can always come back here for support and retraining,"

Sully pointed out. "This will be your home base, your resource center."

"Great," said Jessie, hating herself for her attitude, but hating even more the fact that she was here at all. "Hold the phone while I count my blessings."

Sully refilled his tea glass. For all his charming ways, he was a bit of a slob, hooking an index finger over the rim of the glass as he poured. "You can't stop this from happening. You can decide what you're going to do about it. But I think we'll skip the lecture on how blind people live productive lives and find meaning and fulfillment in their new situation."

"Thank you. I don't think I could stand that."

Irene patted him on the arm. "Sounds like you can take it from here, partner. Take care, Jessie. See you at enrollment."

See you. Jessie shuddered as Irene went inside.

Malachai Sullivan folded his hands on the table and gave her his complete attention. It was gratifying, the way he focused on her. For a moment, she flashed on the idea that her father, had he lived, might look something like Sully, with his neat salt-and-pepper hair, a face lined by experience and a fine mouth that managed to be pleasant even without smiling.

"It's a rough transition for anyone," he said. "It's hard on families as well, but you'll need their support at this crucial time."

"Not me," she said swiftly, appalled. "In the first place, I don't—" Even she couldn't finish that part of the lie. "Look, my relatives are not going to be a part of this. I'm coming here alone, and things are going to stay that way."

"Is that how things were before you became blind?"

"Actually, yes."

"And is that the way you want things to be?"

She thought of Luz, Lila, the boys. Dusty and Amber. Her heart nearly burst with yearning. It took all her strength to say, "Yes. Is that a problem?"

"Maybe, maybe not. To be brutally honest, sometimes the

most loving family members or spouses actually hinder the blind. They try too hard to help, and do too many of the things you're perfectly capable of doing for yourself. Eventually you lose your skills and motivation to succeed. So a too-helpful relative can be harmful."

The exact profile of Luz, Jessie realized, always doing for everyone else. She knew then that when she left, she wouldn't tell Luz where she was going. She'd spare Luz the heartbreak and frustration. "I want to make it through the program on my own," she told Sully. Then she stood. "So is this where I get my tour? I always wondered where they put the blind. I guess it doesn't matter."

"Very funny."

Sully got up from the table and carefully, deliberately, pushed in his chair. Reaching down, he grabbed something from under the table, and Jessie was astonished to see that it was a short leash attached to the U-shaped harness of a large German shepherd, which hastened to its feet and snapped to attention.

Though Jessie made no sound, she must have betrayed her surprise somehow.

"This is Fred," Sully said. At the sound of his name, the dog swished his bushy tail.

"Oh. I—um— I didn't realize—" Flustered, she broke off.

"That I was blind?" He gave the dog a hearty pat, and Fred went around to Sully's left side. "There are times when it hardly matters, like when I'm drinking a glass of iced tea or talking to a friend on the phone. Other times, it's a major consideration, like when I'm crossing the street or playing shuffleboard."

"Playing—" She looked up and down the shady quadrangle, seeing a network of footpaths and gardens.

"I really suck at shuffleboard." He murmured a command, made a nearly imperceptible motion with his wrist and Fred forged to the edge of the walkway. "But I'm a remarkably good bowler."

* * *

The campus of the Beacon was tauntingly close to the University of Texas main campus. Jessie remembered the traffic warning signs along the street: Blind Pedestrian Crossing. Years ago, she'd roared through that intersection without a second thought.

Sully gave her a tour of the facility, which was set up to address a blind person's day-to-day routine, from organizing the bathroom to avoid brushing teeth with hair cream to labeling stove knobs and spices with Braille strips.

"You mean I'm going to cook blind?" Jessie whispered, watching an instructor help an old woman make an omelet.

"Sure."

"Pretty amazing. I never could before."

There was a bewildering and ingenious array of devices in what was known as the library, though it was damned noisy for a library. The new technology was incredible—talking books, narrated movies for the blind, computers that took live and recorded dictation and read text aloud.

"Some work better than others," Sully explained about the movies.

"I can imagine."

"This is generally everyone's favorite part of the tour," he said, leading the way to a gymnasium furnished with obstacles. They stopped in the doorway. A sign labeled the facility as Orientation And Mobility.

An instructor worked with a young, eager golden retriever named Flossie and a woman called Margaret, training the client every bit as intensively as she trained the dog. They went through the routine again and again, with the dog being persuaded, praised and corrected every step of the way. When it worked well, the two moved in a perfect unit; other times, the woman wandered, the dog hesitated and she nearly tripped over a rubber cone or smacked her head on a hanging object. The dog focused and concentrated with an intensity that seemed almost

human. No, better than human. The dog seemed to have no mo-
tive beyond assisting the woman.

"You liked that," Sully said when they left the area.

"Everybody likes pets."

"Fred's not a pet. No guide dog ever is. That's one of the first
things you'll learn." He led the way to an apartment and held
open the door, letting Fred out of his harness. Instantly Fred became a typical dog, leaping on a much-chewed toy and dancing
around the apartment.

"He's as much a part of me as my ears or my hands," Sully
explained, his gentle self-assurance changing to solemn sincer-
ity. "He's more than a set of eyes, too. He thinks and judges for
himself. He makes mistakes and gets things right."

Jessie smiled. She liked Sully, liked him for his honesty, and
for embodying the idea that being blind was not the unspeakable personal tragedy she'd been dreading. She liked the dog,
too. "Is it okay to pet him?"

"Sure."

She stroked the coarse-haired black-and-tan head, earning a
canine groan of pleasure. "You must really love him."

"What I feel for him goes so far beyond love that there's really no word for it." He spoke without false sentimentality.
Reaching down, he held up two pillows from the couch. Each
had been imprinted with a photograph of a child's face. "My
grandkids," he explained. "I love them. They're precious to me.
But they aren't my blood and bone like Fred is."

"Do you see them often? I mean—"

"I know what you mean. Yes, I see plenty of them. They live
over on Shoal Creek, and my daughter brings them to visit a couple of times a week."

She was quiet for a moment. "Have you ever actually seen
them?"

"No. I've been blind since 1972."

"Does it bother you?"

"Sure, I'd like to see their faces. But I've held them. Kissed their cheeks, smelled their skin." Grinning, he touched the strings of a guitar on a stand in the corner. "I've sung them to sleep, read them stories, even written original songs for them."

"You write songs?"

He picked up the guitar, strummed a chord and sang, "Paul Murray Manufactured Homes..."

"Hey. I've heard that on the radio."

"I write jingles. Not exactly great art, but fun enough. What do you do for a living?" Sully asked.

"I'm a photographer."

His smile vanished. "I guess that'll change, then."

Jessie fought a scream, and tried to sound optimistic. "I've always wanted a dog."

CHAPTER 25

Luz had supper with the boys, because Ian had called to say he'd be late bringing Lila and Jessie home from the city. She was used to his missing dinner; that was the price they paid for living so far out in the country. Besides, she didn't mind. There was something oddly comforting in preparing the coveted stovetop macaroni and cheese, and in the uncomplicated chatter of her sons as they consumed impossible quantities of chicken strips smothered in ketchup. Beaver sat at attention, watching the food go from plate to mouth like a spectator at a tennis match.

Although Luz would barely admit it to herself, she felt an easing of tension in Lila's absence. It was a good move, she told herself, letting Jessie take charge of Lila for the day. Luz had to start getting used to the idea that Lila was growing up, seeking other mentors. Now if only she could get used to the idea of explaining Lila's adoption to her.

She'd spent the day with Nell Bridger at her side, taking pictures of other people's children. Once Nell explained the purpose of the article, it was exactly as Blair had predicted—people didn't mind being photographed, even when they were showing raw emotion. In fact, some of them crowded in, craving the val-

idation of being photographed. Luz had faltered at first, then realized that this was little different from photographing her own
children. You simply stepped out of the way and recorded their
pain, relief, confusion, anger. She wondered why she'd stayed
away from this for so long. The work was so gratifying that she'd
nearly lost track of the time, and had to rush to pick up Scottie
by carpool time. Perhaps the most surprising thing of all was that
she actually had a shot at finishing the assignment, provided the
parents and teachers proved to be as startlingly cooperative as
the students were. She'd arranged meetings with several of them
already. She felt a keen sense of their trust. They expected her
to portray them with dignity; they wanted her pictures to show
the depth and magnificence of their grief. And Luz felt confi-
dent in the work she'd done so far. She was good at this, even
with unfamiliar equipment and a novice's point of view.

"Some guy came and talked to our class today," Wyatt said.

Owen made loud chugging noises as he inched a Hot Wheels
Mustang along the edge of the table.

"What kind of guy?" Luz asked Wyatt.

"Some police guy."

"I want to see the police guy," Scottie said.

"What did he talk to your class about?" Luz asked, pushing
preternaturally bright macaroni and cheese around on her plate.

"Safety and stuff."

Owen's Hot Wheels spun out and crashed off the edge of the
table. *"Aaaagh,"* he said. "A hill-hopping tragedy."

"Aaaagh," echoed Scottie. "A hill-hopping tragelly."

"Oh, for heaven's sake." Luz scowled at her middle son.
"That's a terrible thing to say, Owen Earl Benning. Why on earth
would you say such a thing?"

He hunched his shoulders forward and stared at his plate.
Like Jessie, Lila and Luz, Owen had bright red hair and pale col-
oring that blushed like a sunrise. "Sorry," he mumbled.

"You didn't answer my question." She felt Wyatt and Scottie
watching her, wide-eyed. Owen's chin trembled, and her heart

turned soft. "Okay, so it was a bad question. But tell me this. Are all the kids at school talking about hill-hopping?"

Owen nodded.

"What are they saying?"

A shrug, a shifting gaze. "Stuff about Lila's wreck and that kid who got killed."

"We will not make a game out of it, ever. Okay, cowboy?" Luz said.

"Yes, ma'am." He picked up his fork and started eating, and the other two did the same. They left the issue alone like an unwanted vegetable on the plate.

Luz felt a deep welling of love for her boys, mingled with guilt. In all the hoopla over Jessie's arrival and Lila's accident, she'd put her little guys on autopilot. They'd heard snippets of gossip about the accident and were processing it in their own way.

"Here's what I want you to know about the accident," she said, addressing all three of them. "Lila and her friends made some really bad choices. They sneaked out without permission, drank beer and crammed too many kids into their car. And they treated the car like a toy."

Owen's gaze flicked to the overturned Mustang on the floor.

"They weren't being careful and a terrible accident happened and everybody got hurt. Now their lives will never be the same." She was shocked to feel the weight of tears in her eyes. "Lila's life will never be the same."

"So how will it be?" Owen asked.

"Different, moron," Wyatt said.

"She's grounded," Scottie said. "That's like time-out."

"She's grounded because we love her and we want to keep her safe," said Luz.

"She doesn't like being grounded."

"It will give her a chance to think about how she's going to change her life."

Scottie's mouth turned down at the corners. "I don't want Lila to change. I want my same Lila."

"She'll always be your same Lila. And look at it this way—you'll get to see even more of her."

"Because she'll never see the light of day again." With that matter-of-fact pronouncement, Scottie filled his fork with macaroni and cheese. They all fell quiet and finished dinner, more subdued than usual. Wyatt cleared the table without being asked. Owen picked up his Hot Wheels and set it carefully on a shelf.

The sound of a car door slamming disturbed the too-quiet house.

"Dad's home!" Scottie dropped the spoon he was holding for Beaver to lick.

The sound of singing and laughter streamed across the yard from the carport. "Born to Be Wild" was one of Luz and Jessie's favorite road songs from childhood. Luz hadn't heard it in years. Even Ian was singing off-key as they walked to the house and came inside.

Standing in the kitchen, Luz froze.

"You changed your life, Lila," Scottie said.

"She changed her hair, moron," Wyatt said, staring.

"It's like Aunt Jessie's," said Owen.

Jessie grabbed Lila's arm and drew her into the light. "Well?" She turned in a parody of a runway model's slouch, taking Lila with her. "What do you think?"

"You look weird," Owen said.

"Then she fits right in with the rest of us, buddy." Ian grabbed him and pulled him into the kitchen to forage for food.

Luz stood rooted to the spot. Her sister and daughter looked incredible. Now that Lila had Jessie's short, layered haircut, they resembled sisters. Both wore low-slung jeans and cropped T-shirts that showed a hint of midriff, and there, above the waistband of the jeans, was—

Luz scowled, set down her dish towel and bent to have a closer look. "What's that? A stick-on tattoo?"

"I want to see the tattoo!" Scottie yelled.

Lila smiled with more true joy than she'd shown in days. "Aunt Jessie has one, too."

Together, she and Jessie displayed their wares.

"Yuck," Wyatt remarked.

Luz reeled as she regarded the tattoos of constellations. She recognized them from the old map of the night sky posted by the telescope a sponsor had given their mother one year. Pegasus for Jessie, and for Lila, Andromeda, the chained princess. "They're not stick-ons, are they?"

"I'm starved." Lila went to the table, sat next to Ian and attacked the macaroni and cheese.

"What's this about a tattoo?" Ian asked with his mouth full. Luz wanted to smack him. He was so oblivious sometimes.

"It's just tiny," Lila said. "See?"

He glared straight ahead. "No, thanks."

"You know what," Jessie said abruptly, "I have work to do. I need to go have a long talk with the Dictaphone." Before Luz could stop her, she ducked out and disappeared into the night.

Luz burned, but she kept the rage invisible and strictly under control. When had she learned to do this, to hold in the fire, keeping it banked until she chose to let it flare?

Studiously ignoring her turmoil and Lila's new look, Ian took the boys up to get them ready for bed. Lila excused herself to continue the major excavation project that was the cleaning of her room. But she did it with a song on her lips.

As was usually the case in the Benning household, life got in the way of a perfectly good crisis. Deep down, Luz preferred it that way. If she stayed busy enough, she could put off the hard stuff or leave it half finished, like everything else in her life. Homework, baths and bedtime came and went; it was after ten by the time she went upstairs to confront Ian.

He sat in his ancient, overstuffed chair by the window, reading legal briefs from a stack on the floor. Luz loved her husband, but her feelings for him were sometimes tinged with exasperation. Tonight, she was fresh out of patience. "No thanks?" she said, echoing his tone at dinner. "My sister tattoos our daughter, and all you can say is no thanks?"

He took off his reading glasses and set aside the thick document he'd been studying. "I didn't want to look at it."

"That's the problem," Luz said through a flash of anger, hearing the echoes of a thousand previous discussions in his words. "You never want to see. Especially when it comes to Lila. What is it with you, Ian? It's like you're barely there for her."

"She doesn't want me around. To her, I'm nothing but a life-support system for a wallet."

"That doesn't mean you can step down as her father."

"I know that. Hell, Lila knows that. But at her age, she doesn't need me the way she did when she was little."

"She still needs you. Damn it, you wouldn't even discuss that tattoo."

"Discussing it won't make it go away. And guess what, Luz? Getting pissed and fighting about it won't make it go away, either. It happened, okay? We can't erase it. But we can get over it."

Luz deflated onto the end of the bed. She poked idly at a basket of unfinished quilt squares she'd been piecing together for years. He came to sit by her, and the bed made a squeak of protest. The way he massaged the back of her neck never failed to soothe her, even now. "Oh, Ian," she said, "what are we going to do?"

"Hope she doesn't get any ideas about nose rings?"

She leaned her cheek on his shoulder. "You know what I mean. Jessie wants her to know about the adoption. That's really what this is about. She hasn't said anything more, but the haircut and tattoo are speaking loud and clear."

"I've never heard of a kid going haywire because she found out she was adopted," he said. "What do you want to do, Luz?"

She flopped back on the bed, exhausted. "To forget about all this for a little while."

"Now, that's something I reckon I can help with." He slid down next to her.

She knew they'd resolved nothing, but that was the magic of Ian. For these few minutes, he made her troubles cease to matter.

But they were back with a vengeance the next morning. The kids filled the house with commotion as they chomped through breakfast and got ready for school. Luz had to admit that Lila regarded the prospect of school with a more positive attitude than she had before or since the accident. Nothing like a radical new haircut and a permanent tattoo for bolstering a girl's self-confidence. Lila claimed the new design was "itchy" and she "had" to wear a cropped sweater to keep it from being chafed by her clothes.

Luz watched Lila shoulder her backpack and walk up the hill to wait for the school bus. Her heart constricted at the sight of her walking away, as small and slender and determined as she had been ten years before, heading off to kindergarten. Shaken by the image, Luz got Scottie ready for playgroup. Ian dashed off for a meeting with the ACLU and Luz drove Scottie to the church. Afterward, she endured a pained and emotional meeting at the high school with the parents of some of the students involved in the accident. She was moved and humbled by their willingness to participate and share. She captured an image of Nell Bridger holding Dig's football jersey, which she'd rescued from the impromptu shrine that had appeared in front of the school. Luz photographed Sierra's mom and the cheerleading coach sobbing with their arms around each other, and Kathy's father seated alone in the empty stands beside the soccer field, staring out at nothing but blue sky.

By the time Luz arrived home in the late afternoon, she carried other people's sadness and anger as well as her own. She strode across the property to the row of cabins facing the water. Even in the dazzling autumn sunshine, the outbuildings looked gloomy and dilapidated. She had always meant to spruce them up, and had even painted two walls of the first one, but had never gotten around to finishing. Yet already, Jessie had brought her own colorful sense of style to the place, putting a jar of autumn sage and black-eyed Susans on the windowsill, adding a fringed fuchsia shawl as a swag over the window facing the lake.

Luz knocked once and stepped inside. "Hey."

"Hey, yourself." Jessie sat at the table, her chin propped in one hand, a cup of coffee dangling from the fingers of the other. She wore a dress of deep turquoise and a pair of buff-colored cowboy boots that would have been a fashion crime on anyone but Jessie. Blair's recorder sat in the middle of the table. Jessie touched a button to shut it off. "I was working on the article."

All right, thought Luz. They could do their usual dance and talk around this, or plunge right in. Maybe the intensity of her day had affected her. She felt like plunging.

Even so, she forced herself to take a seat slowly and speak calmly. "In what universe is it okay to permanently mark a child who doesn't belong to you?"

Jessie was equally calm and even more implacable. "In what universe is it okay to keep a kid from knowing she's adopted?"

"We discussed this before she was born. You agreed—hell, Jess, you *told* me it would be best not to tell her. And now you're mad because we did exactly what you wanted?"

"Oh, Luz. This is not the sort of thing you get mad about."

"True. It's the sort of thing that calls for permanent disfigurement. Got it."

"Oh, yeah, you get every fucking thing right, Luz," Jessie exploded. "You always do, you with your perfect family and your perfect life."

Luz was too stunned to do anything but gape in disbelief. Jessie was blowing up at her? Then the true impact of the accusations slammed into her, and she buried her face in her hands, howling with laughter. "My perfect life," she gasped, feeling the tears flow.

"You have it all, you're always right, and I'm the flake, gallivanting around the world like a loose cannon."

"My wonderful falling-down house, my husband who's never home. My tattooed daughter, my learning-disabled son." Catching Jessie's expression, she laughed again, verging on hysteria.

"Owen," she explained. "And that's only one of the things you don't know about my perfect life." She stole a sip from Jessie's mug. "God, do you know what I'd give to gallivant? To have a career, a life outside of Edenville, Texas? To see the things you've seen?"

"Luz. You don't want what I've got. Believe me, you don't."

"How would you even know what I want or don't want?" She stood and paced in agitation. Her heart pounded and she realized deep down what was going on. "You're making me compete with you for her."

"What?"

"For Lila. You gave her to me, and now you're taking her away. I had no idea she was on loan."

"Oh, for Chrissake, Luz—"

"You're dazzling her. Sweeping her off her feet. I'm grounding her and making her clean her room while you're taking her to day spas and getting tattoos. Christ, Jessie, don't you think it's hard enough on me to keep her in line without you waltzing in and doing the Auntie Mame thing?"

"Funny you should mention Auntie Mame. Isn't she the one who took her nephew traveling the world?"

"Jess, if you think for one minute you're going to take that girl away, you're dead wrong." Luz planted her feet. She realized that she would sacrifice anything for the sake of Lila. Even her sister. That struck her hard. She would do battle with Jessie if it came down to that.

"Don't even think what you're thinking, Luz. I'm not here to take Lila anywhere."

"You don't have to. For you it's enough to know that she wants to follow you, that she's willing to. She worships you."

"She worships Dave Matthews, too, but that doesn't mean she wants to follow him all over the world. Look, you're her mother. That's the way it's supposed to be. But sometimes—Damn it, Luz, you're so busy being the mother that you forget to be anything else."

"What the hell else is there? It's all I know, Jess. It's not like we were raised by June and Ward Cleaver. I'm making it up as I go along."

"Textbook, Luz. You're forever the mom, and I'm the screwup kid sister."

"Hey, if the shoe fits."

"You know, in your quest to control every possible situation, you're overlooking something, Luz."

"What's that?"

"Lila."

"What the hell is that supposed to mean?"

"You're so busy regulating her life, tracking her grades, monitoring her every move and worrying about her that you forget she's a unique individual."

"That's not true. I resent you coming here, fifteen years after the fact, telling me how to raise my daughter."

"What's her favorite rock group? Her favorite teacher? What stresses her out? Did you know Heath broke up with her and found Jesus?"

That stopped her. "What?"

"That's why she couldn't stay at school. That's why she needed a day away."

"Is that why she needed a tattoo?"

"Maybe *I* needed the tattoo."

"For the love of God, Jess. You already have one."

"Three. I already had three. Now I have four."

"Did you think disfiguring my child would force me to tell her she's adopted?" Luz demanded.

"Nobody's forcing you to do a thing, Luz." Jessie stood and gave the blinds a twist, shutting out the afternoon light. "Coming here was a bad idea."

"Don't you dare say that." Luz hated this feeling—that the foundations of her world were cracking under her feet, and she had to figure out where to jump for safety. "Ah, Jess. I don't want to fight with you. I just wish you'd check with me before doing anything permanent to my kids."

The sound of tires crunching on gravel interrupted them. Luz frowned. "We weren't expecting anyone."

"I was." Jessie put a nervous hand to her hair.

Luz looked out to see Dusty Matlock heading toward the house. When she glanced back at Jessie, she saw something in her sister's face that she'd never seen before, ever. It was a stark, naked emotion so powerful and private that Luz looked away. *Finally,* she thought, feeling some of her anger at Jessie slip away.

Finally. Her little sister was falling in love. It seemed rash to conclude that so early on, but Luz knew she wasn't mistaken. As Jessie watched Dusty coming up the walk, Luz recognized herself watching Ian come home to her. At such moments, a woman's heart filled so full that her expression could not hide what she was feeling.

She liked everything about Dusty Matlock—his mannerisms, his looks, his kid and especially the way he treated her sister. Yet her anger didn't dissipate because Dusty showed up. Luz was finally working to a full head of steam. Jessie's having a date didn't dampen it. The fight stayed open and she fully expected a hangover of emotion and guilt. "So we'll talk about everything later."

"Whatever."

Lila's favorite expression. It was so perfect for people who wanted to be vague and noncommittal. She wasn't through with her sister or this conversation, but it was pointless to pursue it now. She pushed Jessie to the door and opened it.

"My mother wants to meet you," Dusty said, emerging from a veil of shadows cast by the live oaks.

Jessie grabbed Luz's arm. "Oh God, you don't think he's got her with him, do you?"

"Let's go see."

All that had passed between them shimmered briefly and then slid away, burying itself beneath a new moment with a new problem.

"Your mother?" Jessie inquired as Dusty bent to kiss her cheek. "That sounds ominous." Her voice was light, and Luz sensed her sister's profound pleasure at his nearness and familiarity.

"Hey, Luz." He doffed his Matlock Aviation baseball cap in a curiously old-fashioned gesture.

"What's this about your mother?" she asked, raising an eyebrow at him.

"She wants to meet Jessie."

This was getting better and better. "Really. Why?"

"Because Jessie is all I can talk about or think about these days. My mother and I even hunted down back issues of *World Explorer* magazine to see more of her work."

"You're crazy, Matlock," Jessie said.

"Could be," he said. "A little."

She clung to Luz's hand, and Luz suspected she was only half pretending terror. "Don't make me go with him. Don't make me go with the bad man."

"Nonsense." Luz propelled her toward the truck. "You're good at being bad."

"I like that in a woman."

"The other day, you said you liked your women bossy," Luz reminded him.

"Bossy and bad." He winked at Luz.

Jessie made a sign against evil, though she edged closer to the truck. Even as Luz laughed at Jessie's display, she felt a small twist in her heart. This was all in fun, sure, but when a relationship stopped being fun and started feeling like hard work, Jessie tended to disappear.

Don't blow it this time, Jess.

"Where are you going?" Luz asked Dusty. "Are you really taking her to meet your mother?"

"I think I'll save that for another time, when we can spend more time with the old girl."

"Oh, I'm all for that," Jessie said. Then, unexpectedly, she touched Luz on the shoulder. "Are we still fighting?"

Luz hesitated. The Lila issue was not a fight, it was much deeper, more complicated than that. So complicated that she did what she did best—put it aside to worry about later. She answered Jessie's question with one of her own. "Are we still breathing?" She pushed her toward Dusty. "Go. I'll see you later."

Dusty opened the door of his truck for Jessie. "Do you like Mexican food?"

She looked faint with relief. "I adore Mexican food."

"Vaya con dios," said Luz, then stepped back to watch them go.

CHAPTER 26

Jessie fastened her seat belt. She noticed Amber's car seat had been removed. Walking around the truck, Dusty said something else to Luz, but Jessie couldn't make out the words. She couldn't stand having Luz mad at her. What had she been thinking?

She hadn't been thinking. It was always that way with her. She'd always been governed by impulse rather than caution. Particularly yesterday. She'd been given a glimpse of a future she didn't want to face, and had needed to do something crazy that didn't involve firearms or strong narcotics. So she'd tattooed Lila.

And then she'd been surprised to discover Luz disapproved.

As Luz went to the main house, Dusty got in the driver's side. Instead of starting the engine, he slid over on the seat, passing one arm behind her and lowering his mouth to hers, his manner brisk, almost businesslike, but at the same time absurdly sexy.

His kiss was a long indulgence, the feel and taste of him so good that she nearly wept with the pleasure of it. He had a way of putting everything into his kiss—unspoken promises, unvoiced feelings, maybe even dreams. His hand stole inside her blouse. At length he pulled back, leaving her reeling, on fire, aching.

"I've wanted to do that since the first moment I laid eyes on you," he said.

"Do what?" she asked.

"Put you in my truck and feel you up."

"You're such a pervert, Matlock."

"And that's one of my better qualities." With exaggerated reluctance, he disengaged himself from her and slid behind the wheel. Resting his hand at the top of the steering wheel, he said, "Damn. I missed you."

A shiver passed over her. No one had ever spoken to her like this before—directly, honestly. She'd never met anyone like him. He was completely free of pretense. He had survived an unspeakable tragedy and was prepared to go on from there. And when he held her in his arms, he made her feel like the center of the world.

He started the engine and headed up the hill. "I practically had to hog-tie my mother to keep her from coming back here with me to check you out."

"I'm having trouble picturing you hog-tying your mother," she said.

"To tell you the truth, it can't be done. Louisa Tate Matlock is a force of nature. She's dying to meet you."

"Why?"

He reached over and touched her cheek. "You know why, honey."

The possibility that she actually did know why struck her speechless. This was too bizarre. She had managed to live half her life without ever feeling this way, this tumbling glorious, magical way, and now all of a sudden, she did. It was as frightening and as exhilarating as a roller-coaster ride. Except that when you were on a roller coaster, you knew it would be over soon.

Ah, she wanted this. It had taken her half a lifetime to find a man like this, but he'd come along at the wrong time.

He passed the turnoff for his house and kept going. She stayed silent, perversely enjoying the uncertainty of it all. Even when he rolled to a halt at the County Airpark, she didn't allow herself to question him.

"Do you want to know where we're going?" he asked.

"There's no point in my asking," she said.

"Why not?"

"Because my answer is the same no matter what."

"Yeah? What's your answer?"

She placed her hand in his. "Yes."

CHAPTER 27

"I can't believe you brought me to Mexico," Jessie said.

Dusty savored a gulp of his Tecate, the top of the cold can flavored with a squeeze of lime and a shake of salt. "You said you wanted Mexican food for dinner."

Across the round enameled metal table, Jessie looked beautiful, with the night breeze playing with her hair as they shared a meal at the outdoor café. She was excited and maybe a bit sad, and Dusty wondered why. He was glad he'd brought her here. The lone immigration official at the airfield didn't require a passport so long as you had ID and a twenty-dollar bill, but as it turned out, Jessie was in the habit of keeping her passport in her handbag.

It was a perfect Mexican night, the air cool and clear enough to make a roof of stars, the smells and sounds both familiar and foreign.

She squeezed a lime wedge over the top of her beer can. "I love Mexican food. I love Mexico."

I love you. He leaned back in the flimsy folding chair and felt the truth of it in his whole body and soul. No matter how he tried to rationalize or tell himself it was too soon, the fact was as clear to him as the stars in the night sky. There was a certainty within him that he had learned, perhaps with his pilot's instincts, to trust. The rightness of it settled in his heart. She was the one. They were going to be together. He couldn't imagine life without her.

But he didn't want to tell her right now. She'd think he was nuts for bringing it up so early in their relationship. For the time being, he kept the words tucked in his heart like a gift he'd bought and was waiting for the right moment to give her.

And then there was the small matter of whether or not she loved him. He figured she did but didn't know it yet. She was going to, though. That was something else he knew with unapologetic arrogance.

There were a few practical considerations, he reflected. She had to want to be Amber's mother. If she didn't, well, that was a deal breaker. But when he saw the way Jessie was around the baby—caught up in wonder and caring—his hopes soared.

"You're awfully quiet," Jessie pointed out.

"Just enjoying the atmosphere. Candela is one of my favorite towns. I come here a few times a year, just because I can."

She held out her arms as if to embrace the zocalo, a collection of colorful shops and restaurants clustered around the colonial heart of the town. "It's fabulous. How did you discover it?"

"One of Arnufo's nephews works at the air tower over at the landing strip. He makes sure I get a warm welcome every time I head down here."

"Good to know. So no one thinks you're a drug dealer."

"Not that I know of. Who needs drugs?" The proprietors of the café, whom he'd known since he started coming here, tried not to hover and stare, but Felix and Yolanda Molina were too old and cheerful to be subtle. This was the first time he'd brought a woman here, and they were treating Jessie like visiting royalty.

Yolanda had created a feast of roasted peppers stuffed with spicy rice and piñones, chiles rellenos that made him want to howl at the moon and enchiladas sizzling on a hot plate. They ended with sopapillas drenched in honey and cinnamon. Jessie shut her eyes and offered a blissful smile. "I'm going to have to go to confession after that."

"I didn't know you were Catholic."

"I'm not, but I have plenty to confess."

He sensed a solemnity deep beneath the words. "Yeah?"

"You don't want to know."

"Sure I do."

"No, I mean you *really* don't want to know."

"Now you're going to have to tell me for sure."

She shivered a little, pressed her palms flat on the surface of the table. "I don't think so."

He suspected that this was her routine, refusing to share or surrender or open herself to vulnerability. He was about to ask her to dance, to sweep her away and, he hoped, chase the troubled shadows from her face, but something stopped him. "Think again, senorita. I'm your ride home, and if you don't say what's on your mind, I'll leave you to help Yolanda wash the dishes. So spill. Tell me your deepest, darkest secret."

She narrowed her eyes at him. "You first."

He hesitated. Maybe he shouldn't have brought this up.

"Come on, Matlock," she said. "You started this. Spill."

He took another drink of his beer. What the hell. If they were going to be in love, they had to share the hard stuff, the things you confess only to the people you trust. "I'm scared of my own daughter."

Dusty felt as shocked as Jessie looked. He hadn't expected it to be so easy to admit. Maybe it was the beer, the atmosphere or the fact that he was falling in love, but he was finding it impossible to hold anything back from her. "What I mean is, I'm scared something bad is going to happen to her. Every minute. I've been her only parent, and I feel totally out of my depth. If not for Arnufo, I might've done something nuts...handed her over to my sisters or my mom to raise."

"How is that nuts?"

He grinned ruefully. "You haven't met my sisters or my mom. Anyway, when a baby comes along, you do what's best for the kid, not for yourself. I'm raising her because it's the right thing to do."

"Do you disapprove of people who give their babies away?"

"Hell, no. Sometimes it's the best possible choice. But it wasn't for me and Amber. And you're stalling. Come on, Jess. Deepest, darkest. Your turn."

"I had a baby, once, too." The words exploded from Jessie like bubbles from a champagne bottle.

Damn. Maybe she was right. Maybe he really didn't want to know.

She smiled with false sweetness. "Aren't you glad you asked?"

Okay, he thought. This was a test. How bad did he want to love her? Bad enough to take on her burden of sadness? "You feel like talking about it?" he asked.

"It's not mine to tell."

"It's yours, honey. It happened to you." He took her hand in his, stared at their entwined fingers on the chipped enamel table. He felt such tenderness for this woman. She moved him and aroused his finest instincts to comfort and cherish.

She pressed her lips together, then took a deep breath. "I was twenty-one, a senior in college. Gave birth to a baby girl. She was premature, and no one thought she would make it, least of all me. I walked out of the hospital that day and never looked back. I had this weird notion that if I interfered in any way I'd put her chance of survival in jeopardy."

"And she survived," he concluded, not even needing confirmation. "Then what?"

"I can't say any more. This is private stuff."

She drew her hand away and tucked it in her lap. And then, Dusty knew. He reeled, picturing the sullen teenaged girl who'd been giving her family hell. "Damn. Lila."

A single tear tracked down her cheek. "Dusty, you can't say a word."

He frowned. "You mean it's a secret?"

She nodded, tightening her hands into fists in her lap. "When she—when it first happened, I thought...my baby would be better off not knowing about me."

He couldn't imagine not telling Amber about Karen one day. "What do you think now?"

"I don't know." She sipped her beer. "I came home wanting to see her, but my reasons were selfish. I have to figure out what's best for Lila. If we tell her I gave birth to her, she's going to want to know who fathered her, and no one but me knows that."

"Double damn and holy shit, woman. You do have a few issues in your life."

She brushed at her cheek. "You don't know the half of it."

"So tell me the other half."

She hesitated, shifting her gaze away. "I can't. People will be hurt by this."

"You're hurting now, Jess. Talk to me. It helps, I swear it. Those things I told you about Karen—I kept them inside me too long. And after I leveled with you—even with Blair—it didn't seem so bad."

A long inhalation shuddered through her. "It's not like I planned it. I knew Ian before he met Luz. It was nothing. A fling. We had a few laughs, and then we parted ways and forgot the whole thing."

He kept his expression neutral, but it took an effort. "I reckon a fling with you would amount to more than a few laughs, but maybe that's just me."

"It's just you. A few weeks after we parted ways, he met Luz. God, Luz was so happy. I'd never seen her in love before. When we were growing up, she was always the worrier. Our mom wasn't around much, so Luz pretty much gave up being a kid and devoted herself to taking care of us. Then when Ian came along, he made all that go away. It was a magical thing to see. Luz in love was an entirely new person. It was the first time I actually saw the power of love transform a person."

Her breath caught. "Ian and I never mentioned the past. He and Luz made wedding plans right away, and I was accepted for a photography fellowship overseas." She smiled with self-deprecation. "For about five whole minutes, it appeared both Luz and I were finally getting the lives we wanted. Then I found out I was pregnant. I went into a sort of controlled panic. And the guilt knocked me over. Here I was, twenty-one and pregnant by the guy my sister was about to marry. I had always been a wild child, but this surpassed even my standards."

For a moment, Dusty wondered if this meant she wouldn't accept Amber. But he knew instantly there was no chance of that. He could imagine her heartache and confusion back then. She was a different person now, with a heart so ready to love that she had turned her back on the only life she knew in order to come home to her family.

"Trust me, other twenty-one-year-olds have done worse," he said.

She pulled her hand out from under his and took a quick sip of her beer. "As always, Luz came to the rescue. She offered to adopt the baby and Ian agreed. Going by the calendar, he knew there was a possibility it was his. He asked me, and I denied it." She aimed a challenging glare at Dusty. "Nice, huh?"

"I figure you had your reasons."

"If I named him as the father, Luz would have given him up. He would have done the right thing by me and we would have spent the last sixteen years making each other—and our daughter—miserable. Telling the truth would have shattered my sister's world."

"Then you shouldn't have any regrets, Jess. Luz and Ian are great, from what I can tell. Lila's with her natural father and has a stable, loving family."

"I know. I couldn't be more thankful, couldn't have given my baby a better life. But I should have stayed away. I've never been anything but trouble, and this stuff with Lila proves it. When I was young, being a free spirit was fun. Now it's getting old. *I'm* getting old. But Lila... Seeing her again is the only thing that makes sense to me these days. I gave her life, then gave her up. Never let myself think about what I flung into the world, what I let go of sixteen years ago. Now it's all I think about. When you showed up this afternoon, Luz and I were arguing about her. I took Lila out for a day in the city, spoiled her rotten." She touched her midsection, covered by a blue-green dress. "We got tattoos. I wanted to have something in common with her."

He tried to picture Amber at sixteen, getting a tattoo on her belly. "Probably not the best choice for a souvenir."

"I know." She finished her Tecate. "So, Dr. Matlock," she said in an exaggerated German accent. "The patient is a hopeless case, no?"

"You're all going to be fine. You and your sister and Lila."

"Right." She set her empty can on the edge of the table. He caught it before it fell.

"You know what's scary?" she asked him. "I made a point of staying away from Lila for as long as I could. Until I showed up, she'd never met me and hardly knew a thing about me. I was colorful, globe-trotting Aunt Jessie who sent her postcards with exotic postmarks and the occasional e-mail from Internet cafés in Kathmandu or Kuala Lumpur. But even so, she's like me in a lot of ways. It's creepy."

"The kid didn't sneak out and get into a wreck because she's related to you, or because you came to see her. Believe me, that was something that had been brewing for a long time."

"How would you know?"

"Vivid memories of my own misspent youth. Look, whatever's bugging that girl didn't happen overnight. It's not your fault, it's not your sister's fault. It's the fault of hormones and youth."

"Actually," she said, "it's more like brain damage."

"Say what?"

"It turns out that one of the reasons a teenager is so reckless is that her brain—the prefrontal cortex, to be exact—is still immature. The part that controls judgment, emotional moderation, organization and planning is not fully developed. Which explains why teenagers do the crazy things they do. The good news is, if they survive adolescence, the brain matures and they're likely to settle down. I found that out when I was researching an article about the wreck for Blair LaBorde."

"So you're a writer, too?" he asked, impressed.

"Lately."

"Good. I'll be your number one fan." He saw new depths in her now. She'd had a child—Lila—and yet she had never been a mother. That aspect of her both fascinated and touched him. And not once did he doubt that she had the capacity to love a child. She'd just never had the chance. "Look, I don't see the conflict here. You did a selfless thing, keeping Ian in the dark so he wouldn't have to choose between you and your sister. Luz did a selfless thing, adopting your baby. You're both trying to do right and you love each other. That doesn't mean it's going to be easy. You've made mistakes and you'll have to live with them, like everyone else."

She propped her chin in her hand and let out an exaggerated sigh. "Will you marry me?"

He grinned. "Tomorrow."

She stood and lifted the hair from her nape. "Then we'd better go rehearse for the wedding night."

He rose and held out one hand, palm up. "Come here, senorita."

As the mariachis strummed the last tribute of the night, he took her in his arms, this fine, beautiful, tattooed woman he wanted so badly in his life, and he danced with her. He was a lousy dancer, hopelessly out of practice, but he knew how to hold a woman in his arms and how to move with a slow, deliberate suggestion of what he really wanted to do.

"I've got something of my own to confess," he said, and leaned down to whisper into her ear.

"I don't speak Spanish very well," she whispered back.

"I'll tutor you."

The mariachis' soft lament ended with a shimmer of sound.

Dusty paid Felix in American dollars and took her hand. It was a short walk to the Posada Santa Maria, where they were staying the night.

The sleepy desk clerk nodded to them as they passed beneath a stone archway to an inner cloister, arranged in a square around a shadowy garden. Jessie's face shone as they crossed the torch-lit courtyard, where they paused to admire the poinsettias blooming in profusion.

Jessie seemed drawn to a vast climbing vine espaliered along one wall. "Honeysuckle," she said. "Oh, and jasmine. It smells like heaven here." She nearly tripped over the bent figure of a man who straightened up in time to move out of the way.

"Excuse me," Jessie said, then added in rudimentary but adequate Spanish, "I didn't see you there."

"*De nada,* senorita." The workman doffed his cloth cap in greeting. By explanation, he gestured at a flat of plants he was setting in the ground.

"Good night, senor," Dusty said, and guided Jessie toward their room. "You're quiet," he remarked.

"I never thought of someone growing flowers in the dark before."

He laughed softly and kissed her, then led her into the small, rather plain room. He took out his wallet and searched for a condom. Damn. He'd used up his supply the other night and hadn't replaced them. Not surprisingly, he'd fallen out of the habit of looking after this aspect of dating.

"Is something wrong?" asked Jessie.

"No condoms. And I doubt there's an all-night drugstore in this town."

She laid a hand on his arm. "I've been on the Pill. And it's safe. I would never put you at risk, Dusty."

He pulled her to him and kissed her again, his fingers finding the buttons down the back of her dress. He pulled back momentarily to point out an old-fashioned holy water font affixed to the wall.

"We're in a nun's room, aren't we?" she said.

"I think so." He slipped the dress off her shoulders, down her arms.

"Then we're both going to need confession."

"You never know." He bent lower to skim his lips across the lacy edging of her bra. She swayed against him, and threaded her fingers into his hair. Everything inside him seemed to rise up because of that simple, age-old caress, one he hadn't felt in far too long. He shucked his clothes fast, then sank down on the bed, bringing her with him. Leaning against the headboard, he pulled her against his chest and settled his mouth over hers.

Dusty had always liked sex. He liked the way a woman smelled and tasted. He liked the way her skin felt and her breathing sounded in his ear. None of that had died with Karen. But now his liking for sex was a consuming need because it wasn't some vague, generalized discontent that kept him awake, night after night, half inclined to call some of those numbers his mother was always leaving him. That restlessness was over now. After a long spell of indifference, his passion settled on Jessie, and Jessie alone. The notion brought a deep and calm satisfaction to his soul, and when he stopped kissing her, he was content, for the moment, to sit and hold her, savoring her warmth and her smell. A few times in his life, he had felt himself going in a direction that felt exactly right. He knew it in his gut—it was right.

"What?" she asked. "You're too quiet, all of a sudden."

"I was remembering a landing emergency I was once forced to make."

"You must find me very inspiring, then." But there was a smile in her voice when she spoke.

"I was making a run over the Chitina in Alaska, and the valley was blocked with unforecast snow squalls. I was trying to get home before dark. At first, I had a tight little visibility circle, but then the visibility shrank to nothing. Cabin lights failed, too. It was me and the darkness. Visual flight rules were out the window. I was flying blind."

She shivered against him and clung tighter. "So you managed to land."

"Sometimes I don't think it was a hundred percent me. It was sort of eerie. I didn't have a choice. I had to find a way."

"Trust the force, Luke," she said, and her poor imitation made him smile.

"There were one million ways to fail and only one safe landing. I remember seeing the northern lights that night, the way the stars shone through the green and blue streaks. Somehow, I found that one safe place to land." He put his hand on hers, curling his fingers. "That's you, Jessie."

"Your landing strip? Sounds kinky."

"Oh, it is." He played with her lacy, sexy bra, edging it downward. "Ever been in love, Jess?"

"No." Her answer was swift, certain. "I'm not hardwired for it."

"Sure you are." He grinned at her expression. "You've been waiting for me to come along."

Then he reached up with one hand and clicked off the light. Pressing her down to the mattress, he stopped her soft sputter of protest with a long kiss. He liked this silence with her, liked the feel of her hands moving over his face, his neck his shoulders, liked the way they spoke without words. Touching her filled in the spaces where words were not enough; making love expressed things with hands and mouth that he knew she'd understand.

Jessie cherished the darkness. When Dusty made love to her, he opened her to a world of sensation and emotion that had been hidden to her in the bright light of day. There, in the black velvet night, she felt the moist curve of his lips, covering hers; the silky muscled shoulder beneath her sliding hand; the taste of him and the way he touched her so that magic happened. Hurts melted, worries subsided and even the persistent pounding fear of the unknown softened to the rhythmic swish of her own heartbeat.

Deep in the shadows, sex took on new dimensions. Her senses heightened and sharpened until she was overwhelmed. She felt an ecstasy so piercing that it hurt, yet at the same time, his tenderness created in her a haven of hope. She fell into a new form of sensuality, maybe even a spirituality that had its own sort of beauty. In his arms, she found a night garden, a place blooming with a beauty that could not be seen, but must be discovered by deeper senses. Sight could add nothing to the moment.

This was it, she realized. Her heart was going to break. All her life, she'd worked so hard to keep it from happening. She'd pushed people away and fled from them, and all that time, she never knew she was running straight into the arms of this man.

CHAPTER 28

The dawn flight home gave Jessie a dazzling glimpse of the lost maples of Eagle Lake through her narrowing field of vision. The plane swooped from the south to north over the lake, a blue mirror reflecting the cruciform shape of the wings and fuselage, racing over the landscape. The bigtooth maples had turned to russet and sunset, a fire of color amid the dust and sage of the surrounding countryside.

Will I remember this? she wondered, the palm of her hand pressed to the window. Terror and a floating sense of unreality held her silent, yet her thoughts raced. Will I keep this with me, somewhere inside? Or did images fade from the mind like old photographs unpreserved by chemical fixatives? She tried to stop thinking about the fact that this was all going away. After today, she promised herself, there would be plenty of time to wallow.

"You're quiet." Dusty's comment vibrated with the cabin noise.

She took a second to compose her features, then shifted in her seat to face him. In the middle of everything that was happening to her, he was a well of strength and sweetness and joy. Yet like the sweeping vistas of color below, he would soon cease to be real to her, except in some invisible place inside her. "After a date like that, there isn't much to say."

With an endearing, cocky grin, he flipped some switches to prepare for landing. "It wasn't half bad, was it?"

Her whole body responded to him in a wave of craving for physical intimacy. She realized that Dusty was absolutely right about her—she could love him. Unlike her haphazard years with Simon and her flings in foreign lands, this love affair could be different, were the circumstances different. But he'd already loved and lost a wife. Even Jessie wasn't so selfish that she'd hand him the disaster her life was about to become. The only honorable thing to do was to end this before any real damage was done.

But it was too late. Crazy as it seemed, she already loved him.

Though he hadn't said anything specifically, she knew he believed they were going to be together, maybe for a very long time. Maybe forever. He wanted her to become Amber's mother and Jessie yearned to fling herself into their lives. But she resisted the urge.

Like so many other times in her life, she'd reached a crossroads. Like so many other times, she knew she had to go. The difference being, this time would break her heart because what she was leaving behind was all so precious to her—not only Dusty and Amber, but Lila and Luz and the boys. She was entering a world where Dusty didn't belong and would never want to. He had his own life to live, a daughter to raise. The last thing he needed was a blind woman to deal with.

After he drove her back to Broken Rock, she gathered her courage and said, "There's something I need to tell you."

"What's that, gorgeous?"

She nearly choked, getting the words out. "I can't see you anymore."

Standing at the door to her quarters, he hugged her. "Not funny," he said.

"I'm not trying to make a joke."

"Good. Because I'm not laughing."

She wished he wasn't touching her. She wished he would never stop touching her. Extricating herself from his arms, she took a step back. "I never planned on— The fact is, I won't be staying around here much longer."

"You're starting to piss me off, Jess."

"I have that effect on people. Just ask my sister." She felt strangely light-headed, as though she might float away any second. Every word she spoke felt torn from her heart. "Moving on is what I do," she continued. "It's what I've always done."

"What's out there, Jessie, that's got you so all-fired eager to leave?"

"My life." She had hurt many people. Disappointed many people. But she'd always survived the guilt, knowing their hurt and disappointment would fade. She didn't feel that way with Dusty. They had already become part of each other. Leaving him now would scar them both. But staying around would destroy them. "I've got plans. I have to go."

"You're making a mistake."

"It's mine to make."

He took both her hands. "I won't let you go."

"You can't stop me." She pulled away from him.

He was quiet for long moments. Uncannily she could feel the emotions emanating from him—confusion, tenderness, anger, disappointment. *Love.*

Get out now, she silently urged him. Run for cover, before everything falls apart. "Look," she said, struggling to see him, "you need to get home and see that adorable daughter of yours."

"Let's both go see her."

She understood his meaning. He wanted her to cuddle up to Amber. He knew how easy it would be for Jessie to give her heart to the baby. "I can't," she said in an aching whisper.

"You have to. Last night I told you the truth about myself, but I didn't tell you everything."

"What else is there to tell?"

"When Amber was born, I thought I'd have this instant bond with her. But I had a secret."

Fascinated, Jessie fluctuated between the need to know and the need to go.

"There was no instant bond. There was no instant love."

"Are you kidding?" Jessie said, wishing she didn't understand him so well. "You worship that child, and vice versa."

"I learned to do that, Jess, but the way I was loving her wasn't enough. I was...it's hard to describe. I felt so awkward with her, confused and scared, like I told you, and she knows. When things get tough for Amber—you haven't seen one of her epic tantrums yet—she turns to Arnufo, not me. Never me."

He slid his arms around her. "The day I met you, I knew this was going to change. I can't quite put my finger on it, but I'm more easy around her. I want to relax and enjoy loving her, not just worry about her all the time. It's a subtle thing, Jess, but with you in my life, everything's different. Better."

She stepped back, extricating herself from his embrace. "Good lord, don't put that on me. I'm not Mary Poppins."

"True. She left, and you're staying." He laughed at her expression, not knowing it was a mask for heartbreak. "I want you to know, I'm so ready to love you, Jess, and it's making me a better person—a better father."

"Let me get this straight." She honed a sharp edge on her voice. "You want me to stick around so you'll be nicer to your kid."

"You know better than that, damn it."

"You should head home to your daughter," she reminded him.

Pulling her toward him, he kissed her hard, possessively, then walked back to his truck, boots crunching on the dry gravel of the driveway. "I'm not amused by this, Jess," he said over his shoulder. "I'll be back tonight to discuss it."

I won't, she thought, but didn't say so aloud. She stood listening to him go. She could only see him by turning her head and finding a clear field in the lower part of her right eye. As she had with the fiery maples, she tried to fix the image in her mind, as though he were an old photograph she knew she'd study again and again. She couldn't tell whether or not he was waving goodbye, so she lifted her hand, held it there for a moment, then touched her fingers to her lips and finally her heart. Then she went to her cabin to phone for a ride.

Luz's kitchen was the scene of cheerful confusion, the normal state of affairs each morning. As Jessie stepped inside, she was seized by both terror and urgency to leave soon. Moving through striations of light and darkness, detail and shadow, she found Luz at her command post—the butcher block kitchen island. The boys were eating cereal at the table, the younger ones listening, enraptured, as Wyatt read a Harry Potter adventure from the back of the Cheerios box.

"How are things at Mission Control?" Jessie asked, walking into the kitchen.

"Controlled chaos. My specialty."

Jessie tried to gauge her sister's mood, but could only sense the harried energy of Luz in the morning, getting her family off for the day.

Trailing her hand along the counter, Jessie guided herself to the table. The aroma of coffee tantalized her, and she decided to help herself to a cup. Fourth cabinet over. She felt the shape of a thick china mug in her hand and carried it to the coffeepot on the counter. She hooked the tip of her finger over the rim of the mug and poured, but misjudged the flow from the carafe. Hot coffee spilled on her feet as one of the boys from the table said, "Look out, Aunt Jessie!"

She jumped back, stifling a forbidden curse. It was all she could do to conjure a self-deprecating laugh and grope for the roll of paper towels to the right of the sink. "I swear, I am such a klutz," she declared, blotting randomly at the floor. When Luz hunkered down beside her to help out, Jessie felt, along with gratitude, a pinch of resentment. "There you go, wiping up after me again. I think I should be put in time-out." She made her way over to the breakfast table and slid into a seat next to Scottie. "Is this seat taken?"

"Yup."

She tousled his hair and grinned. "I bet you never spill anything."

"Nope."

"Yeah, right." Wyatt helped himself to more Cheerios, then fixed a bowl for Jessie even though she hadn't requested it.

Luz set a fresh mug of coffee in front of her. "That must have been some date last night."

"It definitely doesn't carry a G-rating," Jessie said, with a meaningful inflection.

"Mom only lets us see G movies," Owen said.

"You have a smart mom. G stands for Good," Jessie explained, leaning over to kiss the top of her middle nephew's head.

Wyatt slurped his orange juice through a straw, making such a loud noise that Luz took the glass away from him. "You're the big brother. You're supposed to set an example."

"Want to hear me burp-sing the alphabet?" Wyatt asked.

"Yeah!" Scottie jiggled in his seat and tapped the table with the back of his spoon.

Brown paper crackled as Luz put the finishing touches on the school lunches. "Why, will you look at the time? Two minutes until bus time." Even the ever-patient Luz couldn't keep the relief from her voice.

The two older boys burst into motion, cramming backpacks, tucking shirttails, shoving last-minute permission slips at their mother to sign. They tumbled toward the door, yelling goodbye to their dad, who was still upstairs. Luz stood at the door, waiting to pitch the lunches like airdropped food-aid packets into their backpacks as they passed. She also managed to squeeze in a couple of quick kisses, and then they were gone.

Finally she sank down across the table from Jessie and heaved a happy sigh. "Life among the savages," she said.

"Am I a savage?" Scottie asked.

"Not until you learn to burp-sing the alphabet," Jessie said.

"Thanks a lot," said Luz. "Now he'll be practicing all day."

Catching her sister's flicker of annoyance, Jessie held her breath, waiting for Part Two of the Great Tattoo Debate, but Luz seemed distracted this morning. This was the way they had always fought, ever since they were small—by avoiding the issue and letting it simmer beneath the surface. The method never resolved anything, but at least it kept the peace.

Luz chucked Scottie under the chin and said, "Go finish getting ready, sport. Arnufo is going to look after you today."

"Yippee!" He fetched his sneakers from a tray by the door. Spying his sister coming downstairs, he ran right to her and plunked himself on the floor. "I need you to tie my shoes, Lila," he said, sticking out one foot.

With an exaggerated sigh, she set aside her backpack. "Whatever." Then she bent down to tie his little G.I. Joe sneakers for him. Jessie observed that, even when Lila was in the foulest of moods, Scottie could make her smile, could remind her that she was not the only person on the planet. She narrated the ritual of shoe-tying, making the bunny rabbit ears and knotting them together. She ended with a quick tickle that escalated into a shriekfest.

As Lila and Scottie played together, Luz leaned forward across the table. "So last night. Tell me."

"He took me out for Mexican food."

"I know that."

"In Mexico."

Luz clutched at her chest and pretended to faint dead away on the table. "That is hideously, unforgivably romantic."

"Isn't it, though?" A bittersweet air of wistfulness possessed Jessie. "It was an hour and a half away, in the cutest little town called Candela. We had dinner, and stayed at a colonial inn. Our room was...I barely remember it. There was a holy water font." She thought about all she'd felt last night. The new world of emotion had been a foreign country to her. The sensation of loving a man this way—in every way—overwhelmed her. "He's amazing."

"He's crazy about you, too." Luz knew something was up. Jessie could feel the waves of suspicion, as subtle as fine perfume. "So what about today?" Luz asked. "Maybe he'll take you on a little jaunt to New Orleans."

Lila helped herself to a glass of orange juice and drank it standing up, leaning against the counter. "Dusty Matlock?"

"She said she liked Mexican food, so he took her to Mexico last night," Luz explained.

"Awesome."

While Lila fixed herself a Pop-Tart, Luz bustled around, getting Scottie ready. Under her pajama top, she wore panty hose and a good gabardine skirt. Her feet were stuffed into fuzzy slippers.

"You're only half-dressed, Mom," Lila observed.

"I'll get to the other half after breakfast. Anyway, I'll be up at your school later, doing more pictures for Nell's article." She hesitated. "This is really important to me, Lila."

Lila tossed the hot pastry from hand to hand. "It's cool with me, I guess."

"Way cool," echoed Scottie.

Maybe that was it, Jessie thought with a wave of relief. Maybe Luz seemed happy today because of the photography work. Yet Jessie could feel the tension emanating from her sister.

"How about I push you in the swing until Arnufo comes?" she asked Scottie.

"Yeah!"

Jessie took his hand. "Lead the way, Superman."

He gamely led her outside, and she pushed distractedly at the swing while she experimented with her vision. The pigmentary changes Dr. Margutti had observed were taking over. Colors had lightened, giving the world around her an odd, misty beauty indicative of the end stage of her disease. She was able to think about what was happening in clinical terms. In her mind, she was still in control, matter-of-fact about the dying of the light. That was safer than trying to figure out where she really was in her adjustment. Somewhere between panic and resignation, she supposed.

She heard the sound of a car on the road. *Not yet. Not yet.*

"Arnufo's here!" Scottie left the swing like a stone from a slingshot.

Before relinquishing Scottie to Arnufo, Jessie picked up her littlest nephew, holding him under the armpits so that he was face-to-face with her. "See you around, kiddo. Take care of yourself. Remember, it's bunny-eat-bunny out there."

"Yup."

She kissed his soft, milk-and-sugar face before handing him over to Arnufo.

"You should come with us," Arnufo said.

"Come with us!" Scottie agreed as he grappled with his seat belt.

Jessie swallowed hard. "Too many things to do today," she said. "Give Dusty and Amber my love."

"That is for you to give." Arnufo went around to the driver's side and got in. They took off in a cloud of dust shot through by light from the morning sun.

It took Jessie several long minutes to get a grip before making her way back inside. Luz was wiping down the table while Lila picked at her breakfast. "I don't see why you have to get involved," she was saying. "It's not helping anything."

Jessie realized they were arguing about the article. "Will it make things worse?" she asked, taking a seat next to Lila.

She shifted in her chair. "She interferes in everything else. Why not this?"

"I'd never do anything to hurt you," Luz said. "Is this going to hurt you?"

Be honest, Jessie silently urged her.

"Because if you say yes, I'll quit right now."

Lila's hesitation shrieked with tension. "It's okay, I guess," she said at last. "You might as well. Everybody always goes apeshit for your pictures."

"I think she's secretly impressed," Jessie said to Luz. "And so gracious, too." She quickly changed the subject. "You wouldn't believe what I found out about teenagers' brains when I was researching the article." She explained what she had learned about the prefrontal cortex.

Lila acted nonchalant. "So what?"

"So it means you don't have to be naughty forever." *You don't have to be like me.*

Luz hugged her. "It means you'll grow out of it, and in the meantime, we'll love you, no matter what. That's all anybody needs," she pointed out.

"I guess," said Lila.

Luz excused herself to finish dressing. Jessie and Lila sat alone, Lila with her juice and pastry, Jessie with her cold coffee and breaking heart.

Lila stood and lifted the hem of her shirt, showing off the tattoo that had almost given her mother apoplexy. "Mine's itching a little bit," she said in a conspiratorial whisper. "What about yours?"

"Itchy. It'll go away. Regrets?" Jessie asked.

"Are you kidding?" Lila primped her hair. "I'm a new woman, didn't you know?"

"That's the attitude."

"I was totally bummed about not going to homecoming," Lila confessed. "But I've met this guy named Andy Cruz. He's a senior, training with the volunteer rescue service. He was one of the first ones on the scene of the wreck. He wants to come over to show me some stuff he found at the scene of the accident to see if any of it's mine. After everything that's happened, homecoming seems so...pointless."

"Oh, love, it's not. You're too young to be thinking like that."

"Andy's not going. And he's so totally hotter than Heath Walker you wouldn't believe it. It's not like a date or anything. And if he just shows up, and Mom and Dad are here, that's not violating my restriction, is it?"

"I'm not touching that one." Jessie made a sign against evil, only half joking. Slender and graceful, her daughter was unimaginably beautiful in so many ways. She was a volatile combination of strength and vulnerability, recklessness and caution, youthful impatience and enduring sweetness. Jessie felt a deep regret for missing out on this young lady's life, and finally she acknowledged the envy she felt toward Luz for being a part of something so much bigger and more important than all of Jessie's accomplishments combined.

She crossed the room to where the unsuspecting girl was shuffling through school papers and notebooks.

"I need to tell you something," Jessie said.

"Yeah? What's that?"

Jessie weighed the things she needed to say against the things Lila needed to hear. And she realized they were two different matters. The facts of the past were Luz's to tell—as soon as Luz knew *all* the facts.

Reaching out, Jessie smoothed her hand over Lila's hair. Something in her touch must have alerted the girl, for Lila stopped searching through her papers and stared at Jessie.

"This is a kickass haircut," Jessie said.

"Is it?"

"Yes. And Lila?"

"Yeah?"

"I've been a lot of places in my life. Seen all sorts of people, all over the world. And I want you to know that, sweetie, you're the best, most wonderful thing I've ever seen, the best thing I'll ever hope to see."

Lila shifted, ill at ease. She clearly had no idea where all the sentimentality had come from. "Um, thanks, Aunt Jessie. I, uh, better be getting to school now. The bus'll be here soon." She grabbed her school bag, then stopped in front of the hall mirror for one last peek at her new tattoo. Then, before rushing out the door, she stopped and gave Jessie a hug.

Her arms were firm, her skin soft and sweet-smelling. Jessie shut her eyes and wished she could sneak across the boundaries and take up secret residence in Lila's heart. "Love you," she whispered into the dewy smell of Lila's freshly shampooed hair.

"Love you, too," Lila replied, stepping back and heading for the door. "See you this afternoon. Bye, Daddy," she yelled. "Bye, Mom!"

"Bye, love," Jessie whispered, though she knew Lila wouldn't hear.

A moment later, Ian appeared, wearing what he only half jokingly termed his death row getup—a charcoal-colored suit with a crisp white shirt, conservative navy tie and his one pair of dress shoes. "Morning, Jess," he said, helping himself to coffee.

"Hey."

Acting slightly awkward, Ian said, "I guess I'll see you later."

"Later." She heard him leave, the screen door slapping behind him. Then she thought about what Dusty had said about love and trust and saying the hard things even when it's easier to stay silent. The only thing harder than telling the truth was living a lie. It was time. Past time. And she didn't have much of that left.

She had decided to go quietly and unobtrusively. It was what she had always done, only this time her motives weren't so selfish. She meant to spare Luz from worrying about her or, worse, from trying to control and fix what was going on. Jessie knew Luz's interference, however well-intentioned, could sabotage her plans for complete independence and sever forever the fragile ties that bound them together. There was only one more thing she needed to say. Silence was probably easier, but a stubborn part of her clung to the idea that the truth mattered. A lot.

She followed Ian outside. He was a good man who had been good to her sister for years, and Jessie was terrified of upsetting the balance. She bolstered herself with Dusty's words: *I don't see the conflict here.*

"Ian."

Gravel crunched and then he stopped walking. "Did I forget something?"

"No. I need to talk to you."

"Sure." He checked his watch. "I've got court this morning."

"You're going to want to let your associates handle it."

"What do you mean? What's wrong?"

Jessie pressed her hands on the hood of the car, feeling a faint heat from the rising sun. The days were rapidly getting shorter and cooler. "Things have been so hectic around here, but I think...we should talk about Lila."

"Luz and I agree about telling her, Jessie. But we need to pick the right time."

"I know you will. It's not my call to make." She smiled slightly, gratified by his startled reaction. "That was totally selfish of me, and I'm sorry for pushing it." Do it, she urged herself, shuffling her feet. Don't leave without saying what should have been said long ago. "I haven't leveled with you, Ian. If you and Luz tell her, she's going to want to know who her biological father is."

Even before she said the next words, the color drained from his face. Despite the difficulty she was having with her vision, she could see his Adam's apple slide up and down as realization sank in, then bolted through him like an electrical shock.

He let out a sound of rage mingled with wonder. "I'm her father."

"You've always been her father. You're her father by blood, too."

His eyes watered. "Jesus, Jess. I asked you—"

"And I looked you in the eye and said no. But I can't carry this around all by myself anymore. I'm tired, Ian. I'm sick of pretending. After the wreck, I started to think...you need to know. If not for medical reasons, then because it's the truth. Something's messing Lila up and she doesn't know why. It might mess her up even more to tell her, Ian. But I don't think so. She's nearly grown. She should know who her biological father is. It's you, Ian. I'm sorry I lied but I would do it again."

"Damn it, why? You've held this in for years, Jess. Why speak up now?"

"Because I was too chicken to say anything before. I was afraid you and Luz would be ruined by knowing. You would have felt responsible for me, and Luz would have felt betrayed by us both. We might have done something stupid like get married. Things are different now. You and Luz are rock solid."

"You think?" His color changed from shocked gray to dull red. "Aren't you?"

"Hell, how would I know? I work all the time, she's always wrapped up in some project or other, or the kids. When we see each other, it's to say 'pass the salt' or 'put the clothes in the dryer.'" He mussed his hair. "We're not bomb-proof. Something like this could—"

"You adore her. Anyone can see that. And you've always been the only one for her."

She heard him lean heavily against the car. "Holy shit," he said. Then his voice took on a sharp edge. "I can't believe you kept this from me."

"I didn't know what else to do. I still don't. It's the truth and you deserve to know. Whether or not you tell Luz is up to you. And then you and Luz should decide about telling Lila."

"Yeah." His shoulders sloped downward. He scratched his face as though a beard had sprouted there. "Yeah, okay. Luz needs to know."

"Know what?" Luz crossed the driveway to them. She handed Ian a brown bag lunch and went up on tiptoe to kiss him. Then she caught the expression on his face and stepped back.

In the heartbeat of hesitation that followed, Jessie looked at her sister, perhaps for the last time before she altered her world. This was Luz as she would always remember her—slightly disheveled, her face as open as a daisy, her expression filled with strength and caring. There was a tiny run in her stocking, and she'd broken a nail. The images stained the moment with permanence.

Ian checked his watch again, then let out an unsteady breath. "I'm going to have to get someone to cover for me at work."

"Just tell me."

"Jessie and I were talking about the fact that...we knew each other in college, Luz."

"Really? I didn't know that."

"Before I met you, I dated your sister a few times."

Luz's jaw dropped. "You're kidding."

"It didn't work out," Jessie said hastily. "It was nothing. We never gave it another thought. Then you started seeing him, and it was just...weird. So we didn't say anything."

"You're saying something now."

"We slept together," Ian said, the words sounding wrenched from him. "It was a stupid thing, and then we parted ways. I never gave it another thought until Jess..."

The silence was filled with betrayal. In the distance, a mockingbird called from the maples.

"Oh, dear god. Lila," said Luz, her face turning to stone.

Jessie nodded her head, waited.

"I swear, I never knew. Jess told me just now." Ian took her hand, and when she didn't pull away, he carried it to his lips and kissed it. "I love you, Luz." Even Jessie could hear his heart in the words. "I always have."

She took her hand back and walked around to the passenger side. "Get in the car, Ian." Without waiting to see if he complied, Luz plunked herself into the passenger seat, staring straight ahead as she fastened her seat belt. "Drive."

Tight-lipped, Ian got in and started the engine.

Before they drove off, Jessie motioned for Luz to roll down the window. Bending close to her sister, she studied her face, drawing the image into her heart. She said, "Luz, I'm so sorry."

"Your timing sucks."

Jessie wanted to explain that she couldn't wait any longer, but that would lead to more questions, so she simply said, "I know."

* * *

Luz was aware of Ian beside her, the farm and ranch report crackling from the AM radio, the empty highway snaking between the dusty, sunlit hills. And yet she felt as though she stood apart from the familiar world, thrown there by Jessie's revelation. She had taken a direct hit, and she was in shock, as though the victim of a physical assault. Although she heard Ian speaking as he drove, she couldn't focus on his words.

Then they rounded a bend in the road, and morning sunshine glared straight into her eyes. A moment later, anger thrust itself into her cocoon of numbness. The bottom was falling out of her life, and she felt powerless to fix it. The steady simmer of anger seethed through her like slow poison, waking her up to the fact that everything important to her was suddenly in jeopardy.

Jessie got everything, she thought, and got it first, even Ian. The idea burned through her in a white-hot rage. When she shut her eyes, she could see them clearly, young and laughing, enjoying each other's raw lust with no thought for the consequences.

"...just put it out of my mind," Ian was saying as he drove. "After I met you, I didn't think of it at all."

Luz realized he was talking about his long-ago affair with her sister. *Affair.* She had never consciously thought of that word in connection with Ian.

"And after you realized she was my sister," she said, feeling dizzy, oxygen-deprived. "Didn't it occur to you to tell me then?"

"To us both," he admitted. "But we hadn't seen each other in weeks. I forgot all about her." He pulled off the road at the deserted county park, where a late-autumn breeze was sweeping through the tops of the changing maples. "Listen to me, Luz. A lot of things happened to me before I met you. I got drunk and broke a guy's nose and almost got expelled from law school."

"You never told me that."

"It's not something I'm proud of or care to dwell on. I also caught a trophy bass at Lake Travis, and had my wisdom teeth out. When I was in the sixth grade, I lost a spelling bee on purpose so I wouldn't have to miss pitching in a Little League tournament. I didn't tell you those things, either. So I dated your sister and forgot her, Luz. I fell in love with you."

She stared straight ahead. His litany of things that happened before they met rang false, because nothing on the list involved her sister. Yet she believed him when he said the affair meant nothing. And she believed he was as surprised as she was upon learning the identity of Lila's father. Even so, she felt betrayed by him and Jessie both. She was devastated by the fact that her marriage had been founded on a half-truth. It might not exist at all, if she had known. Did that mean the marriage itself was inauthentic or invalid? And what about the love she felt for Ian? What was happening to that?

"We need to figure out what to say to Lila," she said.

"Why do we need to say anything at all?"

She turned on the seat to face him in disbelief. "You don't think we should tell her?"

He yanked at the knot of his tie. "It's a lot for a teenager to deal with. What's she going to think if we tell her I screwed around with your sister before I met you? She won't care about the sequence of things. Once she gets that in her head, all she'll think about is the fact that Jessie and I screwed around."

Luz winced. A deep and pounding dread filled her. Could they survive this, or had Jessie's confession only held up a magnifying glass to the flaws that were already there? "I don't like lying about this."

"Is not telling her the same as lying?"

"It was to me," said Luz.

After Luz and Ian left, Jessie returned to the empty house, hearing the friendly old creak of settling wood, the hush of the wind through the trees outside, the sucking and lapping of the waves of Eagle Lake down at the shore. She took one last stroll through the home of her chaotic childhood, marveling at how Luz had managed to transform the place into a home filled with warmth. The house had been an empty shell for them as girls. As a wife and mother, Luz filled it with love, populated it with her children, made it a haven as safe and solid as a fortress.

Jessie let go of the envy she felt for her sister. That was one piece of baggage she refused to take with her. One by one, she set aside the others: the end of her career and relationship with Simon. Her unfinished business with Lila. The fallout from dangerous secrets. And finally, her terrible yearning for Dusty. That was the hardest thing of all to surrender. At last, she'd fallen in love, but could not stay to see it through. Against her will, she was about to enter a mysterious new world, and she intended to travel light.

Still, she wanted to take a minute to say goodbye to one that she had only just begun to savor and appreciate. Even facing exile to the Beacon, she had still managed to thrive here, to allow joy into her life.

She found the old wishing jar, and tore a page from Luz's grocery list. Under the scrawled reminder to buy mouthwash and mayonnaise, Jessie scribbled a message which she doubted would be read anytime soon.

She had come here wanting to see her daughter. For her daughter to see her. Only now could she admit that what she had really sought in coming home was absolution. But there was no point in wishing for something that would never happen, only in figuring out a way to reconcile herself. It wasn't enough, nothing would never be enough, not for Jessie.

The crunch of tires on gravel reminded her of what she had to do next. She wrapped the little handwritten note around a penny, pressed her lips to it briefly and put it into the wishing jar. Then she replaced it in the cupboard and stood back to give herself one last look at Luz's collage of photographs on the wall. Squinting through the haze, she focused on the proud poses, the wide grins, the crazy costumes. The images were sewn together like a homemade quilt.

Down in the corner, she spotted a shot of her and Luz, looking so much alike that most people probably wouldn't be able to tell them apart. There was nothing extraordinary about this picture. In fact, Jessie guessed that Luz had taken the shot by setting the shutter on timer and racing to leap into the frame before it went off. They were perhaps thirteen and sixteen years of age in the picture. They filled the frame, their laughing, healthy faces turned toward the camera, their arms twined and held high in the air in a gesture of some forgotten victory, or perhaps of simple joy.

A car horn sounded, signaling that the shuttle van had arrived. The image flickered and swam away from Jessie, leaving only a smear of shadow in its wake. She quickly reached out and pressed her fingers to a photograph that had long ago imprinted itself on her heart.

"See you around, Luz," she said.

PART TWO

After

The death of reason isn't blackness, but another kind of light.
—Kathy Acker, *Pussy, King of the Pirates* (1996)

CHAPTER 29

On a cold, dry day in February, when the legendary hill country heat seemed a mere figment of the imagination, the phone rang. It was the business line in the kitchen, and Luz was busy lugging an overflowing basket of dirty clothes out to the laundry room. She decided to let the machine pick up. Ian had given her the second line as a Christmas gift. It wasn't a terribly romantic choice, but Luz had wanted it. Amazingly she had needed it. In the aftermath of Jessie's disclosure, Ian was trying hard, but dealing with the fallout from this was like putting an octopus in a box.

When *Texas Life* magazine published the article about the tragedy at Edenville, Luz's life had changed in another way. The article had been movingly written under Jessie's byline. She'd sent the piece on disk to Blair before leaving. But the true heart of the piece had been Luz's photographs. Her portraits conveyed, with honesty and sensitivity, the haunted faces of friends and survivors, of family members creating a bittersweet tribute to Dig Bridger. Those were the pictures that stayed with people. Photo editors across the country seemed to recognize this, because the calls had started coming in as soon as the piece was published.

Overhearing the speaker on the answering machine, Luz gathered that the call was in regard to agency representation. Despite the load of sweaty gym socks and ratty T-shirts, she caught herself grinning. Who would have thought an agent would be interested in her? She turned down most assignments; there was the small matter of finding enough time to become the Annie Leibovitz of Texas. But some were too intriguing to pass up, like the Luling Watermelon Thump or a documentary essay on a bereavement camp for children who had lost a parent.

It was all confusing and exciting and extraordinary. The only shadow over the entire picture was Jessie's absence, and the wreckage she had strewn in her wake.

Jessie had left as she had so many times before, giving no notice, no explanation, certainly no forwarding address. Disappearing was her specialty. Luz had a Hotmail address for her, but her messages bounced back, unretrieved by the subscriber. Luz felt justified in her anger at Jessie. Her sister had kept a terrible secret from her for years. To top it off, she'd blown back into their lives, taking Lila to the city for tattoos and sophisticated hairstyles. No one would blame Luz for her cold dismissal of Jessie.

Yet sometimes, regrets came back to haunt her. Until Jessie showed up again, or at least called, Luz wouldn't have the chance to settle things—between her and Jessie, and in her own heart.

Luz's shock about Lila's paternity had turned to anger, then hurt and now it seemed stuck there, no matter how she rationalized the matter. She couldn't control what had happened to Ian before she met him. She understood that he'd had a life before he'd met her. He'd slept with other women. What she didn't understand was why he'd never told her one of those women was her sister. Their marriage had suffered invisible damage, and neither quite knew how to repair it.

"It wasn't important," he'd said at least a dozen times. "I didn't want anything to spoil what was happening between us."

Luz refused to consider whether or not their brand-new love could have been spoiled. She and Ian skirted the topic.

Before she reached the laundry room adjacent to the garage, Luz heard someone drive up. Still lugging the basket of clothes, she stepped out onto the porch. The air nipped at her cheeks and nose, and she was grateful for the thick, warm University of Texas Longhorns sweatshirt and matching rust-colored sweatpants she had thrown on this morning. A bright winter sun glanced off the windshield of the approaching car.

For a single, hopeful heartbeat, she imagined it was Jessie, but the moment the car pulled up she knew better.

Blair LaBorde was already scolding by the time she got out of the car and rushed up the porch to greet Luz. "Put that damned laundry down, woman."

Luz obeyed, only to get another scolding. Blair checked her out from head to toe, taking in Luz's messy ponytail caught up in a scrunchie, and the ill-fitting sweat suit. "On second thought, you actually looked better holding the basket." Grabbing Luz's hand, Blair pulled her inside. "Has anyone called you yet?"

"No. Why?"

"Good. I wanted to see you in person. Hon, I love you dearly, but we really do need to get you a new outfit."

"And I was feeling so fashionable in this," said Luz.

"You're hopeless. But even you wouldn't dare wear that getup to win the Endicott Prize."

The statement didn't really register in Luz's mind. It wasn't until she had poured two cups of coffee and handed one to Blair with her usual half-packet of Sweet'n Low that the words hit her. "I beg your pardon?"

"The Endicott Prize, honey. As in the biggest award a photographer can receive." Blair beamed at her. "It's for—" she consulted a wrinkled fax "—a distinguished example of feature photography in black and white or color, which may consist of a photograph or photographs, a sequence or an album." The winners were announced at 7:00 a.m. Eastern today. Lordy, you should've seen the celebration at the office. We exploded for you."

Luz sat in stunned silence. *Distinguished* example.

"There's a study fellowship attached to the award. Well?" Blair drummed her acrylic nails on the tabletop. "Don't you have anything to say?"

Luz grinned from ear to ear. "I *rock.*"

"Oh, babe, you sure as hell do." Blair lifted her coffee mug and clinked it against Luz's.

This was so amazing, it was almost embarrassing. Luz wasn't quite sure what to do with herself. "God, I wish Jessie were here." The words came out of their own accord, telling her more plainly than daylight that she missed her sister and needed things to be right between them.

"Still haven't heard from her?"

Luz shook her head. "I want her to know. I want her to know so badly." It hit her then that telling Jessie was even more important than telling Ian, or the kids, or her mother. It was almost as though the honor wouldn't belong to Luz until she told Jessie.

"It's no great feat to track someone down," Blair suggested.

"Jessie will get in touch when she's ready. That's the way it works with us."

"What about when you're ready? Haven't you ever needed her rather than vice versa?"

The question took her aback, then forced her to wonder privately if the reason she hadn't knocked herself out to find Jessie was that she and Ian still hadn't leveled with Lila. Deep down, she was reluctant to search for her sister. Jessie had dropped the bomb about Ian, then left the issue of leveling with Lila up in the air. With Jessie gone, Luz simply let it dangle in limbo. She thought constantly about how and when to explain things to Lila.

By reading everything she could get her hands on regarding adoption and adoptive families, she took small comfort in the fact that she wasn't alone in her dilemma. So often, the issue simply wasn't addressed—particularly in families like theirs. The whole world assumed Lila was their natural daughter, and the temptation was strong to stay silent rather than risk making her feel unwanted or confused.

"I'll look into contacting Jessie." Luz gazed out the window at the flat, glassy lake. "I wish she hadn't picked that day to leave. Jessie and I quarreled. It wasn't the first time, of course, but we weren't...finished. At least, I wasn't. Apparently Jessie had other ideas."

"That's a bad way to leave things with someone you love."

"I know."

On the other side of the lake, she saw Dusty Matlock walk down to his floatplane and start the engine. A few minutes later, he took off in a sweeping arc, the spray sparkling behind him. "He was so perfect for her. So absolutely perfect." She often thought about Jessie's whirlwind romance with Dusty. What she couldn't figure out was how even Jessie could bear to leave a man who so obviously adored her. A man who had an angel for a baby and Arnufo for a live-in nanny. It was more than one woman's idea of paradise.

"Do you see much of Dusty Matlock these days?" Blair asked.

"Enough to know my sister broke his heart."

"Small comfort to his legions of fans," Blair commented. "Women still send scads of mail in care of the magazine. I offered to forward everything to him, but he declined. He also gave me permission to screen everything. That's been an eye-opener. I think my favorite so far is the pair of underwear with a marriage proposal taped to it."

Turning the topic back to the award, Blair gave Luz plenty of much-needed information and advice about managing a career in freelance journalism. It all felt a little unreal to Luz, who never thought her career would exceed family photographs or perhaps the occasional community event. Blair came up with suggestions for everything, from agents on both coasts to a makeover and shopping expedition to Neiman Marcus.

"I can't believe it. I am totally unprepared for this," Luz said.

"Now, don't go getting cold feet. Nothing I hate worse than seeing a talented artist run from success."

"I don't have a résumé," Luz wailed. "I don't even have a college degree or work history to put on a résumé."

"Honey, believe me, you've got everything you need." She gestured at the photograph wall. "Absolutely everything."

Luz invited Dusty, Arnufo and Amber over for supper that night and set the table for nine. In a perfect world, they would celebrate by going out for a nice dinner, but with her family's schedule, she'd be lucky to get them all in the house at the same time. So Lucinda Ryder Benning, Endicott Prize-winning photographer, found herself in an overheated kitchen, supervising homework and fixing sloppy joes. And she was doing it with a Texas-sized grin on her face.

Owen and Wyatt's homework session had deteriorated into a sword-fight with pencils, and Scottie came wandering in, looking for something to eat. At the same moment, the phone rang, and Lila, who had been watching MTV, leaped to answer it. She had earned back her phone privileges by getting good marks on her latest report card. Her attitude still needed work, but Luz was mystified as to how to go about fixing it. She was usually good at fixing things. However, in this case, she didn't even know where to begin. She wished there was a pill she could give her daughter, maybe even a surgical procedure. But there was none. She often caught herself studying Lila in silent contemplation, deeply stricken by the inescapable notion that Ian and Jessie had made this child. Yet Lila was so much a part of Luz's heart that she wanted to reject the idea entirely. Tonight, however, Luz refused to let anything dampen her spirits.

Company arrived, and the baby made a beeline for Scottie, whom she regarded with wide-eyed awe. Arnufo handed Luz an arrangement of possumhaw berries and Mexican buckeye. Luz beamed at him. "Keep that up, and you'll be eating here every night."

"Nothing would give me more pleasure."

She waved Dusty toward the refrigerator; by now he knew where to find a cold beer. He was a fine man, this man who loved her sister, who openly admitted that he missed her every day. Like Blair, he understood that it would be a simple matter to locate her.

When they first realized Jessie had gone for good, he and Luz had stood together in the empty guest cabin and debated what to do. Dusty was all for putting out an APB on her, sealing the airports and borders. Luz agreed that, yes, they could indeed locate Jessie. However, her next words had stopped him from initiating a manhunt. "If you find her, then what?"

They hadn't discussed the matter again. They had become friends, united by a helpless love for Jessie and bound by the knowledge that she wouldn't come back until she was ready—and that being ready might take a good long time.

Jessie had left her cameras, including a Hasselblad, Nikon and Sony digital along with a fortune in expensive accessories and lenses. Stuck to the top of the bag had been a note, Jessie's characteristic scrawl even sloppier than usual. *Thanks for everything, Luz. Give my love to everyone. To Dusty and Amber, too. I'll be in touch. Love, Jessie.* That was Jessie—impulsive, extravagant and just plain confusing.

By the time Ian got home from work, the sloppy joes were ready, the coleslaw had been passed around, glasses of milk and juice were being filled. Amber and Scottie created a game of chase that required a good amount of screaming. Wyatt and Owen fought over a Nerf football while Lila turned up the volume on her favorite radio station.

Ian found his way to her, making her laugh by pretending to be a soldier traversing a minefield. He gave her a kiss on the cheek, but before she could say anything, he turned to Dusty. "I'm probably going to be needing a lift on Wednesday if you're available," he said. "I have a date in Huntsville with my favorite psychopath."

In low tones so the children wouldn't hear, the two of them discussed the case. Luz managed to shush the morbid talk, herd everyone to the table, tuck napkins under chins, ladle sloppy joes onto empty plates, pass the coleslaw and potato rolls. She had anticipated an auspicious moment, a pregnant hush during which she would beam at each and every one of them before announcing her news. Clearly that was not going to happen. So as she fed her hungry family and guests, she said simply, "I won the Endicott Prize for my pictures."

"Can you pass me the salt, Dad?"

"Stop kicking me. Tell him to stop kicking me."

"Have you tried fishing with those little metal spoon lures?"

"Mom, there's a tolo dance next Friday. Can I get my curfew extended by an hour?"

"Eew, Amber's eating sloppy joes with her hands."

Luz picked at her food, giving up for the time being. Ian leaned over and patted her hand. "Delicious supper, honey." Before she could respond, he turned to Lila to negotiate the curfew.

"Fantastico," Arnufo added. "But not nearly as fantastic as winning a great prize. Congratulations. Felicitations."

Luz beamed at him. "Thank you for noticing."

"Noticing what?" Wyatt held out his plate for seconds.

"My Endicott."

Owen leaned back in his chair, inspecting her with narrowed eyes. "Where?"

Luz shook her head. "I give up."

She and Arnufo shared a private smile. She had learned much

about the old gentleman in the past few months. He understood the demands and rewards of having a large, busy family, and the virtues of patience and forbearance. Privately she decided to tell Ian her news that night, and the kids whenever she got a chance.

But she never got the chance. The phone rang in the middle of dinner, and it wasn't the business line. Most of the kids' friends respected the dinner hour. Luz picked up, fully prepared to remind the caller of that particular house rule.

"Hello?" There was a beat of hesitation, characteristic of overseas calls. Luz's heart leaped. Finally her sister had decided to call.

"Jessie, it's Simon. God, it's so good to hear your voice."

Frowning, Luz took the cordless phone away from the noisy dinner table. Stepping out on the front porch, she said, "This is Luz, Jessie's sister. Simon? Where you calling from?"

"I'm in Auckland. You sound exactly like your sister," he replied in the gorgeous accent that had so charmed his students when he was a visiting professor at UT. "Can I speak with Jessie, then?"

A familiar, protective prickle touched the back of Luz's neck. According to Jessie, she and Simon had parted ways. So what did he want with her? Luz decided to hedge. "She's not here at the moment. Is it urgent?"

That beat of hesitation again. "Not at all. I wondered...how she was getting on these days. Things were not going well when she left here, as I'm sure you realize."

Luz pursed her lips. She knew, and yet she didn't know. She was aware that Jessie and Simon had been together off and on for years, that Simon was one of the reasons Jessie had given up Lila and taken off overseas. Yet Luz had never known the precise nature of their relationship. Did they love each other? Could Jessie love anyone enough to stay? Which one of them had done the breaking up? Jessie or Simon?

Luz felt exasperated. She wished Jessie was not so intensely private about her relationships. Weighing her words, she said, "She didn't say much about that, Simon. Just that the two of you had broken up. I'm sorry," she added belatedly.

"So am I," he admitted. "I miss her like mad."

Then you shouldn't have let her go, thought Luz. Then she realized she'd done that, too, more than once. She'd let Jessie go.

"She gave me the boot, not the other way around," Simon continued. "I don't care what she told you. That's what happened."

Hearing the waver of emotion in his voice, Luz decided to believe him. On some level, she'd known all along who had done the leaving. "I see."

"So then, did she get in touch with Dr. Margutti?" Simon asked. "Is she enrolled in the program?"

Now Luz was thoroughly confused. Dropping all pretense, she said, "Back up, Simon. You lost me there. Doctor who?"

This time, the hesitation was even tenser. Then he said, "She didn't— Ah, Christ, didn't she—" He cleared his throat and started again. "She didn't explain this to you?"

"I think you'd better fill me in, Simon."

The long hiss of an exhaled breath conveyed frustration. "She went to the States to consult with a specialist about her condition and to take part in a special program. I've been going crazy, hoping to hear there's been a miracle. And then, today I did an Internet search and caught a piece from *Texas Life* magazine on the Web. I saw those photographs she did of the young father. It made me hope to God that she's all right."

Luz sank down to the top step of the porch. The phone receiver slid in her damp hand. Despite the chill of the winter evening, she was drenched in the cold sweat of fear. "Simon, you're going to have to clarify some things to me." Her mind flipped through the nightmare possibilities: cancer, multiple sclerosis, HIV, Parkinson's... "Jessie was here with me for a while, and she seemed fine."

Yet she'd left every piece of camera equipment, and photography had been her life.

Luz forced herself to go on. "Are you saying she's sick?"

"Dear God, didn't she tell you? Luz, your sister has a heart of stone."

"What was she keeping from me?"

"I'm sure she had her reasons for not telling you, but I think you deserve to know."

Luz felt an inner quaking as the edges of her world began to crumble and fall away. "Say it, Simon. You have to tell me."

"Luz, your sister is going blind."

CHAPTER 30

Jessie got lost on her way to group therapy. "I swear, Flambeau, you're a blonde under all that silky red hair. You're not fooling a soul." She began the tedious process of orienting herself and discovered that they had missed a turn and wound up a block west of their destination. Using the techniques she had been studying for interminable weeks, she got her bearings and started off again.

She and Flambeau arrived at the meeting several minutes late. She murmured an apology and directed Flambeau to pick a seat in the now-familiar classroom. Flambeau managed to thrust one chair aside, but Jessie smacked into another and cursed between her teeth.

The group session leader cleared his throat. "We'll just wait while Jessie finds her place."

Jessie felt as though she was in junior high again. "We'll just wait..." she muttered under her breath. "Very funny, Mr. Sullivan." Addressing the whole room, she said, "It's Flambeau, I swear. They're playing a cruel joke on me. They gave me an Irish setter instead of the golden retriever they promised."

In the brief ripples of laughter, she recognized the voices of some of the friends she had made. Actually she wasn't sure she should count them as friends. The relationships formed at the Beacon would never exist if they weren't all blind.

Sully greeted everyone and welcomed two newcomers—Bonnie and Duvall. "Can someone tell us why we're all gathered here for our first meeting?" he asked.

"Too much masturbation," replied Remy, another recent graduate. "We shoulda listened to our mothers."

Sully spoke over more laughter. "Jessie, did you do the readings for today?"

"You mean all that Wordsworth crap about the contentment of the inner self? Yeah, I read it. Or rather, Hal read it to me." Hal was her nickname for the adaptive reading software on her computer.

The woman beside her was nervous. Jessie could tell by her quick breathing and timid silence, and the unfamiliar new fragrance of her cologne. Leaning over, she whispered, "Jessie Ryder and Flambeau, the wonder dog. You must be Bonnie Long."

"That's me."

So this was the woman she'd come to meet. New students were paired with more experienced ones at the beginning of their stay. Jessie couldn't believe she was expected to be someone's mentor, of all things. She didn't consider herself capable of mentoring an insect, let alone a blind person. Yet at the Beacon, they expected the impossible of everyone. "Welcome to blind boot camp."

"Jessie recently completed the program," Sully explained. "I have no idea why we let her come back. We should have kicked her out on her ass."

"I love it when you talk dirty to me." Despite her wisecracking tone, she felt a familiar jolt of terror. Lowering her hand to Flambeau's head, she stroked her fingers through the dog's silky fur. After completing the residential program at the Beacon for the Blind, she'd moved to a nearby apartment. Most clients were eager to rejoin their families and resume their lives.

Jessie recoiled at the thought of going to Luz after all the turmoil she'd caused. She was determined to make some sort of life for herself. She'd dedicated each waking moment to that goal, and was often amazed to realize it was working. With Flambeau, she wasn't afraid of the world. She was adept at talk- and touch-typing and had no doubt she could earn a living. She was out in the world on her own, living independently. A Beacon success story, a veritable poster child for living with a disability.

But she was desperately lonely. Each day, her yearning for Dusty and Amber, Luz and Lila, grew sharper rather than dulling, as she'd hoped.

"Nice," said Sully. "Jessie, why don't you tell the group why you'd characterize the experience as boot camp?"

"Well, let's see. Maybe it was that rigorous battery of physical and psychological tests we're subjected to prior to enrollment."

"Now that you've been through the program, do you see the rationale for that?"

She addressed herself to Bonnie by turning in her direction. "Believe it or not, there is a rationale. You're up at 5:45 a.m. to curb your dog, then you have to feed her, shower and go to breakfast by seven. You'll spend the whole day walking miles of Austin's streets, doing errands, trying not to trip and run into things or fall down stairs. There's a break for lunch and dinner, but we're not back here until final curb duty at 8:00 p.m. Oh, and in between, we'll have life skills, like cooking, talk typing, adaptive reading, learning Braille, laundry, you name it. So anyway, all that takes a bit of stamina."

"I understand. I'm not a young woman, but I've worked all my life and I might as well work on this."

"Excellent," Sully said. "Now, what about the psychological tests?"

"They won't just give a dog to anyone who stumbles in off the street," Jessie assured her. "The fact is, if you're an asshole before you're blind, there's a chance you'll simply become a blind asshole."

"Delicately put," remarked Sully. "Blind people, like every-one else, come in all shapes, sizes and attitudes. If they hate dogs, if they're cruel, they'll fail with the dog. It wastes every-body's time, makes the Beacon look bad and frustrates the dog no end."

Reaching out, Jessie patted Bonnie's arm and wasn't sur-prised to feel a hand knit sweater. "You'll be fine. Sometimes I suspect the success of this program is due to the fact that they reject everybody who'll make them look bad."

"Oh, sure," said Sully. "Then why did we accept you?"

"Because I look like Gwyneth Paltrow, only younger. Slim-mer. Blonder."

"When you're blind," said Patrick, a longtime resident, "all women look like Gwyneth Paltrow."

"You're supposed to be explaining boot camp," Sully re-minded them. "Patrick, what else is in store for our guests?"

"You get a drill-sergeant-type lecture," Patrick said. "Y'all got that, right?"

"The bit about buttering your own bread and cutting your own meat?" asked Duvall.

"Yeah. That's the one. And if you complain that you've never done any of this stuff on your own, they tell you it's about time you started. They'll let you get lost in the halls, put your shirt on backward and miss meals."

"Sounds harsh."

"Going blind is harsh. But not as harsh as giving up. The staff here believe we can do this stuff. And so we do."

At the end of the meeting, Jessie offered Bonnie her arm and grasped Flambeau's halter. "Ever heard of the blind leading the blind?"

"I trust you." A smile warmed the older woman's voice. As they left the day lounge and headed out to the sharp chill air of morning, Jessie recognized the hesitation and faltering steps she herself had exhibited in the early part of her training. To-tally blinded by occluders, she'd taken her first steps here in a rage of frustration. Before long, she didn't need to occlude her sight artificially. Her vision had deteriorated as rapidly as Dr. Margutti had predicted, and the day she had awakened to find herself sightless, she'd been terrified. That first walk, from her bed to the bathroom, had been an act of will, the first steps along a journey she dreaded.

"Listen, I'm glad to have a woman for my sponsor," Bonnie said in a confiding voice. "I forgot to pack a very important necessity."

"Tampons, right?"

"Yep."

"Not a problem," Jessie said. "We're well-stocked." She led the way to the ladies' lounge in the classroom building. "One of our first lessons is getting the proper supplies for this." She'd done the shopping excursion, but had yet to get her period. It was common to be irregular after going off the Pill. But if her cycle didn't start up soon, she'd see a doctor about it.

"Thanks," said Bonnie, then tripped on the threshold of the bathroom.

Jessie put out a hand to steady her, and felt Bonnie shaking. "Don't worry about a thing. I was a total klutz my first week here," she told her. "More than once, they found me crumpled on the floor, lost and sobbing, usually with a bruise or two to prove my incompetence. They showed no sympathy. The first time Sully found me like that, he offered to alert the media to let them know the world was coming to an end."

"You seem so sure of yourself now," said Bonnie.

Jessie felt a flush of wonder. "I do?"

"Yes."

Amazed by the compliment, Jessie showed her the facility—the sensory training rooms, spoken word rooms, obstacle studios, kitchens, gardens. Bonnie's hopes and fears were familiar. She was horrified by being here, yet determined to succeed.

"I have to gain back my confidence, too," she said. "My family needs this as much as I do. After the accident, I pretty much gave up on life. I sat in the house and hid from the world. Medication helped, but what I really need is to be independent and unafraid once again. Not only for myself, but for my kids and grandkids, and especially for my husband."

"I'm sorry, Bonnie. I thought your husband was killed in the accident." Jessie had gone over the files on the computer. She was quite sure of that detail.

"My first husband," Bonnie said with a small hitch in her voice. "I married Roy six months ago."

"Now this I've got to hear."

"Got your attention, didn't I?"

Jessie couldn't get over the idea of a sighted person falling for a blind woman.

"Is he— I mean—"

"He's sighted. I thought he was pulling my leg at first," Bonnie said, clearly sensing her surprise. "I couldn't imagine why he'd want me, when I couldn't see."

"Did you ever ask him?"

"Of course. He was truly confused by the question. The burden wasn't in living with me, Roy said. The burden was in living without me."

"He must really be something."

"Are you seeing anyone special?"

Jessie hesitated. "Actually I have a date tonight. A blind date. Isn't that awful?"

"Not as awful as not having a date," said Bonnie.

It was so pointless, Jessie thought. But she needed the practice if nothing else, and she did want to get out into the world. She figured she'd muddle through somehow, though she truly didn't want to date. She wanted Dusty. Suppressing her yearning was getting harder, not easier.

"Grace in the vet clinic set us up," she told Bonnie. "He works for computer tech support."

"I hope you have a good time. Roy and I never would have met, except that I broke the dishwasher, and he came to repair it. We were married six weeks later." Pride and wonder rang in her voice. "He's been incredible but he needs me to do better. So we had the idea of getting the dog."

"She'll change your life."

"So I understand."

Jessie patted Bonnie's arm as she showed her where the next session was meeting. "You're going to do all right, my friend."

"So are you," Bonnie replied. "Have a wonderful evening."

Jessie's wonderful evening began with disaster and deteriorated from there. She and Tim Hurley had exchanged e-mail a few times, and spoken on the phone once. When he had asked her to the Austin Symphony's open house, she'd been intrigued enough to accept, and it was too late to back out now. The moment he walked into the lobby of her building, he cleared his throat. "Jessie?"

"You must be Tim," Jessie said, getting up from the sofa where she had been waiting with all the clammy-handed anxiety of a teenager on her first date.

"Wow, you're a knockout." At least the wonder in his voice was flattering. "Grace said so, but I thought she might have been exaggerating."

She put out her hand and he took it, apparently assuming she wanted him to drag her somewhere. She laughed and pulled away. "That's some handshake. I like that in a man."

She could feel him checking her out. She could feel his relief at the prospect that she didn't look like a freak. Recalling Patrick's comment this morning, she composed a mental picture of Tim Hurley. He looked remarkably like Joseph Fiennes.

"You have a nice smile," he said.

Maybe this wasn't so bad after all, she thought. She signaled to Flambeau, and the dog came to attention. She sensed the dog checking out the man, too, and to her surprise, she realized Flambeau was indifferent to him. It was something Jessie knew, like knowing it was going to rain by the smell of the air.

Tim exploded with a terrific sneeze.

"Bless you," she said.

"I'm allergic to dogs." He hesitated. "Grace didn't tell me you had a dog. I mean, I should have assumed, but..." He let his voice trail off, then sneezed.

Jessie weighed her options. He was giving her the perfect out, if she chose to take it. But no. It was time to get away, attend the symphony, eat a shrimp cocktail and have a normal conversation that wasn't about closet organizing or avoiding low-hanging obstacles or training your dog not to be distracted by garbage on the sidewalk. It was time to be a woman who happened to be blind rather than merely a blind woman.

"Flambeau doesn't have to come," she said. She could feel the dog deflate beside her. All the way back to the apartment, she reminded both herself and her dog that there were times when they couldn't be together. Dealing with temporary separation had been part of their training, too.

She used a cane to make her way back to the lobby. Getting a whiff of his Stetson cologne, she felt a dart of surprise. "Still here? I gave you the perfect opportunity to escape."

"You won't get rid of me that easily," he said. She could hear a bit of congestion in his voice. "I mean, if it's okay with you to go without the dog."

"It's okay. Unless you're allergic to canes."

Tim gave it his best shot. He offered her his arm and moved along slowly, and he kept asking her if she was all right, if she needed anything. He made hesitant, polite inquiries, as though afraid to offend her. She knew it wasn't fair, but she kept comparing him to Dusty on every level, from his height and the scent of his skin to the way he dealt with her. Tim checked with her about everything. Dusty went for what he wanted. There was something so sexy about the way he had blazed into her life and swept her into his own. He'd hypnotized her with his absolute certainty that, not only did he want her, but he intended to have her. And furthermore, she was going to like it. Of course, Dusty hadn't known the truth about her. That made all the difference.

Pushing aside those thoughts, she accompanied him into the

concert hall. Once seated, she gave herself over to the music, an exuberant celebration of American composers. But at the gala reception for subscribers, Tim fell into a conversation with a fellow programmer about something called PERL, and it didn't take Jessie long to contemplate the entertainment value of listening to paint dry. When the programmer offered to introduce Tim to an associate, he politely asked if she'd be all right on her own for a few minutes.

She gratefully assented and remained standing by a refreshment table that smelled of garlic chicken wings and strong cheese. She stood for several minutes, absorbing snippets of other people's conversations and trying to figure out how to find the ladies' room. One couple kept trying to reach the babysitter on a cell phone only to find the line busy. A woman smelling of Joy and Jack Daniel's walked unsteadily past in stiletto heels. A young boy declared the food "barfy" and whined that he was bored. His mother made an apologetic sound in Jessie's direction, and Jessie favored her with an understanding smile.

"Could I ask for your help getting to the ladies' room?" Jessie asked.

Silence. Damn. The woman had gone already, leaving Jessie to speak to the empty air. She really had to go. I hate this, thought Jessie. I hate my life. I hate everything.

She felt stripped down to nothing. She had no dog, no escort. She'd foolishly left her cane in Tim's car.

"Everything all right, ma'am?" asked a male voice.

The sweet drawl sounded so much like Dusty that, for a moment, hope sang in her veins. But she quickly realized she was projecting an impossible wish onto a stranger. "You bet."

"You look like you could use this." A champagne flute found its way into her hand. He didn't sound like Dusty after all. His voice was more nasal and affected, a Kappa Alpha fraternity twang. Maybe he was a Bush cousin.

Jessie curved her mouth into a dismissive smile. Her back

teeth were floating. She really ought to ask the guy to escort her to the bathroom, but angry pride got in the way. Sometimes she was so good at acting as though she were sighted that people didn't notice. "Thanks."

"What's a pretty lady like you doing here all alone?"

She favored him with a smile. "Trying to stay that way."

Sharp intake of breath. Clearly Cousin Bush was used to getting what he wanted. "With that attitude, you'll have no problem." Leaving a puff of Canoe aftershave in his wake, he left.

She felt physically ill, nauseated by the smell of cologne and food and champagne. All her hard work and training didn't help. At the Beacon, she'd been remade, redefined and managed to remain on a road that ensured her independence. And damn it, she was good at survival. Or was she fooling herself?

On this absurd date, she reflected, she'd been humbled by her own helplessness. Sure, she could avoid getting run over by a truck. But the little, everyday things—like facing desertion in a strange place, or being hit on by a jerk—were pounding her into the ground. She was in no physical danger, but in a way, this was worse. The horror was subtle and she had no solution for it. She couldn't fix this by labeling it with a Braille strip or by counting steps.

"I see you found the champagne," said Tim, rejoining her.

Even as she tried to force a smile, the truth hit her. Everything she'd accomplished, all the skills the sighted found so admirable—all of it was a sham. She was fooling everyone—herself most of all—by trying to prove she could make it alone, in darkness.

She tried to step away from Tim, but there was a cold marble wall behind her.

"Jessie?" he asked. "Are you okay?"

"No," she managed to blurt, just before she threw up on his shoes.

CHAPTER 31

Balancing cold drinks on a tray, Luz walked outside to find Ian and all three boys hard at work on another new ramp, this one leading from the yard down to the dock. Even Scottie lent a hand, clearing broken rock from the path while his brothers hammered down the speed bump strips.

At the top of the shallow incline, she stopped for a moment to watch. It was a misty morning, the air sweet with the promise of spring. Ian wore the tool belt the kids had given him one Father's Day, and a cap embroidered with the logo *Carpe Diem*.

"That's quite a sight," said a voice behind her. "I hope you're prepared for a flock of girls to come calling when Wyatt hits puberty." Glenny Ryder came to join Luz.

Luz took her mother's hand. She and Stu had arrived the day before, having driven from Phoenix in a van that had more bells and whistles than a fighter jet. They had stayed up late the night before, talking about Jessie. Everyone was totally shocked, yet it explained so much. Luz was sick with anticipation. She had wanted to go tearing off to Austin, armed with the information from Simon. She'd burned to track down her sister and scoop her into her arms. In the end, it had been Ian who stopped her.

"Let Dusty do this, Luz," he'd said.

Dusty hadn't had a single doubt. "I'll bring her home. But you're not keeping her. That's my job."

"No one can keep Jessie," Luz had warned him.

"I can love her. I can make her want to stay."

Luz hadn't had the heart to point out that no one had ever succeeded at that before. Not even her baby.

"I'm glad you're here," Luz said to her mother, and she meant it. Despite the complicated threads of emotion and history that bound her to her mother, she loved Glenny and was glad she'd come to visit.

"I can't believe this is happening to our Jessie," said Glenny. "I can't believe she didn't tell us."

"I can," said Luz. "This is her way of protecting us. She's always done this. Most people think I'm the protective one, trying to manage everyone's problems. But Jessie has her own methods. She thinks going away will shield us." Ever since Simon's phone call, Luz kept hearing Jessie's voice: *I just want to see Lila.... I want her to know who I am.... You don't want what I've got.* And deep in the darkest, most hidden part of Luz's heart lay something she despised about herself. Jessie had stolen her thunder again. On the very day Luz found out about the Endicott, Jessie's troubles had eclipsed Luz's shining triumph. And given what Jessie was going through, a prize seemed so trivial.

But not, it seemed, to the world of professional photography. On the heels of the announcement about the award, offers and requests had poured in at a steady rate. Luz was reminded of the magical times in her youth when her mother had won a major title. The heady aftermath of success turned the world into a banquet of possibility. But deep down, Luz still felt like a phony, only playing at being a professional. How could something that meant this much to her actually become a job?

She took a gulp of tea, so cold it gave her a headache. "God, why didn't I realize there was a problem when she handed over all her cameras?"

"How do you guess something like this?" Glenny said. "In the past two days, you've read volumes on the Internet about AZOOR. Could you have seen it coming?"

"No," Luz admitted. "There aren't any predictors, other than a tendency toward myopia. It mainly afflicts females under the age of forty."

"So does VD, but it's not something you think about. Quit trying to take the blame for this, Luz, for God's sake." In a softer voice, Glenny asked, "So do you think this guy—this Dusty—will bring her home?"

"He's not the type to take no for an answer."

"She's not the type to do something because some guy tells her to."

"This is different," Luz said. "There's something between them. The air just crackles when they're together. He's crazy about her. And Jessie—I've never seen her like that."

"Grandpa Stu!" Scottie burst into a run at the top of the slope. "Come and try out the ramp!"

Stuart Burns positioned his wheelchair at the head of the new ramp. The boys hooted with excitement, running along beside him as he navigated the way down to the dock.

Luz felt Glenny tense beside her. Stuart was a fit, good-looking older man who was wheelchair-bound from a climbing accident a decade before. He and Glenny had met at a fund-raiser, and they'd been together ever since. Of all her mother's husbands, Luz liked him the best. He was kind, caring and funny. Unlike his predecessors, he hadn't spent Glenny's money and disappeared.

He made it down to the dock without incident, and Luz saw the tension leave her mother. He, Ian and the boys celebrated with high-fives. Stuart hoisted Scottie onto his lap and treated him to a spin in the chair while Scottie shrieked with glee.

"He's a wonderful grandpa," Luz said.

"Your boys are a handful of fun. Two hands full."

Luz took a deep, nervous breath. "Mom, I need a favor."

Glenny looked at her sharply. She was clearly aware of how hard it was for Luz to ask for something. Anything. "What's that?" asked Glenny.

"Can you and Stu look after the boys today? I thought maybe you could take them to Woodcreek for putting practice."

Glenny's hesitation was weighted with reluctance. "I don't know, Luz. They're awfully active."

Luz ground her teeth. She'd lain awake late into the night, agonizing over her decision. It was going to be so hard. She simply couldn't do it with the guys running around. "Ian and I need some time alone with Lila. Please, Mom. For once in my life, I'm not going to pretend I don't need you. I'm asking for a little help."

Glenny must have heard the desperation in Luz's voice. She took a Virginia Slims and a lighter from her pocket. "Is Lila in some sort of trouble?"

"Not specifically. There's not a crisis like the accident. It's just..." Luz hesitated. "We've decided to tell her about the adoption."

Glenny lit up and gazed out across the lake as she exhaled a thin stream of smoke. "And that'll fix what's wrong?"

"I'm not that naive, Mom. But it's what Jessie wanted before she left us."

"Then you're doing it for all the wrong reasons."

"What's that supposed to mean?"

"You're Lila's mother. Telling her otherwise is only going to confuse the girl."

"Fine. Then you tell me what to do." Luz eyed her challengingly but without any real hope of an answer. She'd been waiting all her life for her mother to make a decision for her, and it hadn't happened yet.

"Don't look to the past for answers," Glenny said, surprising Luz. "Look at what *is*. And don't look at Jessie or Lila. Look at yourself."

"What about me?"

"Did you ever think...maybe you have all this tension with Lila because you're too focused on what you expect of her? Maybe you need to find a way to put the past to rest and find a dream of your own."

"Like you did, Mom?" The sharp note in her voice brought Glenny around to face her.

Luz flashed on a memory of a typical summer. Jessie was in the back seat of the Rambler, lost in another world while Luz tracked their progress on a map, tallied up their expenses in a small black notebook, tried to find a motel that would not set them back too much. Glenny's mind was on her next tournament, her next man, her next move. Luz was always the good daughter, the dutiful daughter, the responsible one. Caretaker and peacemaker.

"Tell me, Mom. When did I ever have time to dream?"

"You make time for what's important."

Luz bit her lip. She didn't want to have to beg, but she and Ian needed this time with Lila. "Look, if I've learned anything from Jessie, it's that keeping secrets is destructive. My God, she couldn't bring herself to tell you or me or anyone what was going on. I don't want to keep secrets anymore."

Glenny finished her cigarette and waved at Stuart and the boys. "Who's up for a round of putting and ice cream at the Dairy Queen?"

"Me!" the boys yelled in unison.

"Into the van, then," Glenny said. "Chop chop."

CHAPTER 32

Each morning when she woke up, Jessie lay still with her eyes shut and tried to think about seeing. There was nothing left of her vision but fog. She thought about colors and shapes. The faces of people she loved—Dusty and Amber, Luz and Lila, Ian and the boys. The sight of snowcapped mountains, gleaming lakes, birds in flight. Even her mother's smile, a cherished gift. Where were those images now? They still belonged to her, didn't they? They hadn't gone anywhere. They were still part of her; they lived inside her.

Then, inevitably, she opened her eyes to the shadowy gray that was her only reality. She despised the fears and humiliations, the clumsy mistakes, the limitations of her condition. She despised the orderly, methodical person she'd become. She missed the mindless freedom of riding a bike, hopping in a car whenever she wanted, even simply jaywalking. Her life had slowed down to a crawl.

She had more time for reflection, Sully and Irene had reminded her. More time for regrets, Jessie realized. When she couldn't simply flee at breakneck speed, she was forced to examine her life and her choices too closely. She wished too hard for things she couldn't have.

Why on earth would she think her road would be easy? Or that she'd have a choice?

Flambeau could never be fooled. Jessie didn't know how she did it, but the dog knew the moment she opened her eyes. Like a persistent toddler, she gave Jessie no time to wallow in despair, but whined softly, her tail a fan that stirred the air. Time for her morning curbing.

"Okay, girlfriend," Jessie mumbled, and went to the bathroom to get ready. A few minutes later, teeth brushed, hair brushed, sweat suit on, she harnessed Flambeau and out they went. She wished she'd brought an apple or something to settle her stomach. The morning air was crisp and dry, and the sun had barely risen. Spring was coming. She caught a whisper of scent from a Ligustrum hedge, felt a waft of warmth on her face. Jessie liked the relaxing early moments of the morning and the muted sounds of traffic on distant MoPac.

She paced back and forth on the sidewalk. Living as a blind person was not the hardest part of the future that lay ahead. Not by a long shot. Her failed date at the symphony had proven that.

Flambeau had a tiny bell attached to her collar. In this way, Jessie could keep track of the dog's morning wanderings. She heard the bell and realized the dog was loping away from her. Flambeau would never run off, but sometimes allowed herself to be lured away by a squirrel. Jessie called out to her.

She heard the dog coming back and could tell she wasn't alone. She could also tell Flambeau liked the stranger. She was prancing and lightly sneezing. Flambeau was an excellent judge of character. But her demeanor clearly indicated that this was indeed a stranger. If the dog recognized someone, she acted differently, announcing that fact with a soft whine.

Jessie felt a disturbance in the air. People who didn't know any better sometimes claimed the blind had special powers of acuity in their hearing or smell or tactile sense, but that wasn't true. Not being able to see simply allowed her to focus on other sensations.

This disturbance was different, fraught with tension. When people approached Jessie, the dog was not protective but she was definitely proprietary. She trotted up to Jessie's side, and Jessie leaned down to clip the walking leash to her collar. Flambeau pranced and then settled at her left side. Jessie lowered her hand to the dog's warm head, but she faced directly forward.

"Hello?" she said.

Long, unhurried strides rang on the buckled concrete sidewalk. Her skin recognized him first. Oh, she felt him, so close, and it was something she had missed with every fiber of her being. The sound of his breathing confirmed it.

"Oh my God." The words rode a soft breath of disbelief.

"Lady, you are some piece of work."

"Don't. Don't yell at me, Dusty."

"Somebody needs to yell at you, Jessie," he said. "Or is that going to make you run again?"

"I wasn't running. I was—" She stopped. "I was taking care of my own private business."

"Right." He gave an angry laugh. "I offered you my damned heart on a platter. And still you left without a word. What the hell were you thinking?"

He had it all wrong, she thought. How could he have it so wrong? "I was thinking that what was happening to me was not the sort of thing I felt like sharing. Particularly with a man who had just lost his wife."

"What the hell's that got to do with it? Do two losses make a right?"

"I didn't want you to suffer, Dusty."

"I fell in love with you, and you left. You think I didn't suffer?"

She jerked her chin up in defiance. "Going blind is bad enough when it happens to one person. Why should I make it happen to the people around me?"

"You are one weird woman," he said, anger crackling around him like a force field. "Damn you, Jess. Why do you believe you can make these decisions for people?"

"Because forcing you to love me like this would be cruel."

"Like what?" he demanded.

She hated him for making her say it. "I'm blind. Don't pretend it doesn't matter. Don't pretend people will understand. The whole world will look at you and think, what a waste. That wonderful man sacrificing his happiness to take care of a blind woman. I won't let you, Dusty. That's why I left, and that's why you should do the same."

He gave a snort of disgust. "You make a lot of assumptions on your own. It's exactly what you did about Lila. You kept the identity of her father from everybody because you thought that would be easier on them."

"And it was."

"That's bullshit, Jess. Jesus, look what it did to you. It made you into a person who can't let herself love, can't trust herself to stay."

She couldn't defend herself against that. He was holding up a mirror, and she recognized the truth. Still, she couldn't take the final step. "If I'd told Luz, she would have tried to fix this. It's what she does. Why should I hand her a problem she can't solve?"

"Sighted or blind, you're a problem, Jess, but that doesn't mean we don't love you."

And then he took her in his arms, and she broke open, all the terror and hurt flowing out of her on a raft of tears. "Damn it, Dusty. I haven't fallen apart once. Not once. And now you come here and—"

"Yeah, I'm here." He kissed her hair, her face—forehead, cheeks, eyes, lips—until the tears were gone. Her senses filled with him—the way he tasted and smelled and sounded, the warmth of him. "Don't you ever do that again, Jess," he said. "Don't you ever leave me."

There was an assumption in his anguished command that she knew she should object to, but it felt too good to hold him, to melt in his arms, to forget for a moment how impossible this all was. She let her mind drift back to the night in Mexico—the lush, decadent romance, the dark, fragrant garden, the mindless pleasure. Finally, she made herself ask the obvious. "How did you find me?"

"Your old flame contacted Luz, looking for you."

"Great. Something else for Luz to worry about."

"I told her not to worry. You're going to be all right."

She put a hand to her hair. "I'm a wreck."

He plunged his hand into her hair. "Do you think that matters?"

They strolled together along the periphery of the park. Jessie's blood sang; she couldn't help it. He shouldn't have come. She should be fighting him off, but she couldn't. "Flambeau likes you," she told him.

"She's going to love Amber and Arnufo, too. I figure she'll put up with Pico de Gallo."

"What are you implying?"

"You're coming back to Edenville with me."

"I don't think so."

"Jesus Christ, woman, would you listen to yourself? Who do you think you are, walking away from me, from your sister, from everyone who loves you?" His anger shocked her and bit deep.

"I'm blind. How can you stand me?"

"I'll pretend you never said that."

Emotions welled up in her, frightening in their intensity. She tried to fight them, to make excuses, anything to keep this from happening. She thought about her sterile apartment, her closed little world. "Who do you think *you* are, barging in here, ordering me around?"

"I would never do that. You're coming because you want to."

"What makes you think—"

"Your sister won an Endicott Prize. Did you know that?"

Wonder broke over her. "Really?"

"Who do you suppose she needed to tell when she got the news? You weren't there for her, Jess. You've got to fix this thing with your sister. She needs you. So do I, even though you're a pain in the ass. I love you, Jessie, and you love me."

For a moment she couldn't breathe. She stepped back and tried to find her voice to give Flambeau the command to take her home, away, anywhere but here.

"Let's go," he said.

"Go where?"

"Back to your place."

"I intend to. But you're not invited."

His laughter washed over her like a song she had nearly forgotten. "Oh, honey," he said, "when has that ever stopped me?"

CHAPTER 33

Lila watched the shiny green van with the bird logo on the side roll away toward town. They hadn't even asked her if she wanted to go to the golf course and Dairy Queen. Not that she would have accepted, but it would have been nice to have the option. Typical. Getting spoiled by grandparents, even funky ones like Miss Glenny and Grandpa Stu, was apparently something else she had outgrown.

Turning from the window, she surveyed her room. True to their word, her parents had made her take down the posters, pick up the mess and keep it that way. Privately she admitted that she preferred her room uncluttered and bright. The only decorations were photographs she had taken herself. Her mother had shown her how to use some of Aunt Jessie's cameras, and Lila had a pretty good eye for taking pictures. But now it seemed sort of creepy, because she knew why Aunt Jessie had left all the photographic equipment behind.

It was a shock, what Mom had discovered about Aunt Jessie. Lila had never known a blind person before. Wandering over to the computer, she read the article she'd found about AZOOR. Acute zonal occult outer retinopathy. According to some famous doctor at Vanderbilt, the condition started with flashing lights and an enlarged blind spot. The visual loss would spread, sometimes to total blindness in both eyes, and sometimes there were even hallucinations. Mom said AZOOR wasn't hereditary. Lila didn't think you could catch something from your aunt, anyway.

Jessie had used what little was left of her diminishing vision so well it seemed as though she could see. Lila had never guessed. Then again, she wouldn't have noticed an air raid if it didn't directly affect her. She vowed to pay closer attention to the people in her life, to care about them more.

She focused on her favorite photograph of Andy Cruz, showing him geared up at the fire station. He liked her, had said so right out. He didn't play games like other guys. When she talked to him about the accident, and he told her it wasn't her fault, she almost completely believed him. Almost. She just wished she could hang on to that belief when she woke up sweating in the middle of the night, her mind screaming with flashbacks.

A light tap sounded at the door.

"Yeah?" Lila called, sitting down at her mirrored vanity. She had been planning on trying out a new tube of mascara. Sable Dreams.

"Honey, can we come in? Your dad and I want to talk to you."

Lila felt a prickle of unease. Usually these talks meant nothing good. "Sure," she said, breaking out the mascara and twisting the wand.

The door opened and in walked her parents. They looked worried.

"Is it something else about Aunt Jessie?" Lila asked.

"Sort of."

"Is she coming home?"

"Dusty went to see her. We all hope she'll come back with him. But...what we've learned from this terrible thing with Jessie is that it's destructive to keep secrets from the people you love."

Lila took out the mascara wand and held the bristled end to

the light. "Look, if this is about that progress report, I've been meaning to tell you—"

"It's not about the progress report." Her mom glanced at her dad. "It's really not even about secrets. It's something we haven't told you yet. We've been putting it off."

Great. Mom was pregnant again. Lila thrust the wand back into the tube with an angry shove. Mom had no idea what it had been like last time for Lila, to have a pregnant mother at her age. Keeping her face expressionless, she set down the mascara tube and tucked her hands between her knees, waiting.

Mom sat down on the papasan chair across from her. Dad stayed by the door as though he wanted to flee. He probably did.

"Well," said Mom with a wavering smile. "I don't quite know where to start. That's one reason we haven't had this conversation."

"What conversation?" Lila asked, losing patience. "You're the only one who's talking and you haven't said anything yet."

Dad's face turned hard, and Lila waited for the expected rebuke: *Don't take that tone with your mother, young lady.* But he surprised her by saying nothing.

So she waited, mystified and unsettled by her mother, who was usually so sure of herself no matter what. Then a horrifying thought smacked Lila over the head. "Oh my God, Mommy, are you sick like Aunt Jessie?"

"No," Mom said with reassuring swiftness. "But Aunt Jessie is...part of this." She seemed to get over her hesitation then. "Dad and I have loved you since the moment you were born. Completely, with every bit of our hearts."

"Okay," said Lila. She wouldn't argue with that. Sometimes she felt completely smothered by love from her mother. There was a whole archive of pictures, starting with the preemie ward where Lila had lain in a special crib, small as a fingerling trout. Her parents had hovered near every second—at least that was the impression she had.

"The fact is, I didn't actually give birth to you, sweetie. Daddy and I adopted you."

Nothing. Lila felt absolutely nothing. The words were not real to her. They sort of hung in the air like a strange fog, and in a moment, the wind would come and blow them away.

Her parents stared at her with an expectancy about ten times as intense as when report cards came in the mail. "Sweetie," Mom began.

Lila's arm shot up like a raised sword. Dad held on to Mom's shoulder. He, unlike Mom, understood what lay in the valleys of the silences. Lila appreciated that about him. She couldn't hear this, not now. She needed silence, complete silence, in order to take in this thing her mother had thrown at her. She would have to inhale it like germ warfare, or swallow it like a foreign body, and later take it out, poke at it and study it like a lab specimen, cut it open and find out what lay at its heart. But right now, she rejected what she'd heard on every level.

It simply couldn't be. That's all there was to it. Adoption was for people who couldn't have babies. Her mother had babies all the time. Lila had seen it with her own eyes. Mom's belly got huge, and out came a baby, and the whole house smelled like diapers and throw-up for months afterward. That's how it happened in this family.

Wasn't it?

She swallowed once, twice. Found her voice. "What are you saying? Are you crazy?"

"I'm saying I'm not your birth mother. Daddy and I adopted you. It's not really a secret and there's nothing shameful about it. But years ago we all agreed that you are our daughter in every way that matters, so it never really came up. It's not something we even think about. It's simply not an issue."

Adopted. That was what you told your brother when you wanted to make him cry. Lila tried to make sense of this totally bizarre development. She'd always known that her parents had only been married a few months when she came along. That was no big deal. But the fact was, her family took pictures. Every event, from the time Mom got her first camera at the age of ten, had been carefully recorded by Mom or Aunt Jessie. And now that she thought of it, they didn't have one single picture of Mom, pregnant with her.

She looked from one parent to the other. This was impossible. She was a Benning. She looked like her mother. She looked like her brothers. Some people even said she looked like her father. She had the same red hair and green eyes as Miss Glenny, as her mom, as—

"Sweetheart," Mom said, "your birth mother is Aunt Jessie."

With a vicious twist, Lila reopened the mascara. Swiveling around on the stool, she leaned toward the mirror and applied the thick, sticky mascara to her eyelashes. She caught a glimpse of her face in the vanity mirror. She could hear them speaking— her *adoptive* parents—and none of the things they said surprised her. Jessie had been young, unattached, all set to travel the world, they said. Mom and Dad were settling down, starting a life.

"You fulfilled us in every way," Mom said, with that little hitch in her voice. "You made us a family. We're sorry we went so long without telling you. Jessie wanted it that way. I kept thinking it didn't matter. How could it matter? From the first moment we made this decision, I thought of you as mine in every way."

Lila hardened her heart. They had kept her from knowing the biggest secret in the world. Who she was.

She swiveled back on the stool. Her face felt like stone, her chest hollowed out. "Who's my father?"

"Back when you were born," said Dad, "Jessie put 'unknown' on the birth certificate."

Unknown.

"Lila, sweetie." Mom crossed the room and took her hand. "Just before she left in November, she finally told us."

Dad went down on one knee in front of her, like he was genuflecting, and turned the vanity stool so she had to face him. "Listen, a long time ago, before I ever met your mom, I went out with Jessie a few times and then quit seeing her. I never knew—"

Oh God oh Jesus. Lila stared at him, wide-eyed, and slowly blinked, the fresh mascara gumming her lashes together. "You mean...you and Aunt Jessie—" She couldn't continue. She was gagging on the words.

Lila took her hand away from her mom's. Not rudely. This wasn't the sort of thing you were rude about. This went so far beyond rude, she couldn't imagine how to respond.

"We want you to be okay with this," her dad said.

Her dad? Which dad? The one who'd married her mother or the one who'd screwed her aunt?

How could she look at them now, either of them, without wondering about the other part of her, that biological part that belonged to one but not the other. Aunt Jessie—her mother—wanted no part of her. Aunt Jessie had gone away and had a fabulous life, and she only came back when blindness destroyed her.

"You want me to be okay with this," she repeated slowly, hoping to bring out the absurdity of the request. "Sure, I'll be okay, knowing you never trusted me enough to tell me the truth."

"It's not a matter of trust," said Mom. Then she said something totally unexpected. "I was afraid, Lila-girl."

No way, thought Lila. Her mother was the most fearless person on the planet, everyone knew that. "Afraid of what?"

"That you would turn to Jessie, be dazzled by her lifestyle and feel deprived."

"Yeah, right. You must think I'm shallow as a mud puddle, to turn my back on my real parents and fall for somebody who walked away from me the day I was born." Lila spoke in anger but she could see her meaning beginning to penetrate.

She heard a car pull up in the drive and knew it was Andy, giving her a lift to the fire station to set up for tomorrow's pancake breakfast fund-raiser. It was something her mother would do, organize a pancake breakfast, but Lila surprised herself by enjoying it.

"Anyway," she said, "you're crazy if you ever thought I wouldn't love you the same, respect you the same, trust you to be there to catch me when I fall." She stood, put the mascara in her purse. "I've got to go now." Impulsively she kissed her dad on the cheek and hugged her mom, feeling their astonishment. "What?" she said. "Did you think it was going to rock my world? I'll be back by suppertime."

She ran downstairs and outside, half diving into Andy Cruz's pickup truck. "Go," she said. "Hurry."

He eyed her sideways as he pulled out of the drive. Just being with him made her feel good about herself. Different from Heath Walker. With Heath, she'd had to be "on," had to appear a certain way. With Andy, she didn't have to worry.

"You all right?" he asked. "Is it something with your folks?"

"I'm fine. Everything's just fine." And then she looked out the window and watched the landscape smear past. She wondered if the new mascara was waterproof.

CHAPTER 34

"You look terrified," said Dusty, slowing the car as he drove Jessie down the last incline to Broken Rock.

"Well, *duh.*"

"Duh," said Amber, wedged into her car seat.

"This is a mistake," said Jessie, tamping down a flutter of panic.

"No," Arnufo said, from the back seat beside Amber. "If you had not agreed to come back here, your bossy sister would have come for you with the *reata.*"

Jessie slid her hand across the seat of the new-smelling car and found Dusty's thigh. The roomy car was just one of the adjustments he'd made for her sake. A car could accommodate Jessie and Flambeau in addition to Amber and her car seat.

My God, she thought. What sort of man could love like that, with such certainty?

She knew what he was pushing her to do. She couldn't commit to him, to anyone or anything, until she fixed things with her family. She wasn't sure she could do that. For the first time in her life, though, she was ready to try.

As a car inched down the hill, she said, "So tell me what I'm getting into here."

"It's all set up for a party on the deck," Dusty said. "There's a banner that says Welcome Home Jessie strung from the live oak, and there are helium balloons tied to pretty much everything. I guess your folks are staying in the big cabin. Looks as though cabin number two has been made up for you."

Jessie braced her hand flat against the dashboard. "Wait a second. I assumed I would be spending the weekend with you."

Dusty stroked her cheek. "I don't want to spend the weekend with you." Before she could reply, he added, "I was thinking of something more along the lines of your whole life."

She couldn't speak. Her mind bounced everywhere. In his aw-shucks, good-old-boy way, Dusty was as stubborn as she was. He was the only person she'd ever met who would not be manipulated by her.

Arnufo made a grunt of satisfaction. Somewhere outside, Beaver barked and Flambeau snapped to attention. "Easy, girl," Jessie said.

"The coonhound is confined to the dog run," Dusty said. "Okay, now everyone's coming out onto the porch. They're all smiling."

"Luz, too?"

"Yeah. Luz, too."

Jessie and Luz had spoken on the phone the previous night. They'd finally told Lila she was adopted and Ian was her natural father. Jessie had no idea how to feel about this news. That was what she'd come here for last fall, but now that it was done, she didn't know how she felt. She had asked Luz how Lila took the disclosure.

"She took it. Nothing I do or say thrills her these days, you know that. But her head didn't explode or anything. Just come home. You need to see her. And Mom's dying to see you."

"Your mother looks exactly like she does on TV," Dusty said. "I guess that's her husband in the chair beside her."

"Stuart. She married him in Vegas a few years ago. I've never met him."

He parked the truck and Amber babbled with excitement

while Arnufo got her out of her seat. The baby had grown so much during Jessie's absence. But Amber remembered her. The moment Dusty had put her in Jessie's arms, she'd clung with innocent and absolute trust.

Jessie had decided to have a sighted guide rather than make Flambeau work during her visit. All the new people and excitement were enough for the dog to handle. She opened the passenger door and stood, then let the dog out, feeling the strong body pour out onto the ground. Flambeau paused at her side, alert and awaiting orders. "It's okay, girl," Jessie said, and turned toward the house. The weather had taken a sudden turn, and warm currents of springtime rode the air.

"Ready?" Dusty offered his arm. Then he all but shoved her forward.

She could hear everyone shuffle their feet in nervous anticipation, and she wanted to scream at them. She thought of the last time she'd shown up here, breaching Luz's fortress against the world, whirling into their lives after a fifteen-year absence. She pictured them standing there, all lined up along the porch, probably holding their breath. Beside her, Flambeau made distinct chuffing noises, and in his dog run, Beaver bayed deeply.

"You hush," yelled a voice. *Luz.*

Jessie's palms were drenched in sweat. She wanted— needed—to pray but only the most childish of thoughts streamed out. Please God, get me through this.

The screen door of the porch opened with a creak and shut with a snap.

The idea of this whole family waiting for her, paralyzed by uncertainty, made Jessie burst out laughing to keep from crying. "Oh, for Christ's sake," she said, holding out one arm. "If somebody doesn't speak up, I'm going to run smack into you and then you'll be sorry."

She heard footsteps. Two strong hands closed around hers and Jessie felt herself pulled into her sister's arms. Luz. Oh God, Luz. Jessie's throat went tight as she hugged her sister.

"You idiot," said Luz, hanging on. "You crazy old thing. I cannot believe you went away like that and never said a word."

"Sure you can," Jessie whispered. "It's my specialty."

"That's going to change."

"Why are you crying, Mom?" asked Scottie.

The sound of her littlest nephew's voice filled Jessie with sweetness. Pulling away from Luz, she found his slightly sticky hand and squatted down beside him. "I made her sad because I was so naughty," she explained. "But now I'm really sorry and she's going to forgive me. Are you mad at me, too, Scottie?"

"Mom said you can't see me."

"That's right."

"How can you see how big I am?"

She grinned. "That's easy." Taking him in her arms, she stood and lifted him off the ground. He smelled of canned soup and washing powder. "Wow, you're *gigundo*."

"Can I play with your dog? Mom said I have to ask."

She set him down. "Flambeau loves being petted, and when she's not helping me, it's fine."

The dog emitted a moan of ecstasy. Jessie put out her hand to Luz. Together, they went to see the others, dispensing hugs made awkward by nerves. When she filled her arms with Lila, Jessie tried to detect something, anything to hint at what Lila thought of all this. But there were too many people milling around, too much going on. Later, she told herself, and was glad she was going to stay the night, after all. Why was Dusty always so smart about things like this?

"Glenny," she said, hugging her mother for the first time in years.

Time melted away, and she found herself surrounded by familiarity. Charlie perfume, Certs and a sweet husky whisper saying, "There's my girl."

Her mother's hands bore the familiar calluses of her sport, yet her skin was papery and more delicate than Jessie remembered.

"This is my husband, Stuart." Her mother guided her hand to a large masculine one.

"Good to meet you at last," he said, and she recognized his pleasant, southern-California voice from the telephone. Oddly he didn't get up to greet her. She found out why a moment later when Flambeau went crazy sniffing and Stuart seemed to glide backward. Her mother grabbed her arm to steady her.

Jessie frowned. "Are you in a wheelchair?"

"Yeah," he said. "Sorry I didn't—"

"No, that's okay. I didn't know. Did you hurt yourself?"

"Ten years ago. I'm fine now."

Jessie wondered how he could be fine if he'd been in a wheelchair for ten years.

Dusty came and kissed Jessie on the cheek. "I'm taking off," he said. "I put all your stuff in your room."

"Pah." Amber leaned toward Jessie and planted a wet kiss on her chin.

"Pah to you, too," Jessie said. "I can't believe you're depriving me of this amazing child."

"I'll be back in the morning. You've got plenty here to keep you busy."

God, he knew. But he was not going to stick around and hold her hand through this. That was the thing about Dusty. He made no apologies for forcing her to do this on her own.

She felt one more kiss, whispering across her lips, and then he was gone.

Jessie could tell the entire family was trying not to act chaotic around her. She imagined Luz calling a meeting to tell everyone that she was blind and needed a calm environment for her and her dog. They had worked on this at the Beacon. Students were prepared for the reaction of friends and family. But they'd lied. Nothing could have prepared her for this.

After supper, Ian, Stu and the boys went to liberate poor old Beaver and have a game of Frisbee up the hill. Jessie, her mother, her sister and Lila sat on the deck overlooking the lake.

"Dinner was unbelievable, Luz," said Jessie, leaning back in an Adirondack chair and patting her stomach. "Those twice-baked potatoes— Lord, you outdid yourself. And chocolate sheet cake. My teeth are singing."

"Lila made the cake," Glenny pointed out.

"It was the best cake I've ever had."

"You don't have to say that," Lila replied.

"Not unless I mean it," said Jessie. She sensed a lingering suspicion and resentment from Lila.

"You've lost weight," Luz said. "I don't want you getting too skinny."

"I haven't been dieting on purpose," Jessie said, allowing her sister to deflect the confrontation—for now. "Four of the eight people in my training group at the Beacon were diabetic so they didn't serve a lot of sweets. After I finished and moved off-campus, I was cooking for myself. Ramen noodles and cold cereal are my two major food groups. And then there's the exercise. When you commit to having a dog, that part is not optional." She dropped her hand to Flambeau's head, and Flambeau lifted her face with the sweet, uncomplicated adoration that had enchanted Jessie since the moment they'd first met.

"How did you pick your dog?" asked Lila.

Jessie smiled. "The person who is blind doesn't get to pick. The instructors do that. They get to know you, and of course they know the dogs because they've been training them for months. They match temperaments and personalities."

"And hair, too," Glenny pointed out. "The two of you are a knockout together. A pair of gorgeous redheads."

"She sure is devoted to you," said Lila.

"Oh, I hope so, love. That's one of the main goals of all the intensive training. Flambeau and I have to bond completely. I think it's working." She curved her hand under the dog's chin. "A guide dog has a rough time of it, early in life."

"What do you mean?"

"Well, Flambeau's not even two years old, and her heart has

been broken three times. They took her from her mother at eight weeks of age, then gave her to a family to raise. After a year of that, she went to an instructor at the Beacon, and she thought he was her person. Finally they gave her to me."

"Poor baby." Lila sounded genuinely distressed. Flambeau's tail thumped the deck. "Some of the 4-H Club kids at school raise puppies for the Beacon. I never understood how they could do it—raise a puppy, train it and love it for a whole year and then give it away."

"Flambeau was raised by a boy from Round Rock," Jessie said. "He came to visit the day the dog and I were matched up. It was—" She stopped, swallowed hard. "It was a day I'll never, ever forget. They brought her to me, and she jumped up to give me a hug. Technically the dogs are supposed to be discouraged from jumping up, but it was something Brian had taught her when she was a pup—to give hugs on command. And that's what my girl did, and it was— I can't even describe what I was feeling. Hope and optimism and finally the certainty that I was going to be okay. And the whole time, I could hear Brian and his mom sobbing away while they stood back and watched us with the instructor. I asked Brian later if he had any regrets, but he said no. He said Flambeau was doing exactly what he'd raised her to do, and that was more important than him keeping her as a pet."

Jessie stopped to take a deep breath. She was amazed at how hard this was. "So you see, I don't dare blow it with her. She got her heart broken a few times along the way, but finally she's in her right place with me, Lila."

Jessie listened to the silence that followed. She was learning to hear the things that hid inside silence. The soughing of the cool breeze through the trees and the lapping of the lake around the dock pilings. Closer in, she detected the creak of Lila shifting in her chair and the soft gasp of her mother's breathing, a muffled sniff from Luz and the sound of her petting Flambeau.

She turned to Lila. "I need for you to be okay with what I did. I need to know you're in your right place."

"It's always been about what you need," Lila said in a harsh, quiet voice. "I'm not a dog. I might be okay with this, or I might not. But either way, it's not going to be because your needs matter."

Jessie could feel the shock emanating from her mother and sister. She sensed Luz gathering breath for a rebuke, but before she could speak, Jessie said, "Well, that's a relief. And here I thought y'all were going to treat me special because I'm blind."

She stood and went to the rail of the deck, bracing her hands on the rough cedar. "Losing my vision forced me to find new ways of seeing. I did some stupid things when I was young. A lot of stupid things. I took my sister for granted and lost touch with my mother. I fell for too many men who cared too little about me. But there's one thing I did that wasn't stupid. It was the smartest thing I ever did. I gave you to your mother. My God, Lila, you're so lucky I did that one smart thing."

She heard Lila drop to her knees and imagined her face-to-face with Flambeau. The feathery tail swished in response. Taking a deep breath, Jessie said, "Brian doesn't love Flambeau any less because he gave her to me."

Lila climbed to her feet. "Yeah, okay." She took a few steps, paused a moment, then left.

In the wake of her departure, Jessie felt drained. "Well," she said, "I guess I blew it."

Glenny surprised her by sniffling. "You see why I don't hang around you girls all the time? You're very intense."

Jessie put out a hand, and her mother took it. Jessie knew then that Glenny had done her best with what she'd had. The heart was a fragile organ, delicate and prone to breaking. Glenny was one of those who armored herself against the assault of everyday loving, so hard on the human heart.

Glenny squeezed her hand. "I have a wall full of trophies and my own fan site on the Internet. I've traveled a lot of miles, but the hardest trip I've ever made was to come here. I couldn't be prouder of my girls."

Jessie was amazed. "You've never told us that before."

"Just because I couldn't always be there doesn't mean I didn't care. But the thing that saved me was knowing the two of you had each other, that you were in your best possible place. If you're mad at each other, then nothing in the world makes sense."

Jessie turned to her sister. "Luz? Luz, please."

Maybe it was Glenny's encouragement or maybe it was the *please* that did it. Luz grabbed on to Jessie and they fell together in a tangle of arms and legs, hugging and letting the tears come at last.

CHAPTER 35

Luz had always regarded the Alamo as a monument to tragedy and failure, haunted by the ghosts of soldiers abandoned to hold out against Santa Ana's legions. Yet on a sunny Friday in late February, Texas's most familiar landmark made its way into her viewfinder. She'd driven down to San Antonio for the afternoon to photograph the First Communion of Arnufo's granddaughter, Guadalupe.

As the solemn processional passed by the Alamo in a traditional march to the historic chapel, Luz found herself enchanted. Against the cobblestones and sandstone-colored mission, the little girls clad in white dresses and mantillas resembled tiny, perfect bride dolls. They went along the West Barracks and past the Cenotaph, crossing Colonel Travis's legendary line in the sand, now a brass bar in the flagstones. Using a powerful telephoto lens, Luz zoomed in close to capture the essence of their childlike purity—large brown eyes surrounded by black velvet lashes, the fall of sunlight on a glossy, waist-length braid, a precious family rosary wound between fingers with nails painted a chipped, dime-store pink. Occasionally she locked onto a not-so-secret smile, punctuated by missing teeth.

Taking pictures had always given Luz a way of putting the world into her own perspective. The Alamo didn't thrill her, but a parade of six-year-old Catholic girls made the tragedy cease to haunt. She caught one last shot of Guadalupe as she passed by her proud parents and grandfather and continued into the sanctuary. Arnufo had invited Luz to join the family celebration after the mass, but she'd declined. That was a time for snapshots and home videos. Besides, Luz needed to get back to Edenville. Life didn't simply stop and wait for her because she had a new career. There was supper to cook, clothes to fold, homework to check, hugs to dispense. A husband to attend to—as much as she ever did these days. She pushed aside the worrisome thought of Ian and concentrated on other, easier matters.

Her mother and Stuart would be leaving soon, and Luz would miss them. It had been a good visit despite the devastating reason for their trip. This past week, Luz and even Jessie had had the most honest conversations of their lives with their mother. Glenny had done the best she could; she honestly had. Now she was teaching the boys to play golf while Stuart surprised everyone by having a fine hand at the bluegrass fiddle. He'd even given Lila a few lessons.

Lila.

As Luz set her bags on the hood of her car to start digging for keys, she yearned for the slow-moving, uncomplicated days of Lila's early childhood, when it was a simple matter to make her laugh and bedtime meant kisses and I-love-yous and when Lila looked at her and said, "Mommy."

This deep gash of separation was supposed to happen, Luz assured herself. In adolescence, teenagers drew away in order to find their own lives. It was a natural progression of things. But Lila's transition was that much more dramatic because of the terror she'd faced in the accident and their disclosure about the adoption.

I think it bothers you a hell of a lot more than it bothers her, Glenny had observed.

Luz found the key, put her gear in the car, then searched under the visor for the parking card. Through the windshield, she glimpsed a familiar figure and blinked, certain she was hallucinating. But no, there across Alamo Plaza was her husband.

Reflexively she started to get out of the car and call out to him, to ask him what he was doing in San Antonio, talking at length to the bell captain of the Menger, San Antonio's most romantic hotel.

But she didn't get out of the car. While the blood chilled in her veins, Luz reached into her camera bag and fit a powerful telephoto lens onto the camera body. Peering through the viewfinder, she brought her husband into sharp focus. He looked wonderful in his best suit, yet his manner seemed a bit bashful, nothing like the crusading attorney known to intimidate sitting judges.

He reminded her of the man she had met in Gutman Library sixteen years earlier.

That memory, like so many others, was tainted now. She used to believe his face had lit up at their first meeting because he found her attractive. Now she wondered if his face lit up because she reminded him of his ex-lover—her sister, Jessie.

She focused on the parcel he held, a glossy black bag from Neiman Marcus. To her knowledge, Ian had never been to Neiman Marcus in his life.

Other lawyers' wives had warned her repeatedly. Don't call him in the middle of the night. Don't follow him to out-of-town depositions. Don't scratch the surface and look at the secrets that lay beneath.

Those warnings had never applied to Luz. She didn't have a wandering husband. Ian would never succumb to the fleeting charms of eager young interns. And yet as he folded a generous tip into the bell captain's hand and then was swallowed by the brass-and-glass revolving door, every warning and doubt Luz had ever had rang in her head.

With shaking hands, she thrust the camera away. This was it, then, the dark side of her deception, punishment for staying silent about Lila, for not seeing the truth even as it stared her in the face. Now she was reduced to peering at her wayward husband like a two-bit private eye.

When her cell phone chirped, she jumped, still unused to having the gadget. Ian had given it to her for Valentine's Day, another wholly practical gift like the Christmas fax and modem line. It had not come in a glossy black bag.

She excavated the tiny phone. "Luz Ryder Benning." She was growing more and more accustomed to her professional name, but it was still a mouthful and sounded made up, as though it belonged to a stranger.

"Mrs. Benning?" His deep, rich voice melted her bones.

"Yes?"

"I have a proposition to make you."

Her heart sped up. "Yes?"

"Get your sweet little Texas ass over here and you'll find out."

The shit. He'd known she was there all along. Before she could reply, he hung up. Feeling both unnerved and foolish, she crossed the plaza to the hotel. The bell captain approached and handed her a key card, directing her to a room on the third floor.

Except "room" was an understatement. It was a suite with soaring ceilings, a canopy bed and bathroom with a marble tub, and an iron-railed balcony projecting out over a patio with a fountain. Ian was nowhere to be found. On the faux Queen Anne luggage rack stood the glossy black shopping bag, which contained a stunning bustier, matching skirt and black sandals. A *bustier?* She did a double take.

Propped against the pillow was a hand-lettered invitation; she was startled to recognize Lila's curly calligraphy. "The pleasure of your company is requested—6:00 at the Rough Rider Bar."

Luz phoned home, and Jessie picked up. "This had better not be my sister."

"Jessie, what's going on?"

"I swear, Luz, you are dumber than a box of hair. Don't you dare call me again." She hung up.

Luz stared at the phone in her hand for a long time. Then she switched the power off.

Two hours later, wearing the slim black skirt and daring bustier, of all things, Luz walked into the Menger Bar. A half-dozen heads swiveled in her direction as she stood in the doorway to let her eyes adjust to the dimness while piano music streamed from a smoky corner. A replica of the House of Lords Pub in London, the bar had a paneled ceiling of cherrywood, booths with French beveled mirrors and decorated glass cabinets.

As she crossed the room, she caught a glimpse of herself in the mirror behind the famous carved bar, reputed to bear the bullet holes of Teddy Roosevelt's Rough Riders, recruited here for the Spanish-American war. She barely recognized her reflection. She was a glamorous stranger with gleaming hair in a French twist, an exotic outfit, a little beaded evening bag.

Ian stood as she approached the richly upholstered booth where he waited. "Wow," he said. "It's amazing what a little hotel shampoo can do."

"Along with a personal shopper."

He took her hand and lifted it to his lips. "Blair LaBorde helped." He laid a slim velvet box in a distinctive color of blue on the table. "I picked this out myself."

A little thrill rolled through her. She could feel every bone of the bustier pressing against her ribs. Judging by the size of the box, it wasn't the usual electronic gizmo or power tool. But this was Ian, she reminded herself. Mr. Apron-And-Barbecue Tools for our anniversary.

Picking up the Tiffany box, she sat down next him at the table and peeked inside. It was a shining gold chain with a trillium-cut emerald pendant.

She snapped the box shut. "You're having an affair."

"What?"

"You're having an affair, and this is a sop for your guilt."

"Very funny, Mrs. Benning." He opened the box and lifted out the necklace. "Here, let me put this on you."

As his fingers clasped the chain around her throat, she felt a flush rise through her. "I'm sorry, Ian. That was petty of me. I'm just...so surprised by all this."

"You're supposed to be." Taking her shoulders, he turned her to face him. "I do want to have an affair, Luz. With my incredible wife. My God, you are gorgeous." He wasn't speaking in the usual way, but with the rare intensity she used to glimpse in him when they had first met.

But old habits died hard. He leaned forward to kiss her and she ended it abruptly, pulling back to say, "So who's watching the kids?"

His jaw twitched. "I think between your mother and Stuart, Jessie and Lila, they can manage. If they need to call in the big guns, there's always Dusty Matlock."

"The only one even remotely qualified is Arnufo, and he's staying with his daughter in San Antonio."

He grinned. "You really believe that."

"It's really true."

The grin disappeared. "Only because you've made it that way by always taking charge. Just let go, Luz. Maybe they're not going to do everything exactly your way, but I think we can safely assume they're all going to be fed and eventually put to bed."

She shut her eyes, thinking about how she always gave Owen a fresh glass of water on the bedside table and how Scottie needed three particular stuffed animals wedged around him just so....

"Luz." His urgent tone startled her, and she opened her eyes. "I need for you to be with me."

She studied his face, the years etched there by laughing and loving and caring. And finally she understood. "All right," she said.

Their love affair had been carefully planned and orchestrated.

After drinks, he took her for dinner at the Anaqua Grill, where she ate things that cost more than a week's worth of groceries at the Country Boy. Amid couples leaning intimately toward each other across linen-draped tables, they dined in a setting of lush gardens, fountains and strolling pheasants. When the small ensemble struck up "Blue Bayou," Ian held out his hand.

"Let's dance."

"You don't dance."

"And you don't—" he leaned forward and whispered a suggestion into her ear "—but there's a first time for everything." After all these years, he could still make her blush. He was a terrible dancer but she felt wonderful in his arms. "This is nice," she said.

"Yeah."

His tone made her laugh. "You hate this."

"All guys hate dancing. We do it so women will have sex with us later."

She lifted her face to look at him. "It's working."

They had planned to take a water taxi back to the Menger, but didn't want to compete with the groups of loud tourists hurrying to the next mariachi-and-margarita stop. Instead they strolled along the Riverwalk, San Antonio's breathtaking thoroughfare lined with shops and restaurants hung with twinkling lights. Luz took off the designer sandals and went barefoot, leaning her cheek against Ian as he walked with his arm around her. Passersby smiled when they saw them, and that made Luz smile, too. "People think we're newlyweds."

"Let's be, for tonight. I'd planned to stop at La Fogada for cappuccino, but hell, Luz. How bad do you need a cappuccino?"

His impatience caused her smile to widen, and then she startled herself by sharing that impatience. "I don't."

"Me, neither."

The hotel room was set for seduction in every sense of the word—dim lighting and a luxurious bed, a bottle of Cristal Rose '95 in a chrome bucket, soft music drifting from unseen stereo speakers. But Luz balked. She had to get to the bottom of this. "Ian Benning, you are genetically incapable of planning an evening like this. Who helped you?"

"Jessie. Your mom and Lila. Blair, too. My Lord, that woman knows how to spend."

Luz dropped the beaded bag on a tapestried chair. "So how about you tell me why."

He looked baffled as he loosened his tie. She saw that it was the Hermès knockoff she'd given him one Christmas. "Because they all love you, Luz."

His matter-of-fact certainty hit her with unexpected force. She often dwelled on how much she loved the people in her life, but it was rare to consider how much they loved her.

"Then what's the occasion?"

Leaving the tie hanging, he went to the armoire and took out a large clasped envelope. "Well, for one thing, this."

She was stunned to see a letter from the University of Texas's Dean of Arts and Sciences, along with a sheaf of forms to fill out. "It says here that, based on my practical experience in the field, they're granting me my degree." Her hand shook a little as she set down the envelope. "Wonders never cease. I finally finished something."

"I'm proud of you, Luz. We all are. But you've never needed an international award or a college degree to make me proud." Crossing the room to her, he took her in his arms. "And I did not arrange this whole thing just because you got a letter."

"Then why?"

"Because we need to find each other again, Luz, and I want tonight to be the beginning of that."

Dear God. She and Ian didn't speak of things like this. Foreboding slipped over her like a phantom chill. "What do you mean?"

An ominous tic tightened his jaw. "You know what I mean. This marriage has been on autopilot for too long. Even the sex—you've been phoning it in, Luz. We need to figure ourselves out again."

She had no reply. His assessment was stunningly, devastatingly accurate.

"I share the blame for this," he admitted. "Hell, maybe it's all my fault we're losing each other."

Pressing her hands to her too-warm face, she knew then that she hadn't begun to deal with Jessie's disclosure. When Jessie told the truth about Lila, Luz and Ian were already in trouble. There were little cracks and fissures in the foundation, and they'd been ignoring them. It was hard, so hard to speak her heart, but she knew she had to. "I feel...threatened," she admitted. "I know I can't control who you knew or didn't know before we met. But the fact you kept it from me—"

"That's the thing that pisses you off, isn't it? That there's a part of me you can't control. Yeah, I kept it from you. So did Jess. And then I forgot about it. Hell, Luz, I was so crazy in love with you that I didn't think of anyone else, and that's the truth. I swear it."

She gathered a deep breath to speak the unspeakable. He deserved the truth about her, finally, and she deserved whatever his reaction was. "The fact is, Ian, I'm jealous."

"No way. Jessie and I—"

"Not that," she said. "I'm talking about Lila. When we didn't know who fathered her, we were both equally her parents. But when Jessie said it was you...the balance shifted, Ian. And I know it's ugly and I know it doesn't make sense but I started resenting you. Lila was yours but not mine. Or at least more yours than mine, and it's been making me nuts."

He was quiet for a long time. Then he said, "Shit. You want to go for that cappuccino?"

She sent him a wry smile. "Look, I don't mean to break the spell, Ian, and I love everything you're trying to do here, but a romantic date is not going to magically erase these issues."

"I don't want to erase them. I want to get them all out on the table so we can figure out the next step."

"This is why I don't talk things out with you, Ian. When you say things like that, it makes me think you want to leave—"

"If that was what I wanted, you'd be the first to know, Luz. Even the problems are part of what we are together, and that's precious to me. I don't lie to you. I never have, and I don't think you lie to me."

"But we keep things from each other," she pointed out.

"Maybe we should change that."

Would he still love her if he knew her secret fears? She thought of the cold panic that had swept over her when she'd spied him in front of the hotel earlier today. "I'll never be as smart or as cute as your interns. You get new ones every year, and they're all twenty-three, and every year I get older. And each morning, you dash off to work as though you can't wait to see them."

"Ah, Luz, if I seem like a workaholic, it doesn't have anything to do with interns."

"Then why, Ian?" The question was a pained plea. She felt the magic of the evening slipping away, but they'd started this and now she had to know.

His next words stunned her. "I've never been the man you want me to be, Luz, and now you've got this photography career going. I've never made enough money, never gave you enough—"

She stopped him by pressing her fingers to his lips. "Oh, Ian Benning, you incredible fool. Where in the world did you get that idea?"

He kissed her fingers, never taking his gaze from hers. "It's in your eyes, every time I look at you. I see you reading travel books about exotic places, collecting pictures of houses we could never afford to own. Jesus Christ, Luz, I want to give you those things, to take you places and show you the world you want to see."

She took her hand away and sank down on the end of the bed. He was right. She'd never said a word, but he saw her clearly. She had spent years dreaming of things beyond her grasp rather than cherishing the life she had. "Oh, Ian. How can you stand me?"

"I can't live without you, Luz. This marriage means too much to me. You mean too much to me. But we need to fix this."

"Okay."

"Starting now."

"Yes."

"Just so you're clear on this," he said, lowering himself to his knees so he was eye to eye with her. "I want you to understand what beautiful is to me, Luz. It's you. You're like a work of art. Every single part of you. The lines around your eyes because you smile so much. Your sweet soft ass and belly that isn't perfectly flat because you bore my children. It's the way your hair smells and the way you look when you get out of the shower. It's the smile on your face when I come home from a long day at work. I miss that, Luz. I want us to find that again. Just tell me what to do. Should I take you to the Taj Mahal or to Paris or—"

"You know what to do, Ian Charles Benning," she said as her heart broke open. "You always have."

She realized then that the carefully crafted romance of the evening was gone for sure. But in its place was something so much richer—a passion heated by honesty, a commitment deepened by a love so sharp and true that she felt pierced by it, a yearning so stark that she could not even put her need into words. What she found so sexy, in spite of everything, was the honesty. She stood, drawing him up with her, and their lovemaking began slowly, with unveiling and exploration. Luz felt slightly absurd in the stiff-spined bustier, but Ian clearly found it a turn-on as he enjoyed the novelty of unfastening the cord down the back.

Luz sighed as her clothes slipped to the floor and she lay back on the downy bed, bringing Ian with her. Simply slowing down yielded a world of remembered delights. She had nearly forgotten the sheer pleasure of weaving her fingers through her husband's hair, gliding her hands over his chest, down his hips. It had been far too long since she'd savored his gasp of lust when she became the aggressor, mounting him and opening herself so he would have access to every part of her.

He could still set her on fire, could still bring her to tears with his exquisite tenderness and generosity. He always could. He wasn't a perfect husband or perfect father any more than she was a perfect wife, but in the bedroom, they reached perfection. This was where he took her away, where she forgave him and he accepted her with all her flaws, where she was so thankful she'd married him, where she acknowledged that she was only half alive without him.

Over the long, dark hours of the flower-scented night, they found the love they'd fallen into sixteen years before, and they fell all over again. Luz felt as though she'd been plunged into a new world; she seemed like a new person. And she knew that she was. Ian had made her see herself in ways she'd been willfully blind to, and it was so simple, really. Her fulfillment always had and always would come from the people in her life, not distant places and risky adventures. It was time, she realized, past time to let go of tired old dreams and begin to cherish newer, truer ones. And she discovered that the real dream had never really left her.

She gave a soft cry of agonized pleasure, and afterward drifted, listening to his heartbeat with her ear against his bare chest, enjoying the way he toyed with her hair. Finally, when it was so late in the night that no one else could possibly be awake, he asked, "What are you thinking, Luz?"

"We might never have Paris, but we'll always have each other. How corny is that?"

"Just don't rule out Paris entirely."

She propped her chin on his chest so she could look at him. "I love you," she whispered.

He settled on top and clasped her hands in his, pinioning her as he slid inside again. "I love you, too, Luz. I always have."

CHAPTER 36

On Saturday morning, Jessie awakened to thoughts of her sister. They had all connived to send Luz away with Ian. Oh, how she prayed it would help. She still felt guilty about the havoc her disclosure had wreaked on their marriage. They loved each other, but they had some serious mending to do. She hoped the stolen evening in San Antonio had been a success.

She went to the main house and was amazed to smell the aroma of baking cookies. "Wait a minute," she said. "Am I in the wrong house? It smells like Luz never left."

"I made a batch of cookies," said Lila. "Want one?"

Jessie sensed her niece was still wary, but at least willing to listen. She took a bite of the warm chocolate chip cookie and made a blissful expression, ignoring Flambeau's frantic sniffing. "You are a domestic goddess in training. I didn't know you were such a good baker."

"Baking cookies is a cinch."

Jessie went to the fridge for milk, frowning when she didn't find the jug in the usual door slot. "Where's the milk?" she asked.

"I moved it down a shelf."

Jessie gritted her teeth, but forced herself to make a joke of it. "When you move something even a few inches, it might as well be in Chicago."

"Sorry."

"Where is everyone?" Jessie asked.

"The boys are over with Miss Glenny and Grandpa Stu. I think Grandpa Stu promised to take them fishing off the dock."

Jessie sneaked another warm cookie from the cooling rack, then made her way to a stool at the kitchen island and sat down. "So what's the occasion?"

Lila hesitated. "There's a thing this afternoon."

"What kind of thing?"

"Just this memorial thing."

"For Dig Bridger," Jessie guessed. She felt a waft of heat as Lila opened the oven and took out more cookies.

"That's right."

"So what sort of memorial is this?"

"There was a fund-raiser to build a new sandbox for the city park, and it's going to be dedicated to Dig. Weird, huh?"

"Why is that weird?" She paused, sensing Lila's discomfort. "I can't hear you shrugging."

"It's a sandbox, of all things. I don't know what I was thinking when I— Well, a sandbox seems weird to, you know, honor a kid who...died."

Jessie got it then. A deep silence filled the room. "Come sit with me, love."

Lila banged the oven shut. They went together to the family room and plunked down on the couch. "I don't know what I was thinking. But my first memory of Dig is when we were really little, playing in a sandbox. That's how he got his name. He loved to dig and dig and dig." Lila's voice cracked with a sob. "Oh, God," she said. "I still dream about it every night. It's like Heath Walker's mother said. The accident was my fault."

"Lila, no—"

"Yes. There was a moment when I could have told Heath to

stop. I knew he was pushing it, but I wanted more and more. I wanted to fly and I didn't care about the landing and I didn't care about the other people in the car, not even my best friend and I know she was scared. I told him to keep going anyway."

Jessie heard echoes of her own carelessness in the confession. "Oh, Lila," Jessie said through tears she could feel on her cheeks. "Hug me hard." As she stroked the girl's hair, she pictured herself, screaming alone through her empty life, hurtling at breakneck speed toward the next shallow thrill.

"You have to stop thinking it's all your fault," she said. "You have to stop regretting the things in the past that you can't change. Every kid in the car that night played a part. Something bad happened, something you'll remember all your life, but you've got to quit blaming yourself."

"Everybody else found Jesus," Lila wailed. "They've all been forgiven. I tried that, I really did, but it felt so phony—"

"Because maybe for you, it is. Ah, Lila. Trust me when I say this. You'll find more grace and redemption in baking cookies and building a sandbox than you'd get from holding hands and singing songs with those kids."

She sniffled and burrowed closer to Jessie. "How do you know?"

"I know. I'm absolutely right and I will not let you move a muscle until you admit it." Jessie stroked her hair some more, putting together the things Lila hadn't told her about the memorial. "You did this, didn't you?"

"Did what?" Lila pulled back and settled against the arm of the couch.

Jessie grinned with pride. "Don't be modest. You know what I mean. You organized this whole thing—the fund-raiser, the ceremony, the sandbox. And you're going to serve these cookies which, by the way, are so good they are probably illegal in most states. My Lord, Lila. You're as good a cook as your mother."

The word hovered in the air between them.

"How could you do it?" Lila asked her baldly. "How could you give me away?"

Jessie took a deep breath and said, "She is the best person I know, Lila. She always has been. When I gave you to her, I gave you a place to grow roots and a family to nurture you. Hell, I know they drive you crazy, but you wouldn't trade them for the world."

"Do you ever wonder what it would have been like, if you had kept me?"

Jessie nodded. "Every day. For me, it would have been wonderful, bringing you along wherever the job took me. But even as young as I was, I knew that was no life for a child."

She gestured at the big room which she knew was cluttered with the flotsam and jetsam of a busy family—toys, books, dishes, shoes, mail...life. "This is what I wanted for you, Lila. I know it doesn't always makes sense now, but—"

"Lila?" Scottie came in, the screen door smacking shut behind him.

"Hey, sport," Lila said. Jessie knew she was dashing away tears, putting on a cheerful mask for her little brother. Just like Luz would do.

"Hi, Aunt Jessie. Hi, Flambeau." Scottie clambered up onto the sofa. "Grandpa Stu says I need my life jacket if I'm going to fish with him off the dock."

"I'll get it." Lila dug around in the mudroom adjacent to the kitchen.

"Can you put it on me?" Scottie asked. "You're the only one who does it right."

"You bet. Here, have a cookie while I fix this buckle."

"These are good," said Scottie. "As good as Mom's. Aunt Jessie, guess what? Lila let me sleep with her last night, right in the purple bed with her."

Jessie grinned as she listened to the two of them together. She knew it was the first time Luz had spent the night away from Scottie. It didn't surprise her a bit that he'd turned to Lila. "Too cool. I never got to sleep in the purple bed."

"I think you're all set, sport."

"Okay. Lila?"

"Yeah?"

"I like your face."

"Aw, Scottie. I like your face, too."

After he left, Jessie was still smiling, though she felt a bittersweet ache in her heart. This was life at its finest, and she'd never allowed herself to truly taste it. She could picture Lila and Scottie together and vowed never to let their image slip away, no matter how much time passed. She felt Lila looking at her and said, "I rest my case."

"Whatever." A smile softened her voice.

"Lila? I want you to know that I've always loved you, every minute of your life. Do you know that?"

"I...guess."

Jessie heard a world of uncertainty and terror in her tone. "It's okay. People who love each other still need to grow and change, and by now you know it sometimes hurts to grow, and the pain isn't always such a bad thing. It reminds us of how important some things are." She clasped her hands behind her head. "So how did I do?"

She heard a decisive snap as Lila put the cookies in Tupperware boxes. "Look out, Dr. Phil."

Laughter and the creak of fishing reels sounded in the distance. "Let me get the camera," said Lila. They went out on the porch. Early spring sunshine warmed the morning air. Jessie caught the scent of roses and knew it was from Luz's ancient rosebush.

"Aunt Jessie, can I ask you something?"

"Sure."

"What can you see? I mean, you turn and face things as though you can see them. Are you still able to see sometimes?"

"Everything that you consider vision is gone, love. I don't live in darkness. It's more like a veil of white smoke or fog."

"You must miss it a lot."

"I'd be lying if I said I didn't. But I don't lie around all day, raging against my lost sight. I promise, I don't. You have to swear you'll never feel sorry for me, and never let anyone else pity me, either."

"Okay." Lila paused awkwardly. "I've been meaning to try this telephoto lens. Can you show me how to switch it?"

"You bet. Good choice. It lets you compress your perspective." Jessie had switched lenses in the dark so often, she didn't need to see as she showed Lila what to do.

Eagerly Lila took some shots of the boys fishing.

"Take a picture of your mom's rosebush," Jessie suggested.

"How did you know it's blooming?"

Jessie grinned. "Magic." Then she switched lenses again, choosing the 100 mm portrait lens. That was Luz's favorite lens style. Jessie wondered if Lila knew that.

"Aunt Jessie?"

"Yeah, love?"

"What are you going to do?"

Jessie should have been prepared for the blunt question, but of course she wasn't. "Well. I suppose I need to figure out a life for myself. I know I'll be a writer. I like it, and it would make me a member of an elite group—John Milton, James Joyce, James Thurber."

"Who are they?"

"Blind writers. Jeez, what do they teach you in school these days?" Jessie paused. "I can't hear you shrugging your shoulders, but I know you're doing it."

"Why can't you stay in Edenville?"

"I don't know how to stay in one place. I've never done it before."

"But you are so amazing. You went blind and you totally figured out how to do stuff. How can anything be harder than that? I know you love us, Aunt Jessie. I know you love Dusty and Amber."

The challenge lay before her, and for the first time, Jessie felt a glimmer of possibility. It was remarkable, she thought, to realize how expressive the human voice could be. She could hear the emotion in Lila's voice, the worry...and the hope.

The click of a shutter broke the silence. "I took your picture," Lila said. "It'll be a beauty."

And it would, Jessie acknowledged. She knew she was smiling.

CHAPTER 37

Jessie awakened from a rare nap, feeling muzzy-headed. Maybe she was coming down with something. She didn't recall inviting Arnufo to stop by that afternoon, but perhaps she had. She recognized the sound of the pickup truck shuddering to a halt in front of her cabin, the rusty creak of its door opening. Flambeau emitted a soft whine of curiosity and bumped her tail on the floor. Jessie gave her computer the verbal command to go to sleep and went outside to greet him.

"Hey, compadre," she said. "You brought a friend with you," she observed, hearing Amber's slow shuffle. She was probably clasping Arnufo's finger as she climbed the two steps to the cabin.

"She is good company," he said.

Amber made a happy little burst of sound, clung briefly to Jessie's leg, then waddled over to Flambeau.

"How was your trip to San Antonio?" Jessie asked.

"Beautiful. I am so proud of my little granddaughter. And your sister, she took many wonderful pictures."

Jessie smiled. If everything went according to plan, Luz had awakened this morning in a fabulous hotel room with her husband and they'd return later this afternoon in a better state. She wasn't naive enough to think a romantic getaway would cure all ills, but the time alone together would surely give them a chance to talk about things that got shunted aside in everyday life.

"Would you like something to drink?" Jessie offered.

"No, thank you. As a matter of fact, I just remembered something. Watch *la pequeña* for me for a moment."

"But I—"

"I will not be long." Giving her no further chance to protest, he left, his boots crunching on the gravel drive.

His swift departure threw Jessie into a panic. She rushed to the door, stubbing her foot on the rubber mat. "Arnufo, what's going on?" she yelled.

No reply.

"Pah!" Amber toddled toward the door, pushing at it.

Jessie thought of the steps, and the woods and the lake, and firmly latched the door. "He'll be back soon," she explained. "We can kill him then."

Amber made a motor sound with her mouth, a steady *burrr* that reminded Jessie of a swarm of angry bees. The baby was headed for the table by the window. Jessie's mind raced. Her computer was there. Before dozing off she'd been dealing with e-mail using her voice recognition system. Cords spilled over the edge of the table to the wall.

What else? she thought, hastily making her way across the room. A hot cup of coffee—

"Amber, no," she said loudly, imagining the child drenched by the burning liquid.

"No!" Amber echoed, her high-pitched voice sharp.

Jessie located her by the table and snatched her up. At first the baby made no sound, then she arched her spine and pushed against Jessie's chest as she gathered air in her lungs. Finally, she exploded with an indignant wail.

"Oh, baby," Jessie said. "Don't do this. I was afraid you'd hurt yourself."

Amber bucked in her arms, still wailing. The tantrum crescendoed into a fury of windmilling arms and force-five screams.

"I can't believe this." Jessie lugged the hysterical child toward the door. "What was he thinking, leaving you alone with me? Arnufo, damn it," she hollered out the door.

"Damn it," Amber yelled.

Only the distant baying of Beaver reached her, and then that was drowned by an earsplitting shriek from Amber.

"Flambeau," Jessie said. "Flambeau, harness."

The dog reported for duty, standing by the hook where her work harness hung. Jessie set Amber on the sofa, and the child immediately raged in protest, dropping to the floor with a thud and thrashing across the room. Jessie was torn—she needed two hands in order to harness the dog, but Amber didn't seem willing to wait for that. Jessie turned away from Flambeau and hastened to pick the baby up again.

"Okay, okay, I won't abandon you." Scooping up the sobbing child, she hurried into the kitchen. "Are you hungry? Here, I've got a banana and let's see...I have some cookies that will make you sing an aria. Lila made them. No? Maybe a cup of milk." With the baby propped on her hip, she opened and reached inside the fridge. "How about a piece of cheese?" she asked. "Yogurt? I know, a pickle!"

All her suggestions were greeted with more hollering. Jessie was horrified. She felt trapped, panicked, completely unprepared. Being set adrift with Amber was like exile to an alien planet, a place where she felt everything whether she liked it or not. What had happened to her life? Her travels and her independence, her ability to brush past people and keep them from touching her? What was this precious mess she now held in her arms? What on earth was she supposed to do with it?

"Come on, Amber," she said, pacing back and forth. "Snap out of it."

The child cried on, her voice growing ragged around the edges.

"Look, here's Flambeau." Jessie knelt beside the hapless dog.

"No!" yelled Amber, and the dog flinched.

Contrite, Jessie stood and paced some more, her ears beginning to ring. She brushed past a plastic bag she'd left on a shelf, and paused. "What's this?" she asked, and for a few seconds, curiosity about the crinkly plastic bag silenced the baby. Jessie reached in and pulled out a small, thick book, shrink-wrapped into a box. "This is for you, Amber. I never had a chance to give it to you. Let's read it."

The baby kept crying, but with less vigor. Her desperate, tremulous breaths tore at Jessie's heart. The little tyke was either wearing herself out or the book actually interested her.

"Lila was with me when I bought this. I sent her a copy, too, a long time ago." She wondered if Lila had ever exploded like this, if Luz had ever felt this helpless.

She brought the baby to the sofa and gathered her into her lap. Amber cried out, clawing at the cellophane-covered book with damp fingers. Jessie opened it quickly and held the book in front of Amber.

"Let's read it." Dear Lord, read it? Her hand shook as she opened the book, and she strained to remember the story. It wasn't much, as she recalled. Something about two kids...Paul and Mary? Paul and Julie, maybe.

The angry buzz started as a low vibration in Amber's chest, and Jessie decided not to waste any more time. "Look, Paul and Julie can pat the bunny," she said, rubbing Amber's hand over the furry patch on the page. "Can you pat the bunny?"

"Pat, pat," said Amber, snuffling.

"Want to turn the page?"

Amber flipped it expertly, revealing a small flutter of flannel. Something about a blanket? No, this was the peekaboo page. "Paul and Julie play peekaboo," Jessie said. Amber's tiny fingers plucked at the flannel. And then, miracle of miracles, a chortle of delight erupted from her. Methodically they went through the book, stopping to examine each little surprise—Daddy's scratchy face, the sweet-smelling flowers, the shiny mirror.

"See the pretty baby," Jessie said, and suddenly her throat felt thick with tears. Oh, how she wanted to see this child, her beautiful face, her bluebonnet eyes. But to her, Amber was made out of bits of voice, a distinctive scent, the brush of cornsilk hair under Jessie's chin.

"Mo'," Amber said when they reached the end of the book.

Jessie turned back to the beginning and they went through it again, page by page. And something happened. Jessie felt herself relax, and then she saw what she was supposed to see—the night garden, a place of unseen beauty. She felt the sweet weight of Amber in her lap, the silky delicacy of her skin, the powder-puff softness of her hair. She smelled the baby's scent of sugar and dew, heard the singsong babble coming from her as she examined the book, over and over again. And finally, in the middle of the fourth or fifth reading, she felt the baby's heavy release as she nodded off to sleep. Oh, she could see her. She could.

Jessie curved both arms around Amber and rested her wet cheek upon the downy hair, nearly overcome by exhaustion herself. She heard another car drive up and decided she would kill the person who woke this child.

She recognized Dusty's gait on the porch outside. Too bad. She would kill even him.

He came in quietly and the sofa creaked as he sat down beside her.

Lifting her face, she turned to him. "I can't do this."

"Jessie." He cupped her damp cheek in the palm of his hand. "You just did."

Jessie told herself she should be used to the raw, exposed feelings his presence stirred, but it only intensified as time went on. While the tears dried on her face, she actually felt a wave of breathlessness, emotion made physical. He claimed he'd brought her here to deal with her sister, but she knew he expected more than that from her. Much more.

"Hey," she said.

"Hey, yourself."

"Arnufo ditched me with the baby."

"I know. He used to do that to me, too, sometimes. Forced me to deal with her, one-on-one."

"And that's okay with you? You don't mind that your preverbal, tantrum-throwing child was left alone with a blind woman?"

"She's sleeping like an angel. You have a magic touch with her." With that, he gently disengaged Amber from Jessie's arms and went outside. She heard him exchange words with Arnufo, and then he came inside empty-handed.

He took Jessie in his arms, and her heart sang and broke at the same time. "I'm not cranky, Jess. Just finished waiting. I've kept my distance all week to let you and Luz sort things out. Now it's time to talk about us."

Apprehension washed through her. *No.* She heard the swish of blood in her ears and pulled away from him. "Listen, I didn't ask you to track me down and drag me back here. But you need to think about what you're saying. You've got a baby to raise. If you need a woman in your life, pick one who can actually do you some good."

"I don't need a woman. I need you. Damn it, Jess, do you think I wanted to love you? Do you think I would if I had a choice? This isn't about doing myself some good. And believe me, loving you is no walk in the park. That was true before your blindness, and it's still true, and it has nothing to do with your vision." He paused. "But I can't stop, I don't want to stop, and I'm not going to stop."

Oh, those words. She wanted to clasp them inside her, to keep them forever. But she feared so much—that she'd be a burden to him, that after a while he'd regret his decision. It wasn't like her to be afraid, but this was new territory for her. "This isn't fair to you or Amber. Or me, for that matter."

"Since when do I believe life is fair?" he asked, his voice edged by irony. "I hate what you went through. I hate it almost as much as I hated sitting in the hospital with Karen, knowing she was gone but keeping her alive for Amber. I know what you're doing—you're trying to protect me from more heartache, like I have some affinity for tragic women and you want to break the cycle. But you're wrong, Jess. You're a miracle to me. Haven't you figured that out yet?"

"I'm a nightmare, and if you think otherwise, you're being naive. It'll be a race to see which one of us drives the other crazy first, me with my blindness, or you with your protectiveness."

"Listen, I don't pretend to understand everything about your blindness, but I swear I won't smother you. I know you, Jessie. You can do whatever you set your mind to. Hell, I used to treat my own kid like a bottle of nitroglycerin, as though she might explode at any minute. But she won't, you know? She might be little, but she's sturdy as an oak. I'm not going to hurt her by loving her." He took hold of her again, opened her hand against his mouth. "I'll never hurt you, either, I swear it. Marry me, Jessie."

The words shot her into the air, sent her soaring. She saw what her life could be, if only she would let it. Her world could be filled with people she loved and moments to give it meaning if only she would get over being afraid, if only she would let it happen.

"Don't do this to yourself," she begged him, taking her hand from his, cradling it in the other hand as though it was wounded. "Don't do this to Amber. Don't love someone like me. You have to let me go—you know you do."

"Why should I?"

"Because I'm blind. I can't look into your eyes and see love or suspicion or joy, and eventually, my eyes will atrophy and they won't say a thing about me. How can I love you if I can't see you?" All her terror and uncertainty rang in the words.

"Ah, Jess. That's the easy part. You do it with your heart, like everyone else. You do it for real, and forever, without caution. And you just hope for the best."

CHAPTER 38

That spike of panic a woman feels when the thought first hits her—*I'm pregnant*—is like no other. That evening, Jessie stunned herself as she started to think the unthinkable.

Dusty had walked out, leaving her to agonize over her decision. Ian and Luz had returned triumphant from their tryst in San Antonio. Jessie had somehow managed to smile and welcome them home. She'd begged off dinner and retreated to solitude, plagued by the question of what the hell she was going to do. She had actually felt queasy as she'd wrestled with her dreams. Could her love for Dusty outweigh her fear of the future? He never made things easy for her, and this was no exception. He'd forced the decision into her hands and left it there. She simply had no answer. She'd been offered the gift of another woman's child, but it was for her to decide whether or not she was worthy of that gift. And then the issue had been eclipsed by a bout of dry heaves.

She couldn't remember her last period. Only today did she dare to think about that.

In a horrifying instant, the world shifted. Dear God, could she be?

Jessie went clawing through her bag of toiletries, her mind screaming a denial.

"Stupid," she said through her teeth. "Stupid, stupid, stupid." She'd stopped taking her pills when she started at the Beacon, but lord knew how many she'd missed before that. One of the many personal hygiene lessons had, of course, been a trip to the drugstore for supplies, and she'd realized then that she was late. Not to worry, the pharmacist had assured her. It was common for the cycle to be erratic, even nonexistent, for a while after being on the Pill for so long.

Flambeau's toenails clicked as she paced, her concern evident.

But she'd still been taking them when she was with Dusty, she thought, trying to calm herself. She found a half-used circle of birth control pills. Even as her frantic fingers identified the empty slots, she realized she'd blown it. She remembered skipping several days during the jet-lagged blur of her trip home, when she'd lost track of what day it was. Having just dumped her lover, she couldn't have known that contraception would turn out to be an issue. Quite possibly, her worsening vision had prevented her from distinguishing the placebo pills from the real thing. She thought about the endless night in Mexico—he'd wanted to go looking for a drugstore, but she'd assured him it was fine. *Stupid.*

"This can't be happening," she whispered, sliding down to the bathroom floor and drawing her knees up to her chest. She felt herself falling into the old pattern of fear and retreat. Her instinct was to flee, but no. Do it the hard way. Take a chance and reach deep inside for the answers. She realized she couldn't make sense of anything until she knew for certain. Instantly she thought of Luz.

Luz.

The last time Jessie had found herself in this predicament, her sister held out the ultimate hand of loyalty.

"Come on, Flambeau," Jessie said, taking down the harness. "We need to go and see Luz." It was early evening; she could tell by the chill absence of light, and she could hear the kids playing football or Frisbee in the distance. She charged into her sister's house, pausing briefly to release Flambeau.

"Luz!" she called, hurrying. "Luz, I—"

"In the den."

"I'll be right there. I need something from the bathroom," she said. Trust Luz to keep a home pregnancy test handy. Jessie remembered finding one under the sink in a wrinkled drugstore bag. Digging around amid bottles of fluid and desiccated sponges, she found the crinkly bag and clutched it to her chest.

She laughed, a harsh sound of desperation. She could not do this without help. Hadn't she learned a damned thing? She'd come so far, and now she was back to being a screwup, pregnant and not married. Not only that, she was running to Luz again.

She clambered down the stairs and headed toward the den, navigating the room in the way that had become second nature to her. "Luz?"

"Over here on the couch, enjoying a couple of minutes of solitude."

"Where is everyone?"

"Mom and Stu are watching TV, and Ian's playing touch football with the kids. Even Lila." A trace of wonder softened her voice.

"Ah, Luz. You need to see how much Lila really loves and trusts you. She's going to be okay, I just know it."

"I hope you're right. The trip was so good, Jess. Ian and I haven't been like that since...I can't even remember."

Jessie forced herself to appear calm. All her life, she'd been bringing her traumas to Luz. Her sister seemed so happy right now, so untroubled and relaxed. And here Jessie was, about to upset her again.

"Anyway, I want to thank you," Luz said. "Ian told me everybody helped in the conspiracy." She took hold of Jessie's hand and pulled her down to the sofa. "I have something to show you."

Jessie frowned as Luz guided her fingertips to soft, smooth skin, then over a series of slightly rough bumps. The texture was familiar to her. "My God, Luz. You got a tattoo, didn't you?"

Luz laughed. "This morning, before we left San Antonio. Can you believe it? It's a constellation—Queen Cassiopeia."

For a moment, Jessie's panic retreated in a wash of bittersweet understanding. "Andromeda's mother."

"Yep."

"Have you shown Lila?"

"Not yet. I wanted to show you first." More laughter. "You should see Ian's."

"I'll pass. Um, Luz—"

"I was working on the family albums." Luz was uncharacteristically self-absorbed as she shuffled books and papers. "I'm way behind."

"Yeah," Jessie said, distracted. "Luz, I—"

"What's wrong?" A book thudded shut as Luz finally became aware of Jessie's agitation. "What've you got in the bag?"

She opened it and reached inside. "I'm going to need some help with this." She took out the unopened box and handed it to her sister.

Luz gasped. "This is a pregnancy test."

"I was hoping it wasn't Preparation H."

"Jess?" Luz's voice trembled with wonder.

"They, um, don't come in Braille. That would be sort of icky, wouldn't it? So I thought maybe you could help me."

Luz's arms went around her and they fell together, laughing through sudden tears. "I screwed up again," Jessie said, "and once again I'm turning to you."

"Don't you know that's what you're supposed to do? And don't you realize how much I turn to you?"

She pulled back. "You do?"

"Absolutely."

"No way." Jessie was incredulous.

"You took care of things after the accident. You shoved me

back into my husband's arms where I belong. None of that would have happened without you. I need you, Jess. I can't believe you don't realize that."

"Oh, Luz. Really?"

"Really."

"So what about Dusty? I got myself knocked up, and now I'm going to go running to him to rescue me."

"In case you haven't noticed, he needed rescuing, too. He was sleepwalking until you came along. You woke him up. He's alive again because of you."

Jessie sat speechless for a few minutes, the tears pouring down her face. If she went through with this, she would be the mother of a child she could never see. The thought stirred a memory of the night garden in Mexico, the elderly caretaker planting in the dark. Just because she'd never see the beauty of a flower again, should that stop her from creating the flower in the first place?

"You understand," she said when she found her voice, "I'm keeping this one."

"Of course." Luz squeezed her again. "Look, this is okay. It's the way things were meant to be. I did the same, having babies unplanned. And look what I got for my troubles—Owen and Scottie." Her grin was filled with warmth. "Sometimes I think the richest things in life come from mistakes."

The bits of hard-won wisdom and home truths rained down on Jessie. "If that's the case, then I'm a millionaire."

Luz sighed happily. "I think I'm going to like being the tattooed aunt. So do you want to do this now, or wait, or...?"

She heard the sound of the evening breeze sweeping across the lake and winnowing through the shedding live oak tree. Faintly, she heard the laughter of children and the bark of a dog and the distant cry of a loon. "Actually, there's something I have to do first."

"Sure, Jess. Anything."

"Can you give me a ride?" This was it, Jessie knew, as joy finally buried her fear. This was the adventure of a lifetime, and she didn't need a passport or a suitcase or anything other than courage. She stood up, turning her face to the warm light streaming through the screen door. "I need to go see Dusty."

ACKNOWLEDGMENTS

Each novel is a journey, and on each journey, I learn and grow from the people I meet along the way. This book begins and ends with my sister, Lori Klist Cross, whose expertise in the areas of blindness and orientation and mobility for the visually impaired is surpassed only by her loyalty and support for her big sister. I will always be older, but only aspire to be wiser and more giving.

The National Library for the Blind provided invaluable resources for research, and I have been privileged to discuss AZOOR with Adrian, Vicky, Jacque, Beth, Leigh... Thank you for letting me into your world.

My first readers are the caring and demanding Port Orchard gang—Lois, Kate, Debbie, Rose Marie, Janine, Susan P. and Sheila. My long-distance friends, Joyce and Barb, never fail to take the time to read my work, as they have for many years. The online RomEx community, including Deb, Lynn and Lynda, always comes through with discussion and inspiration, and I'm grateful for that. Special thanks to Alice and P.J. for critical readings. You are all so generous with your time.

To Annelise Robey of the Jane Rotrosen Agency, whose passion for this story and whose patience with my revisions never flagged—thanks for making me work hard. Thanks to Jane Berkey for her enthusiasm, encouragement and advice. The publishing expertise and commitment of Dianne Moggy, Martha Keenan and their associates at MIRA Books have turned hopes and dreams to reality. And finally, my deepest gratitude is for my agent, Meg Ruley, whose friendship and counsel have been a gift beyond price.